"I've Neve[r] [Seen You] Look [So] Feminine Before."

He reached out to touch the shoulder of her blouse. "I hope it's for my benefit, Gaby," he added, his voice deep, soft.

"You're getting me all mixed up," she said defensively.

"You need mixing up." He tugged a lock of hair. "We aren't going to be enemies."

"I hope not." The way he was looking at her made her nervous.

"You look as if you might jump up and start running any minute. Am I that frightening?"

"It isn't really fear," she said hesitantly.

"Isn't it?"

Her breath began to quicken when he walked toward her. His hands slid slowly to her waist, and he lifted her gently so that she was sitting on the table. Then he moved closer.

She felt her heart begin to race when he bent forward and slowly touched his lips to hers in a whisper of a kiss...

*   *   *

"Ms. Kyle brings all of her instincts for passionate romance to vivid life. . . . And no one, absolutely no one, beats this author for sensual anticipation."

—*Rave Reviews* on *Diamond Spur*

Also by Susan Kyle

Diamond Spur

Published by
POPULAR LIBRARY

FIRE BRAND

SUSAN KYLE

POPULAR LIBRARY

An Imprint of Warner Books, Inc.

A Time Warner Company

POPULAR LIBRARY EDITION

Copyright © 1989 by Susan Kyle
All rights reserved.

Popular Library® and the fanciful P design are registered trademarks
of Warner Books, Inc.

Cover illustration by Franco Accornero

Popular Library books are published by
Warner Books, Inc.
666 Fifth Avenue
New York, N.Y. 10103

W A Time Warner Company

Printed in the United States of America

First Printing: February, 1989

10   9   8   7   6   5   4

For Ann and Muriel who
shared Arizona with me—
and for Stephanie—
with thanks and love.

CHAPTER

One

Just when Gaby thought it couldn't get worse, it started to rain. She groaned as she tried to adjust part of her raincoat over the lens of her .35 mm camera, and kept shooting, aiming away from the red and blue flashing lights and the spotlights so that she wouldn't spoil the shot.

"Are you out of your mind?" the thin man beside her grumbled, jerking her back down just as a bullet whizzed past her ear. "Gaby, that was stupid!"

"Shut up and keep taking notes," she told him absently. The whir of the camera shutter was lost amid the renewed firing. It sounded like an automatic, which it probably was. The armed robber holed up in the old department store building was known to have one. He'd already killed the store manager and negotiations had broken down before they had even begun. "There's a pregnant hostage in there with him. See if you can find out her name."

"Will you stop slinging out orders?" he grumbled. "I know how to cover a story."

Oh, sure you do, Gaby thought irritably, *as long as it's in a boardroom or a good restaurant.* Only fate could have managed to leave Harrington alone in the newsroom when she had needed a photographer. And once the shooting in the street started, Harrington had plastered himself against a police car and refused to move. Gaby had no choice but to give him the note pad.

She pushed back her long black hair and snapped the camera lens cap on to keep the rain out of it. She was drenched already, her jeans and bulky pink knit top plastered to her skin under the concealing folds of the beige raincoat. And while she could take a photograph, Harrington's were better —if he just had the nerve to go with his talent. He was a photojournalist and sometimes did interviews, to fill in for other reporters. He hated taking crime photos.

"I never should have let Johnny talk me into coming with you, you maniac," Fred Harrington muttered. He glared at her through thick lenses that were spotted with drops of rain. She wondered if he knew how big they made his dark eyes look.

"If Johnny were here, he'd be out there where the *Bulletin* guy is right now," she returned, nodding toward a beanpole in baggy jeans with a long ponytail and glasses, wandering into the line of fire. "For God's sake, Wilson, get out of there!" she yelled across the police car she and Fred were crouched behind.

Wilson glanced her way and raised his hand in a friendly salute. "That you, Cane?" He grinned.

About that time, a disgruntled police officer tackled him and took him down, right on top of his camera.

"Good for you, officer!" Fred yelled.

Gaby elbowed him. "Traitor," she accused.

"Stupid people should be trampled," he replied. "Fool! Lunatic!" he called across to the rival paper's reporter/photographer, who was being led away not too gently by his accoster.

"I love you, too, Harrington!" Wilson called back. "Hey, Cane, how about calling this story in to my editor for me?"

"Eat worms and die, Wilson!" she said gaily.

He stuck his tongue out at her and vanished behind the bulk of the angry police officer.

"Will you two keep it down?" one of the nearby policemen muttered. "Honest to God, you reporters are the biggest pests . . ."

"Just for that, I'll misspell your name," Gaby promised.

He grinned at her and moved away.

"You're crazy," Fred said fervently. He was new to the newspaper scene, having preferred photography to journalism—although he could write good cutlines and even do good interviews. He didn't have the wherewithal for this kind of assignment, though. Gaby usually had the political beat. She and Harrington were only here because the police reporter was out sick. And any news reporter could be commandeered to cover police news in an emergency.

Out of the corner of her eye, she spotted movement. There was a uniformed man with a rifle running into a building across the street from the abandoned department store building. "Something's happening," Gaby said. "Look sharp. You might get a little closer to Chief Jones and see if he can fill you in on what the SWAT team's going to do."

Fred glared at her. "Why don't you do it? I can take photos."

"Deal." She handed him the camera and started toward Chief Jones. Then, just as he started shooting, she turned around and removed the lens cap. "It works better that way," she said, before edging her way along the police car line.

"Hi, Teddy," she whispered, easing up beside the tall, distinguished police chief. "What's up?"

"Utility stocks, or so I hear," he mused.

"Dammit, Teddy, stop that," she muttered. "It's been a

long day, and I've got an engagement party to go to when I get through here."

"You getting engaged, Gaby?" he asked. "A miracle." He looked up at the rainy sky.

"Not me," she said through her teeth. "Mary, down in composing. She and I went through journalism school together."

"I might have known." He frowned as his eyes shifted to the roof of the building across the street, where the faint glimmer of metal gave away a marksman.

"Good for you," Gaby whispered, glancing up with eyes that were such a dark olive shade of green that they looked brown. "The robber will take out that hostage if you don't do something drastic."

"We don't like this sort of thing, you know that," he sighed. "But he's killed one man already and there's a pregnant lady in there and he's gone wild. We can't negotiate him out of a damned thing. There's no power or telephone or heat to cut off and trade him things for, and he won't talk to us." He shook his head. "This is a hell of a job sometimes, kid."

"You're telling me."

Three years of work on the *Phoenix Advertiser* had given her an education in police tactics. She stood crouched beside Chief Jones, waiting for the inevitable shot that would drop the gunman. It was like waiting for death, because a head shot was all the sharpshooter was likely to get, if that much. For one long moment, she contemplated the futility of crime and its terrible cost—to the perpetrators, the public, and the police. And then the shot came. It echoed through the darkness with a horrible finality. If death had a sound, that was it, and Gaby cringed inwardly.

"It's a hit!" the sharpshooter called down. "I got him."

"Okay, move in," Chief Jones told his men solemnly.

"Can I come?" Gaby asked quietly.

He looked down at her with mingled irritation and respect. "Sure, you can come," he said. "You'll have nightmares."

"I've always had nightmares," she said matter-of-factly. She went back to get Fred. "Let's get some pix and wrap this up so we can make the morning edition," she told him.

"Pix of what?" he asked.

"Of the gunman," she said patiently.

"You want me to take pictures of a dead body?"

She took the camera from him with exaggerated patience and followed Chief Jones into the building.

Gaby's heart went out to the small pregnant woman, who was white-faced, sobbing, and clearly almost in shock, as she was escorted gently from the building. The gunman lay on the floor. Someone had taken off his shabby jacket and put it over his head. He looked fragile, somehow, lying there like that. Gaby took a quick shot of him without really seeing him. She didn't photograph the hostage. Johnny could scream his head off, but she wasn't going to capitalize on a pregnant woman's terror. Later, she could call the hospital and find out the woman's condition, or she could get the particulars from Chief Jones. She glanced around the room until her eyes caught the sack with the holdup money in it.

A policeman was carefully picking it up, and she looked inside.

"Twenty dollars," the policeman said. He shrugged. "Not much of a haul for two men's lives."

"Does it look like he was a pro?" she asked him.

He shook his head. "Too sloppy. A witness who saw him kill the storekeeper said he was shaking all over, and the gun discharged accidentally while he was trying to get away."

She was writing it all down. "Got a family?"

"Yeah. He's the youngest of six kids. The older brother's a pusher. The mother goes on the streets from time to time to add to her welfare check." He smiled at Gaby. "Tough world for kids, isn't it?"

"For some of them," she agreed. She shouldered the camera and went back to Chief Jones, who'd just finished talking to the hostage. Gaby asked him the necessary questions, picked up Harrington, and drove back to the office in her white custom VW convertible.

"How come you rate a car this fancy?" Fred asked on the way.

She smiled. "I have rich relatives," she said.

Well, it was the truth, in one respect. The McCaydes of Lassiter, Arizona, were rich. They weren't exactly relatives, however.

Her eyes drifted to the traffic. Phoenix was a fascinating city, elegant for its spaciousness, with the surrounding huge, jagged peaks of the southernmost Rockies forming a protective barrier around it. The first time she'd seen the city, she had been fascinated by the sheer height and majesty of those mountains.

In fact, Arizona itself still fascinated her. It was a state like no other, its appearance first frightening and barren. But closer up, it had a staggering beauty. In its vastness, it offered serenity and promise. In its diversity of terrain and cultures, it offered a kind of harmony that was visually melodic. Gaby loved it all, from the wealth and prosperity and hustle of Phoenix, to the quiet desert peace of Casa Río, the twenty-odd thousand acre ranch owned by the McCaydes.

"Doesn't one of your relatives have a construction company in Tucson?" Harrington broke into her thoughts. "McCayde—Bowie McCayde?"

Gaby tingled at the mention of his name. "He's not a relative. His parents took me in when I was in my teens," she corrected. "Yes, he inherited McCayde Construction from his late father."

"There's a ranch, too, isn't there?"

"Oh, yes, indeed, there is," she said, remembering with a smile. "Casa Río—River House. It dates to ten years after the Civil War." She glanced at him. "You did know that most of southeastern Arizona was settled by people from the South—and that during the Civil War, a Confederate flag flew briefly over the city of Tucson?"

"You're kidding."

She laughed. "No, I'm not. It's true. Bowie's people came from southwest Georgia. The first settler was a Cliatt, who married a Mexican girl. There's even a Papago in his lineage somewhere—excuse me, a Tohono O'odham," she said, using the new name the Papago had adopted for themselves. The name *Papago* was actually a Zuñi word meaning "Bean People," so the Papago changed it to words in their own language, which meant "People of the Desert."

"That's a mouthful," Harrington murmured as he shifted uncomfortably in his seat.

"I think it's pretty. Did you know that Apache is a Zuñi word for enemy? And that the word Navajo contains a 'V,' and that there is no 'V' in the Navajo language? Until recent times many scarcely knew of the word, in fact . . ."

"Stop!" Harrington wailed. "I don't want to learn everything about the Southwest in one lesson."

"I love it," she sighed. "I love the people and the languages and the history." Her dark olive eyes grew dreamy. "I wish I'd been born here."

"Where are you from?" he asked.

It was just a casual question, and she'd brought it on herself, but she quickly changed the subject. "I wonder what they'll do to Wilson?"

He glared at her, as she'd known he would. "I hope they hang him from the nearest tree. The fool!"

She smiled to herself. "Maybe they will," she mused.

Her mind wandered as she drove. The rain reminded her

so well of a time in her past—the first time she'd seen Casa Río. It was the night she'd met Bowie.

Just thinking of him made her nervous. In a lot of ways, Bowie was her nemesis. He couldn't be called a brother because she'd never been officially adopted by the McCaydes. She was a stray they'd taken in and assumed responsibility for, but only as a ward. She hadn't wanted them to adopt her, because then they might probe into her past. But she'd covered herself by giving a very plausible story about having moved every other week with her father, and having no permanent address. That much was almost true.

Bowie was twenty-seven years old the night she showed up at Casa Río in the rain. She had caught first sight of him in the barn, where she was huddled and shivering against the faint evening chill of May.

His sheer size had been overpowering. He was a big, rugged-looking blond man with a physique that any movie cowboy would have envied. He was the head of a growing construction company, and over the years, he'd spent a good deal of his time at building sites, pitching in when deadlines were threatening. That explained the muscular physique, but not the brooding look he wore much of the time. Later, Gaby would learn that he didn't smile very often. She'd learn, too, that his extraordinary good looks were deceptive. He wasn't a womanizer, and if he had affairs, they were so discreet as to be almost unnoticed. He was a quiet, intro-spective man who liked Bach, old war movies, and more than anything else, the land upon which Casa Río sat. Bowie was a preservationist, a conservationist. That, in a builder, was something of an irony, but then, Bowie was full of con-tradictions. Gaby knew him no better now than she had that first night. He was rarely ever home when she visited his mother, Aggie—it was almost as if he purposefully avoided her.

That long-ago rainy night, he'd been in evening clothes. Gaby's frightened eyes had followed him as he stared into a stall and rubbed the velvet nose of the big Belgian horse that occupied it. He turned on the light, and she could see that his blond hair was very thick and straight, conventionally cut with a side part, and neatly combed, despite the hour. His profile had been utterly perfect; a strong, very handsome, very definite face that probably drew women like honey drew butterflies. He had a straight nose and a square jaw, and deep-set eyes under heavy brows. His mouth had a chiseled look, and there was something faintly sensuous about it. Gaby tried not to notice sensuality—she was afraid of men.

But masculine perfection like Bowie's was hard to ignore. She watched him as she might have watched a sunset, awed by its impact. The black suit he'd been wearing clung with a tailored faultlessness to his powerful body, emphasizing his broad chest, the length of his muscular legs, the narrowness of his hips, the width of his shoulders. He bent his head to light a cigarette, and she saw the faint orange flair of the match turn his tanned face just briefly to bronze.

She must have accidentally moved and made noise, because all of a sudden he whirled toward her with an economy of movement. His eyes narrowed.

"Who the hell is that?" he asked. His voice was deep, curt, without an accent, and yet there was something faintly drawling about it.

She hesitated, but when he started toward the empty stall where she was huddled in fresh hay, she stood up and moved out into the aisle, terrified of being hemmed in.

"I'm not a burglar or anything," she said, trying to smile. "I'm sorry about this, but it's so cold, mister, and I just needed to get in out of the rain." She sneezed loudly.

He stared at her quietly, his deep-set black eyes frightening. "Where did you come from?"

Her heart hammered in her chest. She hadn't expected that question, and she wasn't used to telling lies. Her father, a lay minister, had drummed morality into her at an early age, and honesty was part of her upbringing. Now, it was hard not to tell the truth. She lowered her eyes. "I'm an orphan," she said miserably. "I was looking for a cousin, a Sanders, but a neighbor said the family moved years ago." That much was true. "I don't have anyplace to go . . ." Her lower lip had trembled. She was so afraid—not only of him, but of having the recent past come down on her head. Her big, olive-green eyes had stared up into his, pleading.

He didn't want her around. That much was obvious. She could almost see courtesy going to war with suspicion in his mind.

"Well, I'll take you inside and let my mother deal with you," he said then. "God knows, she's partial to girls, since she never had one of her own."

She breathed a sigh of relief. She could still see herself as she'd been that night, her long black hair straggly around a pinched white face. Her clothes had been so worn that they had holes in a few places—especially her faded jeans and denim jacket. She'd had only a coin purse with her, which contained a one-dollar bill and some change, and there was a handkerchief in her jacket pocket. There was no learner's license, no credit card, nothing to give her away or help anyone trace her back to Kentucky.

"What's your name, infant?" the big man had asked. He towered over her, enormously tall and powerful. She was five foot six, but he had to be at least six foot three.

"Gabrielle," she stammered. "Gabrielle Cane." That was her real name, but she'd deliberately hesitated before she gave him her last name, to make it seem as if it was a false one. "Most people call me Gaby." Her eyes surveyed the neat barn, with its wide brick aisle and well-kept interior. "What is this place?"

"It's called Casa Río—River House. In the old days, the river ran within sight, but its course changed over the years. Now you can't see the river, and there isn't any water in it for most of the year," he'd replied. "My parents own it. I'm Bowie McCayde."

"Your parents live here?" she asked nervously.

"Yes, they live here." His voice had been curt. "I have an apartment in Tucson. My father is in the construction business."

That would explain his dark tan and the muscles rippling under that jacket. He had big, lean hands, and they looked strong, too. She shifted and sneezed again.

"Come on, we'll go inside." He'd reached out to take her arm, but she moved back jerkily. She had plenty of reason not to like being touched, but instead of being angry, he only nodded at her reticence. "You don't like being touched. Okay. I'll remember," he'd added, and he had.

The biggest surprise of her life had been meeting Aggie McCayde. The only woman she'd known for any length of time had been the matriarch of the big race horse farm where her father had been working, in Lexington, Kentucky. Her own mother had died when she was barely old enough to go to school, so Agatha McCayde came as a very big surprise to a girl used only to the company of her father. Aggie took one look at the sneezing fifteen-year-old and immediately began fussing over her. Her husband Copeland had welcomed the girl with equal kindness, but Bowie had kept apart, looking irritated and then angry. He left for Tucson a day early, as she'd later learned. When he saw how Gaby was fitting in with his parents, his visits became fewer and briefer. He seemed to have difficulty getting along with Copeland and Aggie, a problem that Gaby didn't have at all. She opened her heart to the older couple as they opened their heart and home to her.

For the first time in her life, she was cosseted and spoiled.

Aggie took her shopping, watched over her when the nightmares came and she woke up sweating and crying in the night. The older woman listened to her problems when she enrolled in the local high school that fall, helped her overcome her difficulty fitting in because she was so shy and uneasy. Aggie even understood when Gaby didn't date anyone. That wasn't really so much design as circumstance, she recalled. She wasn't a pretty teenager. She was skinny, shy, and a little clumsy and nervous, so the boys didn't exactly beat a path to her door. Aggie loved her and doted on her, which was why Bowie really began to resent her. She noticed his attitude, because he made no attempt to hide it. But incredibly, Aggie and Copeland didn't seem to notice that they were treating her more like their child and Bowie more like an outsider. By the time she realized it, the damage was done. She knew Bowie resented her. That was one reason she'd opted for college in Phoenix, but it had been difficult there—much more difficult than she'd realized—because her old-fashioned attitudes and her distaste for intimacy put her apart from most of the other students. She formed friendships, and once or twice she dated, but there was always the fear of losing control, of being overpowered, long after the nightmares had become manageable and the scars of the past had begun to heal.

Gaby had had one violent flare-up of sensual feeling— oddly enough, with Bowie. Aggie had pleaded and coaxed until he'd taken Gaby to a dance at college. He'd been out of humor, and frankly irritated by the adoring looks of Gaby's classmates. He was a handsome man, even if he was the only one who didn't seem to know it, and he drew attention. He'd held her only on the dance floor, and very correctly. But there had always been sparks flying between them, and that night, physical sparks had flown as well. Gaby had seen him in a different light that one night, and she let months go by afterward before she went to Casa Río. After that, Gaby began to concentrate more than ever on her studies, and on the job she'd taken after classes at the *Phoenix Advertiser*. Between work and study, there had been no time for a personal life.

Now the job took most of her breathing time. In a city the size of Phoenix, there was always something going on. When she began to work full time, the excitement of reporting somehow made everything worthwhile; she was alive as she never had been before. But the surges of adrenalin had awakened something else in her. They'd prompted a different kind of ache—a need for something more than an empty apartment and loneliness.

She was twenty-four years old now, and while the job was satisfying, it was no longer enough. She hungered for a home of her own and children, a settled life. That might be good for Aggie, too. The older woman had been lonely since Copeland's death eight years before. Gaby helped her to cope after it happened. Bowie had resented even that, irritated that his mother had turned to her adopted child instead of her natural one. But now Aggie was globetrotting, and even though Gaby only spent the occasional weekend at Casa Río, she was missing the small, dark-eyed woman whose warmth and outgoing personality had brought a frightened teenager out of a nightmare.

That bubbly personality was one that Gaby had developed when she had begun to work with the public. Inside, she was still shy and uncertain, and she found it difficult to relate to men who looked upon casual sex as *de rigueur*. In her upbringing, sex meant marriage. That was what she really wanted from life, not an affair. It helped, of course, that she'd never been tempted enough to really want a man. Except Bowie.

She pulled her mind back to the present and drove up in front of the building that housed the newspaper she and Fred worked for. She only hoped there wasn't going to be another

last-minute story to cover. She was tired and worn, and she
just wanted to go back to her apartment and sleep for an
hour before she tried to fix herself something to eat. She
remembered the engagement party and groaned. Maybe she
could find an excuse to miss it. She hated social gatherings,
even though she was fond of Mary, the girl who was getting
engaged.

She and Fred waved as they passed Trisa, the receptionist,
and entered the newsroom. Gaby didn't even look around;
she was so tired that she just dropped into the chair at her
computer terminal with a long sigh. Almost everyone on the
newspaper staff was around. Johnny Blake came out of his
office, his bald head shining in the light, his thick brows
drawn together as he listened to Fred's version of what had
happened.

"That the long and short of it, Cane?" he asked Gaby. As
she raised her eyebrows, Fred mumbled something about
getting the film to the darkroom and eased quickly away.

Johnny glared at her without smiling. "Get the story?" he
asked.

"Sort of."

He stared. "Sort of?"

"It's your fault," she told him. "Harrington and I aren't
cut out for police reporting. You made us go."

"Well, *I* couldn't go," he said. "I'm in management. People in management don't cover shootouts. They're dangerous, Cane," he added in a conspiratorial whisper.

She glared at him. "This, from a man who volunteered to
cover the uprising in Central America."

"Okay, what went wrong?" he asked, sidestepping the remark.

She told him. He groaned. "At least we did get some good
copy," she comforted him. "And I got a shot of the gunman,
along with some swell shots of the police in the rain surrounding the building," she added dryly.

"One shot of the hostage would have been worth fifty shots of the police in the rain!" he raged. "You and your soft heart . . . !"

"Wilson, from the *Bulletin*, got lots of nice pictures of the stand-off," Gaby told her boss, rubbing salt in the wound. "And probably one of the hostage, too."

"I hate you," he hissed.

She smiled. "But the police tackled him and broke his camera and probably exposed every frame he shot."

"I love you," he changed it.

"Next time, don't send Harrington with me, okay?" she pleaded. "Just let me go alone."

"Can't do that, Cane," he said. "You're too reckless. Do you have any idea how many close calls you've had in the past three years? You never hold anything in reserve in that kind of situation, and thank God it doesn't happen often. I still get cold chills remembering the bank robbery you had to cover. I hate asking you to sub for the police reporter."

"It was only a flesh wound," she reminded him.

"It could have been a mortal wound," he muttered. "And even if you aren't afraid of Bowie McCayde, the publisher is. They had words after the bank robbery."

That came as a surprise. Aggie hadn't said anything about it, but she had probably sent Bowie to throw the fear of God into Mr. Smythe, the publisher.

"I didn't know that," she said. She smiled. "Well, he'll never find out about today, so there's no need to worry . . . What are you staring at?"

"Certain death," he said pleasantly.

She followed his gaze toward the lobby. Bowie McCayde was just coming in the door, towering over the male reporters and causing comments and deep sighs among the female ones. He was wearing a gray suit, his blond head bare, and held an unlit cigarette in his hand. He looked out of humor and threatening.

Gaby's heart jumped into her throat. What, she wondered, was he doing in Phoenix? She hadn't seen him for two months—not since they'd celebrated Aggie's birthday at Casa Río. It had been an unusually disturbing night because just lately, Bowie had a way of looking at her that made her nerves stand on end.

Her breathing quickened as he approached, the old disturbing nervousness collecting in her throat to make her feel gauche and awkward. Just like old times, she thought as his black eyes pinned her to the spot while he strode across the newsroom. She was capable and cool until she got within five feet of this man, and then she just went to pieces. It was a puzzle she still hadn't worked out. It wasn't really fear—not the nauseating kind. It was more like excitement . . .

"Hello, Bowie," she said awkwardly.

He nodded curtly to Johnny and scowled down at Gaby. "I'm taking you out to supper," he said without a greeting or an invitation, ignoring her soaked clothes and straggly hair. "We've got to talk."

She wondered if she'd heard him right. Bowie, taking her out?

"Something's wrong," she guessed.

"Wrong?" He waved the unlit cigarette in his hand. "Wrong?! My God."

"Is it Aggie?" she asked quickly, her olive eyes mirroring her concern.

Bowie stared at Johnny until the shorter man mumbled an excuse, grinned at Gaby, and beat a hasty retreat to his office. Bowie had that effect on a lot of people, Gaby thought with faint amusement. He never said anything harsh—he just stared at people with his cold black eyes. One of his construction company executives had likened it to being held at bay by a cobra.

"Yes, it's Aggie," he muttered. Gaby felt faint.

CHAPTER

Two

Bowie realized belatedly why Gaby's face had turned white. "No, no," he said shortly, noting her horrified expression. "She's not hurt or anything."

She relaxed visibly and put a hand to her throat. "You might have said so."

"Are you through here?" He looked around as if he couldn't see what she had to do anyway.

"I need to file my story before I go."

"Go ahead. It'll keep." He walked back out into the lobby and sat down on one of the sofas. Trisa leaned her chin on her hands and sat watching him shamelessly while he read a magazine. If Bowie even noticed, there was no sign of it.

Gaby had to drag her own eyes away. He was most incredibly handsome, and totally unaware of it.

She turned on her word processor, got out her notes, and spent fifteen minutes condensing two hours of work into eight inches of copy one column wide.

Bowie was still reading when she came out of the newsroom, after calling a quick good night to Johnny.

"I'm ready . . . oh, no," she groaned.

Carl Wilson, the *Bulletin* reporter, was just coming in the door with a Band-Aid over his nose, breathing fire.

"So there you are, you turncoat," he growled at her. His ponytail was soaked, and Bowie was giving him an unnerving appraisal. He turned his back to get away from that black-eyed stare. "This is the last straw, Cane," he raged. "I know you've got the whole damned police force in your pocket from your old days on the police beat, but that was a low blow. My camera's busted to hell, my film's exposed . . . !"

"Poor old photographer," she said comfortingly. "Did the big bad policeman hurt its little nose?"

He actually blushed. "You stop that," he muttered. "You told them to do it."

"Not me," she said, holding up one hand.

Bowie had gotten to his feet now and his narrow black eyes were watching closely.

"If you didn't point me out, who did?" Wilson persisted, eyeing Bowie warily as he spoke.

"You were walking right into the line of fire," she reminded him. "We all saw you."

He sighed miserably. "First my car gets towed away, despite the press sticker, because I parked in front of a fire hydrant. Then I get tackled and my film is ruined . . . it's somebody's fault!" he added with a pointed glare.

Gaby grinned. "God must be mad at you," she told him. "He's getting even with you for the Garrison story you conned me out of last week. You do remember having your crony at city hall send me out to the parking lot while you got the final word on the new landfill site?"

He shifted uncomfortably. "That was in the line of duty. We're rivals."

"Yes, and some of us hit below the belt," she added with a meaningful stare. "But I didn't have the policeman tackle you. You should know better than to walk through a hail of bullets. Policemen get nervous about that sort of thing."

"You should know," Wilson muttered. "Didn't you get shot in the last stand-off, after the bank robbery?"

She cleared her throat, aware of Bowie's thunderous expression. "This time, I was safely behind some police cars —not taking a stroll in front of the sniper."

"Is that so." Wilson pursed his lips. "Well," he said slowly, "I might be persuaded to forgive you—if you can spare a shot of the victim."

"No chance."

"Okay, I'm easy. How about the police surrounding the building? Come on, Cane, my job's on the line," he coaxed.

"If Johnny finds out, mine will be, too," she assured him. "Do what the rest of us do. Go and beg from the *News-Record*. They go to press every Tuesday, so this story will be old news by the time their next edition comes out. They'll share with you." She grinned as she said it. The *News-Record* was a small weekly newspaper, but its reporters were always on the spot when news broke, and they didn't mind sharing one of their less important photos with the big dailies—as long as their photographer got a credit.

He sighed. "Well, beggars can't be choosers. Okay, doll, thanks anyway."

He started to bend down to kiss her cheek, but she stepped back jerkily. "You'll give me *Bulletin* germs!" she exclaimed, making a joke out of it.

He shook his head. "Leave it to you. Thanks anyway, Cane." He chuckled, and walked out the front door whistling.

Bowie hadn't said anything. He had a cigarette in his hand, and he was watching her like a hawk. "Bullets?" he asked, moving closer.

"A robbery. The perpetrator got twenty dollars. He killed a store manager and took a pregnant woman hostage, and threatened to kill her. They had to drop him." She lowered her eyes. "He was little more than a boy. The police reporter is out sick, so I had to cover the story. I don't do the police beat anymore," she added, trying to ward off trouble.

"Bullets?" he repeated, his voice deeper, rougher this time.

She looked up. "I'm twenty-four years old. This is my job. I don't need your permission to do it. It was just this one time . . ."

"Count your blessings," he said curtly. He glanced toward the receptionist, who smiled at him, and turned away uncomfortably. "Let's go."

Gaby winked at Trisa as they passed her, but Bowie kept his eyes straight ahead, pausing only to open the door for Gaby and lead her to his black Scorpio.

She sank into the soft leather seat with a sigh, and let her eyes wander over the dashboard. It was a honey of a car. She wished she could afford one.

He got in beside her, making sure her seat belt was fastened before he clicked his own into place and started the car. "Does your receptionist make a habit of staring at people that way?" he asked irritably as he pulled out into traffic. "I was beginning to feel like a museum exhibit."

"Look in a mirror sometime," she murmured only half humorously. "I used to have girlfriends by the dozen in college until they learned that you didn't live at Casa Río. It rather spoiled their dreams of the perfect weekend vacation."

He gave her a cold glance. "I hate being chased."

"Don't look at me." She held up her hands in mock horror. "I'm the last woman you'll ever have to beat off."

"So I've noticed." He eased the car into another lane. "You still don't like being touched, I see."

"Wilson is a womanizer," she murmured. "I don't like that kind of man."

"You don't like men, period. You're damned lucky that

Aggie doesn't know what a hermit you are. She'd have you on the guest list of every party that featured even one single man."

"I know." She sighed and glanced at his perfect profile. "You won't give me away, will you?"

"Have I ever?"

She ran a hand over the back of her neck. "We don't see that much of each other, so how do you know about my social life?"

He lit another cigarette. "You're soaked. Do you want to go to your apartment and change before we go to the restaurant?"

"Yes, I'd like to, if you don't mind." Then she thought about Bowie in her apartment, and something inside her retreated.

He saw that hunted look out of the corner of his eye. "You're safe with me, Gaby. I hoped you knew that without my having to say it."

She swallowed. He read her all too well. She stared at her slender, ringless fingers. "I know. I'm just a little shaken by this afternoon. I don't do police news anymore, and it's been a long time since I've seen anybody shot."

"What a hell of a line of work you chose," he said.

"I like it, most of the time." She clasped her fingers, because reaction was beginning to set in. It always amazed her how calm she was while she was getting a story, but after covering this kind of story she went to pieces after the numbness wore off. Sometimes she had nightmares and there was usually nobody to talk to about them. She couldn't tell Aggie, because the older woman disapproved of her work anyway and had tried to get her to quit. She had no close friends.

"You said you aren't still on the police beat?" he asked conversationally.

"No. Because after Aggie had you tell Mr. Smythe to take

me off it even though I asked Johnny Blake to put me back on he wouldn't." She glanced at him. "I don't miss it anyway. I love political reporting."

"That's reassuring," he said dryly.

"Aggie did put you up to it, didn't she?" she asked. "Speaking of Aggie, what's going on?"

"I'll tell you over dinner." He parked the car in front of the apartment building where she lived—a sprawling white complex with a swimming pool and tennis courts and security people.

"I've moved since you were in Phoenix last," she said suspiciously. "How did you know where I live?"

"Come on. You're soaked."

She threw up her hands. "Do you ever answer questions?"

"You'll catch cold if you don't get out of those wet things," he replied nonchalantly, still sidestepping her queries—as usual.

He got out of the car, opened her door, and let her go first in the slight drizzle. It was getting dark already, and she was too tired to pursue it.

Her apartment was done in whites and yellows, with oak furniture, Mexican pottery, and a few modern paintings. It was bright and open and sunny, and she had plants growing everywhere.

"It looks like the damned Amazon jungle," he observed, staring around him.

"Thank you." She took off her raincoat. "I'll only be a few minutes. There's brandy on the table if you want a drink."

"I'm driving," he reminded her.

"I'll, uh, just get changed," she stammered. He made her feel ridiculously weak. She dodged into her bedroom and closed the door.

It was the first time she'd ever had a man in her apartment. She was all thumbs while she took a quick shower, washed and dried her hair, and put on a neat gray crepe dress with white collar and cuffs, and shoes to match. She curled her hair into a neat bun atop her head, added a dash of pink lipstick, some powder, and a hint of perfume, and went to join Bowie.

He was standing at her window, looking out, his black eyes narrow and brooding. He turned as she came back, his appraisal electrifying as it slid boldly down her body and back up to her face.

"Is it too dressy?" she asked nervously.

"I'd have said it was twenty years too old for you," he replied. "You're an attractive young woman. Why do you dress like a matron?"

She bristled. "This is the latest style . . ."

"No, it isn't. It's a safe style. You're covered from neck to calf, as usual."

Her face was going hotter by the minute. "I dress to please myself."

"Obviously. You sure as hell won't please a man in that rig."

"For which you should be grateful," she said with a venomous smile. "You won't have to fight me off all evening."

He considered that carefully, his sensuous lips pursed, a faint twinkle in his black eyes as the cigarette smoked away in his hand. "I've never made a pass at you, have you noticed? What is it now—eight years?"

"Nine," she said, averting her eyes to the window.

"And I know as little about you now as I did that first night," he continued. "You're an enigma."

"I'm also starving," she said, changing the subject with a forced, pleasant smile. "Where are we going to eat?"

"That depends on you. What appeals to you?"

"Something hot and spicy. Mexican."

"Fine by me." He held the apartment door open for her, one of his habits that secretly thrilled her. Aggie had raised him to be a gentleman, and in times when most men left women to open their own doors and lift their own burdens, Bowie was a refreshing anachronism. He was courteous, but not chauvinistic. Two of his executives were women, and she knew for a fact that he had hired a female architect and several female construction workers. He never discriminated, but he did have a few quirks—such as insisting on opening doors and carrying heavy packages.

They went to a festive Mexican restaurant just two blocks from Gaby's apartment, and were given a table on a small patio near a wealth of potted trees and flowers.

"I love this," Gaby sighed, fingering some begonias in a tub.

"You and Aggie have this hangup about flowers, I've noticed," he murmured. He laid his cigarette case on the table and glared at it. "I hate damned cigarettes."

Gaby's eyebrows lifted. "Then why smoke?"

"I don't know."

"Nerves?" she asked daringly.

He leaned back, crossing his long legs under the table. His black eyes pinned hers. "Maybe."

"About Aggie," she guessed, because she couldn't imagine making any man nervous, least of all Bowie.

"About Aggie," he said flatly. He fingered the case, smoothing over his initials. J.B.M., it read—James Bowie McCayde. He'd never liked his first name, so he'd always been called Bowie.

"What's she done?"

"It isn't what she's done, so much as what she's about to do." He leaned forward suddenly. "She's bringing a man home to Casa Río."

"Aggie's bringing a man . . . I need a drink—something big."

"That's what I felt, too. It isn't like her."

The waiter came, but Bowie ordered coffee, not drinks,

and sat patiently while Gaby read the entire menu twice before settling for a taco salad.

"My God, you didn't need a menu to order that," he said curtly when the waiter had gone.

"You didn't need one to order steak ranchero, either," she told him with a grin, "but you read the menu."

"I wanted to make sure they still had steak ranchero."

She shrugged. "Who is this man?" she asked.

"I don't know him. She met him on a cruise down to Jamaica. His name is Ned Courtland."

"I don't know him."

"Neither do I. She says he's a cattleman from somewhere up north." He glowered at the table. "More than likely, he's got a couple of calves in a lot out back and he's looking for a rich widow."

"Aggie wouldn't get mixed up with a gold digger," she began but she was wondering about it herself.

"Aggie's human, and she misses my father. She's ripe for a holiday affair."

She stiffened. "Aggie isn't the type to have affairs, any more than I am."

His head lifted and his black eyes scanned her face. He seemed to see right into her brain with that unblinking appraisal. It upset her and she moved her hand too quickly, almost overturning her water glass.

"Careful." He righted the glass, his big, lean hand momentarily covering hers. Its warm strength sent an electric sensation up her arm. She lifted her eyes to his, curious and questioning, and he stared back at her with a faint scowl, as if the contact bothered him, too.

She didn't try to pull her hand away. She was nervous of Bowie, but she'd never had any physical distaste for him, as she did with other men. She liked the touch of his skin against hers very much, and every once in a while, she found herself staring at his mouth with frank curiosity. She wondered how it would feel to kiss him, and that shocked her. She'd been kissed, but it had been somehow mechanical. She'd never really wanted it with anyone except Bowie —not that he knew. She'd made very sure that he hadn't. He was the kind of man who took over people. She couldn't bear the thought of that, ever.

He drew his hand back slowly, aware of an annoying surge of pleasure at the feel of those slender fingers under his. Gaby was off limits, he had to remember that. Aggie would cut his hands off if he tried anything with her baby.

Aggie had never made any secret of her love for Gaby, nor had his father. They seemed to stop caring about him the day Gaby had moved into Casa Río, and he felt like a spare person in the family. Gaby had robbed him of his rightful place. He tried not to show that resentment, but he frequently felt it. It had been Gaby at his father's bedside when he died, because his father had called for Gaby before he had asked for his son. By the time he got to Copeland, it had been too late. He'd resented that, too. Aggie hadn't seemed to notice. She was affectionate, but she reserved her displays of emotion for Gaby. Not once in recent years had she offered to embrace her son.

Gaby was blissfully unaware of his anger, but she had her own secrets, he was sure of it. Her attitude had puzzled him for years. It was odd to find a fifteen-year-old alone in a barn, especially one with no apparent background. His parents had been too fond of her to make inquiries, but Bowie hadn't. He'd wanted to know all about her, but he had drawn a total blank. All his contacts and all his money hadn't managed to ferret out one piece of information about her that he didn't already have. He suspected that she had a past, but he had no idea what it was—or even where. She'd covered her tracks with excellent shrewdness, and that made him more suspicious about her.

"Why did you come to see me?" she asked to break the uneasy silence.

"You've got to help me do something about Aggie."

Her eyebrows went up. "What did you have in mind?"

He paused as the waiter put a plate of steak medallions covered with Monterrey Jack cheese, onions, and peppers before him, and Gaby's taco salad was placed before her. Two cups of steaming coffee, with a small pot of cream, came next. The waiter smiled and left.

"Well?" she prompted, her eyes anticipating with delight the fresh slices of avocado and the sour cream topping her enormous taco salad in its crispy shell.

"I want you to take a vacation."

She stared at him blankly. "A what?"

"A vacation. It's May. You didn't take one at Christmas. You could take it now."

"I'm sure you're going to want me to spend it at Casa Río," she murmured. She sighed. "Aggie and a man—my gosh." She looked up, and now she was feeling some concern of her own. "He must be some fast worker if he's gotten her this involved this quickly."

"I know. That's why I'm worried. If I didn't have this project under way in Calgary, I'd camp down there myself. You know Aggie never minds if we come to stay, or how long for." He glowered at the tablecloth. "Why can't she stay home and start a business, or something constructive? Why hare off to the Caribbean and drag strange men home with her?"

Gaby almost grinned, but it was pretty serious. Aggie hadn't dated anybody, except for a friendly dinner now and again with couples from the construction firm, who thoughtfully provided single men for her inspection. That hadn't worked. Aggie was still a dish at fifty-six, and her short black hair was only flecked with silver. She had a nice figure. Gaby's eyes narrowed. Aggie had been alone a long

time; perhaps being flattered and escorted had played on her
loneliness. She thought about some faceless man playing her
adopted mother for a fool and got madder by the minute.

"I'll go see Johnny Blake first thing in the morning,"
Gaby murmured. "I'll ask Aggie if I can stay a couple of
weeks." She looked up. "What if she says no?"

"When has she ever said no?" he asked testily, his black
eyes questioning hers. "I don't know how we can stop her,
but we can certainly slow her down if she's serious. In the
meantime, we'll find out what we can about her beau."

"He could be on the level . . ." she murmured thoughtfully, trying to give him the benefit of the doubt for Aggie's
sake. If Aggie was really smitten, this could prove to be a
nightmare for everyone concerned. Trying to dissuade a determined woman was difficult at best, and Aggie had a
temper that would match even Bowie's when she was
aroused.

"He could be anything or anyone," Bowie countered.
"Confidence men prey on women her age. It's nothing
against her," he added when Gaby opened her mouth to protest the insinuation. "You have to admit that this is unusual
behavior for her. She's been loyal to my father's memory for
a long time."

That was true. Gaby's mind conjured up a picture of big,
blustering Copeland McCayde, Aggie's exact opposite in
every way. He'd been rather domineering and not very affectionate, but Aggie seemed to have loved him dearly.

"People aren't responsible when they're in love," Bowie
said.

She studied him. "Are you speaking from experience?"

He lifted his eyes to hers, catching her startled expression.
"What do you think?" he asked levelly. When she turned her
head, he added, "You can surely see how a woman could get
in over her head—especially a lonely woman with no social
life to speak of."

The way he was looking at her made her uneasy. "We are talking about Aggie, aren't we?" she asked hesitantly.

"Of course." But he smiled in a way she'd never seen him smile. Her heart jumped. "I imagine just having you around will be more than enough of a deterrent," he said easily. He lifted his fork. "Eat that before it gets cold."

She glowered at him. The taco salad was delicious, warm and spicy in its nest of shredded lettuce and cheese with the cool tomato garnish, and just enough. By the time she reached the layer of refried beans at the bottom, it was all she could do to eat half of them.

"No appetite?" he remarked dryly, polishing off the last of his steak and most of the bread.

"I'm not half your size," she replied. "If I ate what you did, I'd have to be carried out of here on a fork lift."

"I'm not that heavy," he said.

"I didn't say you were heavy. You're big." Her eyes slid shyly over his broad shoulders and chest. "I'll bet most of your men don't argue with you."

"One or two try occasionally," he mused.

"And become little greasy spots on the pavement," she concluded.

He laughed deeply, his black eyes losing some of their cold glitter. "Construction people are pretty tough, as a rule," he reminded her. "They'll only work for a man they respect. Pretty words don't put up buildings."

"You've put up your share. I remember when I was still in my teens that you used to go out on the construction gangs with the men when you got behind on a contract."

"I'd die sitting behind a desk all the time," he agreed. "I like the outdoors."

It showed. He was brawny and rock-hard, and his tan didn't stop at his neck. Gaby had seen him without a shirt more than once, and knew that that dark tan went right to his belt, and probably below it. She flushed, remembering the rough texture of his skin, the feathering of hair down his broad chest and flat stomach. What a time to have total recall, she thought frantically.

He saw that hunted expression on her face and wondered idly what had caused it. She was something of a curiosity in his life. He didn't know exactly how he felt about her, but she was definitely a disturbing influence.

"Well?" he asked curtly.

She jumped, gasping.

"For God's sake," he said harshly. "What's the matter with you?"

She flinched at his tone. She couldn't bear a loud voice, and of course, he was used to construction gangs and slinging out orders right and left. "It's the shooting," she lied. "I'm still shaky."

That calmed him down magically. "Proof that you need some time off," he said, because it reinforced his demand.

"Okay," she said quickly. "I'll try to keep the lovebirds in line."

"Good. How about dessert?"

The beast, she thought, observing him. He'd gotten his own way, as usual, and he was feeling smug. She hated that arrogance in his face, but she'd never seen anyone relieve him of it.

"I don't like sweets," she said.

"Pity. I do." And to prove it, he ordered the biggest strawberry shortcake she'd ever seen and proceeded to demolish it to the last crumb.

He drove her back to her apartment. It wasn't until he'd walked her to her door that she remembered Mary's engagement party.

"I forgot about Mary's party!" she blurted out.

"Who's Mary?" he frowned.

"A girl I'm friendly with at work. She's just gotten engaged. There's a party, and I'm supposed to be there . . ."

"Do you want to go?"

She sighed. "Not really, but I should. I'll . . ."

"Come on, then. It's early. You can still go."

She hesitated. "With you?" she asked, her voice softer than she realized.

He stopped and looked down at her, aware of a faint shift in their turbulent relationship. "Yes," he said quietly. "With me."

Her breath had stopped somewhere south of her windpipe. She felt the ground going out from under her. She didn't understand what was happening, and it was a little scary.

Bowie seemed to know that, because he smiled, relieving some of the tension.

"Will she mind if you bring an escort?" he asked.

"Oh, no, of course not. She's wanted to meet you." She hesitated. "If you don't have anything else to do?" she probed delicately.

He shook his head. "I came to see you."

She felt ridiculously pleased. She smiled shyly, unaware of the effect that smile had on her companion. "All right, then. She lives six blocks away, near the interstate ramp."

"Then let's go."

He took her arm slowly, watching to see how she reacted. When she didn't try to pull away, he let his hand slide down until it touched hers, and then his fingers caught hers and linked into them.

She felt her breath catch. It was new and exciting to hold hands with him, although she tried not to read anything into it. Bowie was just being kind, she told herself.

He drew her along with him. He liked that soft, slender hand in his. It made him feel twice as tall as he already was to hold it, but he didn't really understand why. He and Gaby had never been friends. They were more like remote acquaintances, with Aggie their only common ground. But the more he saw of Gaby, the more she intrigued him.

"You're sure you don't mind?" she asked, as he put her in the car again.

He glanced at her quietly. After a minute he cranked the engine. "No. I don't mind."

But he didn't say another word all the way to Mary's house, and Gaby herself fell uncharacteristically silent. Just being near Bowie was suddenly dangerously exciting. She didn't know why, and that was as disturbing as the new emotions that were curling around her like sensuous, seeking hands.

CHAPTER

Three

Mary lived with her fiancé, Ted, in a very nice suburb of Phoenix. The lights were blazing in the windows and music was drifting down to the street, where Bowie magically found a parking space, without even looking. Considering the number of cars, it looked as if Ted and Mary had invited every single person they knew in the world.

"They live together already?" Bowie asked, frowning as he looked down at her when he helped her out of the passenger side.

"Just because you and I were raised with eighty-year-old attitudes doesn't mean the rest of the world was," she said with a rueful smile. "They're engaged, and although it's been a bit rocky, they've been together for a whole year. It's a new world, Bowie."

He looked down at her. "When I care enough to live with a woman, I'll care enough to give her my name first."

She stared into his black eyes, trying to imagine Bowie in love with a woman. He seemed completely self-contained on the surface—a man's man with everything going for him, to whom a woman would be only an amusement. But Aggie

said that he read love poems sometimes in the silence of his
own room, and that he liked Rachmaninoff's Second Piano
Concerto—a romantic piece if ever there was one. He was
fascinating in his complexity—a modern man with a very
old-fashioned outlook on life. Aggie had raised him that
way, just as Gaby's father had raised her in the church, even
though he'd dragged her from pillar to post until that tragic
night they'd parted.

"What are you thinking?" he asked curiously.

"That you're not like any man I've ever known," she
blurted out.

"Should I be flattered?"

"Yes, I think so," she said honestly, her voice soft and
quiet in the stillness, broken only by faint strains of music.

He found himself smiling at the admission. In all the years
he'd known Gaby, she'd always backed away from anything
personal. This had to be something of a milestone. Perhaps
she was lonely, and the loneliness was breaking through that
shell of reserve she wore. He knew the very color of loneliness. It drove him sometimes. He'd been by himself for a
long time, but there had always been the need for another
voice in the darkness—a hand to reach out to when the
world came too close. Gaby stirred that need in him, but he
hesitated to let her get close. There was something vaguely
mysterious about her. It attracted him, even as it made him
wary.

Without replying, he turned and guided her along the
driveway with him, pretending a nonchalance he didn't feel.
He smoked his cigarette quietly. "Looks like a Florida setting, doesn't it?" he mused, nodding toward the grove of
palm trees.

She leaped at the normalcy. The tension between them
was growing. "Yes. Someone told me once that there were
no palm trees around here a hundred years ago. They aren't
native to Arizona—they're supposedly imports."

"Do tell?" He smiled down at her. "How about the rattle-snakes?"

"They're natives," she said dryly.

He chuckled, easing her between two parked cars, so close that her breasts brushed against his chest just briefly in a contact that made him distinctly aware of her.

The smile faded as he held her there, looking down into her puzzled eyes with an equal curiosity. His body throbbed to the beat of the music inside the house while his eyes held hers in a new, different kind of look. Without really understanding why, he moved deliberately closer for just a second, pressing her back against the car behind her, and he felt her breath catch as his body touched hers in a contact neither of them had ever sought before.

Her perfume drifted up into his nostrils. He could feel the faint tension in her posture, the drawing back as her hands came up to her waist in an almost defensive position. He wondered idly if the nervousness was caused by fear or attraction. His eyes fell to her soft mouth and he was surprised to find it trembling.

Gaby had never allowed herself this close to Bowie before, and now she understood why. His size was intimidating, but there was something more—something deep and still and frightening. He made her tremble. It was the second time in her life that she'd felt the sting of pleasure that came from a man's warm, strong proximity. She wanted to run away and toward him at the same time, and her confusing feelings puzzled her.

For long, static seconds, neither of them moved. It took the sudden opening of the back door to break the spell.

Embarrassed, Gaby went ahead of him to be hugged and kissed by Mary, while Ted looked on with something less than joy in his expression at the guests. Mary worked in the composing room of the newspaper, while Ted was assistant sales manager. She'd known them both ever since she'd gone to work at the paper.

"This is Bowie," she introduced the tall, handsome man beside her, hoping she didn't look as disoriented as she felt.

Mary's Ted wasn't bad-looking, but there was only one Bowie. Mary stared up at him with undisguised fascination, barely aware that he shook her hand and said all the polite things.

"My goodness," Mary exclaimed, and then caught herself and laughed. "It's so nice to meet you, Mr. McCayde. Gaby talks about you all the time."

"Does she?" Bowie looked at a beet-red Gaby with undisguised amusement that hid the remnants of an explosive tension.

"She threatens the other reporters with you," Ted said with faint sarcasm, grinning wickedly at Gaby.

"I do not!" Gaby exclaimed.

"Liar." Ted laughed. "She waves you like a flag when anybody comes too close. She's the original 'Miss Don't Touch' at the office."

Bowie's eyebrow went up in an expressive arch, not only at the implication, but at Ted's frankly insulting way of putting it. His black eyes kindled as he stared at Ted.

"Stop embarrassing my friend," Mary said with a nervous laugh, nudging Ted. "Come on in and have some champagne and canapés," she added, taking Gaby away. "You'll have to overlook Ted. He's been sampling too much punch," she added, with a cool smile in her fiancé's direction.

"That's what impending marriage does to a man," Ted replied with just a little too much venom, despite his forced smile. "Why women think all the trimmings are necessary is Greek to me. She's got a house and a man and a good job, but she has to have a wedding ring."

Mary flushed and got Gaby out onto the balcony. "He doesn't want to go through with it," she confessed miserably. "He says that marriage is just a social statement. But my parents don't feel that way, and neither do his." Mary fiddled with the soft ruffle at her bodice. "I'm pregnant," she whispered.

"Mary!" Gaby said. "Congratulations . . .!"

"Ted says he doesn't want the responsibility of a wife and child. But it will just kill my parents if the baby's born illegitimate," she groaned, lifting her eyes to Gaby's shocked ones.

"Ted will get used to the idea," Gaby said gently. "And everything will work out just fine."

Mary laughed coolly. "Will it?" she said. "He's started talking about that new girl with long hair who's working with the Sports Editor." She looked resolute. "If he wants out, he can go and move in with her. My parents said that if I didn't go through with the wedding, I could come home, and I think I will." Her face tautened. "I'm going to let him go. I know that's what he really wants."

"If it's what you really want, too," Gaby replied.

"When you love someone, isn't that the same thing?" Mary asked with a tired smile. She pressed Gaby's arm. "Come and have some champagne. And don't worry about me," she added when she saw the concern on the other woman's face. "I'm not going to do anything stupid."

Gaby took a glass of champagne punch, but she didn't touch it. She wandered around, talking halfheartedly to the other guests while her eyes searched for Bowie. She found him, finally, by the picture window, looking bored. Which was odd, because he'd been cornered by one of the prettiest women who worked at the office—Magda Lorne, the Society Editor.

Magda was small and dark and beautiful. Gaby secretly envied her that petite beauty and her success with men. Although there'd never been any friction between them, the sight of her long, red fingernails crawling on Bowie's sleeves made something explosive stir in Gaby.

She moved toward the two of them, surprised by the expression on Bowie's tanned face when he looked at her. She was afraid her irritation was showing, and she wasn't sure she liked that faint pleasure in his smile.

"I wondered where you'd gone," he murmured as she joined them.

"I was talking to Mary. Hello, Magda," she said politely.

"Hello. I was just getting to know your stepbrother," she sighed, her dark eyes flirting with Bowie's.

"Bowie isn't my stepbrother," Gaby said politely, surprised at the anger that remark produced in her. "We aren't related."

"Really, dear?" Magda asked. "I didn't realize. I'm sure you said something about having a big brother . . ."

"There's Art," Gaby said, nodding toward the reporter Magda was currently dangling from her string. "He's looking this way."

"Oh, brother," Magda muttered. Then she forced a smile and glanced up at Bowie. "Perhaps I'll see you again. I'd love a ride home . . ."

"I came with Gaby," Bowie said, his eyes saying more than he did. "I'll leave with her."

He never dressed up his words, Gaby mused, watching Magda blush at the bluntness of the remark. She stammered something and beat a path over to Art, who beamed at the sight of her.

"Does she make a habit of that?" Bowie asked as he lit a cigarette.

"Of what?"

"Trying to vamp men away from their escorts."

"She's very popular . . ." she began.

"Popular, the devil," he said with a narrow, half-amused gaze. "She's a born flirt with acquisitive eyes and an ego that probably has to be fed ten times a day. She's the type who runs a mile at the first suggestion of intimacy."

Her eyes studied his face inquisitively. "Magda?" She was surprised because she'd always thought of the other woman as being something of a femme fatale.

"Magda." He blew out a thin cloud of smoke. "It's an act, can't you see? A facade to hide her lack of confidence."

"Remind me never to try and hide anything from you," she said with a laugh that hid nervousness. He saw deep.

"And this engagement won't make it to the altar." He lifted his cigarette to his mouth again, took a draw, and put it out while Gaby studied him with wide eyes. "He's cutting at her already. Why? Is she pregnant?"

She gasped.

"I thought so," he mused. "And he feels trapped and wants out. That's what I mean about marriage, Gaby. People who are sure of what they feel for each other don't need a trial run."

"How do you do it?" she asked.

"Do what?"

"Read people like that."

He shrugged. "I don't know. It seems to come naturally." He glanced down at her. "Except with you. Do you know, Gaby, I've never been able to read you. I'd hate like hell to play poker with you. You've got that kind of face."

"Oh, I'm an open book," she said offhandedly.

"No." He glanced around half irritably. "Have you been here long enough? It's been over half an hour since we got here."

He hated parties and dressing up, she knew, and especially when most of the women present were trying to seduce him with their eyes. He had to be the only person in the room who didn't know how devastatingly handsome he was.

"Yes, I've been here long enough," she agreed. "And I'm rather tired." It was all catching up with her—the shooting, the news about Aggie's new man friend, the truth of Mary and Ted's relationship. She'd never been so depressed.

They excused themselves, wished Ted and Mary happiness with forced smiles, and left.

Bowie parked the car in front of Gaby's apartment complex and cut the engine. He leaned back in the seat, his hand loosening his tie and unbuttoning his jacket. His head went back with a hard sigh.

"I've got to get up in the morning and fly to Canada. Damn it, I hate these trips out of the country," he said unexpectedly. "I'm getting too old to enjoy them anymore."

"You aren't old," she protested.

"Thirty-six next birthday." His head turned and his black eyes sought hers in the glaring light from the streetlamps overhead. "Twelve years older than you, cupcake."

She laughed at the description. "I'm not a cupcake."

"That's better. You've been gloomy all night."

"The man they shot was just a boy," she replied. She leaned back, too, her eyes quiet as they looked through the windshield at the city lights and deserted street. "He had a big family and grew up in the kind of god-awful poverty you read about and wish somebody could do something about. He killed a man and died for twenty stupid dollars, Bowie."

He stretched, drawing the fabric of his white shirt taut across the firm muscles of his broad chest and flat stomach. "People have died for less. It was his turn."

"That's unfeeling," she accused.

"Is it?" One big arm slid behind her bucket seat and he studied her thoughtfully. "He tried to hold up a store. That was stupid. There are poor people all over the world who live honest lives and made the best of what they have. A man with a gun isn't going to accomplish a damned thing except his own destruction. That's basic."

"It's still terrible," she said.

"Why don't you find something else to do with your life?" he asked. "You're too soft to be a reporter."

"What would you suggest I do?" she asked.

"You could come home to Casa Río and help me fight the combine that's trying to move in next door to us," he suggested.

"What combine?"

"Some agricultural outfit called Biological Agri-market—Bio-Ag, for short. They're trying to buy up land in the valley to support a superfarm—the farm of the future, they call it. But I'm afraid that what they're actually after is a quick profit and some devastating ecological impact."

"They can't damage the environment," she assured him. "First, they have to file an environmental impact statement; then, they have to go through the planning and development commission . . ."

"Hold it a minute," he said. "Lassiter doesn't have a planning commission, and our particular valley isn't zoned."

She searched his eyes. "Still, won't the development have to go through regular channels?"

"If they can get the land," he agreed. He smiled coolly. "Hell will freeze over before they get any of mine."

"Then you don't have a problem."

"That's debatable." He lit a cigarette, cracking a window to let out the smoke. "Some of the town fathers in Lassiter are being courted by the developers. They're promising jobs and a lavish local economy, and they're greasing palms right and left." He smiled at her. "I had a threatening phone call yesterday. The word is that I'm holding up progress single-handedly by refusing to sell land to the development. It seems that Casa Río has the best soil for their purposes."

"Lassiter could use more jobs, Bowie," she began slowly. "I know how you feel about the land . . ."

"Do you?" His voice was like cold steel. "Apaches used to hunt on our range. My great-great-grandfather made one of the first treaties with the Chiricahua Apaches, and there's a petroglyph that marks the spot where they agreed on it. Cochise camped at one of the river crossings with his people. There was a small fort, and part of the adobe is still standing, where McCaydes helped the Apaches fight off Mexican raiders. There are Hohokam ruins a thousand years old on that land. The Hohokam had a superior civilization that ultimately spawned the Pima and the Tohono O'odham. And the Earps and Doc Holliday rode through on their way to Tombstone. How do you compare that history with a few jobs—jobs that may not even last, for God's sake, if the developers go bust. And what about the ecology, Gaby?" he persisted, eyes blazing with bad temper. "Imagine all that damned silt pouring into the San Pedro and its tributary near us, when we're already facing a devastating future. We've got the Central Arizona Project and the Salt River Project, and cities are buying ranches all over Arizona for the water rights, but we've got to be careful about our water resources, or they may dry up. It's too risky a venture, despite the potential economic value. What's worse, I think those Bio-Ag people really have their eyes on our water rights. First in time, first in right, remember? You need easy access to water to farm."

Gaby studied him quietly. She knew he was a tireless worker for historic preservation. "You're very knowledgeable," she remarked.

"It's an interest of mine. I'm a builder," he reminded her. "I have to know a lot about the environment and the ecology to be responsible. I don't want to leave behind a legacy of ruined land for quick gain. There are too many people doing that already—throwing up buildings for a profit without considering how much damage they're doing to the local ecology."

"I had to learn about some of that for stories I've done," she replied.

"Silt from irresponsible building practices fills up rivers and streams. That has impact not only on our water resources, but on wildlife, and even the quality of life along those rivers and streams," he replied. "It's a subject worth talking about. We've been lucky here in Arizona. We have legislators who were looking out for our water rights years before it was a popular subject. We've done things to ensure a future water supply. Other states haven't been quite as responsible, and they may suffer for it someday."

"But you don't want developers on Casa Río land," she said.

"That's it in a nutshell. Threats notwithstanding, I won't let Casa Río be used to make money for greedy outsiders."

"How do you know they're greedy?" she asked.

"How do you know they're not?" he shot back.

She gave up. It was impossible to hope for more than a draw when she fought verbally with Bowie. "Stalemate," she murmured humorously. "I won't fight with you. I'm too tired."

"You're still coming home to watch Aggie for me?" he persisted.

"Yes. If you think it's necessary." She paused with her hand on the door handle, oddly reluctant to go inside. "Bowie, you don't really think her friend is a gold digger, do you?"

"I don't know, Gaby. Until I do, I have to assume that he is. I don't want Aggie hurt."

She smiled at him gently. "Why do you call her Aggie, instead of mother?" she asked.

"She's never been quite motherly to me," he replied with a narrow smile. "Even if she has to you."

There was a faint bitterness in his deep voice.

Time to go, quick, she thought. She clutched her purse. "I had a good time. Thanks for taking me to Mary and Ted's party."

"My pleasure." He was still staring at her, much too closely. "What day are you going down to Casa Río?"

"Probably Tuesday," she said. "I've got a big political interview Monday afternoon. When does Aggie get there?"

"Tuesday night."

"See?" She smiled. "Perfect timing."

"For God's sake, don't leave them alone for a second."

Instead of frightening her, his irritated expression delighted her. It was nice to know that Bowie was human, after all. At times, he seemed rather impervious to emotion. He was very much a cool, intimidating stranger to Gaby—or he had been, until tonight. She'd learned a lot about him, and she liked what she'd found out.

"Which one of them do you propose that I sleep with?" she asked.

He was still deep in thought. He glanced at her. "Hmmmmm?" he asked absently.

She leaned closer. "Do you want me to bunk down with Aggie, or her new beau?"

"Oh, for God's sake, don't be ridiculous," he muttered. "Just don't leave them alone together for long."

"I'll do my best. But they're both adults."

"I realize that. But he could take over Casa Río. It's happened before in second marriages. He could wind up with everything Aggie owns, and throw her to the dogs to boot! And if he did it in the right way," he added with an intent stare, "we wouldn't have a legal leg to stand on."

"I see what you mean," she murmured. "Well, I'll do what I can. But he may turn out to be a nice man, you know."

His eyes narrowed thoughtfully. "How is it that you don't

trust people, but you never seem to expect the worst until you're confronted with it?"

She shrugged. "It's a knack. Like your uncanny ability to read people's minds. Thank God I'm not on your wavelength," she grinned. "I don't want you wandering around in my brain."

"Don't you?" He reached out and touched her high coiffure, very gently. "I don't like your hair up like that. I like it long and loose. You're too young to walk around like a matron, Gaby—and much too pretty."

She flushed. The touch of his hand on her hair was electric. "I'm . . . not pretty," she stammered, and tried to laugh.

"Beauty is in the eye of the beholder." He dropped his hand and chuckled as he lifted his cigarette to his mouth to finish it and put it out. "When I get that trite, it's time to go to bed. I'm sleepier than I realized."

"Do you have to drive all the way back to Tucson tonight?" she asked, concerned.

"No. I'm staying with a friend."

She felt something possessive stir in her and hoped that he wouldn't be able to see the sudden freezing of her features. A friend. A female friend? She knew that Bowie was no innocent, but until now she'd never wondered about his private life. What if he had a woman here in Phoenix . . .?

"I went to school with him, and we were in the same company for six months in Vietnam, until he was rotated out."

"Oh." She couldn't think of anything to add to that. He was giving her a strange look already. "Well, good night, and thanks for the ride," she said with relief as she stepped out and shut the car door.

Gaby hurried to her apartment. She noticed Bowie didn't leave until she'd opened her door and gone inside. Through the curtains she saw the Scorpio finally pull away.

She didn't move from the window for several minutes. Tonight had been a bad mistake. Going out with Bowie, for any reason, was going to have to be avoided from now on. He made her feel vulnerable, and that was the one thing she couldn't afford to be. Especially not with Bowie.

CHAPTER

Four

In between worrying about Aggie and trying to come to grips with her sudden attraction to Bowie, Gaby spent her weekend going shopping and to a movie. By the time Monday morning rolled around, her eyes were dark-shadowed and she was ready for the diversion of work.

As she plodded through rush-hour traffic, her mind was busy with the speech she was going to make to Johnny Blake about her two-week vacation. It wasn't really a bad time to take one—news was slow. And if she could sell him on covering the story developing in Lassiter, he might see it as a working holiday and be more receptive to it. Lassiter was southeast of Tucson, and out of Phoenix's reporting area, but it would certainly make state news if things got hot enough. She could tell Johnny that, anyway. He liked a story that got picked up by the wire services. It made the paper look good.

Gaby thought that she might even enjoy spending some time at Casa Río. But whether or not Aggie was going to welcome her presence was anybody's guess. How was she going to explain her sudden need for a vacation this time of year?

The other drawback was proximity to Bowie. The night before, she'd seen him in a totally new light. She couldn't forget the touch of his big fingers around hers, or the way he'd suddenly come close to her at Mary's engagement party as they'd gone between the parked cars. Her entire body had rippled with delicious feeling, and that frightened her. She didn't really want to risk letting Bowie come close.

When she got to the office, Johnny was on the phone, murmuring into the receiver while he looked at her with a blank, preoccupied stare.

"That's right," he said. "That's right. Look, why don't you stick around there for another thirty minutes and see if you can't get one of the jurors to one side. We need some idea of what's going on. Don't compromise their integrity— just see if you can get a handle on how the deliberations are going, okay? Good man!"

He hung up with a grimace. "Well, that's as good as it's going to get today, I suppose. I don't know how we're going to manage anything passable about the Highman case unless we can coax a juror into talking."

"Try a juror's wife," she suggested with a grin.

He chuckled. "No wonder I keep you on, Cane," he nodded. "You've got a devious mind."

"Shrewd sounds better. Johnny, can I go home for two weeks? Before you speak," she added, holding up a hand when he looked as if he might explode, "I've got an angle. I need a vacation. But there's a big agricultural outfit called Biological Agri-market—Bio-Ag—trying to buy up land around Lassiter for some huge truck farming operation. It would have a favorable impact on the local economy, but its water usage and destruction of historic landmarks make it pretty controversial. There have already been a couple of death threats. I could sort of get a handle on things and have my vacation at the same time. What do you think? It could be statewide news," she added quickly. "We'd scoop all the Tucson papers. We might even get picked up on the wires."

He was thinking now, his lips pursed. "Statewide, huh?"

"That's right."

His small eyes narrowed. "Is anybody we know involved in this, Cane?" he probed.

She laughed. "Bowie. He's going to fight it tooth and nail."

"In that case, pack your bags. I still remember when he took on that cut-rate construction company project that cost two lives. Anything he does makes news these days. He's a troublesome . . ." He cleared his throat. "Sorry."

"He isn't family," she said, and was suddenly glad that he wasn't. A picture of his hard, handsome features floated unwanted into her mind and she found herself feeling much too eager to go back to Casa Río.

"Yes. I keep forgetting that," he murmured, watching her warm color. "Well, Cane, you have a nice vacation. Don't forget to finish up your assignments today. You can leave first thing in the morning."

"Yes, sir!" She grinned. "Thanks, boss."

"Don't thank me." He held up a hand and smiled modestly. "I am but a poor, humble editor, doing his best to save democracy for future generations. Four score and seven . . ."

"You might write down that speech on the back of an envelope," she suggested as she went out the door of his office. "Who knows? You could go down in history."

He sighed. "Only if I changed my last name to Lincoln. Go to work!"

"You bet!"

The political interview was one she'd been angling toward for weeks. An older state representative—one of sixty representatives in the State House—had been accused of taking kickbacks on a highway project he'd supported. The charge didn't quite ring true to Gaby, who knew the politician. He had a reputation for honesty that was nothing short of fanaticism.

What made the interview so special was that Gaby was the only member of the press that Representative Guerano would talk to.

"Where's Wilson?" the white-haired legislator asked, darting quick glances around as they sat in the comparative security of his office in the state capitol building. "Is he disguised as a lamp?"

Gaby laughed. Her wild journalistic colleague had that kind of reputation, and it was really a pity that he worked for a rival paper. "Despite Wilson's knack for turning up in odd places, he could only know about this meeting from me, and I don't consort with the opposition."

Representative Guerano chuckled deeply. "Good for you. Okay. What do you want to know, young lady?"

"Who's after you and why, of course," she replied with a twinkle in her olive eyes. "I don't believe for a minute that you've taken money from anybody."

He smiled gently. "God bless you for that blind trust. As it happens, you're right. But I only have suspicions, no hard evidence. And I'm hardly in a position to start throwing stones."

"Tell you what," she said, leaning forward. "You tell me who, when, and why, and I'll tell Johnny Blake. We've got an investigative reporter on our staff who can dig blood out of turnips."

His tired blue eyes brightened. "Think so?"

"I do, indeed. Meanwhile, you give me a nice interview and I'll print both sides of the controversy, just the way a good journalist should."

"Isn't this sticking your neck out?" he asked curiously.

She shook her head. "It's good journalism. We like to print the whole truth. Sometimes we can only print half. But we never give up until we get to the bottom of scandals. That's the only way to do it, to be fair to everyone involved."

He nodded. "I can understand that. But meanwhile, a lot of damage has been done to my reputation." He leaned back, looking every day of his sixty years. "You don't know what a living hell it is to be at the center of a scandal, young lady. My family's suffered much more than I have, but even if I'm cleared, the implication is still there. My career is finished, either way."

Gaby was getting cold chills, because she had a pretty good idea of what a scandal could do to even ordinary people, much less people in the public eye. Her background, if it were ever revealed, could do untold damage to the McCaydes.

She snapped herself back to the present. "All I can promise you is that I'll do a good story and that Johnny will put it in a prominent place. If you deny the charges and we can print your side of it, some people may listen."

"If you mean that, about an investigation, I'll give you all the help I can, and so will my staff."

She nodded. "I can promise you that we'll give it our best shot."

"Then, let's get to it. Ask whatever you like."

It was a good piece—one of the best Gaby had ever done. And once it was in print, it would be a good time to leave the area for a while, until the heat died down. She never ran from trouble, but sometimes it was advantageous to walk around it.

Johnny Blake was delighted. He took the few unverifiable bits of information he'd been given and handed them over to Lang, the paper's investigative reporter. Like a bulldog with a bone to chew, the veteran journalist went straight to work. Lang had contacts that none of the other reporters did. His stock of sources read like a *Who's Who* of organized crime, but he always got what he needed, with enough printable sources to support the story. Other papers had tried to lure him away with everything from company cars to incredible salaries, and one of the television networks had even dangled an anchor spot at him. Lang just plugged away at his desk, amused at his notoriety, and never gave it a second thought. Gaby liked him. He was an old renegade, with a shady past and plenty of grit and style. He might not be society, but he was a reporter's reporter. He'd clear Guerano, and Johnny Blake would have his big story for the month. The only casualty might be Guerano himself, because it was hard to undo a public accusation. With the best will in the world, the dirt stuck.

That night as Gaby packed she worried about encroaching on Aggie's privacy, about interfering. She really was concerned, and knew she was just going to have to risk irritating her. The next morning she put two suitcases in her little white VW convertible, left her plants with a neighbor to water, and set out for Casa Río.

The ranch was over twenty thousand acres in size, as many southeastern Arizona ranches were. The sheer immensity of open space was staggering to Eastern tourists. Even to Gaby, who'd lived here for years, the scope of it was almost unbelievable. One mountain was crossed, ending in an endless valley. That reached to another mountain, and beyond it was another endless valley, and so on. Cattle and horses grazed lazily beyond the highway, because open range was the law in Arizona. Considering the size of the ranches, it was understandable. Fencing thousands of acres would cost a fortune, and with the depressed cattle market, ranchers would certainly be hard-pressed to come up with the kind of money Gaby imagined it would cost.

The thought piqued her curiosity. She and Bowie had

- never talked about the cattle operation at Casa Río. Her dark olive eyes narrowed as she drove down the endless highway toward Tucson. She wondered about the impact of an agricultural operation on Bowie's cattle. Not only would the enormous project use great volumes of water—which was still scarce in this part of Arizona—but it would use pesticides that would leach into the soil and add pollutants to the precious water remaining. Arizona rivers, with the notable exception of the Colorado, mostly ran only during the rainy months, when there was flash flooding. Wells provided the majority of the water in southeastern Arizona. There had already been one television special which had alleged that there were toxins in the drinking water around Tucson. Perhaps some conversations with the local U.S. Soil Conservation Service office in Lassiter might be of benefit. Gaby could see that if she wanted to do a proper job on this story, she was going to be involved in a lot of research.

She stopped to eat in Tucson before heading south through Tombstone to Lassiter. This was familiar territory. Lassiter was bordered on the east by the Chiricahua Mountains, where the Chiricahua Apache once reigned supreme. To the south and west was Tombstone, the site of the O.K. Corral gunfight, high atop its mesa. Far to the southeast was Douglas, on the Mexican border, and to the west were the Dragoon Mountains, where Cochise's Stronghold was located. Near Bowie's ranch was the famous Sulphur Springs Valley, once home to the Clanton clan, the archenemy cowboys who had faced the Earps and Doc Holliday at the O.K. Corral in Tombstone. It was a fiercely historic area, and although Gaby had no roots of her own, part of her could understand and appreciate Bowie's love of the land. But as she drove through the desolate country, dotted only here and there with an occasional ranch far off the road, she wondered if Bowie had considered the job potential the agricultural giant would present here. It would require not only laborers, but heavy equipment operators, technicians, engineers, clerical people, truckers, and packers. The people who worked there could spend their paychecks in Lassiter, which would raise the tax base and help increase services to the townspeople. The unemployment ratio in Lassiter had been high, because a number of small ranches had gone under in recent years. Unskilled labor had no place to go except to one of the cities of larger towns in the area. A few local people worked in Tombstone during Hellrado Days in October—the anniversary of the gunfight at the O.K. Corral—where the Old West was re-created for the benefit of hundreds of tourists. But that was seasonal work, and many people in the area needed jobs that would last year-round.

The two sides of the story kept her mind busy all the way to Lassiter. She drove through it with a nostalgic smile. It was typical of most small Arizona towns—a combination of past and present, with adobe architecture in half its buildings, and modern design in the rest.

The pavement was cracked in most places, and the people walking about reflected the poor economy in the way they dressed. There was a lack of entertainment facilities for young people, since most teenagers left Lassiter for work in other towns when they graduated from its one high school. She looked at the landscape and tried to envision Bio-Ag's huge operation settling here. Irrigated fields would spread to the horizon and the desert would bloom. She sighed, smiling at her own vision.

There were only a few shops in town these days, and half of them were boarded up from lack of commerce. The town had two policemen, neither of whom stayed too busy, except over the weekend when the local bar filled up and tempers grew short. There was a fire department, all volunteer, and a motel-restaurant. Several government agencies had offices here, some of which were only open part of the week. There was a newspaper—a very good one for a town that small—

the *Lassiter Citizen*. And there was a radio station, but it was a low-budget operation with high school students manning the control room most of the afternoon and early evening. If Bio-Ag came, there would be some more advertising revenue for the media, and certainly plenty of newsworthy copy to help fill space.

Bowie would fight it, with his environmental priorities, and there were enough special interest groups to help him. Bio-Ag would need an ally. She smiled, thinking of ways to circumvent Bowie's efforts.

The road wound around past the sewage treatment plant and reservoir; then, it became a straight shot out to Casa Río. It was visible in the distance, far off the main highway, on a wide dirt road with fields that combined wildflowers and improved pasture. Bowie's Brahman cattle grazed in that area, where cowboys during roundup would draw straws to see who had to brave the thickets of brush to roust out the strays. Prickly pear cactus, ocotillo, cholla, creosote, sagebrush and mesquite were enough of a threat, without the occasional potholes and diamondback rattlers that could give a horseman gray hairs.

On the other hand, there was clean air, open country, the most spectacular scenery on earth, and the glory of palo verde trees in the spring. There were red-winged blackbirds, sage hens, cactus wrens, and owls. There were rock formations that looked like modern art, and wildflowers bursting from the desert. Gaby had the top of the VW convertible down, and her eyes drank in the beauty of the landscape unashamedly. She had her memories of Kentucky—of lush green pastures and white fences and huge groves of trees—but they were pale against this savage beauty.

She crossed over the bridge that sheltered a tributary of the San Pedro. It was early for the summer "monsoons," so there was barely a trickle of water in the creek bed. It was more of a sandy wash right now than the swollen, deadly

creek it became after a good, heavy rain. Past the bridge was
a long ranch road that led back from the flat valley into a
small box canyon. There, in a small grove of palo verde and
mesquite trees, stood Casa Río.

It was old. The beautiful parchment color of the adobe
walls blended in with the mountains behind it. The house
was two stories high, and despite its stately aged appearance, with wrought iron at the windows, and the courtyard
gate that led to the porch, it had every modern convenience.
The kitchen was like something out of a *Good Housekeeping*
layout. Behind the house was a garage, and adjoining the
house was an Olympic-sized indoor swimming pool that was
heated in winter. There were tennis courts and a target-
shooting range, and a neat stable and corral where the breed-
ing horses were kept. Farther away was the working stable,
the barn, and a modern concrete bunkhouse where the six
full-time bachelor cowboys lived. The foreman, assistant
foreman, and livestock manager—all three married men
with families—had small houses on the property.

The driveway led around the house to the garage, but
Gaby parked at the front gate, leaving her luggage in the
trunk. She admired the only real home she'd ever known.
There were flowers everywhere—pots and planters of gera-
niums and begonias and petunias. There were blooming rose
bushes in every shade imaginable to either side of the house.
The small courtyard garden had a winding, rock-inlaid path
to the long front porch under the overhanging balcony that
ran the width of the house. A staircase with inlaid tiles led
up the side of the porch to the second story balcony through
a black wrought iron gate. There was a towering palo verde
tree just beside it, dripping yellow blossoms, and a palm tree
on the other side of the house. Ferns hung from the front
porch, where wicker furniture beckoned in the shade of the
balcony.

She opened the big black, wrought iron gate and walked

into the garden, smiling with pure pleasure as she meandered down the path, stopping to smell a rose here and there.

"Always you do this," came a resigned, Spanish-flavored voice from the porch. A familiar tall, spare figure came into the light, his silvery hair catching the sunlight. "*Bienvenida, muchacha.*"

"Montoya!" She laughed. She held out her hands, to have them taken in a firm, kind grasp. "You never change."

"Neither do you," he replied. "It is good to have you here. I grow weary of cooking for myself and Tía Elena. It has been lonely without the Señora Agatha and Señor Bowie."

"Have you heard from Aggie?" she asked.

"*Sí.* She arrives today or tomorrow." He glanced behind him and leaned forward. "With a strange *hombre*," he added, "and Señor Bowie does not like this. There will be trouble."

"Tell me about it," Gaby groaned. "He talked me into coming down here as a chaperone, and God only knows what Aggie's going to say when she finds me here."

"When she finds you both here," he corrected.

"*¿Qué hablas?*" she asked, lapsing into the natural Spanish that seemed so much a part of Casa Río because its staff and Bowie spoke it so fluently.

"Señor Bowie came an hour ago," he said. "He seems to have had no sleep, and he has already caused Tía Elena to hide in the bathroom."

She felt a ripple of pure excitement that she shouldn't have felt at the remark. "Bowie's here? But he's supposed to be in Canada . . ."

"Not anymore," Montoya sighed. "He left the project in the hands of his foreman and caught a plane to Tucson. He says that he cannot stand by and let his mother make such a mistake. He is going to save her."

He said the last tongue in cheek, and Gaby smothered a laugh. "Oh, my."

"If you laugh, *niña*, make sure the *señor* does not see you do it," he said dryly. "Or you may have to join Tía Elena in the bathroom. He has the look of the coyote that tried to eat our cat last week."

"That bad, huh?" She shook her head. "Well, I'll go see what I can do. Poor Aggie."

"We know nothing of this man," Montoya reminded her. "He could be right, you know."

"He could be wrong, too."

"The señor?" Montoya put his hand over his heart. "I am shocked that you should say such a thing."

"I'll bet," she mused, grinning as she went past him. "Where is he?"

"In the house."

"Where in the house?"

Montoya shrugged. "*¿Quién sabe?* I have better sense than to look for him."

She gave him a mock glare and went inside. Tía Elena, fifty, and severe as night in her black dress with her hair pulled back into a bun, peeked around the corner, her black eyes wary.

"It's only me," Gaby teased. She hugged the thin older woman and laughed. "Still hiding, I see."

"Is it any wonder?" Elena asked, shaking her head. "I do nothing right, you see. The bed is made with colored sheets, the señor wanted white ones. I have polished the floor too much and he does not like it that it is slippery. The bathroom smells of sandalwood, which he hates; the air conditioner is set too low, and he is roasting; and I am certain that before dark he will find a way to accuse me of having the clouds too low and the sand too deep in the backyard."

Gaby laughed softly. Bowie on a rampage could do this even to people who'd lived with him for years. She patted Tía Elena on the shoulder gently. "It will all blow over," she promised. "It always does."

"I am too old for such storms." Elena sighed. "I will make a salad and slice some meat for sandwiches. The señora and her friend will arrive soon." She threw up her hands. "No doubt the señor will accuse me of trying to poison the meat . . ." she muttered as she went back into the kitchen.

Gaby went down the long hall of the first floor, skirting the staircase that led to the upstairs bedrooms, past the sweeping Western motif of Bowie's study, past the elegant grandeur of the traditional living room, past the library with its wall-to-wall bookcases, pine paneling, and leather furniture, past the huge kitchen, and down the covered walkway to the pool house. And there was Bowie.

He was cleaving the water with powerful strokes, easily covering the length of the Olympic-sized pool and turning with quiet strength to slice back through the water to where Gaby stood watching.

His head came out of the pool, his blond hair darker wet than dry, his black eyes examined her curiously. She was wearing designer jeans, but they weren't tight. The long, trendy, red-and-gray overblouse disguised her figure, except for its slenderness and the elegance of her long legs. Her hair was tied back in a ponytail with a red ribbon, and her dark glasses were still propped on her head.

"Taking inventory?" she asked.

"Not particularly. You're late."

"I'm early, and what are you doing here? You're supposed to be in Canada," she reminded him.

"I couldn't stop worrying about Aggie," he said simply.

He put his big hands on the side of the pool, and with devastating ease, pulled himself out. As he got to his feet, Gaby found herself gaping at the unfamiliar sight of him in nothing but white swimming trunks.

They were very conventional trunks, but they did nothing to disguise the sheer magnificence of his powerful body without clothing. She'd seen him this way before a time or two, but it had never affected her so much. Bowie had a physique that was nothing short of breathtaking. He was a big man, formidable in height as well as size, but there wasn't a spare ounce of excess weight. He was perfectly proportioned—streamlined from his broad, hair-covered chest to his lean hips, flat stomach, and long, powerful legs. He had a natural tan that the sun only emphasized, its darkness enhancing his blond hair and giving his body a particularly masculine glow. He wasn't pale or flabby, and while there was hair on his chest and flat stomach and legs, it wasn't unsightly.

Bowie wasn't unaware of that keen, helpless scrutiny. He rested his hands on his hips, his black eyes narrowed, as he studied her expression with open curiosity. She'd never looked at him in quite that way before, and he found it disturbing. He found her disturbing. It hadn't been only Aggie's unknown suitor who'd brought him here today. He'd brooded all weekend about the way he'd felt when he'd taken Gaby to supper in Phoenix. It had worked on him until he'd put the Canada construction project in the hands of his project foreman and hot-footed it down to Lassiter.

Gaby didn't know that, and he had too much intelligence to let her know. He was sure that if he signaled his interest, she'd turn tail and run. The very way she dressed spoke volumes about her repressions.

"Why don't you get into a suit? I'll race you across the pool," he said with a faint smile.

She lifted her eyes to his and felt her heart race in her chest. "I didn't bring one," she fabricated. She didn't own one.

"There are several in the pool house," he replied.

"I have to unpack," she said. "And get my things out of the car . . ."

"Montoya will already have done that, and Tía Elena will

have your things in the drawers before you can get upstairs," he mused. "If she's out of the bathroom."

"I hear that you sent her in there in the first place," she said with a nervous laugh.

"Lies. All lies. I'm not half as bad as my publicity around here," he told her. He pursed his lips, letting his eyes search over her flushed face. "The water's cool, Gaby," he coaxed, a note in his voice that Gaby hadn't heard before.

Her body tingled. It was so tempting. But she might be unleashing emotions that she couldn't handle. She knew Bowie only as Aggie's son, as the heir to Casa Río. It would be dangerous to start thinking of him as anything more personal. A man his size was a considerable threat out of control . . .

"Maybe later," she said, forcing a smile. "Okay?"

He didn't press his luck. He didn't want to scare her off. He smiled back, his black eyes kind. "Okay, honey."

The endearment made her knees weak. That smile had done some damage, too. Bowie was by far the handsomest man she'd ever seen in her life. She could only imagine how many hearts he'd broken over the years.

"Just what are we supposed to be doing here?" she asked, biting her lower lip. "Aggie's going to be furious, and she'll know immediately why we're here."

"We'll throw her off the track," he promised. "You aren't backing out on me?"

"Heavens, no," she said. "I don't want Aggie hurt any more than you do. But if we look like we're interfering, she may very well send us both packing. Right now, it's her house. We're interlopers, even if we are family to her."

"I know that, too. I don't like trespassing on her privacy. I didn't do it much, even when Dad was still alive."

"I guess you resented me more than you ever said," she ventured, studying him.

He smiled faintly. "From time to time. I didn't fall in line when he wanted me to; then, we didn't speak for two years while I was in Vietnam. After I got back, I worked in a construction gang for a rival company. It was Aggie who persuaded me to talk to my father, and he eventually wore me down. That was the year before you showed up. There'd been no time before, and there was none after. You were their hearts. They both wanted a daughter. They got me."

"I'm sorry," she said softly. "I never knew the whole truth."

"You still don't. But it was a long time ago. No need to brood about it, tidbit. Did you have to fight for your time off?"

"I told Johnny I'd get him a great scoop on that agricultural conglomerate that's trying to locate here."

His face went hard. "Is the job all you think about?"

"That's not fair," she replied. "I had to have an excuse. You don't just walk out the door and tell your boss you're taking a vacation!"

"Why in hell not?" he demanded. "My God, Gaby, you'll inherit part of Casa Río. There's more than enough here to support both of us for life."

"I don't want part of Casa Río!" she shot back. She knew she must be pale; she could feel the blood running out of her cheeks. "It's your birthright, not mine. If there's any outsider here, it's not your mother's friend, it's me!"

He moved toward her, big and confident and a little frightening because of the sheer size of him. She had to look up to see his eyes, and all the while she was aware of the hard muscle of his body, the broadness of his chest, the masculine beauty of the darkly tanned hands holding the towel as he patted his chest with it absently to absorb the moisture.

"I don't think of you as an outsider, despite the fact that we don't see much of each other," he said quietly. "And I don't resent what Aggie feels for you—not anymore."

"Oh, I know that, but it should be yours. You love it more than I ever could. Someday you'll marry and have sons to inherit it..." She stopped because the thought of Bowie marrying someone and having children upset her.

"Oddly enough, Gaby, I don't get along very well with most women," he told her honestly. "I don't flatter, I say what I think, and I expect intelligent conversation." He smiled lazily. "Shall I tell you what most of my escorts expect from me, or are you sophisticated enough to guess?"

She was and she could. "You can hardly blame them," she said defensively, and her eyes ran over him softly, making fires where they touched. "My gosh...!" She averted her eyes from his chest and shoulders.

He felt the impact of her eyes like brands on his skin. He moved a step closer, so that with one more step he could have stood against her. The nearness of her slender body, even in its habitual camouflage, made his breathing rough. He looked at her soft mouth and wondered again how it would taste under his in passion. He wondered if Gaby had ever known passion.

"That wasn't what I meant," he said deeply. "I meant, my escorts expect some tangible evidence of my regard: a diamond necklace, roses at breakfast—that sort of thing."

She lifted her eyes to his hard mouth and forced them all the way to his black eyes. "What a pity they don't know you," she murmured. "You aren't at all the kind of person who deals in buying and selling bodies."

He felt his body go taut and hoped to God she didn't notice what was happening to him. Her unexpected perception aroused him totally. "How do you know that?" he asked.

She smiled softly. "I don't know. Aggie talks about you a lot, and so do other people. I've learned a lot about you that way."

He didn't have room to talk. He'd learned a lot about her

the same way. He liked very much what he saw. She had a lovely figure, and a sexy, soft mouth. Besides that, she had a big heart, plenty of spirit, and an impish sense of humor. He'd never really known anyone like her.

"I've got to get dressed," he said, forcing himself to think sensibly and not give in to the urge to make a grab for her. "Montoya said that Aggie was on the way."

"And you want to be ready—lying in wait to ambush them, right?" she teased, wondering why it felt so natural to play with Bowie.

He smiled back. "That's the general idea."

"It's never wise to mix in other people's business." She sighed.

"I know that, too," he told her. "Get going. I'll be along in a minute or two." He would, when he got himself under control again, he thought ruefully. He was reacting to her in a totally unexpected way. He had to curb his instincts before he frightened her.

"Okay."

It was almost a relief to get away for a few minutes and gather her shattered nerves. Being close to him produced the most incredibly sweet sensations. She wondered how it would have felt if she'd gone in the pool with him—if he'd held her while they were both barely dressed. She wondered if his hands were as capable and expert as they looked, and how it would be if she let him touch her with them. The most erotic images danced in her brain—Bowie towering over her in the shallow area of the pool; his hands peeling away the top of her swimsuit, baring her to his eyes; bending, putting his hot mouth over her soft skin . . .

Blushing furiously, she moved quickly out of the pool area, her legs feeling like rubber beneath her.

She'd only gotten as far as the hall when a commotion outside caught her attention. She went quickly to the front porch, just in time to see Montoya embracing a radiant Aggie. And a few steps behind her was the source of all the excitement at Casa Río—a tall, lean figure of a man about Aggie's age, looking perfectly at home, his eyes, steady and adoring, on Agatha McCayde.

CHAPTER

Five

Ned Courtland wasn't as big as Bowie. He was lean and fairly tall, with dark eyes and skin and silver-streaked black hair. He looked pleasant enough, but there were hard lines in his face and a stubborn set to his chin. Gaby, who'd had years of practice sizing up potential interviewees, would have pegged him as a man who presented a calm front but had a strong will and a formidable temper. He had the look of authority that usually came with money. But all that, she reminded herself, could be part of his act if he was looking to deceive Aggie.

"Hello, darling," Aggie said, laughing as she hugged Gaby. "What in the world brings you down here?"

"A two-week vacation that Johnny talked me out of last year," she said with commendable acting ability. "And I seem to have arrived at a very bad time . . ." Her eyes went past Aggie to Ned Courtland.

"Not at all!" Aggie scoffed, although the man behind her didn't seem overjoyed to find a resident house guest. "Ned, come here and meet Gaby. She's the next best thing to a daughter in my life. I've told you all about her. Gaby, this is Ned Courtland from Wyoming."

"I'm very pleased to meet you, Mr. Courtland," Gaby said politely, and shook hands with him. He had a strong grip, and his eyes didn't waver as they met hers. Good traits, she thought absently.

"Same here, Miss Cane," he replied. "I've been looking forward to meeting you."

"I could postpone my vacation," Gaby offered, feeling guilty and half mad at Bowie for dragging her into this.

Aggie made a familiar gesture with her hand. Her salt-and-pepper hair was cut short, with bangs, and she was wearing a red pantsuit that emphasized her olive complexion and dark, snapping eyes. She was still a pretty woman, and as capable in business as her late husband had been. She was not an easy woman to fool. Of course, she had been lonely, Gaby recalled.

"You aren't about to postpone your vacation," Aggie said firmly. "We'll enjoy having you around while Ned gets an eyeful of the Arizona cattle business. He has cattle of his own, you know," she added, and glanced up at the tall man with pure adoration in her eyes.

He smiled at her just faintly. "Just a few head, Aggie," he murmured. "Don't make me into a cattle baron."

He didn't look like one, Gaby had to agree. He was wearing a simple gray suit, which looked very nice on him, but it wasn't an expensive suit. With it he wore cowboy boots and an inexpensive felt cowboy hat. The hat was cocked at a jaunty angle, but that seemed to suit him. Gaby wondered what secrets lurked in that calm, quiet face. Mr. Courtland didn't look like a gigolo, whatever he really was.

"I have just this minute told Tía Elena to start setting the table for lunch." Montoya grinned. "I will help her get the food to the table. Uh, shall I call Señor Bowie?"

Aggie blinked. "Call him in Tucson, you mean?"

"Actually, he's in the swimming pool," Gaby said, grimacing at Aggie's rapidly changing expression. "He got here just after I did."

"How sweet of the dear boy to come down to meet his tired old gray-haired mother, fresh from the cruise ship in Miami and the plane at the Tucson airport," Aggie said through her teeth and a forced smile. "Do run and have him join us, Gaby."

"I'll do that very thing," Gaby promised. She grinned at Mr. Courtland. "Bowie's nice; you'll like him," she added, ignoring Aggie's raised eyebrows and popping eyes.

"Nice? We *are* speaking of my son?" Aggie prompted.

"The big blond one." Gaby nodded. She cleared her throat and moved toward the house. "I'll go and get him. Excuse me, won't you?"

She whirled and ran like wild for the pool area out back. Now Bowie had done it! It would take Aggie about ten seconds to put the whole plot together, and she was going to be out for blood when she realized what they were up to. She wouldn't consider that they were trying to protect her. She'd think of it as meddling, and what's more, she'd be right!

Gaby opened the door and scanned the pool, but Bowie was nowhere in sight. Perhaps, she thought, he'd already dressed and gone back into the house. But on an impulse, she went to the shower room and pushed open the door, not really expecting to find him there.

It was a mistake not to knock—she realized that immediately. He'd obviously just come out of the shower, because he was drying his hair. He lifted an amused eyebrow at her shocked stance and red face. He was totally nude from head to toe.

"Yes?" he asked in a perfectly normal tone.

Gaby knew that most twenty-four-year-old women had seen men like this. She had, in pictures, once or twice. But in the flesh, it was different, and especially when the man was Bowie. Without the civilizing veneer of clothes, he was devastating. He was tanned all over—lean muscle from head to toe, perfect symmetry, fine lines, blatant masculinity in every ripple and curve. She stared because she couldn't help it. He was magnificent, in every sense of the word.

"I'm . . . sorry," she croaked, trying to avert her eyes. "I didn't think you were in here, so I didn't knock. I should have . . . !"

"It's all right," he said softly. He tossed the towel aside and moved toward her, conscious of her jerky stance, her quick backward step. But he didn't stop until he was towering over her. "There's no need to run, Gaby," he said. "I'm not dangerous."

"Oh, I know that," she wailed. "But Bowie . . . !"

"You've never seen a man like this," he finished for her. "Okay. Now you have. It's no big deal, honey. Even if I'm not in the habit of stripping in front of women, I guess I don't really mind letting you look at me. What's so important that it brought you flying in here?"

She knew her mind had stopped working. He made it sound matter-of-fact, but hadn't he mentioned something about not letting other women see him this way? She was too confused to pick up on that.

"It's Aggie," she said, hot in the cheeks as she tried not to look.

His big hand tilted her eyes up to his black ones. "Aggie and her friend?"

She nodded. "Ned Courtland."

His face went hard and his eyes began to glitter. "So he's here. What's he like?"

"He's tall and rather intimidating, really," she faltered. "Like you," she added with forced laughter.

His fingers touched her cheek and he smiled at her. "Am I? In that case, I suppose I'd better put some clothes on. Hand me my jeans, honey, will you?"

He was getting really free with that endearment, and the thought sent tingling waves of feeling through her slender body. She searched around until she found his jeans, and by the time she had, he was wearing white briefs and shouldering into his blue plaid shirt.

She handed him the jeans with fingers that trembled. They were heavy, sporting the picture jasper belt buckle that Aggie had given him for Christmas last year.

As he took the jeans his free hand touched hers, curling around it. He eyed her with quiet concern. "It's over. Nothing happened. You got an eyeful, but you're old enough. No harm done."

"Except to my nerves," she said with a shy smile. "I'm sorry I came running in like that."

"And I've already told you, I didn't mind. Or would it make you feel better to know that if you'd been any other woman, I would have minded?"

She lifted her eyes, frowning. "Why?"

He shrugged. "I've got my own hangups." He pulled on the jeans and fastened them with quick, deft movements. His lean fingers worked at the buttons of his shirt, concealing the thick hair and hard muscles of his chest while he studied Gaby's frankly curious eyes.

"Then I'm flattered," she said, and tried to appear less embarrassed than she was.

He tucked his shirt into his jeans, and his black eyes held hers. "I've never made love to a woman, except in the dark."

"Oh." She shifted restlessly. Now that she'd seen him, all sorts of thoughts were flailing about in her brain—shocking things. She turned away while he got into his socks and boots.

"How did Aggie take your arrival?"

"Fine—until Montoya told her you were here," she told him, glancing back with a nervous but mischievous smile.

"She's livid. I think we're both going to be on the lunch menu as entrées."

"Think so?" He got up, pausing to run his comb through his thick, straight hair in the mirror. It looked like burnished gold, and he kept it conventionally short and neatly trimmed. She loved the very way he moved, with such elegance and grace.

"I offered to go back to Phoenix, but she wouldn't hear of it," she said, searching for something to break the silence.

"You can't go back to Phoenix and leave me here to deal with this," he said shortly. He pocketed the comb and turned, looming over her. "Aggie's obviously in the throes of infatuation, and God knows what kind of man he is."

"You might give him the benefit of the doubt," she suggested, brushing back an irritating strand of black hair.

"Not before I size him up." He looked down at her for a long, tense moment, until her knees felt rubbery all over again. "Don't start avoiding me now," he said unexpectedly. "I'm not embarrassed, and there's no reason for you to be. Okay?"

She nibbled her lower lip. "Okay." Her eyes fell to his polished boots. "You have this way of making the most extraordinary things seem perfectly natural."

"I don't think I've ever been called extraordinary before."

She glanced up, laughing, because his tone had been droll and dry. His eyes were twinkling with humor. All the tension left her. "Pity," she murmured and turned away quickly.

He chuckled, moving to open the door for her. "Next time, go swimming when I ask you to," he said at her temple when she passed him, "and you'll know when I'm in the shower."

She met his eyes briefly. "I haven't been swimming in years, you know," she said abruptly, without even meaning to. "I don't own a bathing suit."

His eyes lost their amused glow and narrowed, searching

hers in a silence that took fire. "Don't you think it's time you stopped hiding your body and took a woman's natural pride in it, little one?" he asked quietly. "Wearing a sexy outfit isn't going to put you in danger with me. And I'll fight off the rest of the male population for you, if that's what frightens you."

For once she was without her customary defenses. "You would?" she asked hesitantly, her olive eyes wide and unblinking.

That gaze knocked him in the stomach. She had eyes that seduced. She probably didn't even know it, but she was working on him in ways he hadn't expected.

"Yes," he said, answering her at last. "I would. I might take you out to dinner and dancing one night."

Her breath stilled and then became quick and sharp. "You might?"

His lips parted. He was talking to her, but the words were superfluous. The real communication was between his black eyes and her olive ones, and the tension was beginning to build in a feverish way.

"Why not?" he asked, his voice becoming deep and slow, like dark velvet. "Do you dance?"

"Not really. Don't you remember? At that dance in college, I stumbled all over you and finally gave up."

He did remember, all too well.

"You might try teaching me again," she ventured.

He felt his body going taut. The effect of the words was visible and he thanked his lucky stars that she was too green to see it. "Yes. I could teach you." It wasn't dancing he was thinking about. His eyes dropped to her soft mouth and lingered there. He could teach her passion. It was there, inside her, he knew it. All it would take was a little tenderness . . .

"Bowie?" she whispered.

His eyes lifted slowly to hold hers. He was close enough that she felt the warmth of his body striking into her, and she could feel the coiled strength in him as his hand came up very slowly to her upper arm. His fingers spread over it, encompassing it, testing its silky warmth.

"I want your mouth," he whispered. His hand pulled her gently toward him, moving her inches closer, so that they were almost touching.

She let him. The sensations she was feeling were new and overwhelming. It was like being drugged, she thought, and the dragging sensation in her stomach and upper thighs was oddly crippling. She was trembling inside, in a way she'd never expected. Her breasts ached. It was as if just the feel of those black eyes on her mouth had made some basic change in her chemistry. She felt the threat of his great strength at the same time she wanted to feel his body against the length of hers. She wanted to put her arms around him and be hugged until her breasts ached, kissed until her mouth was swollen and sore. She went pale. Was she going to be able to face the past at last and move into womanhood?

It almost seemed so. Her lips parted on a shaky breath, and her eyes searched Bowie's fierce ones.

"Do you want my mouth on yours, Gaby?" he asked huskily, and his head started to bend. His gaze fell to her parted lips. "Do you want to feel me kissing you?"

"Oh . . . God," she groaned, her legs going weak as the passionate need snapped in her. "Bowie . . . !"

She was reaching up to him, shaking with anticipation. And that was when the voice, stark and bleak, shattered the fever that was building in the pool house.

"Sēnor Bowie!"

Bowie's hands contracted sharply on Gaby's arms, almost bruising. His eyes met hers, black with frustration and shocked fury. Then she was free and he was striding out into the hall.

"What is it, Montoya?" he asked in a steely but perfectly normal tone.

"Lunch is served, sẽnor," Montoya called, grinning at the end of the hall. "Is Gaby with you?"

"She's around somewhere. I'll go hunt her up." He paused, waiting until Montoya disappeared back into the dining room before he turned and motioned to Gaby.

She walked out into the hall on shaky legs, avoiding his eyes. But he didn't move and she cannoned into him.

"It's only a reprieve," he said quietly, holding her wide eyes. His face was hard and his expression dogged. "I'm going to have that kiss. I'm going to take the breath out of your body and the strength out of your arms, and you're going to want me like hell. That's a promise."

He slid his hand into hers and pulled her along with him toward the dining room, his profile intimidating. His fingers contracted and he glanced down. "Don't start looking for excuses, either," he added. "You and I aren't related in any way. We can hold hands, we can go on dates. We can even make love. There aren't any barriers."

Her breath felt shaky. "That's what you think," she said under her breath.

"I'll get past those hangups, honey," he mused. "I'm not a rounder by any stretch of the imagination, but I know very well what to do with a woman. I won't hurt you—not ever."

She wanted to argue, to tell him that she couldn't, she wouldn't. There were so many secrets from the past, so much hidden pain and fear and guilt. But she couldn't pour all that out. She couldn't let Bowie know what had happened—she couldn't let him get close to her at all. That knowledge was like a thorn in her heart. She wanted him—really wanted him. It was a new and exciting feeling. But what a pity to find it now, with the one man in the world she didn't dare love. Her love could destroy everything the McCaydes had built up for themselves. And she couldn't even tell Bowie why. She should never have gone near him in the first place.

She tried to disengage her fingers from his strong, lean ones, but he refused to let go as they walked into the dining room.

When Aggie looked at them, she knew why. Aggie had been sure that Bowie and Gaby had come down to protect her from her new friend, but when she saw them holding hands and felt the blinding tension radiating from their set faces, she formed a new opinion. She pursed her lips and her eyes began to show sheer pleasure rather than astonishment.

Gaby looked up at Bowie to see a raised eyebrow and an amused twinkle in his dark eyes. She glared at him. So that was his game—throwing Aggie off the track with a red herring. She wondered how much of what he'd said to her in the pool house had been part of the plan. Had he meant it, or had he just been stirring her up so that Aggie would read even more into her expression?

She didn't trust men at the best of times, but she'd always felt that she could trust Bowie. Now she wasn't sure anymore. She felt vulnerable and afraid.

"Hello, mother," Bowie said. He let go of Gaby's hand and seated her before he leaned over to kiss Aggie's cheek. "How was Jamaica?"

"Jamaica was lovely," Aggie murmured dryly. She glanced at her friend and put her thin hand over his big one. "Bowie, this is Ned Courtland." She made a caress of his name.

"How do you do?" Bowie said pleasantly enough, but his features were rigid and his eyes were already damning the other man to hell.

"I'm fine, thanks," Ned returned in a slow drawl. "How are you, son?"

Bowie bristled, but he didn't rise to the bait. He smiled coolly. "I hear you run a few head of cattle." He sat down beside Gaby and lit a cigarette, his first that afternoon. "What do you think of the Japanese outlook?"

Ned raised thick eyebrows. "Well," he began, "I don't much care for Japanese food, to be honest, but I guess I could learn."

Bowie's expression, in another place, would have been comical. He leaned forward, his smoking cigarette in one lean hand resting on the other forearm. "I meant the export of beef to Japan."

"Oh, that." Ned smiled. "Damned if I know much about it."

Bowie's eyes were speaking volumes, and Gaby could see Aggie starting to fidget as Montoya brought coffee and Elena set platters of food on the table.

"There's been a movement afoot to encourage the Japanese to import more American beef," Gaby began, trying to help things along.

Ned glanced at her in an odd way. "Is that so?"

"There's a hell of a lot more to the situation than that," Bowie said irritably, glaring at her.

"I refuse to talk shop at the table," Aggie said shortly, her dark eyes challenging her son. "Eat your lunch, Bowie, then you and Gaby and I might show Ned the operation here."

"What a wonderful idea," Gaby agreed enthusiastically. "Casa Río has some beautiful purebred Brahmans."

"I hate Brahmans," Ned said pleasantly, and smiled as if at some secret joke, his lean hands ladling chili into a bowl from the red pot on the table. "Ugliest damned cattle in the world."

"Yes, they are," Aggie chuckled, "but very suited to desert conditions."

Bowie finished his cigarette and put it out with a deliberate motion that meant trouble.

"What breed of cattle do you like, Mr. Courtland?"

"Call me Ned." He pursed his lips as he sampled the ham. "I like red and white ones."

Gaby picked up her napkin and smothered a helpless

laugh in it. Aggie was doing the same thing. Bowie looked as if he might take a bite out of his plate and then Mr. Courtland.

"Have some ham, Bowie." Gaby offered the platter to him quickly.

He searched her eyes with pure malice, but he took the hint. He fell to eating while Aggie and Gaby caught up on each other's gossip. Mr. Courtland seemed pretty intent on his own food, but there was a definitely amused gleam in his dark eyes the one time Gaby got a good look at them.

After lunch, Gaby stuck to Bowie like glue, torn between her growing attraction for him and her need to help Aggie ward off his temper before it exploded over Mr. Courtland.

The pasture stretched all the way to the main highway. Parts of it were fenced, only to keep in certain cattle. The rest, like most ranch land, was open range, and the cattle wandered where food and water were available. Bowie had plenty of windmills that pumped out groundwater into troughs for the cattle. All the same, the groundwater table on his land was dropping steadily. There were small streams running out of the mountains, but not nearly enough to supply his vast herds of cattle with adequate drinking water. It was this facet of ranching that the proposed agricultural project threatened. Agriculture used tremendous amounts of water for irrigation, and drawing it out of an already stressed aquifer only made the water table drop even lower. Besides that was the danger of pesticides leaching into that ground water and contaminating it, and the erosion from the disturbed soil. Agriculture was big business all over Arizona, but more and more farmland was being sold as agricultural ventures failed. Farmland was being developed into housing and business enterprises, which used less water.

But Gaby had a sneaking suspicion that Bowie would be just as opposed to a housing project or an industrial park on his land—maybe more so. It was the history and heritage of the land that he wanted to preserve, and its natural beauty. He had a keen sense of continuity, of saving his heritage for posterity—laudable goals that were hard-kept against the kind of public opinion that was polarizing against him. Unemployed workers wanted jobs. Conservation was all well and good, but it didn't pay bills and feed hungry children.

"We have some fine grazing land here," Aggie was telling Ned, sighing over the panorama that spread to the mountains on the horizon. "Despite the desert environment, there's plenty of food for the livestock."

"We can even feed them prickly pear—cholla and ocotillo, too, but the thorns have to be burned off first," Bowie offered.

"How do you get enough water to them?" Ned asked.

"We use windmills to pump it out of the ground," Aggie said.

Ned frowned. "Why not pump it out of the river?"

Aggie laughed. "Ned, our rivers aren't like yours up in Wyoming. Ours only run during the rainy season. We wouldn't know what to do with a river that ran year-round."

"My God," Ned said reverently.

"Do you have prickly pear up your way, Mr. Courtland?" Gaby asked politely.

He shook his head. "Lodgepole pine, aspens, prairie grass. It's an easier country for cowboys, except in the winter. We lose a hand or two every winter to warmer country. Six-foot snowdrifts just don't appeal to everybody."

"We get snow here once in a while," Aggie said. "Up around Tucson, the saguaro cacti get a white dusting of it. It sure is pretty. Did you know that saguaro grows nowhere else in the country except in southern California, Arizona, and Mexico?"

"I thought I'd seen a few in west Texas and New Mexico." Ned frowned.

"Organ pipe cactus, maybe, or cardon cactus." Aggie

nodded. "But not saguaro. There's a lot to learn about them."

"For example?" Ned grinned.

"Well, they can live for over a hundred and fifty years. They can weigh up to three tons. They're pleated so that they can expand during the rainy season like an accordion. They're woody inside. The fruit was and is gathered by the Papago Indians to make jelly and a fermented drink . . ."

"Tohono O'odham," Gaby corrected. "They changed the name."

Aggie made an irritated sound. "You and your Papago history. Well, I can't pronounce that and I won't try."

"Yes, you will." Gaby chuckled.

"Yes, I will," Aggie sighed. "But it's hard."

"All the same, it's their own word, in their own language, not a borrowed name in Zūni, which Papago is," the younger woman replied. "Tohono O'odham means 'People of the Desert.' "

"You people sure do know a lot about where you live," Ned commented.

"Oh, we haven't started yet." Aggie smiled. "We'll have to take you out on the reservation and show you the White Dove of the Desert—the San Xavier Mission—and buy you some Papago fry bread and take you through the Saguaro National Monument and out to Old Tucson where they make Western movies."

"And that's only the tip of the iceberg," Gaby added as they walked toward the fence. "You could stay busy for weeks and still not see half the sights. Tombstone is just a few minutes down the road, and it's a must-see."

"Will it spoil your day if I tell you I've been there?" Ned chuckled. "When I was a boy, it was the dream of my life to stand where the Earps did. I spent a week in Tombstone when I was in my twenties, and I've never forgotten a thing about it."

"So this isn't your first time in Arizona?" Bowie asked as he bent his head to light a cigarette. He was bareheaded, and the sun burnished his blond hair like a halo.

"Not hardly," Ned returned, his eyes secretly amused.

"It's heating up," Gaby remarked, "and I came out without my hat."

"So did we all," Bowie agreed. His eyes slid over Gaby's face. "You're asking for sunstroke," he mused.

"I'll have company," she said with a pointed look at his thick hair.

He smiled faintly. "I guess so." He held out his hand and waited until she put hers into it, oblivious of Aggie's surveying gaze.

He drew her along with him, leaving Aggie and her Wyoming man to follow slowly behind them. Bowie's eyes were brooding as they went back through the wrought-iron gate toward the porch.

"Don't spoil it for her," she whispered.

He glanced down. "Honey, I'm not going to spoil anything. I just want to be sure of my ground. He's hiding something. I can feel it, can't you?"

She moved restlessly. "Yes."

"Let's find out what before we join his fan club."

She sighed, her slender hand moving closer into his. "Okay."

He tugged her close for an instant, his eyes kindling as he looked down at her. "You feel it, don't you, Gaby?" he asked, his voice deep and rough. "Fires, building between us."

Her lips parted. "Don't . . . don't rush me."

"I won't." He searched her eyes slowly, and let his fingers curl into hers. "You're a virgin, Gaby," he said softly. "You tell me if I'd expect you to climb into my bed like some casual conquest."

She let her eyes slide to his chest as she pondered that. "No," she said at last. "You wouldn't."

"So, no pressure. No underhanded tactics. Most of all, no seduction." He pinched her fingers gently to bring her eyes jumping up to his. "That works both ways. You have a way of looking at me lately that stirs me."

Her face did a slow burn as she remembered just how she'd looked at him earlier, in the shower room.

"That wasn't what I meant," he murmured with dry perception. "I mean the way you stare at my mouth, or didn't you think I'd noticed?"

Her breath sighed out through her teeth. "Sorry."

"Don't be." He smoothed over the back of her hand with his thumb. "I'm just as curious about you that way as you are about me. In point of fact, Gaby," he added slowly, searching her eyes, "I'd like to pin you to the wall with my body right now and kiss you until your knees buckle."

Her eyes lifted with faint surprise, reading the frank hunger in his eyes. His words allowed her to paint a mental picture that was graphic and exciting—Bowie's big, lean body crushing down against her breasts and hips and thighs, the cold wall at her back, and his warm strength holding her there, his mouth settling slowly over her parted lips, kissing her as she'd watched people kiss in movies. It was violently arousing to think of Bowie holding her so intimately, to think of his mouth warm and moist and demanding on her own.

She drew in a sharp breath and a tremor ran through the fingers he was still holding. His black eyes flashed. He took a step toward her, his face going hard as his warmth began to envelop her in the cool shadow of the balcony over the porch.

"We can't . . . !" she burst out, aware of murmuring voices somewhere close by.

"Like hell we can't," he said shortly. "Come here . . . !"

But even through the fever that was consuming him, he heard the footsteps coming up behind them and the soft creak of the wrought iron gate.

He stopped in his tracks, his eyes blazing with sudden need. "What are you doing to me?" he asked huskily.

"I could ask you the same question," she said in a shaky voice. She gently disentangled her fingers from his and turned away, thoroughly disoriented, as Aggie and Ned joined them on the porch.

"Ned wants to meet some of my friends," Aggie said, leaning gently against Ned's hard arm. "So how about helping me organize a party, Gaby?"

CHAPTER

Six

That Bowie was furious about the upcoming party became quickly evident. He excused himself and went out the back door with his pearly gray Stetson tilted at a furious angle across his brow. He didn't come back until late evening, then he walked straight into his study with only one long, hungry glance in Gaby's direction before he vanished for the rest of the evening.

"Bowie's going to be one big headache, isn't he?" Aggie sighed after Ned had gone to bed. Bowie was still shut up in the study with the phone, making business calls.

"He's worried about you," Gaby said simply. "He just doesn't know how to express it."

Aggie's eyes narrowed. "Are you worried?"

Gaby lowered her gaze to the floor. "Aggie, your life is your own business. I really shouldn't interfere."

"But?" the older woman prompted with a knowing smile.

"What do you know about Mr. Courtland?" the younger woman asked.

Aggie curled up on the sofa in her stocking feet. "He's kind. He doesn't put on airs. He likes children and animals.

He doesn't drink or smoke. He was married, but his wife died of cancer nine years ago. They had no children of their own." She lifted soft eyes to Gaby's. "And I think I'm in love with him."

Gaby whistled noiselessly. "Oh, boy."

"But how he feels is anybody's guess," Aggie added solemnly. "He seems to enjoy my company, and he didn't start looking for excuses when I invited him here. But he's very close-lipped about his feelings." She seemed to slump. "He hasn't even kissed me. He's very old-fashioned. There were younger women making a play for him on the cruise. Even for his age, he's very attractive, but he didn't give them the time of day. He stayed with me." She smiled, reminiscing. "I got lost in Montego Bay and couldn't find my way back to the tour jitney. He rescued me and got me back to the hotel. After that, he was always around when we went sightseeing. After the second day, we seemed to be inseparable."

"He seems very nice. But . . ."

"But what?"

"There's something hidden in him," Gaby replied, her eyes narrowing thoughtfully. "Not something devious, just secretive. He seems to find Bowie's attitude amusing, although he hides it well. And he'd better." She chuckled. "Your son seems to be searching for a way to get at him."

"Something I noticed immediately. I noticed something else, too," she added, eyeing Gaby. "You and Bowie were holding hands."

Gaby hated the flushed skin on her cheeks. She picked at the sofa. "Yes, we were."

"Has he made a pass at you yet?" Aggie grinned.

"Not a real one."

"That will come," The older woman said. "He may not seem like a ladies' man, my darling, but you'd better believe that the experience is there. Don't ever underestimate him."

Gaby looked up. "Shame on you," she said gently. "Bowie's the last man on earth who'd ever seduce me out of some casual need."

Aggie's eyes widened. "Well, my goodness . . . !"

"He scares me, Aggie," she burst out involuntarily. She wrapped her arms around herself. "But it's not a kind of scared that I've ever been. He . . . shakes me up inside."

"I can identify with that," Aggie laughed softly, and her face was young all at once, excited. "You know, I loved my husband," she said, "but his whole life was the company. He was always working—nights, weekends, holidays. I lived in his shadow and took what he gave without making any demands on his time, but it was a shallow relationship. I gave, he took. With Ned, it's . . . different. I can talk to him. He doesn't shut me out. He tells me what he feels, what he thinks. I feel so close to him, even when we aren't touching." She shrugged. "Imagine, at my age, feeling like a shy girl with a man."

"I think it's wonderful," Gaby said quietly. She studied the high-cheekboned face that had, in its day, been beautiful. "You've been alone for a long time. Don't be afraid to go out and get what you want, Aggie. It's a different world today. Don't let Bowie overwhelm you. He means well, but he doesn't see both sides of issues. He only sees the side he's fighting for."

"Yes, I know. Copeland raised him that way. He loves me, in his fashion, but I was never able to get close to Bowie. He shut me out. In a way, he's still doing that." She laughed gently. "You were so much easier to love, my darling. My son is a hard case."

"He loves you, though," Gaby said. "He really does."

Aggie's dark eyes were suddenly piercing. "What do you feel for Bowie, Gaby?" she asked softly.

Now there, Gaby thought dazedly, was a question. Her heart ran wild. What did she feel for him? Just a fiery arousal of the senses, a stirring of physical sensation that she'd never known? Or was there more to it—feelings that she'd submerged for years: It was a question that she might have to answer all too soon, and she was nervous of it.

"I don't know," she said, her voice a shadow of its usual self.

Aggie pursed her lips. "Well, don't brood about it, darling," she said gently, and patted the other woman's hand. "Time takes care of most everything. Now. Whom shall we invite to my 'coming out' party?" she asked with twinkling dark eyes.

It was just the right diversion. They made a list of prospective guests—mostly from Aggie's friends, but a few from Bowie's.

"Probably that is a mistake," she mused, pointing to two of Bowie's boyhood cronies. "Ted and Mike were always all for anything Bowie wanted to do, and they still are. He'll sic them on me, too."

"I'll save you, Aggie," Gaby assured her.

"Will you, really?" The older woman grinned. "Then who's going to save you?"

That was an interesting question, and Gaby didn't have a pat answer for it. Disturbing images of Bowie as she'd seen him at the pool house drifted across her mind while she listened to Aggie ramble on about the guest list and the catering. His sudden and unexpected ardor had startled her. It had been so sweet, feeling that way about a man for the first time in her life—feeling wanted without fear. Bowie was experienced, all right—she didn't need Aggie to tell her that. She'd known just by the velvet soft tone of his deep voice, by the look on his face, the intent in his dark eyes. He'd stirred her so easily with just his voice, without even touching her. She could hardly breathe when she tried to imagine what it would be like to have him kiss her in passion.

But it worried her as well. Bowie was coming on strong, and she was a cautious woman—very cautious. She didn't want to involve herself in a situation that was totally without resolution. Being physically attracted to Bowie was one thing; contemplating intimacy with him was something quite different. She couldn't tell him why she was afraid of lovemaking, or that she was concerned that she wouldn't be capable of giving herself in intimacy. The lack of explanation would disturb him, but his ego would suffer if she led him to believe she wanted him and then pulled back. She'd been accused once of being a tease, which was almost laughable, considering her past. The man hadn't been anyone she cared about; in fact, he'd been a pest. But the sharp memory had stung her pride, and she didn't want Bowie to say such things about her.

The thing was, she had no intimate experience with men, and it put her in a bad situation with Bowie.

Aggie had just penciled in the name of a caterer when Bowie came out of the study with a cigarette in his hand. His head was bare, his boots off, so that he was walking around the floor in his white stockinged feet. His shirt was out of his jeans and open down the front, and Gaby felt her heart racing at the sight of all that lean, tanned muscle, with its rippling mat of hair running down past the hand-tooled leather belt with its fancy picture jasper buckle.

Bowie liked the way she was looking at him. He could pick the thoughts right out of her mind. He smiled slowly, a predatory kind of smile that made her blush.

"Did you get through with your work?" Aggie asked him.

"Most of it," he said. "We've got an apartment complex going up in Colorado that I may have to check on later in the week. I've got a good crew up there, but I like to make sure."

"How many crews do you have?" Gaby asked, because

she was genuinely curious. "You sent one to Canada, you said."

"That's right. I've got several gangs of workers," he replied. "We're a big company, Gaby. We bid on jobs all over the country, and even in other countries."

"But how do you know how much to bid?"

He laughed softly. "That's a long story. I have people who can estimate a job right down to the last nail. After that, it's a matter of averaging out the cost of the job with an acceptable profit, and still undercutting the competition."

"Copeland was a past master at it," Aggie recalled. "He taught Bowie."

"Losing two big jobs in a row at the beginning taught me a lot, too," Bowie murmured dryly. He stretched, muscles rippling under dark skin. "God, I'm tired. Did you two iron out the guest list for the party?" He glanced at his mother. "I hope you remembered to put Ted and Mike on the list."

She glared at him. "How could I forget? But don't you dare incite those boys to join your plot against me, Bowie. And don't forget that two can play at that game."

He pursed his lips. "Game?"

"The Academy Awards have already been doled out," Aggie said imperturbably as she got to her feet. She glanced from Bowie's speculative gaze at Gaby, to Gaby's flushed cheeks, and smiled. "Come on, Gaby," she murmured with a speaking glance in Bowie's direction. "We'll go up together. You can get the lights, can't you, dear?" she asked her son.

"I can get the lights," he agreed with narrowed eyes. "Good night, Mother, Gaby."

Gaby nodded. She didn't dare look at him, because he'd see her disappointment. She'd thought that Aggie might go to bed and leave them alone, and if she did, Bowie might kiss her. The thought had made her body sing with anticipation, but Aggie was going to put paid to that sweet hope.

The message was getting through, loud and clear. If they were going to interfere, so was Aggie.

"Sleep well, darling," Aggie told her son with a wicked smile. She went up the stairs beside Gaby, humming a cheerful little tune.

Behind them, Bowie was watching their progress with eyes that were as amused as they were frustrated. He wondered if Gaby was as disappointed as he was, and if his mother intended to spend her time at the ranch keeping them apart. She was telling him that he'd better keep his nose out of her friendship with Ned Courtland.

Ned Courtland had been much on his mind. He'd heard from Aggie that the man supposedly lived in Jackson, Wyoming, but his discreet telephone inquiries tonight hadn't netted him any information about their mysterious house guest. He was even more suspicious now than he had been. Who was Ned Courtland, and why was he after Aggie? Somehow, he had to find out before any damage was done.

Gaby took a shower and changed into her nightgown, a brief, yellow silk impulse of a luxury that fit her body like a second skin. It was cut low in front, emphasizing her high, firm breasts and narrow waist, flaring to softly curved hips and long, elegant legs. Her figure was a perfect twelve—not quite voluptuous, but very noticeable—which was why she spent so much time camouflaging it. She didn't like men staring at it. On the other hand, it didn't bother her to think of Bowie looking at her.

She flushed, remembering the exquisitely masculine lines of his own body without clothing. She hid her face in her hands and wondered if she'd ever forget what she'd seen. The newness of her attraction to him was as disturbing as his sudden interest in her.

She lay down on the cover of the bed, her eyes on the ceiling. Even though she had every reason to be afraid of men, she wasn't afraid of Bowie. She wanted to kiss him.

She wanted to feel his arms and his hands on her. She wanted . . .

She actually moaned, stretching sensually on the covers, her body on fire for the first time in her life. She didn't understand the trembling need in it, the stark hunger for something she couldn't even put a name to. She closed her eyes and forced her mind to focus on the party. Bowie was making her all too vulnerable.

Aggie was up at the crack of dawn, standing outside on the patio to watch the sunrise in her neat white dress, when footsteps sounded behind her. She turned to find Ned there, bareheaded, his dark, silver-streaked hair still damp from a shower, his gray plaid shirt carelessly unbuttoned at the throat. His face was pensive as he studied her.

"Your son doesn't want me here," he said quietly. "He thinks I'm a gigolo on the make. What do you think?"

Aggie smiled at him shyly. "I think you're a very nice man with impeccable manners who made my holiday unforgettable." She lowered her eyes to his chest. "I'm sorry Bowie's such hard going. He thinks you may be a permanent guest, I suppose . . ."

"He thinks right." He moved closer, no trace of amusement in his dark eyes as he stopped just in front of Aggie and pulled her against him. "I want you." He bent his head and kissed her.

At no time in her life had Aggie been kissed like that, not even by her late husband. She gasped under his hard mouth and stiffened, but he didn't back away so much as a fraction of an inch. His hard arms tightened and the kiss deepened. She was shocked to find that she could still feel desire. She reached up and slid her arms around his neck, letting him hold her more intimately. Her body trembled against his, and she heard him whisper something roughly under his breath.

As the kiss grew harder, Aggie let her eyes close helplessly. Love, she thought, could be so painful at her age.

A long moment later Ned lifted his head. He had tasted tears on her soft mouth. His dark eyes searched hers. "Why the tears, Aggie?"

"You'll go home ...!" she whispered, and her voice broke.

"No!" His lean hands came up to frame her face, to brush away the tears. "My God, I'm not leaving you—not now, not ever! Aggie," he breathed, "I love you!"

She wasn't certain that she'd heard him, but he repeated it. When he kissed her again, it echoed in her whirling mind, bringing spring to the winter of her heart, blossoming in her like roses in a barren garden. She whispered the words back to him, glorying in the newness of loving. She thought she heard a sound nearby, but she was too lost in Ned to care what it was, or whom.

By the time Gaby woke up, dressed, and got downstairs after a totally disturbing night, the rest of the family was already at the breakfast table. Bowie was wearing a chambray shirt with jeans and boots, brooding as he ate.

Aggie was talking to Ned Courtland. His hair was faintly disheveled and his face was closed. His thin lips pursed as he listened to Aggie, but his mind was obviously somewhere else. Aggie herself had dressed to the teeth in a white, Mexican-style dress. With her hair neatly brushed and makeup on, her dark eyes sparkled with new fire. She was actually glowing.

"Good morning," Gaby told them, sitting down next to Bowie. Aggie was at the other end of the table, and Ned Courtland was at Bowie's other side.

"Good morning," Aggie said.

Gaby felt a little uneasy in her form-fitting olive green blouse and neat jeans. Her tanned arms were bare under the short sleeves and the vee-neck was more revealing than anything she'd ever worn before. She felt Bowie's eyes on her.

"I hope you slept well, Mr. Courtland?" she asked.

"I slept very well, Miss Cane," he replied. He smiled back at her, but when his eyes moved down the table to Aggie, his smile changed. "Aggie and I were up at dawn, watching the sunrise."

"It was lovely," Aggie said, and blushed.

Bowie clanged his fork against his plate. "I've got to help Montoya do some work in the garage this morning," he muttered, rising. "One of the trucks is running rough, and Bandy's busy breaking new horses for the remuda."

"Bandy's too rough with them," Gaby murmured, glancing at the other three faces. Something was very wrong. She could feel the tension in the atmosphere, and she wondered what she'd missed.

"Can't be helped," Bowie said quietly. "We don't have time to gentle each horse individually."

"I'd make time," Ned Courtland said, lifting his head. "A horse is a creature with feeling and intelligence. Raking him with spurs will break his spirit."

There was a distinct challenge in the very set of the older man's head, and Bowie smiled coolly as he met it head-on. "We don't use big roweled spurs on our stock," he told Courtland. "When Gaby says that Bandy's rough, she doesn't mean that he whips the horses bloody or beats them. He simply rides them down until they give in, and the horses always have an equal chance. Bandy's had two broken ribs in the past six months."

Courtland had started to speak when there was an interruption from the hall.

"Señor Bowie, there is a man to see you," Montoya called from the doorway.

Bowie glanced at Gaby with an odd expression before he nodded curtly to the family and strode out.

"I'm getting pretty tired of this verbal wrangling, Aggie," Ned said. There was steely purpose in his dark eyes. "I've already taken more from your son in two days than I'd take from most men in one. We've got to get this thing settled."

Aggie grimaced. "You can see what it's going to be like," she told him earnestly.

"I don't care," he replied stubbornly. "I want it out in the open."

Aggie glanced apologetically at Gaby. "Ned's asked me to marry him," she said, and blushed again, remembering how he'd asked her.

"Oh, how nice," Gaby said, and wondered what in the world she and Bowie were going to do now.

Aggie gave her a hard look. "So I'm going to have to fight you, too, is that how it stands?"

"Of course not," Gaby said quickly, because if she voiced her suspicions or made waves right now, she might accidentally push Aggie away. She got up and hugged the older woman, placating her. "You know I only want the very best for you."

"Yes, I know that, baby girl." Aggie hugged her warmly. "Be happy for me."

"I am." She congratulated Mr. Courtland, noticing the curious way he eyed her, as if he saw right through her pretense.

"Now all we have to do is convince Bowie," Aggie murmured with narrowed eyes.

"He's not going to take it lying down," Ned said quietly. "He'll fight it with his last breath. You need to talk to him."

"Bowie doesn't listen." Aggie replied. "He likes his own way."

"I like my own way, too," Ned said. "And I'll get it."

Gaby felt cold chills at the way he said that. She'd have to talk to Bowie, and fast.

"It's my own fault," Aggie was saying. "Bowie and I

were never close. He and his father tried to be, but they were both too cool and distant to make a go of it."

"I hope he doesn't decide to make trouble," Ned said, almost to himself. "Not before I . . ." He stopped, as if he was aware of Gaby's scrutiny.

Aggie didn't notice the thought voiced aloud; she was brooding again. "Maybe if we tied him up and put him in the closet," she mumbled, "and got a head start, we could get to Wyoming before he missed us."

Gaby grinned. "He'd cut himself loose and come after you," she said. She glanced at Mr. Courtland. "So you're in the cattle business, Mr. Courtland?" she began with her best reporter's smile.

"In a very small way," he returned. "I'm more of a horse man myself." He pursed his lips and glanced at Aggie with a calculating look. "Not that I've got much capital to invest in them."

"Are you from Wyoming?" Gaby persisted.

He frowned. "Well, no. Not originally."

"Where did you . . ."

"Stop doing your reporter number, Gaby, or I'll kick you," Aggie threatened. "Which reminds me, how long are you staying?"

Gaby was suddenly under fire, and her mind threatened to shut down. Aggie had seen through her questions. "I'd sort of like to stay for two weeks, if you don't mind. I'll be quiet as a mouse. In fact, I'll hang out with the coyotes and chase cats or something."

Aggie's face lost its coolness and she laughed. "As long as you aren't underfoot all the time, I don't mind. Stay as long as you like." Her eyes narrowed. "How about Bowie?" she asked with a calculating smile. "Does he want to stay two weeks, too?"

Gaby flushed, which helped drag the red herring right under Aggie's nose. She looked delighted.

"He can stay, too, unless he gets in my way," Aggie added firmly. She glanced at Ned, feeling girlishly young. "After all, courting couples need a little time alone together, you know."

Bowie would love this. Time to get more involved, he'd be thinking, and Gaby was really suspicious now about Mr. Courtland's motives. He sounded and looked more and more like a threat. But what could they do? Aggie was far past the age of consent. If she wanted to get married, it would take more than Gaby and Bowie to stop her.

"Are you going to tell Bowie what we've decided?" Ned asked unexpectedly, staring at Gaby.

"He's sure to find out," she hedged.

"I was afraid of that." Ned Courtland sighed heavily. "Sure as God made little green apples, he'll sew his shadow to my boots and trail after us like a kid."

"He'd better not," Aggie muttered. She was girded for battle, and Gaby didn't like that determined look. "Gaby, don't you say a word to him about the marriage, or I'll throw you all the way back to Phoenix. It's my right to tell him."

Gaby grimaced. She didn't want to promise, but if she didn't, Aggie was quite capable of telling her to leave, and that would ruin everything. "Okay," she said. "I'll let you tell him—but don't take too long."

"I won't," Aggie said. "I don't want to hurt either of you, but I don't have to have permission to get married."

"Of course you don't," Gaby agreed, faking a smile.

She got up. "I'll just move along and let you two have a few minutes to yourself," she said. She glanced at Mr. Courtland with a cagey smile. "What breed is a red and white cow, do you know?"

"It's a Hereford," he said. He studied her for a minute. "And if you want to know, the Japanese trade agreement has already gone through. We'll be sending more beef over there."

"Why did you send Bowie off on a tangent by pretending not to know?" she asked softly.

"He expected me not to know," Ned returned easily. He leaned back. "You know, trust is hard to get these days. I understand the misgivings he has, but a woman shouldn't have to fight her own kids to be happy. No child has the right to tell his parent how to live."

"On the other hand," Gaby replied, "a child has every right to try to protect that parent when he or she is vulnerable."

He cocked an eyebrow and smiled. "I wouldn't know. I don't have any kids."

She glanced toward Aggie. "If you marry Aggie, you will have," she promised dryly. "A two-hundred-and-twenty-five-pound son."

Ned's dark eyes twinkled. "As long as I don't have to bounce him on my knee, we should manage all right."

Gaby smothered a laugh. "I'll see you both later."

She smiled at Aggie, but when she was out of the room, the smile faded. Things were so complicated. She could see why Bowie was worried about the elusive Mr. Courtland. He was like two sides of a coin, and she couldn't decide which face was the true one. He acted so suspiciously, as if he had an amusing secret and was playing a part. If he was a con man, there was every good reason to make sure he didn't get Bowie out of the way. Aggie was so obviously in love with the man that it was going to be difficult to convince her that he was a scoundrel, even if he turned out to be a bank robber. She went out the front door, having forgotten all about Bowie's visitor until she heard the curt anger in his deep voice.

"I've told you how I feel about this," Bowie was telling a small, wizened man in a suit. "I won't sell land to a potential polluter. My God, man, can't you see the impact that outfit would have on the water table around here?"

"It's a sound financial venture, Mr. McCayde," the older man said. "And a number of people in Lassiter are in favor of it. You're not a popular man right now. You have the best land for the project, and it would mean a great deal to the local economy..."

"Not in the long run," Bowie said stubbornly. "The answer is no."

"Won't you reconsider?"

"I will not."

"Mr. McCayde." The small man smiled, spreading his hands. "Surely you don't intend to go on with this one-man crusade to preserve the land intact. It isn't realistic—not at all. You can't hold back progress."

"Stand back and watch me."

"The town will fight you," he assured Bowie, "tooth and nail. And you'll be the only loser... Mr. McCayde!"

Bowie had picked the little man up in mid-tirade and was calmly carrying him to his car. As Gaby watched, torn between shock and hysterical laughter, Bowie put the man into his car, closed the door, and walked off toward the garage. The visitor, whom Gaby finally recognized as a local realtor, fumbled his engine into life and took off jerkily.

It was several minutes before Gaby could stop laughing long enough to go in search of Bowie. His actions were typical of his hard-bitten personality. Like many desert-bred men, he was nothing if not blunt and forthright about things. But he had a unique way of settling arguments, she thought. That poor realtor wasn't going to forget his reception at Casa Río for a long time.

She could understand his point of view, and Bowie's. But it was hard to match heritage against hungry children and unemployed people. Bowie was so stubborn, she wondered if anything would change his mind. If the townspeople of

Lassiter were really up in arms, she could see trouble coming in swarms. But the land question wasn't as urgent as Aggie's situation was.

Out in the corral, Bandy was breaking another horse, his small, grizzled figure clinging stubbornly to the saddle of a bucking gelding. Outside the fence were several small Mexican boys, children of the workers, who were too young to be in school. The woman who was supposed to be watching them was busy putting a basket of laundry into a beat-up pickup truck, to be taken into town to the laundromat.

Bandy was suddenly thrown and landed with a "whump!" in the dust, while the angry horse threw up his hind legs and bucked around the corral, trying to get the saddle off.

"Sorry, Bandy!" Gaby yelled at him. "Are you okay?"

"Everything but my pride is." He chuckled, dusting himself off as he walked toward her. "Good to have you home, kid."

"Good to be home." She liked Bandy. His father had been a friend of the infamous Pancho Villa, and Bandy could spin a fine tale about the old days down in Douglas, on the border, and the excitement of watching the Mexican Revolution from the rooftops of that small town.

The pale blue eyes studied her warily from a face like scorched leather. "You down here because of Miss Aggie's house guest?" he asked pointedly. "Because I'd bet money Bowie is."

"Shame on you for gossiping," she chided.

"Should be, I reckon. He's no lily, that Wyoming fella," he said, nodding toward the newcomer, who was walking toward the corral with Aggie. "Look how he walks—just like a cowboy. Nothing in the world more ungainly on the ground than a . . . Good God!"

The exclamation came at the sight of one of the small boys tearing into the corral, laughing as he taunted the bronco. The other boys egged him on with loud cries of encouragement.

"Get the hell out of here!" Bandy yelled.

The bronco was still bucking, incited by the child waving his arms. The boy was laughing, not paying a bit of attention to Bandy. He thought it was a great game, but the bronc wasn't playing.

"Do something!" Gaby cried.

Bandy ran toward the bronc, only to be knocked to the ground by the shoulder of the frightened animal. Gaby started over the rails in pure terror, but a lean, strong hand caught her and held her back.

"Get me a rope, quick," Ned Courtland demanded, his lean face set and ruthless as he watched the bronc start to chase the boy.

Bowie had heard the urgent sounds and came out of the barn at a quick, hard stride.

"Bring a rope!" Courtland yelled, and climbed deftly to the top rung of the corral.

Bowie reacted instinctively to the sharp command. He grabbed up a lariat and threw it to Courtland. The older man caught it and quickly made a loop, which he sent singing out from the top of the corral fence. It caught easily around the bronc's neck. Courtland jumped down, his booted feet planted firmly so that his heels dug into the soft ground. His lean strength slowly brought the animal to a standstill while Bandy got the boy out of the corral. Then it was a treat to watch Courtland gentle the gelding.

He didn't jerk him around or mistreat him, or even use a great deal of force.

He talked to him, softly, quietly, standing still with the rope taut as the animal stood panting and wild-eyed. The boy had been caught and whacked soundly on the bottom by Bowie, who told him off quietly and effectively in flawless

Spanish and sent him running, with his friends, to his mother.

Courtland was moving toward the horse now, while Aggie, Bowie, and Gaby watched, fascinated. The older man began to stroke the horse's soft muzzle, still talking to him. He smoothed the mane, the long, elegant neck. All the while, he spoke to the horse, as if it were as intelligent as he'd said only minutes earlier. Then he turned and led it gently back to the barn door and handed the reins to Bandy.

"My God," Bandy shook his head. "I've heared of men who could do that, but I've only seen it done a time or two. That was a real treat, Mr. Courtland."

Courtland only nodded. He walked back to the fence, vaulted over it with the ease of a man half his age, and took off his hat to wipe away the sweat.

"How's the boy?" he asked Bowie.

"His bottom is pretty sore," Bowie said quietly. "Otherwise, he's fine. His father is one of the cowboys here." His eyes narrowed. "That was a hell of a bit of roping," he said speculatively. "And I gather that you know something about horses."

"Oh, I used to ride some when I was younger," Ned Courtland said, pursing his lips amusedly. "I like horses."

"They seem to like you, too." Bowie bent his head to light a cigarette. "Bandy's been working that little white-eyed horror for three days, and it's nearly killed him once that I know of."

"I got lucky. Aggie, let's get along. We're going up to see something called Cochise Stronghold," he told the others, sliding a casual arm around Aggie's shoulders.

"We're going to stop for lunch while we're out," Aggie said, beaming as she nestled closer to the lean man. "So don't wait for us."

"We won't," Bowie agreed. "Have a good time," he told

his mother, but absently, because he was still digesting what he'd just learned about her suitor.

He watched them walk away with Gaby, thoughtful and silent, at his side.

"That man knows ranching," Bowie said. "I'd bet money on it. But why is he so damned secretive? And who is he? I can't find anybody in Jackson who knows the cattle business who's ever heard of Ned Courtland."

"Maybe he isn't from Jackson," she suggested. "Maybe he's trying to throw you off the track."

"My God, the man may have a criminal record that he's trying to hide," he said shortly. "What if he's on the run?"

CHAPTER
Seven

Gaby thought about what Bowie had said before he stormed off into the garage to work on the truck. She didn't really think that Ned Courtland was a criminal, but what if he was? They were going to have to find some way to check him out.

She spent her morning telephoning invitations to the people on Aggie's guest list. The party would be Friday evening, and it was already Wednesday—hardly enough time to have invitations printed and get them mailed. Gaby wondered what would happen when Bowie found out that not only was his mother in love with Ned Courtland, she intended to marry him. She had to talk to him, to soothe him down, before Friday.

Montoya had come in to fix lunch, and while he and Tía Elena were working on it, Gaby slipped out to the garage to talk to Bowie.

She heard a lot of angry banging from underneath one of the pickup trucks, and saw a familiar pair of big booted feet sticking out on one side.

Bowie was under the truck, flat on his back, wielding a wrench and turning the air blue.

Gaby, now wearing her jeans, sat down cross-legged on the concrete floor of the garage beside him without a word.

"Hand me the socket wrench," he said curtly, holding out a big, greasy hand for it.

She looked at the red container of socket wrenches. "There must be twenty of them. Which one . . . ?"

He told her, and she found it, pressing it into his palm. The arm disappeared. There were metallic sounds and then a lot of muttering. "That damned real estate agent had better not come back here again," he said shortly. "I've warned him about coming out here and bothering me."

"It sounds as if the situation is getting serious, Bowie," she said quietly.

"It was never anything else." He banged something else. "Did you hear what I said?"

"Yes."

"You're a reporter. Start digging."

"I'm going to do that. But you aren't going to change my mind about the state of the local economy and the need for an additional tax base," she said.

"You and these damned liberals," he said shortly. "You'll sacrifice the whole quality of life for a few dollars."

"It's not like that at all," she said. "There are two sides to every story, I know, but the unemployment rate here is terrible. You have to have industry or new business to keep people working. And I know about the danger of pollutants in the groundwater table—I've done several articles about water quality and conservation. But you can't just leave the land as it is forever, Bowie! Desert serves no one except itself."

"Take your damned sermon out of here," he said, his voice cutting. "I've got more than land on my mind right now, and you know it."

She sighed. "Yes. I know it."

"She's out of her mind," he said audibly.

"She's lonely, Bowie," she replied gently.

He made a sound and held out his hand. "That's the wrong size," he said, handing the wrench back.

"That's what you asked for," she pointed out.

"Then read my mind next time. Give me the next smaller size."

She searched for it, found it, and handed it to him.

"Damned imports," he mumbled.

"This isn't a foreign truck," she pointed out.

"Wyoming imports!" he corrected shortly. "Him!"

"Oh."

"My father's only been dead eight years," he said angrily. "And that yahoo from the Tetons isn't a patch on him, even if he can spin a rope and talk to horses."

She had to hide a grin at the way he'd put it. She wondered if his pride was sore because Courtland had jumped in with that rope before he could. He wasn't the kind of man who liked being stuck on the sidelines in an emergency.

"I guess it would be hard to watch Aggie marry someone else," she said quietly, feeling his pain even through the anger.

There was a hard pause. "Harder than you know." He tightened another bolt. "What about your own mother, Gaby?"

She studied a spot on the knee of her jeans. "I don't remember her very well," she said, finding it easier than she'd dreamed to talk to him about it. "She died when I was about five or six. Then Dad and I traveled all over, anywhere he could find work. He wasn't the best father in the world, but he was good to me."

"Where is he now?"

"He's dead." She bit off the word. It hurt to say it. She'd never really come to grips with his death, and it hadn't been until she went to work in Phoenix for the newspaper that she'd learned about it. That was all she'd found out, though

—nothing about the people who'd been involved in her mad
flight from Kentucky and her father's agonizing last year of
life in a mental institution. She'd been afraid to pursue that
line of questioning in her research, for fear that it might give
the people in Kentucky some clue to her whereabouts. The
last thing she wanted was to have the past revealed. It would
inevitably involve the McCaydes in a terrible scandal, and
that she couldn't have.

Lost in her thoughts, she hadn't realized that Bowie had
spoken again. "I said, are you listening?" he repeated.

"Oh, were you saying something? My mind drifted
away," she said lightly.

"I said, you never talk about the past."

"It's all long forgotten. Do you want another wrench?"

"No." He slid out from under the truck and sat up. He was
wearing a white, short-sleeved T-shirt dotted with grease. It
clung to his powerful chest and shoulders and arms like wet
silk, and Gaby caught her breath at the impact of all that
vivid masculinity so close. He was sweating, and the damp-
ness made the fabric cling to his breastbone. Under it was
the faint shadow of thick chest hair. She couldn't imagine
why it should affect her so strongly lately, but ever since
she'd seen him without a stitch of clothing on in the pool
house, she'd had such erotic thoughts about him.

She forced her eyes away from his torso and up to his
face. He was so unbelievably handsome—every line of him
was perfect. His black eyes narrowed at her scrutiny while
he pushed back a sweaty strand of blond hair. Her eyes
glanced off his and she colored.

"Do I have spots on my nose?" he asked pointedly

"No." She shifted, studying her boots. "Sorry."

"You stare at me a lot lately," he observed. "Mind telling
me why?"

She smiled self-consciously. "For the same reason other

women do, I guess." She looked up and then quickly down again. "You're very handsome, Bowie."

He made a sound and tossed the wrench he was holding into the tray of tools. "Hell."

"Well, you are."

"Hand me that piece of cloth, and a cigarette."

She tossed him the cloth, watching him wipe the grease from his big, lean hands as she pulled the cigarette package from the pocket of the shirt he'd tossed aside before he had begun working on the truck. "Do you have matches?"

He searched in his jeans pocket, tightening the fabric over the powerful muscles of his legs. She felt pleasure ripple through her at the sight, and blushed when she realized what was happening to her.

He saw the blush and his eyes narrowed. He calmly lit the cigarette and propped one leg up, dangling the hand with the cigarette over it. "Nervous, Gaby?" he asked with a faint smile.

"A little," she confessed, deciding that it was always best to fight fire with fire. "Things are getting very complicated around here."

"Oh, it's not so bad," he said. He took a draw from the cigarette, still studying her. "Courtland will go home soon, Aggie will get back to normal, and the agricultural combine will discover that when I say no, I mean it."

Her olive eyes danced. "Nice to be so certain of things," she murmured, because he didn't yet know what his mother had in mind.

"Why the transformation?" he asked, reaching out a hand to touch the shoulder of her sexy blouse. "I've never seen you look quite so feminine before. I hope it's for my benefit, Gaby," he added, his voice deep, soft.

"You're getting me all mixed up," she said defensively.

"You need mixing up." He tugged a lock of her hair, savoring its soft texture with his fingers. "We aren't going to be enemies," he said quietly. "No matter what happens here with Aggie or the land. You and I are never going to be adversaries."

"I hope not," she agreed. She felt shaky. The way he was looking at her made her more nervous than ever. It all came flooding back—the things he'd said in the pool house, the way he'd started to kiss her, the tension that had been steadily building between them ever since. It was in her eyes, in her face when she stared back at him.

"You look as if you might jump up and start running any minute," he mused. "Am I that frightening?"

"It isn't really fear," she said hesitantly.

His black eyes darkened even more and his hand stilled on the lock of hair he was holding. "Isn't it?" His fingers tightened. "Come here."

She wasn't sure, and it showed. "It will . . . change everything," she whispered.

"Everything is already changed," he said quietly. "This has been building between us ever since that night in Phoenix. Every day it gets worse. Do you know, I almost came to you last night?" he asked, his voice deepening at her scarlet blush. "It took all my will power to stay in my own bed."

She remembered her own anguish the night before, the way she'd wanted him. It was uncanny that he should have felt it, too, but that only increased her fears. She felt her nerve deserting her. She tugged her hair away from his confining fingers and jumped up, moving away from him toward the wall.

"Don't say things like that," she whispered huskily. "It isn't right!"

"You're twenty-four, for God's sake!" He got up, too, gracefully for a man his size, and walked toward her with the smoking cigarette in his hand. "We're not playing games, Gaby. This isn't some mild flirtation because I'm bored and looking for a diversion. And you won't make me believe that you react to me any differently than I do to you."

She didn't know what to say. She knew her legs were trembling. She was afraid of what he might expect of her. He was worldly and sophisticated and she was a novice—A very nervous one, at best. She shifted so that she was standing with her back to the long worktable against the wall. "Bowie, you're going too fast," she said, her voice husky with feeling.

"No. I'm just refusing to put off the inevitable any longer. My God, I want your mouth," he breathed roughly.

Her lips parted as she felt the impact of the words, saw the need in his black eyes. She couldn't speak.

He studied her expression closely. In a few seconds he dropped the barely touched cigarette to the concrete floor and ground it out deliberately under his booted foot. He hadn't shifted his eyes one inch, and she felt the purpose in that steady gaze grow.

Her breath began to rustle quickly in her throat when he walked toward her. His hands slid slowly to her waist, clasped it, and lifted her gently so that she was sitting on the table. Then he moved closer, between her jean-clad legs, his hands still on her waist.

In her high sitting position, his eyes were on an unnerving level with hers, and she could feel the pervasive warmth of his big body, smell the scent of tobacco and cologne and sweat that mingled sensually and drifted into her nostrils. His black eyes searched hers until she flushed, and then they fell with obvious intent to her lips. She almost swooned with the need to feel his mouth. For two days now, she'd gone hungry for him, but there had never been the opportunity for them to be alone. Now they were, and it was going to happen, at last . . . !

She felt her heart begin to race when he bent forward and slowly touched his hard lips to her soft ones in a whisper of a kiss, his smoky breath mingling with hers in a silence that magnified the sound of her own rapid heartbeat. She stiffened a little at the intimacy of his mouth against hers, the newness of being so close to Bowie. His lips were hard and warm, and he brushed them lazily over hers, nudging them apart. Her hands gripped his shoulders, half in fear and half in anticipated pleasure. The strength of his body was all too evident in the near-intimate embrace.

He lifted his head enough to see her eyes, and he read very accurately the apprehension there. "This is all I want of you right now," he said quietly. "Just your mouth under mine. Relax, little one. I won't hurt you. I'm only going to kiss you."

The complete control he displayed and the laziness of his movements took the rigidity out of her spine. She stopped trying to fight it. Her breath rippled against his hard lips as he bent again. This time the kiss lingered. His mouth brushed at hers again with slow, expert sensuality until he made her lips part. Then he moved forward, feeling her starkly open eyes on him as he turned his head slightly and covered her mouth completely with his lips.

She gasped. It was the most sensuous thing she'd ever done with a man in her life, and to do it with Bowie was shattering. She stared up at him, meeting his steady, curious eyes.

"I feel it, too, baby," he said quietly, his voice rough with emotion. The unfamiliar endearment sounded so natural, yet he'd never used it with her before, and it sent delicious chills up her arms. His nose rubbed softly against hers as he bent again. "Lift your arms around me."

She didn't understand why it was imperative that she obey him, but it was. She slid her hands behind his head, where they touched, tentatively, the thick hair at his nape and entwined there. Her mouth yielded to the slow crush of his and she was staggered at the flash of emotion it ignited.

His big hands left her waist to slide up her back and pull her closer into his warm, enveloping embrace. He half lifted her against him, her breasts crushing softly against his broad, hard chest. His mouth grew just slightly harder on hers, brushing firmly at her lips to make them part even more.

She felt a sting of pleasure that ran down her taut body and settled in her lower stomach. She heard herself make a sound deep in her throat and pulled her mouth from under his.

"It frightens you, doesn't it?" he asked with a faint scowl on his face. "Haven't you ever felt passion before?"

She swallowed. She shook her head, beyond words. Her lips were tingling, faintly swollen from the long touch of his mouth on them. Her eyes fell to his mouth and found it equally swollen. Her breasts shook with her heartbeats. He was very close, and the intimacy of the hold he had on her was making her body throb in the most disturbing way. She felt herself tremble and wondered what to do about it.

His hands moved, raising her higher against his chest, while his lips paused just above hers. "I won't let it get out of hand, if that's what you're nervous about. Give in to me," he whispered sensually. "I'll teach you what you want to know without making you afraid."

The words didn't really make sense until his mouth settled down on hers and began to rub against it, parting her lips with slow expertise while his hands slid to her hips and slowly, achingly, drew them completely against his.

She'd never felt a man's aroused body before—not like this. Not so that she was a willing participant. Her mind was drowning in the sweetness of a heady pleasure like nothing she'd ever known before. She clung to Bowie's powerful neck and didn't protest the intimacy of his hold, not even when his fingers contracted hungrily on her hips.

He felt that submission with a thrill of pride, because he

could feel her innocence. Very likely, this was the first time she'd even been kissed properly, much less anything more intimate. His body sang with delicious sensation, rippled with it. He breathed in the gardenia scent of her and put his tongue delicately against the inside of her upper lip, teasing it. He felt her mouth begin to open, welcoming him, and with a groan of pure anguish, he pushed his tongue inside it, his arms swallowing her hungrily, crushing her against his body.

She tightened her arms, feeling him pull her up as he rose, feeling his body absorb her weight as her feet hung off the ground in his bearish embrace. His mouth was doing the most intimate things to hers, and she loved it . . . loved it! Her body throbbed where he held it to his. His mouth was the center of the universe. She was living only through it, and if he stopped, she was going to die . . . !

When he suddenly put her down and started to move back, she cried out and clung to him, her eyes opening like dark olive flowers, helplessly caught in his black gaze.

His eyes were full of thunder. His heartbeat was so hard and heavy that it shook her, and he was breathing as roughly as she was, but he seemed to be in complete control. The hands that put her quietly away from him were deft and completely steady.

She tried to speak, but tears spilled down her cheeks. The intensity of emotion was new, just like the helpless trembling of her body.

"No . . . !" she protested helplessly when he moved away from her, and then flushed at her own boldness.

"I promised you I wouldn't let it get out of hand," he reminded her. "No normal man can keep that up for very long," he said with a gentle smile. "You get my meaning, I believe?"

She did, all too abruptly. The changed contours of his big

body would have been enough to bring it home, even if his wicked smile hadn't.

She caught her breath, wrapping her arms around her breasts. They felt oddly swollen, like her mouth.

"My gosh," she whispered aloud, as the intensity of what they'd shared loomed over her like a threat.

"Want a cigarette?"

She shook her head as he flicked a match and took a draw from the cigarette. He seemed perfectly at ease, except for a faint glitter in his eyes.

"You and I are explosive together," he remarked.

"I never dreamed I could let anyone kiss me like that," she whispered, without meaning to give herself away so completely.

"You don't trust me enough to tell me what happened, but I think I've got some of it worked out. Somewhere along the line, a man lost control and frightened you."

She swallowed. There was a glimmer of truth in what he'd guessed, but he hadn't come near the real story.

"Something like that," she agreed, to placate him and keep him from probing further.

"Were you raped?" he asked.

She felt her face going scarlet, because she hadn't expected that question. "No!" she burst out automatically.

"Talk to me," he said gently. "I'm not going to look down my nose at you or give any lectures."

"I can't!"

She was almost in tears. He gave it up. Upsetting her was the last thing he wanted to do. He moved closer, pulling her forehead against his T-shirt and holding it there. "Stop it," he said softly. "I won't pry. One day, you'll tell me everything." His mouth brushed gently over her temple.

"I never meant to let this happen," she whispered tearfully. "It's all so complicated. I can't . . . I can't ever be intimate with a man, Bowie. I can't . . . !" She looked up with tragic eyes.

He touched her lips with a lean forefinger. "You can be intimate with me," he whispered. "Not right away. Maybe not for a long time. But sooner or later, you'll tell me all about the past, and I'll ease you through the first time." His black eyes narrowed. "And it will be the first time, won't it, Gaby?"

Her eyes couldn't move. He'd trapped them. "Yes," she breathed. "But I won't be able . . ."

His mouth brushed hers into silence. "Suppose you get on the phone after lunch and invite John Hammock to that party Friday night?" he asked, changing the subject with remarkable ease.

The suddenness of the remark startled her. "What?"

"I want you to invite John to the party," he said simply. "Aggie used to be sweet on him, and his wife died last year. He's good-looking and a conservationist."

"Bowie, I don't think it's going to work. Your mother is really interested in Mr. Courtland."

"Mr. Courtland is going home. He just doesn't know it. Humor me—I know what I'm doing." He smiled wickedly. "John's got a way with women."

"You might not believe it, but so does Mr. Courtland," Gaby said firmly. "He's not what he seems. And I don't think he's an escaped convict. Did you see how he handled that rope, and the horse?" she persisted. "Even Bandy isn't that good, and he's been a horse wrangler his whole life. Mr. Courtland has a rare talent, and there's something very authoritative about him."

"Well, he seems pretty ordinary to me," he replied. "His clothes are off the rack, and he doesn't know a damned thing about cattle, even if he can throw a rope."

"Bowie, after you left the table, he told me what he thought about the Japanese import deal."

His black eyes searched hers. "Did he?"

"And he knows what a Hereford is. Are you sure you checked with the right people in Wyoming? Because I'd bet money that man has an interest in cattle, somehow or other."

He pursed his lips. "Then that might be a good project for you. Ask him a few leading questions. Dig out some information."

"I tried. Aggie stopped me. Do you have any ideas?"

"I might fly up to Jackson the first of next week." He frowned. "That might be the best way. I've got to get this foreigner out of here before Aggie does something stupid."

Gaby moaned silently. She'd never been so confused and uncertain. She hated acting behind Aggie's back, but like Bowie, she couldn't sit on her hands and do nothing. "He seems like a very nice man, Bowie, and he looks at your mother as if she's his whole world."

"That's a talent any man can fake, and don't you forget it," he said.

"Were you faking what just happened, to get me on your side?" she asked, her curiosity aroused.

His dark blond eyebrows shot up. "You think a man can fake desire?" he asked with real surprise.

Then she remembered the feel of his body against hers, and she burned all over.

"My God, Gaby," he mused as she turned quickly and moved away from him. "I'll call the *Guinness Book of World Records* right now. There can't be another woman your age in America who could second that opinion . . ."

"You stop that," she muttered as he fell into step beside her and they walked toward the back door of the house. "I wasn't thinking."

He laughed softly. "You're going to be an education for me," he said thoughtfully. And when she looked at him angrily, he added, "and I suspect I'm going to be a hell of an education for you."

She wouldn't have touched that challenge with a ten-foot pole. She moved quickly to the back door, trying not to notice his amused glance as she fumbled the screen open and almost fell into the kitchen in her haste to get away from his taunting presence.

Montoya looked up as they came together into the dining room. "Ay! Tía Elena will have a fit if you sit down like that, Bowie." The older man shook his head.

"What's wrong with me?" Bowie demanded.

Gaby had to bite her lower lip to keep from giggling. His white tee shirt was covered with grease. So were his brawny, hair-covered forearms, and there was even a streak of it in his hair.

"Grease," Montoya said politely. "You should work well now, since you are liberally anointed with it."

Gaby couldn't hold back the laughter. Bowie gave her a dirty look and glared at Montoya.

"I'm not that dirty."

Just as he said it, Tía Elena came in and a veritable torrent of rapid-fire Spanish left her lips. Bowie answered her in the same tongue, with equal fluency, and they went back and forth for several seconds before he threw up his hands and strode out of the room.

"I'll take a damned shower," he was muttering. "My God, you have to be scrubbed with lye soap and disinfectant before you can get a meal in this house . . . !"

"Just remember the doctors say that we should all cut down on grease, Bowie!" she couldn't resist calling after him.

He said something stormy in Spanish that made Tía Elena blush as she hurried into the kitchen to get the coffeepot.

"There is something you should know," Montoya said.

"What?"

"Bowie wishes you to invite Señor Hammock to the party,

in hopes that his mother will notice him and forget her new friend."

"Yes," Gaby agreed. "Well, she might," she added doggedly.

"Señor Hammock is newly engaged to Señora White," he said with a sigh.

"Great," Gaby moaned. "That was our last hope." She looked up at him. "We'll have to think of something else, and quick."

"He seems not a bad man," he said. "Are you both so certain that he is up to no good?"

"We don't know, because we can't find out anything about him," Gaby replied. "But we're working on it."

"Work fast," Montoya advised. "Marriages are difficult to put aside."

"You're telling me!"

Meanwhile, her mind was working overtime. In between fighting progress and a stepfather, Bowie was finding incredible ways to get under Gaby's guard. He was taking her over. But he didn't realize the threat the past held, and she did. She was as vulnerable and as out of control as Aggie. She was frightened, too. It gave her a new and binding kinship with the older woman, but it also made things worse.

CHAPTER
Eight

Gaby didn't share what she'd learned from Montoya with Bowie. They ate a brief, pleasant lunch, except that Bowie's black eyes kept straying to Gaby's mouth, and she knew that he was remembering, as she was, the fever that had sprung between them in the garage.

She had to get out of the house, even if only for a little while, so she went driving into Lassiter.

Bob Chalmers, the editor of the *Lassiter Citizen* was a friend of Aggie's, and she stopped in to say hello. Bob was a former Phoenix resident, and he knew Johnny Blake.

"Haven't seen him in years, though." He grinned, offering Gaby a seat in his office. Out in the newsroom, several girls were setting type, proofreading, laying waxed copy on the pages, and talking on the telephone. Gaby also noticed through an open office door that a middle-aged, rather heavyset man was talking on the phone while he typed on an enormous electric typewriter.

"Looks unfamiliar to you, I suppose," Bob mused, watching her expressions change. "We get out one issue a week, on Tuesday, and the paper hits the stands late Wednesday afternoon. We have eight employees, of which only three are full-time, and one reporter—Harvey Ritter." He cocked his head toward the open office. "Harvey used to work for one of the big San Antonio papers before he moved here. Judy, sitting at the typesetting machine, has been here for ten years. And Tim, back in the darkroom, almost came with the newspaper. He used to run the linotype machine before we went to offset press and retired hot type."

"I don't know much about weekly papers," Gaby confessed, "but I've heard editors say that a daily is much easier on reporters, because there are plenty of people to do the support jobs. Here, a reporter has to be a jack of all trades, doesn't he?"

"That's for sure. Harvey threatens to quit every Thursday." He leaned forward, chuckling. "That's the day when everybody reads the mistakes in the paper and calls to complain. I myself always leave the office to have lunch with someone or other in Tucson."

"You coward," she teased.

"I've lived this long," he pointed out. "Why don't you quit that Phoenix rag and come to work for me," he said suddenly. "You're a top-notch reporter, and you aren't afraid of controversy. Harvey does good political columns, and he's pretty expert on water and agriculture, but he doesn't like stirring up trouble. Right now, we need somebody to stir things up."

"I saw last week's front page," she said hesitantly.

He cleared his throat. "And, probably, the editorial page?" he suggested. "I cut your stepbrother to pieces. I won't apologize—I think he's wrong. We need jobs in Lassiter. We can't afford to put the emphasis on heritage to the point that it leaves hungry people in its wake."

"Oh, I agree," she said, and didn't correct his assumption that Bowie was her stepbrother. It was a common one, and it did no good to try and convince people that there was no connection between them. She usually just let it go. "In fact, that's why I'm here. Johnny wants me to do a piece on the agricultural outfit that's trying to buy land from Bowie. I thought you might be able to point me toward them."

He beamed. "Could we get you to do a sidebar for us, after you run your story?"

She smiled. "I think I might be able to talk Johnny into that."

"Great! Come on, I'll take you around to the real estate office where Mr. Barry works. He's acting as agent for the agricultural combine. I understand he had words with Bowie this morning?"

Gaby felt her face go hot. This was going to be a rough assignment. "He had several words with Bowie."

"Well, we'll work it out eventually," he said. "Controversy doesn't last long, which is good news for local citizens and bad news for the papers."

He led the way out the door. "Hey, Harvey, Gaby's going to do us a sidebar on the combine project! She's going to stir up a hornet's nest!"

Harvey stared at her through his thick glasses, but he didn't smile. "That's nice of her," he said, and abruptly picked up the telephone to start dialing without another word.

"Don't mind him," Judy whispered as they passed the petite blonde. She grinned. "He's just mad because Bob asked him to do it and he wouldn't. You're stealing his thunder."

"I hope I won't cause you any trouble," Gaby told Bob.

"Not a bit of it. Come along."

He introduced her to Alvin Barry, the real estate agent Bowie had ousted from Casa Río only hours before.

"This job is getting me down," Mr. Barry said, shaking hands with Gaby. "I never realized that Mr. McCayde would take such a hard line. He's going to find himself in a mess of trouble before this is over."

"He usually does," Gaby murmured dryly. "But he has his point of view, Mr. Barry, and I feel that he's entitled to it, despite the fact that it conflicts with yours," she added, wondering why she felt driven to stand up for Bowie when she disagreed with him as much as everyone else did.

Mr. Barry cleared his throat and looked embarrassed. "Sorry, Miss Cane, I'd forgotten the family ties. What can I do for you?"

"I want to know about the agricultural project," she said simply. She sat down and dug out her pocket tape recorder. "I'd especially like to have the names of the executives, so that I can contact them and discuss it with them as well."

"Good idea," Bob agreed as he sat across from her in front of Alvin Barry's big oak desk.

"They're rather hard to track down at times," Mr. Barry said, "but I'll do what I can. They, uh, sent me some press kits, just in case they were needed. Here you go. Mr. Chalmers already has one."

"Yes, I do." Bob pursed his lips as he watched Gaby thumb through the slicks of harvesters at work on huge planted fields, and agricultural irrigation in full swing.

Gaby was frowning. She looked up. "I understood that this was to be a kind of big truck farm—you know, one of those 'come and pick your own produce' kind of things— but this is cotton. These slicks show nothing but cotton production."

"That's in other states—Southern states," Mr. Barry said easily. "The main thing is to get the land, you see. Mr. McCayde has ten thousand acres that would suit admirably. It's level—although the agricultural people now use laser-leveling to make the fullest use of irrigation water—and it's near a major highway."

Gaby felt a niggling doubt in the back of her mind. Something wasn't right here. She didn't feel comfortable. That was usually her first indication that people weren't on the level with her.

"How about using effluent for that irrigation?" she asked.

Mr. Barry blinked. "I beg your pardon?"

Even Bob looked momentarily blank. "Effluent is recycled waste water," she explained. "It's much more economical, and less damaging to existing water supplies, to use that for agriculture in some instances."

"Well, that's not really in the projection," Mr. Barry said.

"Then what provisions are they going to make for contaminants leaching into the groundwater table? And exactly what amounts of groundwater do they envision pumping out? Can they adhere to the Groundwater Management Act with what they plan on doing here?"

"My God," Bob said, his voice soft with respect as he stared at Gaby. "You've done your homework."

"Unfortunately, I haven't done mine," Mr. Barry said with a grimace. "I have to admit that I can't answer your questions at this time, Miss Cane. Mr. Samuels is our executive vice president in charge of acquisitions, and I know he'll be eager to tell you what you want to know. This is, uh, for the Lassiter paper, is it not?"

"Oh, no," she shook her head. "I'm with the *Phoenix Advertiser*."

Mr. Barry looked frankly uncomfortable. "I can't imagine that such a big newspaper would be interested in our speculative efforts way down here in Lassiter," he said with a growing ruddy complexion.

"Ours?" she latched onto the word. "I thought you were only acting as advance man."

"Well, I do have a small interest in the company," Mr. Barry said.

"I see." Gaby pursed her lips. "Well, do you have a telephone number where Mr. Samuels can be reached?" she asked.

"Yes, of course." He fumbled in his desk and produced a business card. "Terrance Highman Samuels, Jr.," it read, "Vice President, Bio-Ag Corporation." The headquarters were in Los Angeles. Gaby looked up from it. "Isn't this a long way for this corporation to come looking for land?" she frowned.

"As you know, Miss Cane, land is growing higher in price near cities, and a great deal of good agricultural land is being diverted for industrial parks and housing. Arizona is one of the last frontiers, so to speak, in agricultural land."

"And one with growing water supply problems," she pointed out. "The Colorado River is Arizona's biggest water resource, even if we do have to share it with four states and Mexico. But it's on the other side of the state. Tucson is going to benefit from the Central Arizona Project, but we aren't. And the Gila River's water, which flows north of us, is already under siege. We have small water resources around Lassiter, and agriculture is one big water user."

"You really must speak with Mr. Samuels, I'm afraid," Mr. Barry said, and stood up, smiling as if he had to force it. "I'm sorry I know so little about my subject. Perhaps that press kit will be of some assistance."

"Perhaps it will. Nice to see you, Mr. Barry, and thank you for your help," she added politely.

"Some help," Bob scoffed when they were walking back down the sidewalk toward the newspaper office. "The press kit seemed straightforward enough. I used most of the slicks they sent, along with the announcement that they were going to try to locate a project here. But until you started asking those questions, I didn't realize how much I took at face value. Where did you learn so much about water?"

"I'm Johnny's resident expert," she said with a faint flush. "Somebody had to go to the meetings on the Central Arizona

Project and sit in on round-table discussions about water. I was picked. I don't even mind. Water is a fascinating subject."

"I gathered that."

"I don't know nearly as much as I'd like to," she added. "I'm a novice. But I know how to ask questions, and I can sort of understand the answers. Plus, I have sources that I can call to ask questions if I need to."

"I thought this project was a dream come true when it started," he mused. "But now, I've got questions."

"I'll contact Mr. Samuels," she promised, "and see about getting some answers. Mr. Barry doesn't know much, and that's really understandable. The project is still on the drawing board. Presumably, the organizers haven't had time to come down here and talk about it."

"That will probably be their next step. I'll bet you money that Mr. Barry is on the phone to them right now."

She grinned. "In that case, I may not need this phone number after all."

"Be sure you don't lose mine," he said. "And while we're about it, will you think about that proposition I made you? You'd be one hell of an asset to us. I'll even match whatever Johnny's paying you."

She was flattered—very flattered. "I'll promise to think about it."

He beamed. "Thanks."

She did think about what he'd said, all the way back to Casa Río. It would be a challenge to work for a small weekly paper, but in some ways, less of a hassle. She'd be near Bowie . . . She knew that was where her train of thought was leading her.

All day, she'd thought about his ardor in the garage, about the way he'd held her and kissed her, about the things he'd said. She'd gone into town to avoid him, because it was all going too fast. He was backing her into a corner, and she was afraid of what could happen.

The odd thing was that he didn't frighten her physically. She found him terribly attractive. Despite her mental scars from years past, he was the one man who didn't bring them open again. He was tender and slow, and she loved what it felt like to be in his arms.

But she didn't dare allow her emotions to become involved. It was too much of a risk. On the other hand, she didn't know how she was going to manage to keep him at arm's length.

When she arrived at Casa Río in her white convertible VW, Aggie and Courtland had already returned. Apparently she was late for supper.

Gaby had changed this morning to go into Lassiter. She was wearing a white sundress, white pumps, and she'd put her hair into a neat, cool bun tied with a white ribbon. The look Bowie gave her when she sat down at the table was intense and extremely flattering. It made her pulse race wildly.

"You look nice," he remarked, smiling at her. "Very cool."

"It's blazing hot out," she said, "I went shopping," she lied, because it was too soon to tell him what she was up to, "but I didn't find anything I liked."

"It's too hot to shop, darling," Aggie murmured, smiling at her and then at Courtland. "We had a nice trip up to Cochise Stronghold, and we stopped at Pearce to let him see the museum there. You remember it, Gaby, in an old country store."

"Yes. It's got everything from antiques to signed posters of John Wayne's movies."

"And some fascinating remnants from the mining era," Bowie added.

"Did you get the telephone calls made, darling?" Aggie asked Gaby.

"Every last one."

"*Every* last one?" Bowie queried with a raised eyebrow.

She nodded, and he smiled secretively as he lowered his eyes back to his plate. Gaby wondered what he was going to think when he found out that John Hammock was engaged to be married.

Bowie was called to the phone during the meal. He discovered he had to fly out to Canada suddenly to take a look at his project, which had developed a hitch. After everyone was finished, he drew Gaby outside with him to the Scorpio he drove.

"Keep an eye on them," he told her, nodding toward the house. "Don't let them out of your sight for a minute."

She lifted her eyebrows. "Not even to go to the bathroom?"

He glowered at her. "Don't be absurd." He checked his watch. "I've got to run. I won't be back until Friday afternoon, but I'll do my best to be here by the time the party gets under way."

"Okay."

He tilted her chin up to his and searched her olive eyes. "You've been trying to avoid me since this morning," he said quietly. "Why?"

Her face colored. "It's too soon," she blurted out.

"No. You've just got to have a little time to get used to me in a different light." He bent and brushed his hard lips slowly across hers. "Don't close your mouth like that, baby," he whispered. "Open it and let me kiss you properly."

"Someone might see . . . !"

"To hell with that," he whispered. "Open your mouth, Gaby."

She did. His lips parted against hers, and pushed down. She reached up to hold him hungrily, as his mouth worked on hers, hard and warm. He dropped his briefcase, and his big arms swallowed her against him while the kiss grew harder and rougher in the stillness of late afternoon light.

"You taste sweet," he whispered. "I think I'm going to get addicted to your mouth."

"I'm plain," she whispered back, her mind in limbo. "And there are things you don't know..."

He kissed her again, more tenderly this time. "You'll tell me what I want to know one day. I can wait. And I won't rush you any more than I already have." He smiled wickedly. "As for rushing you," he mused, looking down at the high, square bodice of her sundress, "you don't have a single cause for complaint. Yet."

She felt the heat sing through her at the way he was looking at her body.

"I don't go around showing myself to men," she said with a lightness she had to force.

"Yes, I know. I don't go around showing myself to women. Only to you," he added with a wry smile, delighted at the color that rose suddenly in her cheeks. "You needn't blush. You didn't look away all that quickly, as I remember."

"Bowie!"

He laughed softly. "I'll stop. Goodbye, Gaby."

He let her go, picked up his briefcase, and got into the car without another word or a backward glance. She stood watching him drive off, wondering how much more complicated things were going to get.

Aggie and Courtland were sitting on the living room sofa together watching a television special when Gaby excused herself and went to bed. Their heads were close together, their hands linked. They looked almost like one person in the pose, and when Aggie lifted her eyes to his, his whole face softened magically. If Aggie was besotted, so was the mysterious Mr. Courtland. She hoped Bowie got lucky in Jackson. If he didn't, they had no hope of postponing the wedding. Poor Aggie. Gaby really hoped Mr. Courtland was a good guy.

Gaby tried to contact Mr. Samuels with Bio-Ag the next day, but she was told by his secretary that he was out of town until the following Tuesday, so she settled down to helping Aggie finalize the catering and music for the party and making decorations with Tía Elena to brighten up the patio, where most of it would be held.

She hadn't realized how much she needed a vacation until she was at Casa Río. The past few months had been hectic, and the shooting she'd covered before she left Phoenix had dwelled on her mind. It was a relief to be away from work temporarily, even though Bowie's disturbing presence and Aggie's explosive engagement could yet threaten her peace of mind.

Ned Courtland slowly became less reserved when Gaby was around. He had a dry wit, and he spoke his mind with unaffected honesty. Gaby was beginning to see why he appealed so much to Aggie. He was a strong man, and he had some fine qualities.

Friday was a long day, fraught with preparation. Gaby chose a simple, Mexican-styled white dress with exquisitely colorful embroidery down its bodice and around the hem of its full skirt. She tied her hair back with a ribbon and decided that it wasn't so bad, looking feminine. But she knew that it was only because Bowie was around that it didn't bother her as it had in the old days.

Bowie had called from Tucson just after five, to tell them he was on his way down. He arrived as the buffet table was laid, wearing a handsome tan suit, his blond hair clean and neatly combed despite his long trip.

"I'm on time, I suppose," he said as Gaby greeted him at the door, her eyes bright and soft.

"Exactly. People should be getting here any minute. How was your trip?"

"Busy," he said. He glanced around at the piñatas, colored lanterns, and streamers. "Nice. Did you and Aggie do it all?"

"Tiá Elena and her sisters helped. You look tired, Bowie."

"I am." He stared at her for a long moment. "I stopped over in Jackson on the way home."

She moved closer, glancing warily around them, but Aggie and Ned still hadn't come in from the patio. "And?"

"I drew a blank," he said. "There are no Courtlands where he said he hailed from. There used to be," he added with narrowed black eyes. "But that was almost a hundred years ago. I don't know who Aggie's suitor is, but he's sold her a pack of goods. I've got to talk to her."

"Not now," she pleaded. "Let her have the party."

He glared down at her. "What will that accomplish? She's got to know about this man."

She didn't know why she argued. Perhaps it was because she'd never seen Aggie so happy. What would a few more hours hurt, after all?

"Humor me. Just for tonight, let her be the belle of the ball and don't cast shadows," she pleaded.

"I gather there's a reason for your intervention?"

She smiled dryly. "I'm not defecting to the enemy camp, but I do like Mr. Courtland."

"Traitor," he accused.

"I know." Her olive eyes studied his handsome face, taking in the new lines. He worked so hard, and he never seemed to slow down. It bothered her that he was looking so worn.

"I like the dress," he murmured, letting his eyes slide down it. "You've never worn anything quite so colorful before."

"It's a festive night," she said, and worried about how he

was going to react when he discovered what Aggie and Ned Courtland were really up to. She should have told him. But Aggie would—she'd promised.

"I'd better go and change. This is a bit too formal," he indicated his suit. "John Hammock is coming?" he asked.

Gaby smiled. "Yes."

His dark blond brows drew together. "But . . . ?"

She laughed. "But, nothing. He's coming. Honest."

"All right, then." He moved closer to her, stopping her smile with just the heady threat of his big, muscular body. "Did you miss me?"

"You weren't gone long enough to be missed, and I was busy."

"That's right. Busy missing me," he said, and smiled wickedly. His black eyes danced. "Aggie hired a band, I see," he said, nodding toward the cowboy quartet tuning up on the patio. "Good. You can dance with me."

She met his eyes curiously "I can't dance," she confessed.

"You what?"

"I told you before—I can't dance." She smiled shyly. "I never liked it, so I never learned. You said you'd teach me."

"I can teach you a lot of other things, too," he said. He touched her hair, running his hand along a silky strand of it. "I'd like very much to drag you off into a corner right now and kiss the breath out of you."

She wanted that, too, but it wasn't the time. "You'd better change," she said nervously.

He sighed. "I suppose so." He tugged her hair and smiled as he let it go. "Watch out for Ted and Mike. I've got plans for them."

"Don't you dare try to mess up Aggie's evening with those two clowns," she said.

"I'd never do that to Aggie," he said, and then his eyes

twinkled with pure mischief. "Of course, Ted and Mike might."

"I'll tell on you," she threatened.

He only laughed. "No, you won't." He winked at her lazily, making her heart race, and started through the house to the staircase, whistling something under his breath.

Gaby watched him go. She'd been right. This was going to be one long, miserable evening. And when Aggie and Ned made their announcement, she hoped that Bowie didn't go through the roof.

CHAPTER

Nine

Aggie came in from the patio wearing a long white caftan with gold braid on one sleeve—a designer gown that suited her dark tan and eyes and her gray-streaked black hair. Ned Courtland was wearing dark slacks with an open-necked white shirt and a parchment-colored jacket with black threads in it. He looked elegant himself, and his arm never left Aggie's waist. Gaby sighed at the oneness they radiated. It was something she'd never known with anyone, except for that brief interlude with Bowie in the garage.

Bowie was almost rubbing his hands with glee, when John Hammock walked through the door. He shook hands with the white-haired man, all smiles.

Gaby joined them, privately thinking that Mr. Hammock wouldn't suit Aggie in a million years. He was an agricultural equipment salesman with a paunch in front, and he liked nothing better than football, which Aggie hated.

"How are you, Mr. Hammock? Good to see you again," Gaby said, smiling as she shook the man's pudgy hand.

"It's nice to see you, too, Gaby." Mr. Hammock grinned. "Who's that man with Aggie?"

"Just some man she met on the cruise ship," Bowie said shortly. "He'll be leaving in a day or so."

"He looks familiar." Mr. Hammock frowned.

Bowie was immediately all ears. He'd changed out of his suit into tan slacks and a white silk shirt with rolled up sleeves. He looked casually elegant, and to Gaby's eyes, the handsomest man in the room.

"You know him?" Bowie asked, lowering his voice. "He says his name is Ned Courtland and he's from Jackson, Wyoming."

"Courtland. Courtland." Hammock shook his head. "No, I don't know the name. I meet so many people, you see, it's kind of hard to keep the names and faces straight!" he grinned. "Bowie, Gaby, I want you to meet someone. Ellen, come here." He drew a handsome older woman to his side. "This is Ellen Thurmond White. She's my fiancée."

Bowie looked crestfallen, but he regrouped instantly and smiled at the lady. "Nice to meet you. Both of you, have some hors d'oeuvres and punch. The table's right over there, where Aggie and Courtland are standing."

"Thanks, Bowie, don't mind if we do," Hammock said, nodding. He escorted Ellen away and Bowie gave Gaby a hot glare.

"Did you know about that?" he demanded.

She nodded. "Montoya told me. He hears all the local gossip, you know."

"Why didn't you say something?" he persisted.

"You wouldn't have believed me. Don't you want some punch?"

"No." He glared toward Courtland, who was shaking hands with Mr. Hammock. His black eyes flashed. "She can't be serious about him."

"Bowie..."

At that very moment, Aggie was holding up a crystal glass and tapping it with a teaspoon.

"I'd like to make an announcement," Aggie called in her musical voice. She held up a glass of punch. "I want you all to meet Ned Courtland. He's from Wyoming . . . and I'm going to marry him."

There was a shocked silence. Bowie didn't say a word. He stared at Aggie, taking in her defiant but hopeful glance and Courtland's dark scowl at Aggie without reacting to either. He turned on his heel and went out the door without a word, giving the assembled guests some juicy gossip to chew on.

"You promised you'd tell him before the party," Courtland said to Aggie, his voice deep and slow.

"He was late," Aggie faltered. She colored. "And anyway, it was safer this way—I told you it would be."

"Aggie, I'm not afraid of him," he said quietly. "It was his right to be told first."

"I'll smooth it over later. Right now, there are some people I want you to meet." She clung to his hand and tugged him along with her, her face still flushed and nervous.

Gaby followed Bowie out into the darkness, watching him light a cigarette as he strode angrily toward the corral, his bare head catching the faint glimmer from the windows and patio of the house.

He leaned against the corral fence. He couldn't believe what he'd heard. Aggie was going crazy, that was it, marrying a total stranger—a man about whom they knew absolutely nothing. He didn't know how he was going to survive having a new man in his father's house, using his father's things, living with his mother.

A light touch on his forearm made his head jerk up. He stared at Gaby without expression.

"You knew," he said accusingly.

His pain was so intense that she could almost feel it, and her tender heart ached for him. He didn't show it, but she knew that he felt things deeply. "I wanted to tell you, but it wasn't my secret. It was hers." She sighed. "Besides, I didn't know how to tell you."

"My God." He took a draw from his cigarette and stared out into the darkness. "My God. I don't think I can stand it."

"You may like him when you get to know him," she said, her voice hushed and caring. "I do."

"He isn't marrying your mother."

"Well, I never really knew my mother. Aggie is special to me. I wouldn't want her to make a terrible mistake, either. But Mr. Courtland, if that's his real name, is still very much an unknown quantity. He wanted to tell you about the engagement two days ago."

"He could be anybody."

"I can't argue with that," she said. "But wouldn't you be distrustful of any man Aggie brought home?"

"Probably," he admitted. "But I'd feel a lot better if I knew him myself. And if my mother had known him longer than a couple of weeks," he added darkly. "The plain fact is, I don't want him here."

"He knows that, but he's staying anyway. Doesn't that tell you anything?"

"It tells me he doesn't know what he's getting into. I won't have it, I tell you," he began, his voice like a whip. "No way on God's green earth is my mother going to marry some damned gigolo and put Casa Río in his hands! I'll see him in hell first—I swear I will!"

"Bowie . . ."

"Damned Wyoming import," he muttered. "I've got half a mind to go back in there and plant one right in his mug." His dark eyes glittered dangerously. "In fact, that's the best idea I've had all night."

He meant it. Gaby bit her lower lip, trying to think of something to say that might stop him. On the other hand, it was a much better time for action. She didn't have time to think about what she was going to do, because he was already grinding out his cigarette.

She jumped up on the lowest rung of the corral fence and slid her hands nervously around Bowie's neck, feeling him tense with surprise.

"What are you doing?" he asked. He turned to catch her waist and keep her from pitching headfirst off the fence as she lost her balance. Her mouth was just under his, and proximity solved all her problems at once.

"You can't punch out Mr. Courtland," she said in a breathless tone. "He looks the type of man who'll punch right back. You can't let Aggie's party turn into a brawl."

"Can't I?" he asked, but his eyes were on her mouth now.

With her last shred of nerve, she moved the scant inches necessary to bring her soft lips over his hard ones. Her hands clung to the nape of his neck, and she opened her mouth the way he had in the garage when he'd kissed her, pressing her body hard against his and moving it with what she thought was gentle sensuality.

To Bowie, it was something else again. He shuddered at the unexpected movement that roused him beyond thought, and he moved toward her without a single hesitation. "Gaby!" he bit off against her mouth, his body rippling with shocked hunger.

"Yes," she whispered, enticing him. This would get his mind off Courtland, and she did love kissing him. "Teach me how to kiss, Bowie," she breathed into his mouth.

He wanted to teach her a lot more than that. The feel of her soft body moving against him so sensually had shattered his control. He wondered if she knew how fiercely she was arousing him, and why. But his mind wasn't working properly, and he couldn't fight it. He'd barely slept since the morning in the garage, his mind full of Gaby, his body aching for hers. He'd never wanted anyone so much.

His big hands spanned her waist and jerked her closer as

his mouth pressed down hard over hers and grew slowly, steadily more demanding. The darkness closed in on them. She felt his breath going roughly into her open mouth as his tongue teased her lips, tracing them until they parted in faint protest. And suddenly, without warning, his tongue pushed past them and deep into her mouth in a hard, slow thrust that made her legs shudder.

She made a tiny sound deep in her throat, because he'd kissed her that way in the garage, and it was fiercely stimulating. But the hunger in it made her nervous, and when she felt his body begin to tremble faintly against hers, she started freezing up. He didn't seem to notice, and that worried her. She put her hands against his broad chest. His lean fingers began to stroke upwards from her waist and toward the upward thrust of her firm breasts, until she panicked.

This was the one thing she hadn't counted on—that he might want more than a kiss. The feel of his hands against the sides of her breasts frightened her.

"Bowie?" His thumbs were suddenly touching the outside of her breasts with an erotic rhythm far beyond her experience. "No, Bowie, you mustn't!" she whispered, and began to twist in his embrace.

He moved, drowning in his anguished need for her. She'd thrown him off balance and he was ravenous to touch her, to feel her soft body under him. He pinned her to the fence— not roughly, but firmly—his arms against the fence at her sides, his hard-muscled body holding hers immobile while he kissed her with feverish hunger. His lean hips brushed against hers. And in that close embrace, she felt the full force of his arousal and realized how dangerous the situation had become. There was a deserted barn not twenty steps away . . .

"Bowie . . . please . . . no!"

Her frantic plea got through the sensuality that had fogged his mind. He lifted his head, his body still pinning her hips, and stared down into her eyes with frustrated acknowledgement. Her fear was clearly visible.

"Gaby," he said gently. He forced his hips away from hers and leaned against his hands on the fence, taking deep, shuddering breaths while he fought for control. "It got away from me. I'm sorry."

Her tense body began to relax. The quietness of his tone, his lack of anger, reassured her. She leaned back against the fence, trembling a little, and watched him.

"Have I . . . hurt you?" she whispered unsteadily.

He managed a wan smile. "I won't die," he promised. He took another slow breath. "Don't look so guilty. It's a normal reaction to frustrated desire."

She lowered her eyes to the mouth that had kissed hers with such aching hunger, and delicious sensations washed over her. "It's my fault. I didn't want you to hit Mr. Courtland. But I didn't realize that . . . that kissing you would," she swallowed, "would do that to you."

He actually laughed, very softly. "My God."

"I don't know much about men."

He laid a lean finger over her lips. "All you have to remember is that when you grind your hips against mine like that, you'd better want me on the spot, standing up," he said, with a rueful smile at her blush. "I've been without a woman for a long time, and I have a rather potent reaction to you."

"Are you all right?" she asked softly.

He nodded. "I will be, in a minute." He leaned his forehead against hers while he got his breath back. "What frightened you?" he asked.

She closed her eyes. "You pinned me against the fence," she whispered, feeling the nightmares in the back of her mind. "I couldn't get away."

He lifted his head and her eyes opened. He searched them

quietly. "I won't make that mistake twice," he replied. "There's nothing to be afraid of. I won't hurt you."

"Oh, I know that," she whispered tearfully. "I'm so sorry, Bowie!"

He gathered her close, leaving space between his hips and hers, his head bent protectively against her own. "We've got a long way to go, haven't we, honey?" he asked quietly. "Trust is going to take time."

"It . . . it isn't you," she whispered. "Really, it isn't. I have some old mental scars."

"I realize that." He brushed his mouth softly over hers. "We'll take it one day at a time. Don't start running."

"I won't," she sighed. She couldn't—he was already such a part of her life that it was painful to imagine his not being in it. She reached up and touched his hard mouth. "I've never been able to go that far with anyone else," she told him, because it was important that he know.

He frowned and sighed heavily. "Gaby, was it only my strength that frightened you?" he asked intently.

She blushed, because she knew what he was asking. "Yes."

"That response," he said quietly, "is something a man can't help. It's automatic. I can keep from letting you feel it, but I can't stop it from happening."

"I'm not afraid of you . . . like that," she whispered huskily. "It's just that I don't know if I'm capable of intimacy." Her eyes searched his worriedly. "You understand? It's the thought of giving in, of giving up control."

He pushed the damp hair away from her face. "You can learn to want me," he said quietly. "I'm in no flaming rush for it to happen. I can wait. Does that reassure you?"

"What if I can't, ever?" she groaned.

"Let's live one day at time, honey." He caught her by the waist and lifted her clear off the ground, smiling as he brought her soft, swollen lips on a level with his. "Kiss me and go inside. I've got some plotting to do."

"I won't hurt you again?" she whispered worriedly.

"Not if I know you're going to do it," he murmured dryly. "Come on, come on, I don't have all night."

She laughed delightedly and put her mouth against his, floating as he returned the kiss gently.

"I'm going to teach you what passion is one day," he whispered into her parted lips. "That's a promise." He put her down abruptly. "Now, go inside before we create any more problems."

"All right." She searched his eyes. "Bowie, you won't ruin Aggie's party, will you?"

He sighed heavily. "No," he said angrily. "But I won't let up on Courtland. I have to protect her."

"I hope you're right. Because if you aren't," she added, turning away, "she may never forgive you."

He knew that. He watched her go with a rough curse. Life was getting pretty complicated, and Courtland was the reason. Not that Gaby was going to be any less of a problem. If she really wasn't capable of intimacy, he didn't know what he was going to do. She was becoming necessary to him. But he knew himself well enough to know that he couldn't settle for a platonic relationship with her. They couldn't have anything together unless he could convince her that passion wasn't the terror she thought it was.

He turned and strode off down the path that ran along the pasture fences. He was too stirred up and furious at his mother and Courtland to go inside until he'd cooled down. He'd promised Gaby that he wouldn't make trouble, but he was sure as hell tempted. The thought of losing Casa Río to an outsider was depressing. The thought of losing his mother to a gigolo was even worse.

Gaby, meanwhile, was making her way through laughing guests when she came face to face with Aggie at the staircase. Aggie's eyes were dark and apprehensive. "How is he taking it?" she asked, her face drawn.

"Badly," Gaby said. She'd gotten herself under control, except for a faint residue of embarrassment at her own boldness. She should have known better; she knew her limits. She'd just wanted so badly to overcome them. It looked as if that was going to be an uphill battle. She knew that Bowie couldn't settle for friendship, but if she couldn't get past her hangups, that was all she could offer him. She wanted to sit down and cry.

"I was afraid he'd dig his heels in," Aggie said miserably. "It's what I expected, after all." She glanced toward Ned, who was talking to some of the other men. "Ned told me that Bowie was going to be a problem, but I hoped that my son might care enough for me to let me have what I need to be happy."

Gaby studied the older woman quietly. "What about what Bowie needs, Aggie?" she asked softly. "A child who feels loved isn't going to react that way to a stepparent—is he?"

Aggie actually went pale. "That wasn't fair," she said stiffly.

"No, I suppose not, but is it true?"

The older woman sighed and turned her attention to Ned. "Yes. I was never able to get close enough to my son to tell him that I cared about him. He's so like Copeland was, Gaby—so reserved, so remote. He has this way of making you feel like an alien when you're around him. I don't know how to reach him." She looked at Gaby levelly. "Do you?"

Gaby did, but not on a conversational level. "You might try just talking to him," she suggested.

"I have. He changes the subject or walks away."

"Then, will you try to see things from his perspective?" Gaby persisted, glancing toward the very loud band playing country-western medleys. "You come home from a cruise with a man you've known less than two weeks and announce wedding plans in front of a crowd without giving him any idea what you're planning. The man you're going to marry is someone he doesn't know and can't find out anything about."

Aggie looked worried. "That doesn't mean he's a desperado or something," she said restlessly. "He's just a poor, working cowboy, but I don't care." She said it as if she were trying to convince herself. "I don't care, do you hear? I can live in a line cabin if I have to." She lifted great tragic eyes to Gaby's. "I love him so much. He can't be after my money, Gaby, he just can't!"

"I don't like to think that he could, either, but none of us knows anything about him . . ."

"You're just like Bowie," Aggie said with fierce anger, flushing. "You both think I'm a flighty old woman who hasn't got enough sense to see people for what they really are! Well, Ned is my business, and if I want to marry him, I will. The two of you can go hang!"

"We love you, Aggie," Gaby protested.

"No, you don't! Bowie just wants to make sure a stranger doesn't get his hands on Casa Río, and you're afraid of the same thing. I can't believe you could be so ungrateful—not after the way I took you in, without any questions about your past, and took care of you all those years!"

Gaby lost all her color. "Aggie, I don't want you to get hurt," she began.

"Ned wouldn't hurt me half as much as my so-called family already has!" she said icily, then turned and walked away, leaving Gaby feeling as if she'd been kicked.

Gaby had had enough. She went up the staircase with tears running down her cheeks. She'd rarely cried in her life, but she had good reason tonight. Bowie was going to hate her because she couldn't even let him touch her, and now Aggie was furious with her. She didn't think she could take much more pressure. Maybe she should go back to Phoenix tomorrow and let them fight it out among themselves. She was tired of being caught in the middle.

Outside, Bowie was still smoking and grappling with his anger.

The sound of footsteps nearby caught his attention. He turned to find Ned Courtland wandering down the path, bareheaded and scowling, with a cigarette in his hand. It was the first time Bowie had seen him smoke since he'd been at Casa Río.

"Looking for somebody?" Bowie asked coolly. "Or are you just checking out the assets before you move in?"

Courtland stopped just in front of him, his usual easygoing manner as absent as his casual attitude. "Don't ever get the idea that I need your permission," Courtland said curtly. "Not to move in here, marry your mother, or generally do whatever else I damned well please."

Bowie's eyebrows arched. "Well, well. Gloves off, I gather?" he asked with a mocking smile.

"Count on it." The older man leaned back against the fence and smoked quietly. "Aggie promised me she'd tell you about the engagement before the party. She didn't, I gather."

"Does that really make a difference?"

"To me, one hell of a lot," Courtland replied quietly. "The whole situation is getting out of hand. I came here so that Aggie and I could have some time together, away from people, to get to know each other. I wanted to see how and where she lived . . ."

"I'll just bet you did," Bowie said insolently.

"Keep pushing," Courtland invited with eyes as cold as Bowie's. "I've taken more from you than I've ever taken from another man. I've had enough of you and your damned sarcasm, and your cynicism is even getting a hold on Aggie. She's started looking at me as if she expects me to take her for every dime she's got and walk off."

"You mean it hadn't crossed your mind?" Bowie asked.

"The whole point of this trip was to make sure Aggie could accept me as I am," he replied. "I didn't want to rush into marriage with a woman who'd become infatuated with the idea of a poor, lonely cowboy on holiday."

"How did you afford Jamaica?" Bowie asked narrowly.

"I saved up for years," came the quiet reply. "It's the first vacation I've ever had—the first time I've been out of Wyoming for any length of time since my wife died."

"Your wife?" Bowie asked, frowning. Aggie hadn't said anything about his being a widower.

"She died nine years ago of cancer," he replied. He stared off at the distant house, his eyes narrow and thoughtful. "I hadn't even looked at another woman until Aggie got lost." He shrugged. "I spend most of my life looking out for stray things, mostly calves. She kept getting lost, and once a foreign tourist got a little too overbearing with her, and I stepped in. After that, we just sort of drifted together, both lonely, searching for something." He sighed. "I got in over my head before I wanted to. Now I've got to work things out." He glared at Bowie. "In spite of you and Gaby and your overprotective attitude. Hell, I don't want Casa Río, I want Aggie!"

Bowie didn't like the man. It irritated him that he wanted to. "Maybe she'll decide she doesn't want you," he replied coldly.

"That's her decision, not yours. If I could, I'd pack her up and take her home with me. But I've got a couple of spinster sisters living with me, and they'd give her the same treatment you're giving me. I can't do that to her."

"Sisters?" Bowie asked. "How about your own kids?"

The look on Courtland's face was puzzling. It was cold and hard, and then angry. He stared down at the ground, then suddenly flung his cigarette there and put it out under his boot.

"I don't have any kids," he said shortly.

"I'm sorry," Bowie said curtly, looking away.

"You love your mother, boy," Courtland said heavily. "I can't fault you for that. If I could have had kids, I hope they'd have loved me half as much." He leaned wearily against the fence. "My wife used to cry in her sleep. She never let me see her do it, but I knew just the same how it hurt her to be childless. We had twenty wonderful years together, and I ran my pickup into the river the day she died." He laughed bitterly. "But I had a man on the place with an overworked sense of responsibility. He pulled me out a few seconds too soon."

Bowie was getting a terrifying picture of this man—someone who loved so fiercely and completely that he'd rather have died with the woman he loved than to have gone on living without her. Bowie himself couldn't conceive of that much emotion, that depth of commitment to one woman. He knew for a fact that his father hadn't felt it for Aggie. Copeland McCayde wouldn't have run his pickup into a river if Aggie had died—he'd have been too busy cursing the funeral for keeping him away from work. That was a disloyal thought, and it made Bowie angry.

"Aggie loved my father," he said defensively.

"Of course she did," Courtland replied. "She loves you, too. But she's still a woman. There are things she needs emotionally and physically that a son can't give her."

Bowie glared at him furiously. "And you can?"

"Yes, I can," Courtland replied hotly. "And don't you raise your fist to me unless you want it back in spades. I'm just as old-fashioned as Aggie is. We aren't sleeping together, and we won't until we're married. I'm a churchgoing man."

Bowie unruffled, but Courtland had startled him. He couldn't imagine his mother wanting a man.

"When are you planning the happy event?" Bowie asked through his teeth.

"God knows. Aggie's got to be willing to live on a ranch in the Tetons, where she won't be Mrs. Agatha McCayde of Casa Río," he said resignedly. "I don't like crowds and exotic places, and I'm not a partying man. The Tetons suit me. They'll have to suit her, and so will being a ranch wife. A real one—not a figurehead dripping diamonds."

"My God, don't tell me you'll expect Aggie to milk cows!" Bowie exploded, because that was what it sounded like.

Courtland arched an eyebrow. "Why not? I do."

"She'd be dead of overwork in a month!"

"Oh, hell, she'd love it as much as I do. Half her problem is boredom. A rancher's life is close to God. It's better than what passes for life in the fast lane." His dark eyes narrowed on Bowie's hard face. "And you damned well know it. You're no more a high roller than I am. You're a rancher yourself. If you didn't care about land and animals, you'd sell this place in a minute instead of fighting half of Southern Arizona to hold on to it!"

Bowie didn't have a leg to stand on. He glared at the older man. "I don't want a stepfather," he said finally.

"I'm not thrilled with the idea of you for a stepson," Courtland shot right back, "but we all have our crosses to bear."

"You haven't leveled with me," Bowie said abruptly. "There are no Courtlands in Jackson."

"I didn't say I was from Jackson; I said I lived there."

"There are no Courtlands living there who own ranches."

Courtland stuck his hands in his pockets and pursed his lips. "You've done your homework. All right, I'll give you a little more rope. I moved to Jackson when my wife died. Up until then, I lived and worked in San Antonio."

"Courtland can't be your legal name," Bowie returned.

"You're sharp." Courtland lit another cigarette. "No, it's not all of my legal name. But I'm not on the run, and there's nothing about my past that I'm ashamed of."

"I don't like lies."

"Neither do I, son," Courtland said quietly. "But sometimes a little subterfuge is necessary. You'll understand it all one day. Now, shall we go back inside before your neighbors carry our dirty linen home and give it to their wives?"

Bowie shrugged. "For Aggie's sake, I suppose we should present a united front." He glared at the older man as they started back to the house. "But don't expect me to call you daddy."

"God forbid," Courtland said easily. He glanced sideways at Bowie. "I don't suppose you'd go away if I offered you a quarter?"

Bowie had to stifle a grin. "No."

Courtland shrugged. "It was worth a try."

Aggie was waiting nervously on the patio, her dark eyes full of fear and sadness.

"We didn't come to blows," Courtland assured her, sliding an affectionate arm around her shoulders. "But don't offer him any quarters to make himself scarce. You can take it from me that he can't be bribed."

Aggie smiled nervously. "I'm sorry," she told Bowie. "I should have told you."

Bowie studied her quietly. "No harm done." He glanced at Courtland. "But I hope you like milking cows."

"What?" Aggie asked.

"Never mind," Bowie said. "I guess I'll go circulate. Where's Gaby?"

Aggie grimaced. "She's gone to bed. I had words with her," she said miserably. "I didn't mean what I said."

"You can patch it up in the morning," Courtland said. "Come on. Let's see about our guests."

Bowie watched them go, still half mad and undecided. He

put out his cigarette in the silent butler, talked to a couple of people on his way out of the room, and sauntered up the staircase.

He knocked on Gaby's door and waited. Barely a minute passed before she opened it. She hadn't undressed, and her eyes were red-rimmed and miserable.

The evidence of tears on her face bothered him. He couldn't remember ever seeing her cry. "Aggie didn't mean it," he said gently.

"I guess not," she said, forcing a smile. "But it hurt."

"You'll patch it all up tomorrow, honey. I was going to invite you to go sightseeing in the morning, but I've got a meeting in Phoenix." He smiled. "You could come with me."

"I have to do an interview," she concocted. She needed a little breathing space, and she wanted to get Johnny's story done. She wondered if Bio-Ag had a Tucson office. She decided to go by the newspaper office in the morning and see if Bob Chalmers could help her do some digging. It would save her a flight to Los Angeles if she could luck up on some official nearby.

"Okay," he said, searching her eyes. "I may go on up to Canada for a day or two, as well, but I'll be back early next week," he added pointedly. "So don't get any ideas about haring back to Phoenix for good."

"Would you really mind?" she asked with downcast eyes. "I don't know if I can . . ." She shrugged helplessly.

He tilted her sad eyes up to his, and his own narrowed. "That's something you and I will find out together," he said quietly. "But there isn't going to be any pressure, or any repeats of what happened outside. The next time we make love, I'll make damned sure I don't pin you."

She tingled from head to toe, because he didn't sound as if he intended to give up on her. She managed a shy smile. "Okay."

He bent and brushed his lips over hers in a caress that was as reassuring as it was tender. "You excite me more than any woman I've ever known," he breathed against her mouth. "You can't imagine what it's like to touch you and know that no other man ever has."

He lifted his head and smiled at her expression. "Go to bed. I'll see you in the morning."

"Aggie really isn't mad?"

He shook his head. "She's just under the spell of the Teton man," he mused. His face hardened. "Courtland came out to talk. He says he expected Aggie to tell me before she made the announcement."

"Yes," she agreed. "He told her so at breakfast yesterday."

He shifted, his eyes cold. "If I knew him, I might like him," he said grudgingly. "But I don't know him, and I don't want Aggie mixed up with a man on the take. Anyway, she'll get over him."

"What are you planning?" she asked suspiciously.

His lips pursed. "Curious? Well, hold your breath, honey. That's going to be my little secret. Good night."

She watched him walk away with open curiosity. Poor Aggie. She turned back into her room, smiling a little at the hope that had come out of such a surprising night.

CHAPTER

Ten

Gaby hardly slept at all. Her dreams were of Bowie, and hopelessly erotic. She tossed and turned until dawn, and when she woke, the sheets were damp with perspiration. She remembered the night before, the way Bowie's body had tautened and hardened when hers was pressed against it. She felt her skin go hot as she savored the memory. If only he hadn't grown so demanding. But his lack of restraint had brought back painful memories. She knew about lack of control and terror: she'd always associated them with men. Bowie couldn't possibly understand what overpowering ardor did to her. She closed her eyes and saw blood . . .

She dressed quickly and left the room, forcing herself not to remember the past. She was safe now; she had to remember that. The terror wasn't ever going to touch her life again, because she'd covered her trail very well. That gave her an odd kinship with Mr. Courtland. He, too, had secrets. She wondered if his were as dangerous as her own.

She went downstairs reluctantly. Aggie would still be angry at her. That had hurt, along with the harsh words. She and Aggie had never argued before. Bowie would be there,

too, and she was nervous of him, even though she was
bathed in excitement because of the newness of their fragile
relationship.

He looked up when she came in the door. His eyes, as he
smiled, were soft and full of lazy appreciation.

She reacted to that appraisal by tripping over her chair at
first as she tried to sit in it.

She felt very feminine in her white culottes and red polka
dot blouse. She was wearing boots with the outfit, and had
her hair loose around her shoulders.

Bowie looked his usual handsome self, but he wasn't
wearing casual clothing. He had on a pale tan suit with a
patterned shirt and tie, dressed for travel.

Aggie was staring at her. Gaby averted her gaze as she
reached for the coffee carafe.

Aggie remained unusually quiet. Bowie ate a huge breakfast, obviously enjoying the tension he was creating with his
irritating replies to Ned Courtland's conversation. In fact, he
was sick of the whole damned situation, and Courtland was
number one on his list of straws that broke the camel's back.
His continued presence at Casa Río was like a rash.

"Are you going somewhere, dear?" Aggie asked with a
cool smile.

Bowie lifted his face and smiled mockingly. "How astute
of you to guess, Aggie," he replied. "I'm going to Phoenix,
to a meeting. I'll be there overnight, and I may go from
there back to Canada to check on my gang."

"I thought you were having a holiday," Aggie mused,
smiling to herself.

"It started out that way." He finished his eggs and took a
sip of coffee. "I'll be back Monday or Tuesday. And Gaby
isn't going anywhere."

"Just up to Tucson," Gaby replied, her eyes lifting shyly
to his and then dropping to her plate.

"Oh, Gaby," Aggie said miserably. She shrugged. "I

thought you and Ned and I might all go sightseeing together," she began in a conciliatory tone.

"I'm afraid I can't today," Gaby said tautly.

"Giving up so soon?" Courtland asked Bowie with a smile guaranteed to enrage him.

"Nothing of the sort," Bowie assured him. "I expect to do some hunting while I'm away, so enjoy it while you can."

Ned smiled to himself. "Oh, I expect to, don't worry."

With a cold glare in Bowie's direction, Aggie slammed her fork down beside her plate and stood up. "Gaby, could I see you for a moment?"

"I'm not quite finished," Gaby said stiffly.

Aggie squared her shoulders. "Please?" she added.

Gaby got up, dreading the confrontation as she followed the older woman into the hall.

"I'm sorry," Aggie said curtly. "I didn't sleep all night after the things I said to you." She suddenly burst into tears and pulled Gaby close. "Oh, Gaby," she wailed. "I'm sorry I ever started this. It's not going to work. Ned's poor and I'm not, and even though I love him, I don't know if I can live the way Ned does," she added in a worried whisper. "What if I fall flat on my face? I've never done housework, you know, and I can't even cook. I'll be a liability!"

Gaby patted her shoulder gently as she hugged her. "Aren't you worrying about things that may be a long way down the road?" Gaby asked softly. "Why don't you just enjoy yourself and try to live one day at a time?"

Aggie pulled away and wiped her eyes on the back of her hand. "I'm not enjoying myself, though. Bowie's making sure of it. Every meal is like civilized warfare!" She looked up at Gaby. "You aren't thinking of leaving, are you? Please don't go. Bowie will come back with both barrels blazing and I'll have no peace. You won't let him have a clear field to torment me, will you? Even to get even for the things I said last night? I didn't mean them, darling, I didn't!"

Gaby was too soft-hearted to bear grudges, especially against Aggie. She could feel the older woman's pain. "I know that," Gaby said with a gentle smile. "You're just in love, that's all."

"Love hurts," Aggie sobbed. "It's not what the poets say."

"It is. You've just been reading the wrong poets. I'll take Bowie off your hands," she promised. "Now stop worrying, or Ned will think you've got cold feet."

"I have," Aggie confided. "I don't know if this is what I really want, and Bowie won't give me any time to find out."

"He's going away," Gaby said, trying to feel relief when she was miserable at the thought. "You'll have some time alone with Ned, really you will."

Aggie sighed. "I don't think time is going to work in my favor. I never should have pulled the engagement announcement off like I did. Bowie's furious, and he's going to make Ned pay for it. They were out by the corral talking last night, and I think they argued. Bowie is still riding him, and Ned seems amused about that. And the two of them are talking in riddles, have you noticed?"

"Your Mr. Courtland is a shrewd man," Gaby said. "I imagine he and Bowie laid their cards on the table last night. That may help to defuse the situation—which is not to say that they're ever going to be bosom buddies."

"I suppose not." She studied Gaby quietly. "Bowie is attracted to you, have you noticed?"

Gaby sighed. "Attracted, yes. But that's all, and I'm not . . . I'm not much good around men, Aggie." She laughed nervously. "Can you really imagine a man as handsome and eligible as Bowie getting serious about a woman who looks the way I do?"

"But you're lovely, Gaby," Aggie said, and meant it. "You have a sweet nature, and you're very independent. You have wonderful qualities."

She lowered her eyes. "Aggie—there are things about me that you and Bowie don't know."

Aggie touched her hair gently and smiled. "Whatever it is, it wouldn't matter to me. I love you. You're my baby girl."

Gaby had to fight back tears. "I love you, too." She averted her gaze and pulled herself together. "Now, that's enough mushy stuff." She laughed self-consciously. "I've got to get going. I have to find the man who owns this agricultural operation and find out a few things."

"That would be a good idea. Meanwhile, Ned and I will have a little time to get to know each other. Originally, that was why I invited him here. I thought it would be a nice, peaceful visit." She grimaced. "I could kick myself."

"Bowie does love you," she said. "He just doesn't know how to express it."

"Couldn't you teach him how?" Aggie asked with a smile. "It might be the very thing for both of you."

"Don't rush me," Gaby said, smiling. "And Bowie and I may yet square off over the land deal."

"The agricultural project? Yes, I know about it." Aggie sighed. "It would do so much for the economy, but Bowie will die before he lets go of a single acre of Casa Río." She frowned thoughtfully. "You know, Gaby, if he didn't have controlling interest in the ranch, he might try to see the other side of the issue."

"Don't do anything silly," Gaby pleaded, afraid that Aggie might think of making Ned Courtland a present of part of her shares in the ranch. That would be the last straw.

"Not to worry, dear," she patted Gaby's shoulder. "I was just thinking out loud. Now, let's get back before they miss us."

The two men were finishing their breakfast, and actually talking, in a way.

"...I can't move them to high pastures because there

aren't any," Bowie was explaining with exaggerated patience. "This isn't the Tetons. Our mountains down here are just big, rocky hills."

"The house backs up into a canyon," Courtland pointed out as he finished his eggs. "Good water, plenty of shade. You could utilize that."

Bowie's eyes narrowed. "Possibly." He stared at Courtland. "You know a lot about cattle for a horseman."

"A rancher worth his salt had better know a lot about both. Ranching goes back three generations in my family." He stared at his plate. "I suppose it will end with me. There were only the three of us kids, and my sisters never married." He looked bitter for a minute, then looked up and saw Aggie, and smiled. His whole face changed, softened. "Everything okay?" he asked her.

She smiled like a girl. "Everything's fine," she said and winked at Gaby.

Bowie drained his coffee cup and stood up. "I hope you noticed that I'm leaving without the quarter," he said to Courtland. He leaned over and kissed his mother absently on the forehead. "Montoya will be skulking around, so don't you and the Teton man start sneaking into dark corners with the doors shut," he said firmly, ignoring Courtland's surprised chuckle behind him. He glanced at the older man. "I know your kind," he said. "Just keep in mind that my shotgun is loaded and standing in a corner."

Courtland smiled. "In that case, I'll stake Montoya out on an anthill and carry your mother upstairs."

Aggie laughed with pure delight, almost clapping her hands with glee. "I'll get you some rope, Ned!" she said.

"My secretary knows where I'll be if you need to reach me," Bowie told his mother. He dug his car keys out of his pocket and his black eyes went homing to Gaby. He wanted to ask her to walk out with him, but she looked nervous and uncertain this morning.

He settled for a warm smile. "Keep an eye on these two," he mused. "I'll see you when I come home."

"Take care," she said softly. Her eyes were puzzled, because she couldn't read any emotion in his at all, and he managed not to sustain that look for very long, either.

He dragged his eyes away and went out the door.

"Couldn't you put your story off until tomorrow and keep us company?" Aggie asked when Bowie had driven away.

Gaby forced a smile as she finished her coffee. "I wish I could, but I don't get paid for lying around. I'll be back by dark. I want to drive into Tucson and talk to some people."

"All right, dear. Be careful."

During the long drive up to Tucson, Gaby tried not to think about Bowie at all. She turned up the radio and drowned herself in country-western music. Maybe he'd decided that kissing her was self-defeating. She couldn't really blame him. She'd probably hurt him badly last night, and he didn't want to risk being that vulnerable with her again. But it made her uncertain and wary. It was hard to reconcile what he'd said last night with his behavior this morning. And she didn't really want to start worrying about it. She had too much to do.

There definitely was a field office of the Bio-Ag Corporation in Tucson. Mr. Barry hadn't told her so at the meeting in his realty office, but Bob Chalmers had ferreted out the information for her when she had stopped by to see him on her way out of town that morning. Gaby had to search to find the office, and when she got there, she discovered it was very small and in an out-of-the-way building near the barrio. Since it was Saturday, she hadn't really expected to find the office open, but it was.

"Hello. How may I help you?" the very young secretary asked with a smile.

"I'd like to see Mr. Terrance Highman Samuels, Jr., please, if he's in," Gaby said, smiling back. That was a calculated bluff, because she knew the vice president in charge of acquisitions was supposed to be in Los Angeles.

"Mr. Samuels?" She frowned. "Oh. You mean the vice president of the company. I'm afraid he doesn't work out of this office. He's in Los Angeles. Our manager here is Mr. Logan."

"Then, could I see him?"

"Just a minute—I'll see if he's free. May I tell him your name?"

"Yes. I'm Gaby Cane, from Lassiter."

She buzzed the intercom and gave someone on the other end of the line the information, and was told to send Gaby in.

Gaby was ushered into a small office furnished with an old desk and some rickety-looking furniture, where a small, thin man rose from his chair to greet her.

"I'm Jess Logan," he introduced himself with a smile. "You're from Lassiter, are you, Miss Cane? Perhaps you know that we're trying to acquire a large parcel of land there for a new project."

"Yes, sir, I'm aware of that," she said.

"Well, we'd be grateful for any help you could give us," he said. "We have a petition here that we're planning to present to the mayor and city council of Lassiter, protesting the efforts of a man named McCayde to block our very beneficial development."

Gaby felt her hackles rise. She should have introduced herself immediately. It was rather dishonest not to have, but now she was glad she hadn't.

"A petition?" she asked in a sugary tone.

"That's right. Here." He pulled out a sheet of paper and put it before her. It was typed, but poorly, and there was a misspelled word right up front. It wasn't the best wording, either, but it got the point across. Bowie was holding up progress out of a dim-witted attempt to keep the land safe for snakes and coyotes. At least, that was the tone of the document. There were some fifty signatures on it so far, most of them barely recognizable scrawls, and none names that Gaby recognized.

"High-pressure tactics?" she asked with a faint smile.

He looked uncomfortable. "Heavens, no. We just can't find a better site for our purposes, and the man is a local landowner with more power than he needs. We want to do something for the economy in Lassiter, and we can. We're no fly-by-night proposition. We're a legitimate business with offices in six states, and this isn't a new venture for us. We have a very successful cotton operation in Kansas."

Gaby stared at him for a long moment. "Perhaps I should have presented my credentials before we began." She took out one of her business cards and pushed it across the desk to Mr. Logan.

He went red, but she detected no outward sign of anger. "A reporter. Yes, we know the *Phoenix Advertiser* very well," he said, smiling. He quickly put up the petition, as if he'd never shown it to her.

"I'm doing a story on your project," she said.

"We sent press kits to all the newspapers . . ." he began.

"I don't use press kits, Mr. Logan," she said with quiet firmness. "I find that they frequently depend on outdated information and stock photos. I prefer to do my own leg-work." She pulled out her pad and pen, set her tape recorder on his desk, and turned it on, smiling reassuringly at him as it began to run. "Now. First, I'd like to know if you propose to drill wells to supply your irrigation water, or if you plan to depend on existing stores in Lassiter."

He simply stared at her. "As you're surely aware, Miss Cane, whoever buys the land buys the water rights along with it—in Arizona, at least. We'll have Mr. McCayde's water rights, which are considerable."

"You'll have Mr. McCayde's land over his dead body," she mused. "So what are your alternative sites?"

"You seem to know the gentleman?"

"I should. I've lived with him for almost ten years. His family adopted me when I was fifteen," she said. It wasn't completely the truth, but it was close.

"I see," he said coolly. "And can I expect an objective story from you, in that case?"

"You'll find that my job is sacred to me," she said. "I don't take sides, even where family is concerned. In fact, Bowie and I had words about the project. I tend to favor progress in areas of economic depression."

Mr. Logan smiled his relief. "Thank God. I was afraid I'd really put my foot in it. We're so enthusiastic about this land, Miss Cane. We think we could do a lot for the local economy, and we're willing to bend over backwards to do what we can to employ large numbers of local people. Here, let me show you the projections."

He drew out maps and documents, and outlined the entire project for her. It was much like the press kit, except that he didn't mention the kind of crops the conglomerate would plant and she couldn't quite pin him down on it.

"That all depends on soil studies," he said, "after we purchase the land. Uh, about that petition," he added, "that's privileged information, and you didn't announce your profession when I showed it to you."

"It's still part of the story," she replied. "Mr. Logan, I print whatever I get. I don't play favorites, and I don't cover up information. A petition isn't a bad idea, so long as the names on it can be verified as accurate. And believe me, Bowie will insist on it."

He sighed. "I knew that already. Very well, I won't attempt to tie your hands. But do try to remember what our goals are."

"Why won't you consider an alternative site?" she asked curiously.

"Because there really isn't one. Arizona is big, I grant you, but water is our primary interest, and Mr. McCayde has the only tract of land that would provide enough for our uses. Water is scarce, and growing more so. We have to locate where we can find adequate stores of it."

"There's land on the Santa Cruz and the Colorado," she pointed out.

"I'm afraid we can't afford land in those areas," he said sadly. "We're rather limited about ready capital. But we're very dedicated to helping small communities, and we have a great track record. We don't mind at all if you check us out, Miss Cane. I can provide you with references, I'm proud to say."

She let him give those to her and she began to wonder if she hadn't been suspicious for no reason. They seemed very open and aboveboard about their operations. Could Bowie be wrong about them? Or was she being carefully led?

After the interview, she treated herself to lunch at a Chinese restaurant, just to have a break from Mexican food. She dreaded going back to Casa Río. At least she and Aggie had made peace, but she was afraid of the future. There was so much at stake. She couldn't bear the thought of having Bowie hate her, and he might, if the past ever came out. Even if it didn't, her fear of intimacy might make a relationship between them impossible. It might have been better if she'd never let him kiss her, but the thought of giving up the memory of that sweet pleasure was too terrible to bear.

Maybe she should join a nunnery, she thought half-seriously. In her present condition, she had no business at all around men.

She finished her lonely lunch and went on to the Lassiter office of the U.S. Soil and Water Conservation Service, where she lucked up on one of the employees who'd come in

to pick up some papers he'd left on his desk. He was concerned about water, himself, and didn't mind taking time to
discuss it with the press. He gave her an earful about herbi-
cide and pesticide contamination, silt and erosion damage to
flowing streams, water conservation and groundwater scarcity. By the time she'd finished collecting data, she was
more nervous than ever about the strain on the aquifer from
an agricultural operation. Lassiter's groundwater table had
dropped in recent years, and there was already a ban on
outdoor watering. Presumably the city fathers hadn't yet
considered that a big agricultural project would drain the
aquifer even more, and possibly threaten existing water supplies for Lassiter.

Bowie was careful about how he used water in his cattle
operation, and he didn't waste anything. He kept small
ponds and drilled wells, and he didn't exhaust the land trying to make a quick profit. A big operation like Bio-Ag
might not be so careful. They were outsiders, and making
money was their primary objective. Gaby knew from past
research that an uncaring agricultural operation could lay
waste to the land and make it virtually unusable for years to
come. There were dangers such as leaching, which could be
controlled, but was an added expense that many growers
didn't like to provide for. There was the strain on the under-
ground aquifer, and the silt from the disturbed soil that went
into the river—when it ran—although even silt was beneficial, in some instances, because it slowed down the water
flow and therefore conserved it sometimes.

Even so, there were many dangers. If Bio-Ag made a
quick profit and took off, those local people they hired
would be quickly out of work again, and the situation would
be even worse due to the pollution.

It was difficult to know where to put her faith. Bowie was
a reactionary and he hated progress, despite his work as a
contractor. He'd automatically fight anything that threatened

to change the landscape. The agricultural people wanted to use the land to make money and boost the local economy, but they weren't looking at the overall picture—only the part of it that affected their finances. It was a case of both sides being basically right, and both wrong.

Gaby sometimes hated reporting. She hadn't really been able to take sides since she'd started the job. It was too easy to see both sides of any public issue, and too hard to put one above the other—usually, at least.

She drove back to Casa Río late that afternoon with a full pad and two full tapes from her tape recorder. She didn't know what she was going to write. Tomorrow, she'd go to the library and back to the newspaper office to search through Bob Chalmers's research files. No, she reminded herself, tomorrow was Sunday. She'd go Monday.

Ned and Aggie were just sitting down to supper when she walked in, tired and hungry.

"Have a seat and eat something," Aggie invited. "You look terrible."

"I feel terrible," she murmured. "Must be the heat. I don't like what I found out."

"They're opportunists, out to strangle the land?" Ned asked with a faint smile.

She shook her head. "They're nice people with praiseworthy goals, but they could do a lot of damage to the aquifer. On the other hand, they'd bring in a lot of new business and jobs."

"Jobs won't make new water," Ned replied. "Bowie's right."

Aggie's eyes almost popped. "I don't think I heard you right."

"Sure you did. Water is a touchy issue these days, even up in Wyoming, where we've got plenty. Any big operation is after money. I could tell you horror stories about what greed has done to areas of the Great Plains."

"Please do," Gaby invited.

He did, over dinner, telling about how the land had been devastated by saline seep and tilling, the natural grasses destroyed and the land unfit for anything after the conglomerates got through with it.

"But we're not prairie," Aggie began.

"No, you're desert, which is worse." He stared at her. "And you're going to be Teton material, not desert, if you marry me. I won't live on Casa Río."

She toyed with her coffee cup. "Yes, I know."

"Aggie's adaptable," Gaby said in the older woman's defense. "She'll fit in just fine."

"Will I?" Aggie asked under her breath, but no one heard her.

Gaby got up, having only half finished her meal. She missed Bowie, and Casa Río just wasn't the same without him. "If you don't mind, I've got to type up some notes. Is it okay if I use the computer in the office, or will Bowie have kittens?"

"He won't mind, darling." Aggie smiled. "You go right ahead. Want to watch a movie with us on the VCR?"

"I wish I had time," Gaby laughed, lying through her teeth, because they needed time alone, "but I've got to boil down these facts so that I'll have something to feed Johnny on Monday over the phone. See you later."

She went out quickly, glad that they hadn't seen through her gaiety to the sadness underneath. She could hide in the office until bedtime, if she could stand the memories of Bowie that it would bring back. Then she could go to bed and try to stop worrying about the future. Time would tell if she and Bowie had one together, but nothing she could do right now would affect it, one way or another. She had to trust him not to hurt her. Trust was something she had very little of for anyone, and especially for men. Even Bowie.

CHAPTER

· Eleven

It was late Tuesday before Bowie came home. Meanwhile, Gaby had spent her days searching out more information on the proposed agricultural project and trying to decide how she was going to write the story so that it reflected both sides of the issue. Unfortunately, one of them had only one proponent—Bowie. Or that's what she thought until Bob Chalmers invited her into his office Tuesday morning to talk to a couple of local residents.

"This is Señora Marguerita Lopez," he introduced a dark-haired woman with silver streaks in her elegant coiffure, "and her son, Ruíz. This is the lady I told you about," he said to them. "Miss Cane works for the Phoenix newspaper, but I hope soon to convince her to work for me."

"Con mucho gusto en conocerles," Gaby said, extending her hand to the woman, and then to her son.

"I speak English." Marguerita grinned. And she did, with barely a trace of an accent. "It's nice to meet you, too. I understand you're Bowie McCayde's stepsister."

"No, I was just adopted by the family," Gaby faltered.

"No matter. We think he's right," Ruíz interrupted, his

dark eyes smiling at her. "We represent a small group of landowners on the fringe of Casa Río. And this is what we're afraid of."

He tossed some photos on Bob's desk. Gaby picked them up slowly, turning them in her hands. They showed the devastation of blowing topsoil which had literally buried a ranch up to the third rung of its corral fence.

"That is erosion," the young man said, nodding toward the photographs. "It's the result of too much tilling on desert soil. As you can see, those of us who will live near the project have as much to lose as Bowie does. He isn't alone, you see. He has support in Lassiter."

"There are two sides to every story," Gaby agreed. She sat down and smiled at Bob. "Do you mind?"

"Feel free, if you're applying for work," he said, tongue-in-cheek. "Come on, Gaby, give it a try. You'd love it in Lassiter."

"I always did," she sighed. "I'm thinking about it," she said, without mentioning how tempted she was.

She turned on her tape recorder and proceeded to get a stimulating interview from the Lopezes.

Dinner was over when she got back to Casa Río, and Aggie and Ned were nowhere in sight. She smiled to herself, thinking about Sunday, after the three of them had come home from church. She'd gone looking for them, and had found Aggie held fast in Ned's arms under a palo verde tree out back, being kissed in a way that made Gaby faintly envious. She couldn't imagine that kind of passion. She'd never felt it, although she liked kissing Bowie and being held by him. But the way Aggie had been clinging to Ned had convinced Gaby that there was much more to kissing than just faint pleasure. She wondered if she'd ever be capable of feeling what they obviously did for each other.

She went into the kitchen to find Tía Elena gone and Montoya muttering softly to himself.

"What's your problem?" she asked with a smile as she poured herself a cup of coffee from the carafe on the counter.

"Tía Elena has gone to comfort Aggie," he sighed.

Gaby turned, staring at him. "Why?"

He shrugged. "They have had their first argument."

"How bad?"

"Señor Courtland left for the airport an hour ago."

She whistled softly. "Ooops."

"He was in, how you say, a rage, and Aggie was crying. We do not know what happened—only that something has gone very wrong between them. I was afraid of this. It was too soon," he said. "They know so little about each other."

"Bowie will be delighted, I'm sorry to say," Gaby muttered. She put down the coffee, untouched. "I'll go up and see about Aggie."

"Bowie phoned from Texas," he called. "He expects to be here by dark."

"Aggie will love that." She stopped in the doorway, frowning. "Texas?"

"Texas."

She pursed her lips. "Did he talk to Ned or Aggie?" she asked suspiciously.

He shook his head. "Only to me."

There was one possible reason for the breakup out of the way, she thought as she went upstairs. Her heart lifted at the thought of Bowie coming home again, and fell at the realization that nothing had changed. She was still the same person she'd been out by the corral when he'd kissed her too roughly and pinned her against the fence, and the situation was just as impossible between them. She could certainly sympathize with Aggie, she thought with a rueful smile. She had her own problems with relationships.

Aggie was facedown on her huge canopied bed, wailing.

Tía Elena was hovering, looking worried, until she saw Gaby.

"*Gracias a Dios,*" she whispered under her breath. She and Gaby exchanged looks and Tía Elena made a quick but dignified exit.

"Aggie, what's wrong?" Gaby asked softly, sitting down beside the older woman.

"He's gone," Aggie sniffed. She sat up, throwing her arms around Gaby. "He's gone away, and it's all my fault!"

"What went wrong?"

"He wanted me to give up Casa Río," she said, sobbing into her handkerchief, "and go off to live in the wilds of Wyoming with grizzly bears, and to milk cows and cook homemade bread . . . !" She sniffed again. "His wife did all those things. I'm sick of hearing about his wife. She must have worn a cape and made America safe for the elderly!"

Gaby had to fight down laughter, but it wasn't really funny. She smoothed the silver-threaded short hair gently. "Did you really give it a chance, Aggie? You had so little time together."

"Time enough to know that I'm not cut out for the life he had mapped out for us," she said miserably. "I know I'm flighty, and I can't keep house—why else would I have Montoya and Tía Elena? I can't cook, because I've never had to. I couldn't milk a cow on a bet. He's unreasonable!"

"What did you tell him?" Gaby asked.

"That Lincoln freed the slaves over a hundred years ago, and that I wasn't about to give up Casa Río for a shack in Wyoming," she said stiffly. "And I'm not. I like my life as it is. I can get over him. It was just a holiday infatuation." She lowered her eyes to her lap. "He said I was too modern to suit him, too," she added in a subdued tone.

Gaby frowned. "Too modern?"

She colored a little. "I didn't mind if we slept together before we got married, and he got all stern and arrogant and said where he came from, people didn't do that sort of thing." The color got worse. "Well, they don't where I come from either, but I did want him so terribly," she whispered huskily. "So much that I was shaking with it, and he just got up and walked away!"

Gaby didn't understand—she couldn't pretend to. She'd never felt like that. But she patted Aggie's shoulder and made soothing noises.

"He won't come back, you know," she said. She sat up straight and dabbed at her red eyes. "I've told everyone we're engaged, and now I'll have to live it down." The tears came back again. "Oh, Gaby!"

"You worry too much about what people think," Gaby said sternly. "At least, from time to time you do," she amended dryly. "Now, dry your eyes and let's go have a nice cup of coffee. You have to get yourself together before Bowie gets here. You wouldn't want him to gloat . . . ?"

"Bowie's coming home?" She groaned. "When it rains, it pours. He'll laugh himself sick!"

"He will not," Gaby assured her. Not if I have to have Montoya tie him up, she added silently. "Now, come on. You'll feel better when you've had something to drink and eat. Have you had supper?"

She shook her head. "No appetite."

"No wonder you're miserable. Your blood sugar's low. Come on, now, Aggie, it will all work out. And I wouldn't sell your Mr. Courtland short, either," she added, remembering the stubborn determination she'd seen in that gentleman's hard face from time to time. "He isn't like a lot of men."

"That's right," Aggie agreed. "Most men these days don't expect their wives to milk cows and pull a plow!"

Gaby just shook her head as she coaxed Aggie downstairs.

They had small sandwiches and coffee, and only a little later, the sound of Bowie's car driving up broke the silence.

"Go and watch TV, Aggie," Gaby said gently. "I'll break it to Bowie."

"If he laughs, you hit him, Gaby," the older woman said coldly. "Just as hard as you can!"

"He won't laugh. I'll be back in a minute."

Gaby rushed out the front door and through the wrought iron gate. Bowie was just getting out of the car, holding a suitcase and an attaché case linked in one hand while he closed the door. He looked up and his black eyes danced as Gaby ran to him.

"Well, what a nice surprise," he murmured, putting down the cases. "Come here, cupcake."

Before she had time to say anything, he lifted her by the waist and kissed her softly on her cheek, drawing back instantly as he set her on the ground again.

"I got sidetracked down to Texas making inquiries about our Mr. Courtland." He grinned. "I hired a private detective to speed things up. Speaking of the gentleman . . ."

"He's gone."

He didn't seem to move. "Gone."

"That's right. Back to Wyoming." She drew in a slow breath, a little stunned by his brief kiss and brotherly manner. He didn't act like a lover—he acted more like the stepbrother everyone seemed to think he was to her. Had he decided that he didn't want her anymore? Had she turned him off altogether with her reticence? It didn't even bear thinking about—not when she'd ached to be with him for days and dreamed of him every night.

"Why?" he asked, frowning.

"Aggie doesn't want to milk cows and pull a plow," she explained with wide eyes. "And Lincoln freed the slaves, and besides all that, he wouldn't go to bed with her because they weren't married."

He actually leaned back against the car. "I beg your pardon?" he asked curtly.

"Older people do sleep together," she reminded him. "They were in a clinch out by the stable Sunday that would have kept you awake for days running. They want each other, but he's one of those Puritans who won't allow himself to be coaxed into bed without a wedding ring. Aggie got mad and sent him away."

"Because he wouldn't sleep with her?!" he burst out, aghast. "My God, we're talking about my mother . . . !"

"Yes, I know." She smiled shyly. "Isn't it exciting? And I thought I'd be bored down here without gun battles and political in-fighting."

He lit a cigarette. "Damn it, I'd almost quit," he muttered, glaring at the cigarette. "Now she's set me off again." His black eyes held Gaby's. "Courtland's gone home? For good?"

"Looks like it."

"They fought."

She nodded. "Because he wouldn't go to bed with her, if we're making guesses. I don't think milking cows had a lot to do with it. I think Aggie's frustrated."

His chest rose and fell in a huge sigh and his black eyes slid down Gaby's gray dress, over her high, firm breasts, narrow waist, sensuous hips, and long, elegant legs. "I know all about frustration," he murmured to himself. "But I can't picture my mother feeling that way."

"She isn't ancient," Gaby pointed out, trying not to flush at his explicit appraisal. She'd worn the tight belt with this dress for the first time today, and had been amazed at the pleasure it gave her to emphasize her small waistline and look feminine. "And they're in love, or I miss my guess."

"That doesn't matter, as long as he's out of the picture," he said curtly. "Thank God! I was afraid I might have to resort to blackmail to shoot him out the door."

Gaby was shocked and looked it. "Bowie, she's your mother. You have no right . . ."

"I have every right," he returned coldly. "This is my birthright, and I have an obligation to my father to preserve it for Aggie as long as she's alive, and for myself afterward. I'm not handing it over to any gigolos without a fight." His lean hand lifted the cigarette to his lips. "What's mine, I keep, honey. And Casa Río belongs to me."

"You're so stubborn," she muttered.

"My father taught me to see one side of any issue—my own. That way, I don't make the mistake of trying to be too understanding."

"But it's ruthless, don't you see?" she argued, her olive eyes pleading with his. "You're not the only one with rights."

"Where Casa Río's concerned, I am." He touched her hair. "I like it long, like this," he mused.

"What are we going to do about Aggie?" she persisted, and her body rippled at the gentle touch on her hair. "She's been crying ever since he left."

"We'll show her some family movies and take her up to Tucson for the rodeo tomorrow," he said. "It's about time we did a few things as a family. That'll cheer her up."

"Tomorrow?" she said. "Bowie, I've got to fly out to Los Angeles and see the vice president of this agricultural business. And tomorrow night, the Lassiter city council meets. I'm going."

The cigarette poised in midair. "If you go to that meeting, I'm going with you," he said. "No way are you going to drive around this territory at night without protection."

The way he said it, and the look on his face, startled her. "I don't understand."

"Don't you? I told you in Phoenix that I'd had threats. They haven't stopped just because everything's on hold."

She didn't like the intrusion of that possibility into her

mind. She stared up at Bowie and tried to think how she was going to feel if anything happened to him. It was simply unbearable.

"You could back down," she suggested, knowing even as she said it how impossible it was for him to give up when he wanted something.

"I could take up knitting, too," he returned. He smiled faintly. "Worried about me?"

"Of course I'm worried about you," she said coldly. "You could get yourself shot over a few acres of land!"

"A few thousand," he corrected.

"Whatever! It isn't worth your life!"

"Anything worth having is worth fighting for, Gaby," he replied. "If I didn't feel that way, I'd have let you run back to Phoenix the day after you got here, because you wanted to run."

She felt the ground giving way under her. She couldn't meet that level, intent stare. "Maybe I did," she said. "But staying here hasn't been much more sensible." She drew in a slow breath. "Bowie, can we be friends?"

"Friends and nothing more?" he said for her, without a smile. "That's what you mean, I gather?"

She leaned against the car beside him, staring at his light suit jacket. "I watched Aggie kissing Mr. Courtland Sunday," she said slowly, choosing her words. "It . . . I don't know, it shook me a little, I think. You see, Bowie," she said in a weary breath, "I've never felt that kind of emotion. I don't know if I *can* feel it. I only know that passion is as alien to me as the lack of it would be to you." She looked up at him, searching his narrowed eyes. "I don't want to know the kind of pain Aggie's feeling right now. I think it might be that bad for me if we . . . if we grew any closer, and it fell apart."

"You don't want the risk."

She shifted. "No."

"And if I could teach you passion?"

The deep, frank note in his voice ruffled her nerves. She looked up at him with curiosity and fear mingling in her soft eyes. "Can it be taught?"

"Stick around and let's find out," he returned. He didn't make a move toward her. He smiled. "Nothing ventured, nothing gained, honey."

"There must be dozens of women who'd jump at the chance," she murmured, her eyes delighting in his extraordinary good looks.

"Dozens who'd love my money," he returned with faint cynicism. "Not many who'd want me without it."

"I've got to get you a good mirror," she said, shaking her head, "and maybe some glasses. Have you really taken a good look at me?" she asked with a short laugh.

His black eyes narrowed and he took a draw from his cigarette before he answered her. "You're soft-hearted. You like animals and sunsets and romantic music. You day-dream. You stick to your guns when you think you're right, and you're loyal to the people you love. You're generous, hard-working, and a good companion." He leaned closer. "And you're just pure sweet heaven to kiss. Yes. I've taken a good look at you. I like what I see."

She blushed at the way he said it. Her eyes slid to his stubborn chin and lingered there. "Aggie said that you liked poetry," she said absently.

He traced one of her dark eyebrows. "Did she? Do you?"

"Oh, yes, very much," she whispered.

His lean finger moved down to her lips and touched them with lazy delicacy. "'. . . Desire still on stilts of fear doth go. And yet amid all fears a hope there is . . .'"

Her heart jumped at the softness in his slow, deep voice. It was perfect for reading poetry, she thought, even as she tried to fit the sonnet with its elusive author.

"Sidney," he said, smiling down at her. "Sir Philip Sidney, a sixteenth-century Elizabethan gentleman. Sidney died with utmost chivalry on the field of Zutphen, and Spenser was sufficiently moved to dedicate his own work, *The Faerie Queene*, to him."

"I never thought of you as a student of literature," she said softly.

"But then, you don't know me, do you?" he asked, his voice deep in the stillness. His finger traced her upper lip with an intensity that made it tremble.

Her instinct was to catch his strong wrist and pull his hand away, but she fought with it. She liked the sensations he was causing. Her eyes sought his in the growing darkness, and when he dropped his cigarette and moved closer, she lifted her mouth without protest.

He brought his hands up to frame her face and held it firmly as he bent slowly toward her hungry mouth. His breath rustled against her parted lips and she could feel the heat from his big body. It would be rough this time, she thought while she could, and for the first time, the threat of it didn't frighten her. She wanted him to be rough, just once —to kiss her with the same hard passion she'd seen when Ned Courtland had kissed Aggie . . .

The front door opened and Bowie's hands contracted. "Oh, God, no, not now!" he bit off, his lips almost touching Gaby's.

"*Señor, gracias a Dios. Lo Siento, pero su madre . . .!*" Tía Elena was rattling off her perfect Spanish, gaily oblivious to the explosive kiss she'd just prevented.

Bowie stamped out the cigarette burning in the dust with a violence Gaby had rarely seen him display. "*Yo sé*, Tía Elena," he said shortly. "*¿Donde esta mi madre?*"

Tía Elena answered him, holding the gate while he and Gaby walked into the courtyard and up the steps. Bowie put his cases down in the hall for Montoya to deal with and went into the living room, where Aggie was waiting. He didn't look at Gaby. He couldn't, just yet. He was all but shaking from the fever of so nearly having her in his arms again.

"Go ahead," Aggie said through her teeth. "Laugh."

"I'm not laughing, Aggie," he replied. He sat down beside her, his black eyes searching her wan face. "I'm sorry."

"Are you?" she demanded. "You wanted to break us up."

"I wanted you to be happy," he returned. "Maybe I went a little overboard." He shrugged. "And maybe I forgot that you're still human, even if you have got a few gray hairs," he added with an amused, knowing smile.

Aggie actually flushed, and then she laughed. She started to touch Bowie and suddenly drew back.

"What's wrong?" he queried with pursed lips. "Are you afraid you'll get warts if you hug me?"

Aggie flushed again and laughed, and abruptly reached out toward him. With a deep laugh of his own, he gathered her into his arms and rocked her, because she was crying again.

To Gaby, it looked very much like a milestone in their relationship. It delighted her to see mother and son so close, probably for the first time in Bowie's adult life.

She went to get coffee, and by the time she and Montoya got back, things were back to normal—on the surface, at least. Bowie was telling Aggie about his trip to Phoenix. Gaby noticed that he said nothing at all about going to Texas as well, and she didn't give him away.

They settled down to watch television while they sipped coffee, but the news was the only thing interesting, and it dealt with a subject guaranteed to curl Gaby's hair—an assault on a local woman.

She got up as soon as she decently could and announced that she was going to have an early night, hoping against hope that Bowie wouldn't offer to walk her up. She didn't want to have to explain her nervousness.

He seemed to know, all the same. He wished her a pleasant good night, along with Aggie, and watched her retreat with quiet, curious eyes.

She pulled on her soft cotton gown and climbed into bed, hoping that the news story wouldn't affect her sleep. Of course, inevitably, it brought the nightmares back.

With her body bathed in sweat, she relived those frantic minutes in the Kentucky stable, the brief terror that had colored her life, steeled her to living as a solitary woman. Not even a woman—a neutered thing, a shadow of her true self.

She felt again the hands tearing at her clothing, smelled the whiskey, heard the drunken laughter. She knew the helpless revulsion of hands on her skin, of a heavy, hurting body bearing down on hers. And then, to add to that horror, there was the sudden curse and the hard blow and blood everywhere. Blood . . . !

"Gaby!"

She fought the hands that were holding her arms, struggling, her teeth clenched. "I'll . . . kill you . . ." she panted. "I'll kill you! Let me go!" she cried piteously.

Suddenly she was jerked upright and shaken with tender ferocity. Her eyes flew open and Bowie's hard, concerned face was there. She was awake. It had only been a dream, after all—a nightmare.

Tears streamed down her cheeks and she was breathing in shaky gasps, her face white, her eyes enormous. She shook helplessly.

Bowie didn't know what to do. He was afraid to upset her any more by taking her in his arms, because it was quite obviously memories of a big man that had left her this way to begin with. But he couldn't walk away, either.

"I want to hold you," he said gently. "That's all. Just until you stop shaking. Come here, Gaby. I won't let anything hurt you, not ever again."

She lifted her arms. "Bowie," she whispered through her tears.

He gathered her up with breathless tenderness, amazed to find himself bristling with protective instincts. If only he could find the man who'd done this to her, and beat him into pulp!

"It's all right, baby," he whispered in her ear. "I've got you. There's nothing to be afraid of."

He stood up, his powerful muscles rippling as he took her weight, and walked the floor with her. Holding her close against his heart, he whispered soft endearments as she cried out the pain and fear of the last few minutes, clinging to his neck.

"I've soaked your shirt," she whispered brokenly when she was calmer, her fingers touching the sodden collar of his blue striped shirt. He'd worn that with his suit, but now his tie and jacket were off, and the shirt was completely unbuttoned down his broad, hair-roughened chest. Her eyes went down to it, fascinated. She hadn't paid much attention at first, but now she was mesmerized by the expanse of tanned skin and the pure maleness of him. Odd, she thought dazedly, that she wasn't afraid of him this way, especially after the nightmare she'd been having.

"It'll dry," he murmured. He saw where her eyes had fallen and guessed, mistakenly, that the sight of his bare chest was frightening her. "Here, I'll button it," he murmured, and set her back on her feet.

"It's all right, Bowie," she said, her voice soft and husky. "I'm not afraid of you." She lifted her eyes to show him that she wasn't, and surprised an indescribable look on his face.

"I don't suppose it would do any good to ask what you were dreaming about?" he asked quietly.

She shook her head. "I can't talk about it."

He took a slow breath. "Well, I hope you realize I can't leave you here alone like this." He searched around the room until he found her robe and eased her into it without looking too pointedly at the way her cotton gown clung to her body. He belted the robe and bent, lifting her into his arms again.

"Where are we going?" she asked, because he was headed for the open balcony window, from where he'd obviously come.

"Your bed's too short for me," he said without looking at her. "So it'll have to be mine."

Her heart stopped beating. "Bowie . . . ?"

"I won't leave you in there alone in the dark," he said curtly. "And if you have to ask about my intentions, I'm going to stand on the balcony railing and jump off."

She hid a smile at that threat, because at the moment he looked capable of it. She sighed and laid her cheek against his hard shoulder, which would probably tell him all he needed to know.

It did. It made him feel as if he'd grown an inch, and aroused him until he wanted to throw back his head and scream, but he didn't let her know it. She was going to get comfort and protection and nothing else. He had to have her trust before they went any further.

She'd only been in his room once or twice, and never when he was in it. It was huge, like he was, and decorated in browns and tans and greens—earth colors that suited his personality. His bed was king-sized, a four-poster, with an Indian print comforter carelessly thrown back to reveal tan and cream sheets already turned down.

"I was just about to turn in myself when I heard you," he said. He laid her down, pulled the sheets over her, robe and all, and leaned over her with his arms catching his weight. "You're going to sleep with me—just sleep—and I'm going to wear pajamas, so you needn't look at me with those huge, shocked eyes. There's no need, anyway—I don't have anything you haven't already seen," he mused dryly as he got up and went to search through his dresser for the one pair of pajama bottoms he owned.

She remembered very well what he looked like without clothes, but she wouldn't have dared mention it under the circumstances.

"What will Aggie say?" she asked nervously.

"We'll cross that bridge if we ever come to it. I expect to be awake and get you out of here by daylight." He found what he was looking for, closed the drawer, and paused to look down at her on his way to the bathroom to change. "Are you afraid of me?"

She searched his hard face. "No, Bowie," she said softly.

"That's something, I guess," he said ruefully, and went off into the bathroom.

CHAPTER

Twelve

Gaby curled up next to Bowie with her head pillowed on his bare shoulder, and noticed with secret delight that he was outside the covers with a serape pulled over him in the air-conditioned room.

"Won't you be cold?"

"With you next to me?" he asked, smiling as he finished his cigarette. "I hope you don't snore."

"I hope you don't, too," she mused. She watched him put out the cigarette and turn to snap off the lamp by the bed. He was so handsome, and the feel and smell of him made her giddy, like lying beside him in bed. She'd never have dreamed anything could be as sweet. Even on the heels of the nightmare, she couldn't be afraid of Bowie. That should have struck her as unusual, but she was too shaken to think.

"Comfortable?" he asked, his voice subdued, deep, and a little tired.

"Very. Are you?"

"I'll do."

She sighed, searching for someplace to put her free hand.

Finally, she settled for curling it up on his shoulder. He laughed.

"You can put it on my chest if you want to," he said in a whisper. "As long as you don't start rubbing your hands over it and smothering me in open-mouthed kisses, it won't bother me."

"Bowie!" she gasped, stiffening.

"I thought it might reassure you," he said with evident amusement. "You don't have to be that careful, honey. I'm so tired. I've been halfway across the country, and I didn't get much sleep last night. You're perfectly safe—tonight, at least."

"Okay. I just didn't want to make you uncomfortable," she said, letting her hand slowly go to the serape over his chest and flatten there, very still.

His big hand pressed over hers. "You won't have any more nightmares tonight," he said quietly. "I'll hold you while you sleep. Close your eyes, *adorada*."

"What did you call me?" she asked drowsily.

"Never mind. Go to sleep."

She drifted off with the soft Spanish word echoing in her tired, worn brain. Adored one—wasn't that what it meant? She smiled against his shoulder, savoring his unfamiliar tenderness. She'd always thought that he had that capacity, but she'd never really seen him use it, except with children or young animals. Now she knew that he could feel it with her, and it was reassuring. If only she could count on it at that most basic of moments—when he was aroused. But men seemed to be uncontrollable at that stage, and it was the one time when she was the most afraid of strength and violence.

She slept finally, lulled by the deep thunder of Bowie's heartbeat and the slow sound of his breathing. Something woke her at dawn—a soft rasp, followed by running feet and voices. Like insects, she thought drowsily, humming...

"Oh, hell!"

She heard the deep, sleepy curse and opened her eyes. The ceiling was there. She looked down and felt her body go very still. Bowie's arm was around her—she could feel its warm strength—and one of his long legs seemed to be thrown over both of hers. They were curled together, under the covers, both of them. Bowie's head was raised, and he was glowering at someone. There, at the foot of the bed, stood Mrs. Agatha McCayde.

Behind her and beside her were Tía Elena and Montoya. Gaby knew her face was scarlet as she sat up, still in her robe. "Bowie?" she asked, her voice wavering.

"I know. I had hoped they were just a bad dream," he mused, dragging himself up against the headboard to light a cigarette. "Go ahead, say it," he invited his mother.

"Say what?" Aggie sighed. "If it was anyone except Gaby, I could seethe and rage and spout platitudes. But if you're in bed with Gaby, it's because she had a nightmare and you didn't want to leave her alone." She threw up her hands. "Damn it, there's no excitement around here any-more—no parties, no surprises in the coat room, no drunks with guns . . . Montoya, you'd better bring them some coffee so they can wake up. I'll have mine out on the patio. No hose fights on the lawn . . ." she was muttering as she left with a softly laughing Montoya and a giggling Tía Elena at her heels.

"Well, I like that," Gaby muttered, glaring after them. "They find me in bed with you, and nobody even shakes a finger."

He threw off the covers and stretched lazily. "They know you too well."

She turned, her hair disheveled, and looked down at him. "Bowie . . ."

"What?"

"Did Aggie ever really find you in bed with a girl?"

He chuckled. "Not at Casa Río," he murmured dryly. "I

had too much sense to bring any of my women here." His black eyes narrowed thoughtfully. "And there weren't that many, Gaby. I've spent a lot more time making money than I have spending it."

"I know. You work terribly hard," she agreed. Her soft eyes ran over his hard, bare chest, lingering on the thick hair that ran down over his lean stomach and into the low band of his pajama bottoms. It shouldn't have affected her, because it hadn't before—not to any real extent. But she looked at him and wanted suddenly to touch him.

He knew too much about women to mistake the look. It fascinated him, and aroused him helplessly. His jaw tautened as he stared down at her, aware that she was seeing that vulnerability, and for the first time, understanding it.

Her soft eyes levered back up to his while her heart ran away with her. She didn't say anything because she couldn't think of anything that would suit the occasion and spare her modesty. She simply looked at him.

"And now you know something more about men, don't you?" he asked softly. "Don't be embarrassed. Men have these crosses to bear." He sighed heavily, lifting his cigarette to his mouth. "It was easier around puberty, before girls started getting so knowledgeable about why boys walked bent over double from time to time."

She laughed. It was unexpected and amazing to her, but his droll humor always had the power to bring her out of nervousness or awkwardness.

"Aggie looks less miserable, at least," she remarked when he grew silent.

"Why shouldn't she?" he sighed. "She's found plenty of diversion in here this morning. The way we wound up didn't help the situation, either."

She remembered how they'd been wrapped together. Her shy eyes sought his. "I guess you're sort of used to sleeping with someone," she said hesitantly.

"Not all night, honey," he replied. He took another draw from the cigarette and put it out. "In that respect, you were my first," he added with a dry smile.

She felt outrageously pleased. "Anyway, thanks for letting me stay with you," she said with averted eyes. "I was pretty scared."

"So I noticed." He got up lazily, stretching again. He couldn't remember when he'd had a better night's sleep. He'd awakened early to find Gaby curled up against him, and the pleasure of it had made him feel warm and tender. She was getting under his skin already, even if he did have some less than obvious motives for his active pursuit of her in recent days. Aggie was out to get him for his part in the Teton man's exit, and he could almost read her mind. He'd have bet ten to one she was going to give Gaby controlling interest in Casa Río to get back at him. Well, if Gaby was his, that would backfire—at least, that's what he was telling himself. The new and fragile tenderness he felt for Gaby was something he tried to push into the back of his mind, for the time being, anyway. "I can't remember when I've slept better. What do you have planned for today?"

She couldn't remember what she had planned, because the sight of him like that—powerful muscles rippling as he reached toward the ceiling—knocked the breath out of her.

He glanced down and lifted an eyebrow at her rapt stare.

"I'm sorry, what did you say?" she asked dimly.

He laughed. "Never mind." He reached down and caught her under the arms, swinging her out of the bed. His hands linked behind her back and he studied her flushed face. "You look pretty first thing in the morning," he remarked. "Very virginal and sweet."

"You don't look bad, either," she said softly. He was smiling at her, and she felt as if she had the world in her pocket. She smiled back. And for one long, exquisite minute there wasn't anyone else in the world.

"Ah, ah." Montoya broke the silence, making clicking sounds with his tongue as he brought in a tray with a pot of coffee, two cups, cream and sugar. "If you continue to look at each other that way, the shotgun behind the door may be loaded for you, Bowie."

He pursed his lips, still staring down at Gaby. "Suppose we tell them what really happened last night?" he asked speculatively.

Her eyes widened. "What do you mean, what really happened?"

"Montoya's not unsophisticated," he mused. "Are you, Montoya?"

"No, and I'm not stupid, either." Montoya grinned. "Pull the other one, Bowie."

Bowie glared at him. "If you'd cooperate, I might browbeat her into an engagement."

"Oh! Excuse me!" Montoya looked at a stunned Gaby and cleared his throat, putting a lean, dark hand over his heart. "Señorita, I am shocked at your behavior. How could you corrupt so worthy a gentleman as Señor Bowie?"

"Corrupt?" Aggie was at the door again, obviously going past it. "Did you say corrupt?!"

"She took shameless advantage of me," Bowie accused, staring at Gaby. "I think it's only right that she make an honest man of me. Don't you?" he asked Aggie.

"What a lovely idea, dear," Aggie murmured, glaring at him. She smiled wickedly. "And I'll give you all the help you gave me."

"I knew it," Bowie sighed as she went past the door. "She isn't over the Teton man—not by a long shot."

"That is obvious, since she cried most of the night," Montoya said at the doorway. He glanced back at Bowie. "She puts on a brave act, but there is pain underneath it."

"All the more reason for Gaby to marry me and give her

something to occupy her mind," Bowie agreed. "Get out and let me propose in peace."

"My pleasure, señor." Montoya grinned again, and carefully shut the door on his way out.

"You're joking," Gaby stammered.

Bowie turned to face her. "No, I am not," he replied.

"We'll buy a ring and take it one day at a time." He pulled her back up again. "If you trust me enough to sleep in my arms, there's every hope that one day you'll trust me enough to give yourself to me. I can wait."

"We'd be taking a terrible chance," she whispered huskily, and all the while she was thinking of the future, of the sweetness of belonging to him and having him belong to her. She had slept with him, without protest. It might be possible, one day, to go all the way.

"I don't mind taking terrible chances," he replied quietly. "Say yes." His black eyes twinkled. "Your reputation is ruined, and so is mine, so you might as well. Tía Elena will have it all over the valley by dark, and most people don't know us as well as she does. Believe me, you'll be a scarlet woman by sunset."

"That isn't a good reason to get married."

He framed her face in his big, lean hands and bent to brush his mouth over her soft lips. "We get along well together most of the time, don't we?"

"We did, until we started taking sides on this agricultural thing," she agreed.

"You'll change your mind."

"No, I won't, Bowie," she said. "I think they're right."

His black eyes narrowed. "And I think they're wrong. But that's one issue. On most of the others we agree. You can keep on working, if you'll come home and work for Bob Chalmers, and when and if you like the idea, we'll make a baby together."

Her face went scarlet and her breath caught at his wording. She buried her hot cheek against his chest, trembling at the knowledge of what they'd have to do to create one. But it was a new kind of trembling, and it wasn't from fear.

"You've got a natural maternal streak," he said softly, "and I love kids. That's another thing we have in common. But I won't rush you. Just say yes, and let's go and tell Aggie. She'll have the time of her life plotting ways to break us up to get even with me for sending the Teton man packing."

She lifted her head. "Bowie, you didn't," she said.

He smiled. "I wish I could take credit for it, but I didn't do anything. He went home on his own, with a little help from Aggie herself. I told you she wouldn't want to milk cows."

"Yes, I guess you did, but she's going to be terribly lonely."

"She'll have us," he replied. His eyes searched hers quietly. "Marry me, Gaby."

She smoothed her hands over his bare chest gently, so that she didn't disturb him too much, even though he did stiffen. "Bowie, is it just that you want me? Or is it Casa Río?"

He hesitated, but only for a second or two. "I want you," he said. "And I do feel that you're more likely to tone down your campaign to develop the land if you're married to me," he added with complete honesty. "But there's something more. You feel it, just as I do. A tenderness between us—a kind of empathy. I touch you and I feel whole. I think you feel the same way, despite those scars in your mind."

She looked up at him. "Yes," she whispered, glorying in the newness of what they were sharing. "I feel it, too."

"Then marry me. Give it a chance to grow."

She reached up and touched his handsome face, trailing her fingers lovingly over his high cheekbone. "I could . . . love you, I think," she whispered shakily.

His heart skipped and his hands on her upper arms contracted at the words. "Could you?"

"Oh, yes, I could," she whispered, trembling a little when his blond head began to bend.

"Softly, *adorada*," he breathed as his mouth met hers. His arms pulled her gently closer, wrapping her up. The kiss was like none they'd ever shared—tender and slow and ever so soft. She felt as if he'd wrapped her up in cotton, as if he were cherishing her. She relaxed completely and gave him her mouth with exquisite delight.

"This won't be enough for you, eventually," she whispered worriedly when his head lifted, because even at the chaste distance, she recognized the tautness of his body, the coiled need.

"Maybe it won't be enough for you, either, eventually," he whispered back and smiled. "Don't worry so. We've got all the time in the world to discover each other—mentally, emotionally, and physically. All right?"

She smiled with pure adoration. "All right."

"You'd better go and get dressed before Aggie hears the news from Montoya. The element of surprise is on our side right now."

"She won't mind, will she?" she asked, frowning.

"Is that likely?" He smiled again, and watched her go out the balcony doors and on to her room. When she was out of sight the smile faded. He had his own doubts about whether or not Gaby would be able to give him what he needed. In the meantime, he'd foxed her into an engagement and he could stop her from selling out Casa Río to the enemy. He could watch her; he could even take care of her. Most of all, he could indulge the new feelings she aroused in him and find out what and why they were. He'd never loved; now he wondered if this was it.

He turned back to his closet and started to dress. At least the Teton man was out of the picture. Now all he had to do was get Aggie back to normal and put Gaby in his pocket. He felt on top of the world. Everything was going his way.

Bowie was downstairs before Gaby, so he broke the news to his mother alone. Aggie took the development with a pointed smile. "My, my, you're making sure, aren't you?" she asked.

He glowered at her. "I care about Gaby."

"You care about Casa Río," Aggie replied snortly. "You broke up my engagement to keep it, and you're not beyond appropriating Gaby to keep it. Tell me you love her, Bowie."

He couldn't—not yet. His jaw tautened. "Love will come."

"Will it? You want her—a blind man could see that. But she'll need careful handling and a lot of love. I don't think you're capable of it. If you were, you'd never have gone to such lengths to try and break up my relationship with Ned. I know why you went to Texas, Bowie. You and I share the same lawyer," she said, noting his surprise. "He called to tell me what you were up to, and I told Ned. That was the straw that broke the camel's back. He said that if I trusted him, I'd marry him on the spot, before you started digging deeper, but I refused. I said that if he loved me, he'd tell me the truth. One thing led to another, and I sent him packing —because of you, dear boy," she muttered.

He sighed wearily and lit another cigarette. He seemed to have done nothing but smoke lately. "I'm sorry," he said tersely. "I didn't mean for it to happen that way. I had every intention of checking him out and shooting him out of here," he added, his black eyes flashing as they caught hers. "But I wouldn't have done it under the table."

"I'd like to believe that," she said. "But I know how you feel about the land. Copeland drilled heritage into you until you're bloated with it."

"I care about you, too, in my way," he returned curtly. "Even if Gaby and Courtland do rate first with you."

Aggie avoided the accusation in his dark eyes. "Well, what's done is done, isn't it? I can't go back and undo the damage I've done, any more than you can. Maybe if I'd been a little more attentive to you, you wouldn't have resented another man here." She lifted her face proudly. "None of that matters now, though. You've done what you set out to do. Ned's gone, and he's too proud to come back after the way I refused him."

He sighed heavily. "It could have been infatuation."

"Like what Gaby feels for you?" she taunted, and watched the dart hit home. "She's into her first real crush, and you're it. How does that feel, when she's getting so deep under your skin that you can't move for feeling her there?"

His eyes narrowed dangerously. "We won't discuss my feelings."

"How could we, when you won't even admit them?" she challenged. "You're leading Gaby up the garden path, but when she finds out why, her infatuation is going to die a nasty death. And if your heart is vulnerable, you may find that love hurts more at your age than it does at hers," she added curtly. "You may eventually understand how devastated I am to lose Ned. If that happens, I may even feel sorry for you."

"I don't need your damned pity," he shot back. "I don't think I love her."

Which was just what Aggie was trying to pry out of him. She smiled coldly. "As I thought," she said softly. "Don't underestimate her, my dear. Gaby isn't a fool, even if you're playing her for one. You knew what I intended doing all along, didn't you?"

"I had my suspicions," he replied.

"And they were justified," she replied. "I'm tired of being a pawn in your lust for Casa Río. I spoke to my attorney in Tucson this morning. I'm going on an extended holiday, and I'm going to start things in motion signing over the property to you and Gaby, with one minor variation on your father's theme," she added with a cold smile. "Gaby gets fifty-one percent, you get forty-nine. If you go to war over the agricultural conglomerate, Gaby wins. Put that in your cigarette and smoke it, damn you."

She got up and walked out of the room, leaving Bowie grim and silent with rage. He'd expected it, but it was devastating all the same. Aggie had made him admit his motives, and he wasn't too pleased with them. They tarnished in daylight, and made him feel cheap. But there was more to it, his mind protested. It wasn't all because of Casa Río. Gaby made him feel protective and tender. She aroused desire in him, but a new kind of desire that wasn't selfish or cruel. She made him want children and a family of his own to love and be loved by. He couldn't tell Aggie that. He didn't want to face the implications of it, because they made him vulnerable, for the first time in his life.

Gaby, blissfully oblivious to what had just happened in her absence, was just coming down the staircase as Aggie started up it.

"I've just given you controlling interest in Casa Río," Aggie told her. "I'm going into Tucson to sign the papers, and then I'm going down to Nassau for a few weeks. I still have the money Copeland left me when he died, and a good bit of my own. I don't need Casa Río. I'm tired of having Bowie interfere in my life over love of it. But I've complicated things for you, and I'm sorry."

Gaby felt a rush of fear. Now she could never be sure if Bowie wanted her or Casa Río. He was fanatical about it, about his heritage. He'd proposed this morning, but had he suspected what Aggie was going to do? He read people so well.

"It's because of Ned, isn't it?" Gaby asked with cold chills running up her arms. "Bowie did do something to help break you up."

"You think I'm getting even?" Aggie sighed. "I don't know. Maybe I am. I hurt, Gaby. I hurt as I haven't since Copeland died, and Bowie's to blame—at least, partly. I have to get away. I don't want to fight anymore; I just want to be left alone." Tears stung her eyes. "I'm sorry."

"There's nothing to be sorry for," Gaby said gently.

"Isn't there?" The older woman searched her eyes. "You're in love with Bowie."

That was the first time Gaby had heard the words. She'd intimated to Bowie that morning that she might be able to love him, but she'd never admitted that she already did. But of course she did, she thought, amazed. Or why would she have let him carry her to his room? Why would she have slept beside him all night without a protest?

"Yes," Gaby said huskily.

Aggie kissed her cheek gently. "Maybe it will work out for you. If you care, try to make him see that land, even heritage, aren't as important as people."

"I'll try. What about you?"

Aggie's thin shoulders rose and fell. "I'll go to Nassau and stay with some friends. I don't know, after that. I just want time to try and forget Ned." Her voice broke and the tears came again. "God, Gaby, it hurts so much!"

Gaby was beginning to realize that. She was in love with a man who might only be using her to get his hands on a piece of land that should have been his to begin with. It didn't bear thinking about.

CHAPTER
Thirteen

It was the longest week of Gaby's life, despite the fact that it seemed to begin on Wednesday. After she accepted a job with the *Lassiter Citizen* she got together all the factual information she'd been gathering on the Bio-Ag project, together with interviews from the environmental people and quotes from Mr. Barry, the Lopezes, and Mr. Samuels of Bio-Ag. When she finished the story, it was a well-done piece, she felt, carefully neutral, but presenting both sides of the explosive issue as well as she could. Even so, it still leaned toward Bio-Ag's position, and she grimaced as she tried to imagine Bowie's reaction when it was published. He wasn't going to like it, but she hadn't prejudiced the article to reinforce her own feelings. Her own feelings were rather vague right now. What she'd been told about the project only made her more curious. She felt that the organizers of the proposed agricultural project were deliberately withholding information about their intent, and that was disturbing.

She had every respect for agriculture and farmers. Considering the tiny percentage of the population that worked so hard to feed everyone else, it wouldn't have been politic to antagonize this project. On the other hand, the water table was dropping, and agriculture was the biggest user around. When water ran out for drinking and bathing, did agriculture have the right to put its needs above those of the populace? She groaned. The more she tried to think it out, the worse it got. Jobs, she told herself—Bio-Ag would bring in jobs. Then she thought about the future and the scarcity of water in the desert, and the slight possibility that the whole thing could be a dreadful fraud. She couldn't leave it like this. She had to dig deeper—she had to be *sure* before she threw her vote to Bio-Ag, for the sake of the community and her conscience.

Meanwhile, Aggie signed the necessary papers for the transfer of Casa Río to Bowie and Gaby which would take several weeks to effect, and then got quietly on a plane for Nassau. The older woman looked drawn and unhappy, and Gaby's heart went out to her. Aggie had decided to leave while Bowie was still in Tucson, and that was going to hurt him, but then, Aggie had reason to be angry at both her son and Gaby. Their interference had led to her present state. She couldn't understand that their only concern had been to protect her from a con man. Gaby didn't really believe that Mr. Courtland was a con man, not anymore, but it was too late to worry about that. She had enough problems to concentrate on.

She'd asked Aggie if she minded her living at Casa Río, and Aggie had just laughed. The house belonged to her and Bowie now, she had said gently. She was more than welcome to live in it, as long as Aggie had visiting rights now and again. That had brought forth a well of tears, and Gaby had cried like a child. Aggie seemed to be losing everything. It was almost unbearable to see her misery and feel that she had had even a small part in it.

Bowie brooded when he realized his mother had left without a goodbye. All the years he'd felt left out because of

Gaby had come back to haunt him. He could have had a closer relationship with his mother, perhaps, if he'd tried a little harder. It was pride that had held him at bay. Now it might be too late to work it out. He hoped not.

He drove Gaby up to Phoenix to resign. While they drove she talked about carefully neutral subjects, and didn't mention the article she had in her purse to give to Johnny Blake as a going-away present. She knew Bowie was going to explode. Part of her wanted to tell him about the hard work she'd put into the story, and how carefully she'd managed to tell both sides without prejudice, but she was reluctant to disrupt the peace between them.

She was sad to leave the job she'd held for three years. Johnny let her go without a fuss, and with the proviso that she keep him posted about Bio-Ag's progress. Gaby knew she was going to miss the hectic pace, but the Lassiter paper had a charm all its own. She knew she was going to like it there. And Bob Chalmers had been overjoyed at her acceptance even if Harvey Ritter hadn't.

Her one regret about the week was missing the city council meeting. Bob had sent Harvey to cover that, but since Bowie would have insisted on going with Gaby, perhaps it was for the best. She could always pump Harvey for information about the project.

But as she prepared to start her new job on Monday, an unpleasant thought crept into her mind. Bowie might be regretting his proposal of marriage. He'd been quieter and more thoughtful than usual lately. She knew he was upset about Aggie, but he had hardly touched Gaby, except with lazy affection now and again. Although they spent time together over the weekend, and went to church on Sunday, there seemed to be more distance between them now than there ever had before. It wasn't a cold or angry distance; it was more like a slow wall moving down, cutting them off from each other. Gaby mentioned it to Bowie, but only once. He clammed up and walked off, as he usually did when he didn't want to discuss something, so Gaby went her own way, wondering if Bowie only wanted to make sure of Casa Río by proposing. Maybe Aggie had said something to upset him, but she couldn't find out what it was.

She was at work by eight-thirty that next Monday, dressed to the teeth in a denim skirt and lacy blouse and high heels. The office staff gave her a sideways appraisal with raised eyebrows and went back to work in their jeans and T-shirts.

"Am I overdressed?" she asked Bob stealthily.

"Not for Phoenix," he replied, tongue-in-cheek. "And not if you're planning to go out on an interview. But to work around town—yes, I think you're a bit overboard."

"Okay." She chuckled. "I'll get it right next time. What do I do?"

He outlined her job and gave her her own office, right next door to Harvey Ritter's. She noticed that Harvey didn't look up or offer any welcome. She understood that. He'd been the only reporter on the staff for several years, and he had to resent her presence.

"These are all the local numbers." Bob pointed to a sheet by the phone. "Police, fire department, civil defense, and so forth. When you get time—not today, because we're going to be pushed for time trying to get enough copy to fill the paper before we go to press at noon tomorrow—it would be a good idea for you to go around to all the various city departments and introduce yourself. They're nice folks. You'll like them."

"I'll do that," she promised. "What would you like me to do meanwhile?"

"Harvey's doing a last-minute story on a new business that just located here, and then he'll get the police news. You might check around for fires that happened over the weekend, and see if anybody knows anything about a drug bust," he added under his breath. "Harvey won't ask, but I hear it involved some bigwigs."

"I'll need to go to the police department for that," she said, "and look at the arrest record."

He gaped at her. "You're not afraid to do that?"

"Of course not."

He grinned. "Welcome to Lassiter."

She did the rounds, mostly running, because one tidbit of news led to another and it took most of the day to run down the true story about the drug bust. But she got it all by closing time and took it home with her to write.

Bowie frowned when she asked for access to his computer.

"You don't need to bring work home, do you?" he asked.

"I won't usually," she said, "but I'm new, and I'm a little slow at learning the routine of a weekly newspaper. They say the resident reporter shies away from controversy."

"But you don't, do you?" he asked with narrowed eyes. "You don't mind where you hit, or how hard."

She colored, because her story for the *Phoenix Advertiser*, about the proposed agricultural enterprise, had just been released the day before. Obviously, Bowie had read it.

"I gave both sides of the story," she said.

"Sure. Yours and theirs."

"Bowie . . ."

"I don't give a damn what you write, I'm not backing down," he replied quietly. "You don't have to understand my point of view to respect it."

"And I do," she said, almost pleading. "You aren't alone. There are at least two environmental groups supporting you, and several local people. It's just that I have to tell it the way I see it."

"We can debate that until hell freezes over," he returned. "You love your work, don't you?"

He made it sound like a disease. "Maybe I'm addicted to adrenalin," she hedged. "I need to work on this."

"Be my guest. I'll use the phone in the library." He walked out without another word, leaving her to it. He went out shortly afterwards, without a word. By the time she went to bed, he still hadn't returned.

The story was a blockbuster, complete with names, dates, places, and perfect sources, all printable. She took the disk in to the paper in the morning and called it up on the computer so Bob could read it. He just shook his head. "Great," he murmured. "Really great. Now, if we can just get it to work properly through the printer. . ."

He carried the disk into the make-up room, slid it into its slot on the huge printer console, and pushed some buttons. The machine made clicking sounds. "It takes a little while," he explained. "This is the newest thing I could afford. It's been obsolete for years, of course."

Minutes later, he had offset copy in perfect column form, ready to cut into manageable strips and run through the waxer, then paste onto the pages. "We'll run it four columns with a banner headline," he murmured. "Too bad we don't have pix. Maybe Harvey has something we can use to balance the page."

She went back to her terminal and began to type up the newest things that had come in—mostly society news and tidbits about local people that had been mailed or brought in. She set those up to help Judy, who was up to her eyebrows in legal advertisements, obituaries, and want ads. The display ads were made up in the composing room by Bob and Harvey, she learned.

Tuesday had to be the most awful day in the week, she thought as she got used to being on her feet all day helping to paste copy onto the sheets, ran back and forth to help answer the phone, and talked to customers who wanted to place ads, pull ads, or provide news.

"What's this?" Harvey demanded just after lunch, when he joined the others in the composing room to help lay in ads. He was reading the front page, and his broad face was red. "Who did this?" he demanded. "This was a story I meant to get for next week!"

"It would have been old news by next week," Gaby explained. "I had the time, you didn't, so what difference does it make who actually did the legwork? Aren't we a team here?"

"That's right, Harvey," Bob said calmly as he used the scissors carefully on a newly set up want ad. "No sweat."

Harvey glared at Gaby's byline on the story, and then glared at her. "I don't think there's enough news in this little town for two reporters," he said icily.

"You'd be surprised how much there is," Bob replied. "Now stop bristling, Harvey. You aren't going to be out of a job just because I hired Gaby. She'll be doing a lot of things you hate anyway, like all that controversial stuff."

Harvey shifted irritably. "I suppose I'll be stuck with obituaries and politics for the rest of my life."

"Of course not," the boss assured him. "I've been thinking of adding a sports page. You could cover football games."

The heavy man actually flushed. "I hate sports."

"It was just a thought." Bob smiled and stared at the man until Harvey muttered something conciliatory and began pasting up copy.

But it was a rough beginning, and it got worse. Gaby found herself fighting for every bit of news she got. Harvey always seemed to know what she was going to do, and got there first. Since he knew the town and all the public officials, it was understandable that he had the edge. Gaby was left with the police beat and not much more. Not that weekly papers seemed to have beats, like big-time papers did. And the jobs were interchangeable—she had to set her own copy in type, and help Judy when she was overworked, handle subscriptions, bag and wrap papers in the back every Wednesday for mailing, take ads over the phone, and even rush out to take photos when they were needed. She wound up taking a lot of pictures of giant vegetables and wrecks while Harvey got pix of visiting dignitaries, beauty queens, and fires. Harvey, in fact, was giving her fits.

"He'll adjust to you," Bob said quietly when she finally complained about it, after the second week at work. "Give him time."

"Must he fight me every step of the way?" she asked miserably. "I love this job, but he's making it impossible for me to do it. Can't we each have definite assignments, so that the divisions are clear?"

Bob lifted a thin eyebrow. "There's an idea. Okay. Give me a few days to work it out."

"Fine. Thanks!"

After that, they each had clear-cut assignments, which made Harvey all the more irritating, and unsettled Gaby. He was the kind of reporter who'd look for things to dig up on people. She'd already overheard Harvey asking pointed questions about her connection with the McCaydes and her background. She felt a new kind of tension around him. He seemed like a vengeful man, and she had a feeling that he was going to cause her grief before he was through.

Her home life wasn't much better. Bowie had been in Tucson during the week and out of town most weekends since Aggie had been gone. At first Gaby thought it might be to preserve the conventions, but she began to realize that it was simply his old lifestyle. He was making no concessions whatsoever to being engaged. Ever since the newspaper story had come out, he'd been cold toward her. There had been no more mention of the future—even of an engagement ring. She began to think Aggie had been right about his motives.

"The city council meets tomorrow night," she mentioned over supper.

"Again?" Bowie asked, barely glancing up from the legal document he was reading as Montoya put food on the table.

"It's been a month since their last meeting," she replied.

He looked up then, and his black eyes searched her face. She looked thinner, and there were circles under her eyes. He'd been so involved with work the past month, and so irritated at her public defection to the enemy camp, that he'd forced himself not to go near her. But now he was seeing her, for the first time in weeks, and he felt a twinge of guilt at the way she looked. Maybe she'd expected something more from their engagement. So had he, but the one time he'd made a move toward her physically she'd backed away, as if even being kissed was too disturbing to contemplate. He'd been overwhelmed with memories of what Aggie had said to him about Gaby only being infatuated, and it could be true. He was trying to find out if she really cared, without the enhancement of physical infatuation to blind her, but it hadn't worked. Her bulldog attitude toward her work, her lack of loyalty to him, and even her physical reticence had combined to enrage him. He'd withdrawn from her, but now he felt bad about it. She was showing the effects of his coldness, and hurting her was the very last thing he wanted to do. Then he remembered, too, that he hadn't even bought her a ring.

"I've neglected you," he said quietly.

"Yes, I know." She searched his eyes. "Something's worrying you."

"A lot of things, honey." He sat back. "Including your stories on the agricultural project. Do you really think they're unprejudiced?"

"They may seem slanted, I agree," she said honestly, "but I'm honor bound to present both sides. I have to be objective."

"Well, I can't be," he said. "I still think there's something not quite aboveboard about the whole operation. They leave out too many points in their explanations."

"I'm not blind," she replied. "I've noticed the omissions. And I'm not just sitting on my hands ignoring them. Bowie, I'm a journalist," she said steadily, her eyes on his. "I can't take sides, even if I'd like to. I have an obligation to my paper and to my own conscience about the things I write. If I fail to do my job and people are hurt because of it, I have to live with that. I'm going to dig as deep as I can, as fast as I can, and if there's anything shady about the operation, I'll print what I find. So will Bob Chalmers. I know you don't like him, but he's a good newspaperman."

He relaxed a little. "Okay. I'll give you the benefit of the doubt."

"It's Aggie who really worries you, isn't it?" she coaxed.

He grimaced. "She didn't say goodbye. I knew she was mad, but I didn't think she felt that bitter. I was trying to protect her. I've had some difficulty expressing what I felt, but I never meant to hurt her. I guess I've left it too late."

"When she's had time to think things out, she'll come back and you can get it all straightened out," she said.

"Think so?" He sighed, dropping the subject. "What's this garbage about a petition?" he asked suddenly.

She blinked at the quick change of subject. "The Bio-Ag petition? Yes. I saw it. They're presenting it at the city council meeting. Mayor White even asked if I was going to be there." She grimaced. "They're expecting a record turnout of voters."

"Of course they are. Crowds always gather at bloodlettings."

She knew about the latest death threat. Bowie hadn't told her, but Montoya had. A deep, grizzly voice over the phone had threatened Bowie with a bullet and hung up before he had time to reply. He'd raged for half an hour before he had gone out to check fences with his foreman. He hated checking fences, and rarely did it. Mostly, he left the management of the ranch—only twenty-two thousand acres, and small by Arizona standards—to his foreman, Jeff Danvers. He was much more occupied with the construction business than he was with the cattle, although he did love the land passionately.

"What are you going to do if somebody tries to shoot you over this?" Gaby asked tightly.

"Shoot back, of course," he replied lazily. He leaned back in his chair to study her. "I carry a rifle in the pickup when I drive it, and I've got a .38 police special that I carry around in a holster when I'm out at night. I have a permit for it. You know that."

She knew what a dead shot he was, too, but that wouldn't help if he was ambushed. This was wide open country and incredibly big, with open spaces where not a soul would be seen for miles. At night, it would be so easy to sit and wait for a particular vehicle to pass and slide a bullet through it.

"I don't want you to get hurt."

"What an odd way you have of showing it," he returned with a cool smile.

Her eyes ranged lovingly over the handsome angles of his face, lingering on his thick blond hair and deep-set black eyes. He delighted her in every way, but if he even wanted her these days, it didn't show.

"I'd better see if Tía Elena needs any help," she said in a subdued tone, and got to her feet.

"Sit down," Bowie said curtly. "I'm getting pretty damned tired of having you run like a rabbit every time I come into a room."

Her eyes widened. "But I don't," she protested. "You're never here!"

"What would be the use?" he asked wearily. His eyes slid

over her body with faint longing. "You don't want me. You never have and you never will. You're dead inside."

She knew it, but to hear him put it into words in such a way was devastating. She had to swallow down a knot of hurt anger before she could even speak.

"You haven't touched me, or even offered to, since the morning you asked me to marry you, Bowie," she reminded him in a stiff, wounded tone. "Only once, and even that was because you seemed to think I was expecting it. You even said so." She lowered her eyes. "I would have tried, you know. But it's difficult for me to . . . to . . ." She made an expressive gesture with her hands and turned away. "It's no use, is it? The engagement was all a sham, anyway, just like Aggie said it was, to keep me from opposing your stand on Casa Río."

She turned and left the room, her back ramrod straight, her heart worn and leaden in her chest.

She went up to her room and stretched out on her bed with a long sigh. That should have done it, she thought. Now he'd have his inheritance back and he could stop pretending that he wanted to marry her. He was free.

The door opened and closed again, and Bowie came and sat beside her on the bed.

"I've gone about this all wrong," he said quietly. "Perhaps you still don't realize how difficult it is for a man to try and conduct a relationship with a woman who starts backing away the minute he touches her. I haven't started anything because it's painful when I have to draw back from you." His black eyes fell to her body. "The wanting hasn't stopped, Gaby, but I know you don't want me. That's not much of an incentive to do anything about our situation."

"I could try," she whispered, her voice shaking.

His eyebrows drew together as he caught her eyes. "Is that an invitation?"

"It will have to be very slow," she got out. "And you . . .

when you lose control, I may fight you . . ." Her eyes closed. "But I'll try."

"You'll suffer me, isn't that what you mean?" he asked coldly. He laughed. "Thanks. My ego can use that kind of boost."

"You don't understand," she bit off.

"How can I, when you won't tell me what happened?" he demanded. He glared at her. "I don't read minds. So a boyfriend got out of control once and frightened you. So what? That happens to a lot of girls, but it doesn't turn them into cakes of ice!"

Her eyes closed. "I let you think that," she replied. "But that wasn't what happened." She didn't want to tell him, and she couldn't tell him all of it, but she had to make him understand. "All right, Bowie. I'll tell you." She took a slow breath, aware of his stillness. "The man was the brother of my father's boss," she whispered, shocking him into listening. "He'd had his eye on me for a long time, and I was careful to keep out of his way. But one afternoon the bus broke down and I was late getting back from school because I had to walk from the main highway. He was waiting for me. He dragged me into the barn," she choked, her face going white at the memory, "and pushed me down on the floor. It was dark, but I could smell the whiskey on his breath, and I knew he'd been drinking. He was as big as you are," she continued, her voice shaking, "and strong. I fought and fought, but I couldn't get away from him." Tears ran down her cheeks, over their pale coolness. "He tore my clothes and touched me," she cringed, her eyes closing as she shuddered. "He pinned me down with his body, and I knew then that I couldn't stop him, that he was going to hurt me in that terrible way, and I screamed and screamed . . ."

"Oh, my God." Bowie felt sick at his stomach. He'd never suspected anything like this. He hadn't imagined that a grown man had tried to assault her.

"He was stopped in time," she whispered hoarsely, trying to forget how he'd been stopped, trying not to see the blood that had been everywhere. "But I had nightmares for years afterward, and I couldn't bear for a man to touch me, or hold me against my will. I still can't. Only . . . only you," she added, her wet eyes seeking his in the stillness. "When you touch me, it doesn't make my skin crawl, and it's so sweet to kiss you. I didn't think I could ever do that with anyone, but it's so natural with you."

She made him feel ashamed—of the way he'd treated her, of his lack of understanding.

He reached down and drew her up, lifting her across his legs to hold her gently, her cheek pillowed on his hard chest, against the soft white silk of his open-necked shirt. "Why couldn't you tell me this years ago?" he asked quietly.

"I've never told anyone. And . . . that's not all of it," she whispered brokenly. "But I can't tell you the rest." Her voice broke and she wept helplessly. "I wanted to . . . to die!"

His arms gently pulled her closer. His head bent against hers and his breath caught at the pain he could feel in her. "It's all right," he whispered huskily. "You've got me now. Nobody and nothing will ever hurt you as long as there's a breath in my body!"

He sounded as if he meant it, Gaby thought dazedly. And he didn't sound angry anymore, at least. She closed her eyes, dabbing at them with her fist.

"Here," he said, drawing out a handkerchief for her. "What about your father, Gaby? Didn't he do anything? Why did he let you run away, alone?"

"There was nothing he could do," she said miserably. And there hadn't been; he'd done what was necessary. Then he'd given Gaby what little money he had, and he'd said they had to separate, so that their chances of getting away would be as good as possible. She'd cried and begged to go with him, but he'd been adamant. Just in case, he'd said, crying, too, it would make things bearable if he knew that she'd made it to safety. He had to have that hope. There was a cousin in Arizona; all she had to do was get out there. Her last sight of him had been blurred, because the tears hadn't stopped. But people were already running back and forth, and sirens came shortly afterwards. There was no time to waste in protests. He'd gone out through the tobacco field at a dead run, and Gaby had run through the tall grass in the other direction toward the highway, everything she had left in the pocket-book she'd carried home from school. Inanely, she thought that her schoolbooks must have still been in the stable when the police came. She shivered.

Bowie touched her hair gently, smoothing it away from her face. "You make me feel about two inches high," he said quietly. "I thought it was a boyfriend who'd gone too far. I had no idea it was like that."

"He was a lecher," she sobbed. "And he drank like a fish. He was always after the young girls, when he wasn't hanging around the bus stop. Everybody knew about him, and I was warned. But I just never thought anyone would try to do that to me—not even him. I'm not pretty."

"A man like that doesn't look at a woman's face," he said shortly. His temper was aflame at the thought of how helpless she'd been. "He should have been shot! Do you know what happened to him after you left? We need to get in touch with the family..."

"No!" She went stark white and sat up on his lap, her eyes wide with terror. "No, you can't! I won't tell you who they are, or where—I won't...!"

"Calm down." He touched her mouth with his fingertips, his eyes speculative. "It's all right, Gaby. I won't do anything that you don't want done. I just think it's unfair that a man should be allowed to do something like that without being punished for it."

"It was ten years ago," she hedged, lowering her frightened eyes. "It's too late."

And it was, but not for the reason he thought. She shivered a little with reaction and dabbed at her eyes.

"No wonder you've lived the way you have," he said, his voice still and tender. "I used to be curious—about the way you dressed, your lack of boyfriends. Now it makes sense."

"I thought about going for therapy once," she confessed. "But I couldn't trust anyone enough to talk about it. Eventually, I decided that I'd just be an old maid."

"And then I took you out to supper," he mused, smiling as he tilted her face up to his dark, quiet eyes. "And the world shifted ten degrees."

"You fascinated me," she confessed softly, searching his face. "Everything about you. You always had, but lately," she averted her eyes, "after I came down here, I started having these dreams about you."

He saw the color tint her cheeks. He traced them gently, amazed at the intensity of feeling she aroused in him. "Erotic dreams?" he asked softly.

She nodded. "That was the first time I'd ever had them in my life. And the night I came looking for you, when Aggie announced her engagement . . ."

"I frightened you," he recalled curtly.

She looked up. "Yes, but even then, I felt something," she whispered. "Something new and a little scary. I started getting wobbly and I had the oddest feeling deep in my stomach." She smiled sheepishly. "And in my legs. It scared me."

He was very still. His eyes held hers. "A kind of dragging sensation," he said softly.

"Well, yes," she said curiously.

A light began to glow deep in his eyes. "When I traced around your breasts," he added.

She shifted her attention to his collar. "And when you backed me into the fence," she added, forcing a smile. "It wasn't altogether being overpowered that scared me so badly."

"This probably isn't the best time for it," he said as his lean hands slid to her waist, "but I think it might be as well to show you what those dragging sensations really are."

She looked up without totally comprehending, until she felt his thumbs edging against her breasts. She stiffened, but he shook his head slowly, holding her eyes, and she subsided.

He watched her face the whole time. His lean hands were expert, slow, and very wise. He traced from the outer edge of her breasts almost to the nipples, with a touch that was almost like a faint breeze, light and teasing. But it was fiercely arousing, and in seconds, she was stiffening in a new way. Her hands caught his upper arms, but for support, not in protest. Her breathing began to change and she looked up at him with an expression in her eyes that made him feel fiercely male.

His hands turned, so that his thumbs were doing the tracing now, and his nose rubbed softly against hers as he searched for her mouth. He touched it with his, nuzzling it with deft laziness, so that its soft movement both relaxed and stirred her. And still his hands were making magic on her body, his thumbs coming closer and closer to the suddenly hard tips of her breasts.

"I don't . . . understand," she got out.

"Open your mouth a little," he whispered. When she complied mindlessly, his lips moved between them and so did his tongue. At the very instant his tongue went deep into her mouth, his hands claimed her breasts.

She moaned. She'd never done that before, except in her dreams of him, and her body trembled.

"Yes, you like it, don't you?" he whispered into her mouth, and his own smiled faintly as he probed at her soft lips. "Bite me."

He enticed her teeth against his lower lip, teaching her the tender pleasure, and his thumbs began to rub with delicious abrasiveness against her hard nipples. She shuddered with each wave of pleasure they caused, her breath rustling against his hard lips, her body moving helplessly toward his hands while she held on for dear life.

Her nails were digging into him, and she wasn't even conscious of it, the little kittenlike movements making him even hungrier.

Her breath was catching. It made it hard to speak. "Bowie, it . . . makes me so weak," she whispered shakily, "and I ache."

"So do I, baby."

"You only call me baby . . . when you kiss me," she recalled.

He smiled against her mouth. "It seems to suit, doesn't it?" His lean fingers went to the buttons and she looked up into his black eyes without making a sound. "I'm going to bare you to the waist," he whispered, holding her eyes. "All right?"

Her body trembled. "All . . . right."

His head spun with the realization that she actually wanted this. She was feeling the same fierce excitement he was.

The impact of his eyes was frightening, she thought as she watched him peel away her blouse and stare quietly at the lacy bra that covered her breasts. Her nipples were so hard that they pointed against the thin fabric, and that was where his eyes lingered, even when he reached behind her for the catch and loosened it with one deft flick.

Her hands instinctively came up when he started to pull the straps down. She held the bra to her trembling body, her eyes wide and uncertain and a little frightened now.

CHAPTER

Fourteen

It would send Bowie through the roof, she just knew it. She closed her eyes, waiting for the explosion.

But he didn't blow up. He caught her hands gently, and with a patient smile, he pulled them away from the blouse.

"None of that," he said softly. "You and I are going to get married. It's perfectly acceptable for me to look at you. And that's all I really have in mind right now. We're going to do it in easy stages, little one. This is only the first step."

He made it sound so easy, and it was. He moved her hands aside, tossed the blouse to the bed beside her, and lazily slid the bra off her. His black eyes held hers all the while, until the lacy garment was lying on the bed and she was bare to the waist in the stillness of the room.

Only then did he look down, his face tightening a little. His eyes glittered, but not in a frightening way. "Venus," he murmured, delighted at the soft pink contours, the tilted tips, very hard, their mauve darkness contrasting so beautifully with the creamy perfection of the rest of her skin.

"Will I do?" she whispered nervously.

"You're perfect," he replied, letting his eyes move up to search hers. "Perfectly formed. Elegant."

Her lips parted, and only then did she realize that she'd been holding her breath. It was broad daylight, and she was letting him look at a part of her that even her assailant hadn't seen in the dark barn. It was new—wondrous, in the best sense of the word. His eyes told her that she was beautiful, and she felt it.

"Still afraid of me, Gaby?" he asked, and a faint, tender smile smoothed his rigid features.

"How could I be, when you look at me like that?" she whispered huskily. "Oh, Bowie, you . . . make me feel beautiful."

"Is that so surprising, when you are?"

"I felt dirty afterwards," she said in a hushed tone, meeting his gaze. "He handled me, and even though he didn't see me, I couldn't look at myself in the mirror without feeling ashamed."

He felt a surge of pure rage against the animal who'd done that to a fifteen-year-old girl. "The shame was his, not yours. That's over," he said quietly.

"Not . . . while I can still feel his hands," she whispered, flushing as she tried to get across to him what she wanted. Her shy gaze fell to his chest. "Could you . . . touch me?"

"If you want it, yes," he said huskily, his pride kindled by the soft question, by the courage it must have taken to ask it.

She moved a little closer. "It won't bother you or anything?" she asked worriedly.

He smiled. "Of course it will bother me," he murmured. "But I want it as much as you do."

That was a hopeful sign, she thought, because it had to mean that he still wanted her, that he wasn't giving up on her. She steeled herself not to fight him or flinch or draw back.

As it turned out, none of those things happened, because

he didn't touch her with his hands. He bent, and his warm mouth brushed softly over the curve of one firm breast, in a touch like warm sunlight, like a summer wind.

She gasped. She hadn't expected that. Her body trembled with a whisper of pure pleasure, but he felt the ripple and lifted his blond head to search her eyes quietly.

"I didn't know you were going to do that," she faltered.

"I'm going to be very gentle, Gaby," he said quietly. "I won't hurt you. Watch . . ."

She'd never dreamed of anything half so erotic. Her shocked eyes watched his mouth smooth over the creamy skin, and she gasped again at the sting of pleasure as his lips parted and moved closer to the small, hard tip.

One lean hand was at her back, holding her. His other hand was at her rib cage, making warm, lazy patterns on it. All the while, his mouth grazed leisurely back and forth, back and forth, each movement sensual and delicious as he teased the swollen contours and threatened the hardness that was growing more sensitive with each pass.

Her cold fingers moved into his thick blond hair. She didn't know what she was doing, but she knew what she wanted. She began to pull gently.

He lifted his head, pleased to find her eyes misty and half-closed, her face not frightened, but faintly aroused.

"I know what you want," he whispered. "But let's not rush it, little one. I can make the pleasure so much more intense this way, if I take my time."

Her breath was unsteady. "It's very . . . sweet," she managed, trying to convey what she was feeling.

Sweet wasn't the word he wanted from her, but passion would be difficult for her—he understood that. His mouth went back to its silky teasing. He lifted her a little closer, but he was still denying her what she wanted most.

She moaned under her breath, biting back the sound. Her fingers contracted in his hair, loving its cool softness. Something was building, deep inside her—the same shuddery feeling she'd known only once before, when Bowie had kissed her so hungrily.

His mouth opened, moist and deliberately sensual, his tongue touching her skin now, still smoothing lazily toward the object of his attentions.

She arched helplessly, needing something she didn't even understand.

But he seemed to. All at once his mouth moved to cover that hard, aching tip. He took it inside his lips, and she shuddered as a flush of heat ran through her body like fire. Her fingers caught in his hair and forced his mouth hard against her. She gasped, her lips moving against his hair tenderly, encouraging him.

She felt him lift her and lay her against the pillows, but she didn't open her eyes. She felt nothing except the warm delight of his mouth on her skin, learning her body with tenderness and expertise, making her arch and tremble as it drew a new kind of pleasure from the recesses of her mind and brought it into the light.

When he finally could force his mouth away from the sweet perfection of her breasts and sat up, he hardly recognized the woman lying so helpless on the pillows. Her face was warm with color, her eyes drowsy with pleasure, her lips slightly swollen.

He leaned over her, his black eyes searching as he balanced himself above her, careful not to threaten her with his weight.

But Gaby was in the throes of her first experience of desire. It was only a spark, but the impact of it was shattering. She reached up with trembling hands and began to unbutton his shirt.

"I . . . I want to touch you, too," she whispered apologetically.

"My God, don't apologize," he said huskily. He clenched

his hands beside her head and tried not to groan at the fumbling slowness of her fingers undoing the buttons. Finally, she got them open and tugged his shirt out of the way. Then he felt her hands, and he bit back a curse and shuddered. Even untutored, those soft fingers made him feverishly hungry.

When she lifted, unconsciously seeking a contact that he wanted just as badly, he forgot everything but the fierce need she was kindling. He let his weight down over her and dragged his hair-roughened chest against her breasts in slow, achingly tender patterns that widened her eyes and made her arch up again to make the contact even closer.

"If I give you my weight, are you going to scream?" he whispered roughly.

"No . . ." she whispered uncertainly, because what he was doing to her made her feel oddly weak.

With a harsh sound, he levered down over her, his long legs tangling in hers, his fierce arousal so obvious that it must have been faintly uncomfortable for her with his weight behind it. His mouth searched for hers and opened it, and he held her in an embrace that drove sanity, convention, everything from his mind except the fever of desire.

He moved against her in a way he never had, in an intimacy he never had. She felt him that way and gasped at the explicit motion, the shudder that rippled the heavy, hard muscles of his big body. He was so huge, and she began to grow frightened. He was moving sharply now, his hips grinding down against hers while his mouth demanded something she didn't understand. One lean hand suddenly curved around her upper thigh, and she felt him surge against her with a feeling of frank terror.

"Bowie . . . !" she cried out, stiffening.

He heard the fear in her voice and had hell stopping. She was soft under him, and only a faint layer of fabric stood in his way. He could remove that barrier and drown himself in her. His control was all but gone. But then sanity began to return, and he knew that he couldn't do it. He had to stop. He had to . . .

He forced himself to roll away from her, but he couldn't get off the bed. He lay there in agony, his face contorted with the desire he couldn't express or satisfy, his body arching helplessly, shuddering with its need. His hands clenched in the pillow under his head and he groaned harshly.

Gaby had never seen a man like that. She reached out to touch him and thought better of it. She didn't know what to do. She knew there were things a woman could do, but she didn't know what they were, and she was too shy to ask. She felt terrible guilt at having let it go that far. But it had been so sweet to be held and touched and kissed like that. She hadn't dreamed how quickly it could get out of hand for a man.

"What can I do?" she whispered unsteadily. She was sitting up now, her body still trembling as she stared at him with helpless concern.

"Nothing." His voice sounded unfamiliar. His teeth clenched.

"Bowie," she whispered miserably. She was near tears. She hadn't known that men could be that helpless, that vulnerable. He was obviously in pain, and she couldn't do anything to help.

He jackknifed and managed to drag himself off the bed and into the bathroom. The door slammed behind him and Gaby sat there shivering, too shocked and upset to get dressed. She pulled the cover up to shield her breasts and waited.

Several minutes passed before he came back. He was white in the face, and his hands shook as he lit a cigarette. He sat down heavily on the side of the bed next to her and pulled an empty candy dish on the bedside table toward him to use for an ashtray.

"I think I'll just shoot myself and be done with it," she whispered tearfully. "I hurt you."

He could barely get words out of his tight throat. Subconsciously he'd known that once she started touching him, he wouldn't be able to control his need. She might as well know the truth.

"This is why I've kept my distance," he said heavily. "Inevitably, one day I'll lose my head completely. I almost lost it just now." He searched her eyes. "Gaby, I don't think I could live with myself if something happened against your will. But marriage should be . . ."

"It should be a complete commitment," she said for him. "Physical, as well as emotional. Yes, I know." She lowered her eyes, hurting. She only wished she could tell him why she always drew back at the last minute. Being overpowered was her greatest fear. "Bowie, I think we should break off the engagement."

He stared at her without knowing what to say. That was the last thing he'd expected from her. "Break it off?"

"Yes." She wiped the tears away. "I never dreamed it would hurt you so much to have to draw back, and it will only get worse. I just can't make myself do it, Bowie." Her big, wounded eyes lifted to his, filled with apology and fear. "You know it's for the best. You can't go on like this. You deserve so much more than I can give you."

He couldn't remember ever feeling so helpless. He knew she loved him. It was more than just virginal fear, he was sure of it. There was something she was holding back—something she wasn't telling him. He wished he could make her trust him enough to tell him all of it, but she had to come to that realization herself. In the meantime, he didn't know what to do. He didn't dare pressure her anymore. The hell of it was that she was right about his own limits. He couldn't go on like this, even if he hated admitting it, hated seeing that tragic sadness in her olive-green eyes.

"Are you sure that this is how you want it?" he asked quietly.

"No, but it's how it has to be," she said. She felt like half a woman. The odd thing was that she'd almost wanted him. If only she could get over the past. And it wasn't so much what had happened to her as what had come after it. The violence was what frightened her, much more than the intimacy.

She wished she could tell him the whole story, but he'd hate her. Not only that, the risk was too great. The scandal would be devastating—especially now, with things so unsettled at Casa Río.

"It's just as well that we didn't make an announcement or buy a ring, isn't it?" she said hesitantly.

"I guess so." He ran a big hand through his sweaty hair. "I thought I could make enough concessions—that I could be patient, until you were ready for intimacy. But I've been too long without a woman, and I'm too much a man." He looked up. "I don't mean that in any conceited way. I need a woman. I can't settle for companionship. It would be a disaster to try and suffer a platonic marriage."

"You don't have to explain," she said gently. "I understand. I'm not blaming you. The pattern was set a long, long time ago. I had hoped that I could break it, but I can't." She stared at her hands, clenched on the sheet. "I should go to Phoenix and get my old job back," she began.

"There's no need. You'll be happy enough working down here. I'll be in Tucson during the week, and I've got my own job to keep me busy," he replied. "There's no reason you can't stay at Casa Río. You'll have to, now that you own the biggest part of it."

"I don't want it," she said coldly.

"Aggie wants it." He got up slowly, and his chest rose and fell in a heavy sigh. He'd buttoned the shirt back up, but he could still feel her hands on his chest, the softness of her breasts under it. He groaned inwardly.

"What will we tell Montoya and Tía Elena?" she asked.

"I'll tell them."

He went to the door and glanced back at her with barely contained desire. "It's a hell of a waste, I'll tell you that," he said curtly. "You were made for a man to love."

"In my dreams, I was able to love you," she whispered sadly.

He ground his teeth together to stop from groaning aloud. "Dreams aren't enough for a flesh and blood man," he replied. "I won't stop wanting you."

"You'll find someone else," she said, almost choking on the words.

His black eyes narrowed. "Will I?" He laughed coldly and went out, closing the door behind him.

After that, Gaby threw herself into her work. She enjoyed her job well enough, and it was a godsend that things started heating up during the following week. She didn't have time to dwell on her shattered future.

Bowie went back to his apartment in Tucson for most of the time, appearing at Casa Río just briefly when he was needed to see about ranch business.

Monday, three days before the city council meeting that had been postponed suddenly last week, the agricultural combine called a press conference in Lassiter. The announcement that they were being denied land by a local landowner made statewide headlines and opened a can of worms that polarized the townspeople. Gaby was sent to cover it, because Harvey was conveniently busy. She knew he'd done it deliberately. It was going to be devastating for her to have to deal with the conglomerate now, and Harvey knew it. It was just one more way he was using the job to needle her.

But she went, and she covered the story, and she wrote it

without a single bias. Bob Chalmers loved the article. It was front page, of course. The *Phoenix Advertiser* carried it with her byline and gave credit to the Lassiter paper. Johnny Blake called her personally to ask her to cover the story as it developed, and because Bob knew him and respected him, he agreed to let Gaby do it.

Bowie read the headlines and came home in the middle of the day, breathing fire.

Gaby took one look at his face and knew that she was going to have hell staying in the same country with him now.

He slammed the Phoenix paper down in front of her, where she was sitting on the sofa watching the news while she ate a quick lunch. His big body seemed to vibrate with contained fury.

"What the hell are you trying to do, incite a riot down here?" he asked in that quiet, measured tone that meant bloodshed.

"Bob sent me to cover the story, and he gave me permission to let Johnny Blake have it, since his paper could get it out before ours could," she murmured, averting her eyes to his polished tan boots. She thought inconsequentially how well they contrasted with the pale tan suit he was wearing. "If I hadn't done it, Harvey would have. I gave both sides."

"That's your eternal argument, isn't it, Gaby? Fair coverage. But this is going to stir up a damned hornet's nest!"

"I didn't call the press conference," she protested. She pushed away the plate with her half-eaten sandwich. He sure was hell on the appetite.

"That wasn't a press conference, it was character assassination," he returned. He lit a cigarette. "Now I'm holding up progress, it seems. I'm a one-man reactionary who befriends rattlesnakes and Gila monsters!"

"The environmental people think you're a hero," she said gently. "They've been singing your praises all morning."

She smiled shyly. "I'm doing a whole article on their point of view."

"Great," he muttered. "Just what I need—endorsements from the radical right."

"They aren't radical. They're concerned about habitat and the ecology," she muttered.

He turned, glaring at her. "What are you concerned with?"

She felt under attack. She hated the accusation in Bowie's black eyes, the sense of inadequacy and failure he made her feel. She was subdued these days—a shadow of the woman she had been. And the strange thing was that since she'd seen Bowie like that, vulnerable and in pain, sex had slowly become a natural physical act, not some ritual torture for a man's sole pleasure. Just knowing that Bowie was vulnerable had lessened her fear of him, but it was far too late to tell him now. And she couldn't be sure of her reaction until they went too far, and she hurt him again. She really couldn't put him through that anguish twice.

"I'm concerned with my job, I guess," she said dully. "Nothing more."

"In a few weeks, you'll own controlling interest in Casa Río," he said stiffly. "I suppose the agricultural combine would settle for your twelve thousand acres, if you sold it to them."

She started to protest, to tell him that she'd never dream of cutting the ground out from under him in such a cruel way. But the realization that he believed her capable of it stilled her tongue. How could she deny it without telling him she loved him? Not that he'd believe it now. If she loved him, she wouldn't have pushed him away—that was how he'd look at it.

Her eyes fell to the floor. "Aggie shouldn't have done that," she said. "She wouldn't have, if you hadn't hurt her so badly over Mr. Courtland."

"Damn Mr. Courtland," he said icily. "I've got a few things to say to that gentleman, if I can ever find him. I've got private detectives combing the hills and they haven't turned him up yet."

"Do you realize that we don't know where Aggie is?" she asked suddenly, looking up.

"What do you mean? She's with the Sevrils in Nassau."

She shook her head. "I phoned her last night, to talk. She left there last week and didn't tell anyone where she was going. They don't know where to reach her, either."

He drew in a rough breath. "My God. When it rains, it pours. Well, I'll have the detectives trace her, too. Courtland has turned the world upside down around here."

"Your reaction to him did that," she reminded him. "If you'd kept out of it . . ."

He turned, his eyes blazing. "My mother's welfare is my business."

"Everything seems to be your business," she said sadly. "Work is your whole life—that, and Casa Río. You're going to be just like your father when you get to his age. You're a company man from the head down."

"At least I'm not frozen solid from the head down," he returned with a cool smile.

She didn't flinch, even though it was that kind of blow. "You're right about that," she said with forced gaiety. "At least I'm a good reporter, even if I'm a total failure as a woman."

She got up and picked up her purse. "I have to get back to work."

But as she started past him, he caught her upper arms and held her just in front of him.

"I didn't mean that," he said quietly. His chest rose and fell heavily. "God, I'm lonely, Gaby."

She swallowed. "So am I," she said in a thready whisper.

His big hands brought her against his chest gently and he

wrapped her up, holding her. He closed his eyes and rested his cheek against her high coiffure, feeling at peace for the first time in days. Just having her with him was heaven. He'd never been so miserable or unsettled in all his life, and his temper had become a local legend at the office—all because Gaby didn't want him in bed.

"What are we going to do, baby?" he asked heavily.

"You could find someone else," she suggested bravely.

He only laughed, the sound deep and bitter. "I don't want anyone else. I can't even get aroused by anyone else." His lean hands slid lower and pulled her gently to him, letting her feel his body's instant reaction to her closeness. "This only happens with you, Gaby."

Her arms slid around him and she held him gently. "I love you, Bowie," she whispered softly, closing her eyes against the tears. "I'm sorry I couldn't . . ."

He lifted his head and looked down into her misty eyes. "Say that again," he breathed huskily.

"What, that I love you?" she asked, blushing. "Didn't you know?"

He shook his head. His breath sighed out and one hand came up to touch her face and trace her soft mouth. "My God."

"You mustn't mind," she whispered. "I'll get over it. You need someone who can give you what you need from a woman. You need . . . someone whole."

His hands framed her face and he searched her eyes slowly. "Do you think that makes it any easier," he asked softly, "when I go to bed aching for you every night?"

Her eyes closed painfully. "So do I," she whispered. "I don't know what passion is, but I know what it is to love, now. You can't imagine how I hate myself for what I've done to you."

He bent and put his mouth very gently against hers, loving the way it accepted him, parted for him, adored his touch.

His breath caught at the love in her voice, in her face, her lips. If she loved him, there was still hope. One day, somehow, she might be able to accept him. If he could learn patience and control, and exercise it . . .

"I thought I'd come home for the weekend," he said, lifting his head. "You and I could go sightseeing. There's a place over near Cochise Stronghold where nobody ever goes. We run cattle there in the spring and fall, but it's deserted right now. There are some Hohokam ruins on it. I've never shown them to you."

Her heart lifted as she searched his hard face. "Can you really bear to be around me . . . ?"

His fingers stopped the words. He drew a breath. "After we look at the ruins, we could have a picnic. Sunday, we'll go to church together."

"It isn't because you feel sorry for me, is it?" she asked miserably.

"I feel sorry for both of us, honey," he replied quietly. "Because love is best expressed, for a man, in the act of love. But I'm desperate enough to settle for companionship, if that's all you can offer me." He smiled bitterly. "Don't you know how I feel? Isn't it painfully obvious by now?"

Her heart was going like a trip hammer. The look on his handsome face almost drowned her in tenderness. "You want me," she began.

"A man who feels nothing but desire isn't going to suffer the tortures of the damned just being away from the woman he wants," he said stiffly. "I've driven work crews until they're talking assassination, I've harassed secretaries—I've even tried to pick a fight with one of my gang foremen. He very rightly told me that what I needed to do was go and see the woman who was driving me crazy." He smiled faintly. "So I did. The story was just an excuse." His big shoulders lifted and fell. "I've missed you."

She could have walked on air. The words rippled over her

like magic, and her wide, olive eyes held his without blinking until her toes curled. "I thought I was going to die," she said, trying to smile. But the smile dissolved into tears, and as her lips trembled, his covered them very softly.

He lifted her and sat down with her on the sofa. "Whatever happens, it's you and me," he whispered against her cheek. His lips touched her closed eyelids, sipping away the tears. "If all we do for the rest of our lives is sit and hold hands, that's all right, too."

She really cried then, clinging to his neck, shivering with the anguished pleasure of having his arms around her, feeling his powerful body so close and warm against her. The fragrance of his spicy cologne filled her nostrils, the scent drowning her in sensation as his mouth parted against hers and he began to kiss her with a startling tenderness.

"Don't cry," he whispered.

"I thought you hated me," she mumbled tearfully. "I wanted to run the car over a cliff . . . !"

"And I'd have been two steps behind you," he bit off against her mouth. "My God, don't ask me to try and live without you! I can't bear the thought of it," he groaned.

She couldn't think. His mouth was slow and warm and exquisitely demanding. She lifted her arms around his neck and clung to him clumsily, but he didn't seem to mind. He cared for her. Just knowing it made everything all right, made the world bright with color again. Bowie was the world.

She found his hand and took the cigarette from it, leaning over to toss it into an ashtray.

"Weren't you through with it?" she whispered.

"I didn't even remember that I had it," he whispered back, smiling.

She caught his fingers in hers and brought them gently to her breast, feeling his whole body go taut as she uncurled them against the warm, soft rise.

"I'm going to try, so hard," she whispered, looking up into his black eyes as he held his hand against her body. "Because I don't want to spend the rest of my life as I am, Bowie."

He looked down at the soft blouse where his hand rested. "We can't go as far as we did the other night. I'm afraid to risk it."

"Then, one step at a time," she whispered. "The way you said we would."

He searched her eyes. The love shining out of them made him feel humble. "Gaby . . . could you forgive me, if it ever did go all the way?"

She reached up and touched his hard mouth. "I love you," she said simply. "Of course I could." She nuzzled her forehead against his chin, loving the soft caress of his fingers, the sound of skin against fabric loud in the stillness even though the television was still blaring. She liked the sensations she was feeling, and the fear had already diminished. She smiled. "Bowie . . . I'm sorry I hurt you that time, but it changed things for me."

He kissed her forehead. "How?"

"Because I didn't know that men were vulnerable, too."

He lifted his head, frowning. "What?"

"Well, it was always that loss of control that scared me so," she explained. "But when I realized why you lost control, it put a new perspective on things. You were as helpless as I was, weren't you?"

"I don't damned well like admitting it," he said irritably. "But, yes, I guess men are helpless when they get that hot."

"It made me feel less threatened," she said. "Do you understand? It made everything so much less frightening."

"There's something else you don't know," he replied quietly. "Something you haven't considered."

"About you?"

He shook his head. "About yourself. When a woman is

properly aroused, Gaby," he said, his voice deep and quiet, "she doesn't think. Not about pain, or being overpowered, or anything else except fulfillment."

"What is fulfillment?" she asked, curious.

He let out a breath and actually laughed. "Ask me that when I'm a little calmer, and I'll try to explain it to you. Right now, I have to get back to Tucson. And you have a job to go to yourself."

He got up, putting her on her feet. He didn't even look like the same man who'd barreled into the house an hour ago.

"Even though we disagree," she began, "I'm not trying to tilt the stories in the conglomerate's favor."

"Hell, I know that. Do what you think is right, honey," he said. "I'm not mad at you. I couldn't be. The land is important to me, but just lately I've had a slight adjustment in priorities." He tilted up her chin. "I've decided that Casa Río can go hang if I can have you."

She beamed at him. "Really?!"

He chuckled. "Not completely. I'll still fight to preserve that land. But I'm not going to let it come between us. Do what you please with your half of it, Gaby. I'm not going to lay down any conditions. I'm going to go back and give my gang foreman a raise."

"Will you be here tonight?" she asked hopefully.

He shook his head. "I've got a banquet tonight, and a meeting afterward, and a trip to Texas tomorrow to check with the private detective about Aggie." He grimaced. "Maybe if I can find Courtland, he'll know where she is."

"She was pretty upset when she left," Gaby sighed. "Maybe he is, too."

He smoothed over her nose. His eyes were steady and quiet. "If they felt like I feel, I don't doubt it. I may have made a hell of a big mistake, Gaby. I don't like to think about the grief I could have caused Aggie. She said that love was painful at our ages, when she was warning me about putting Casa Río above you. Now I know what she meant."

"It will all come right, somehow," she said. "You do think she's all right?"

He sighed. "I don't know, but I'm going to move heaven and earth to find her. Are you covering that meeting Thursday night, or is your bosom buddy at work?"

"Harvey isn't my bosom buddy. If they burned me at the stake, he'd cut the firewood."

His eyebrows arched. "You'll win him over. But I'm taking you to the meeting," he added quietly. "I won't have you on these roads at night alone."

"But you can't go to the meeting," she said, worried. "Bowie, it will be a lynch mob!"

"I'll go where I please," he said. "I'm not afraid of a few dissidents."

"But . . ."

"Go to work, honey. I'll come down Thursday, and then I'll stay over the weekend. And for God's sake, stay off the roads at night."

"All right," she said. "You be careful, too."

"Kiss me."

She stood on tiptoe, thrilled at his commanding tone and thread of soft humor under it. She smiled against his hard mouth, loving the way it felt to be at peace with him.

"See you," he whispered. He kissed her back, hungrily, then let her go and walked out without a backward glance. Gaby stared after him with stars in her eyes for a long moment before she could force her legs to carry her out to the car. Despite the turmoil around her, something wonderful had come out of the day.

CHAPTER
Fifteen

Gaby was dressed at five to go to the city council meeting, even though it didn't start until seven thirty. She paced the floor, very trendy in her full circle denim skirt and white silk camisole top and boots. She left her hair long and brushed it until it shone with dark highlights, and put on her best blue earrings. She experimented with makeup, too, because she had so much extra time. She wanted to look her best for Bowie.

She'd halfway expected him to phone the past two nights, but he hadn't. Probably, she reasoned, he'd been too involved with business to think about her. But just remembering the things he'd said and the way he'd looked at her put those thoughts right out of her mind.

Bowie came in a few minutes after she was dressed, looking worn and half angry, but when he saw Gaby, his face lit up and his black eyes smiled.

"Pretty thing," he murmured. "Do you know, Johnny Cash did a song a few years back with June Carter Cash. It was called *Darlin' Companion*, and I don't think I've ever seen anyone it fit better than you, right now."

She beamed and blushed, all at once. "Thank you. Are you going like that?" she asked.

He was wearing gray slacks with a white silk shirt, a beige jacket, and brown tie. His blond head was bare and he looked impossibly handsome. "Will I do?" he asked.

"You'd do if you went in a gunny sack," she sighed. "If there are any women at the council meeting, you'll be raped."

He laughed delightedly at her use of the term without flinching, and impulsively, he picked her up by the waist and put his mouth hard against hers.

He was smudging her lipstick, and she didn't even care. Her hands clung to his nape and she returned the kiss as fully as he gave it, only vaguely aware of a cleared throat behind them.

Bowie reluctantly lifted his head and put her down, glaring at Montoya.

"Well?" he asked curtly.

Montoya grinned. "Supper. You have time to eat before you leave for Lassiter, surely?"

"I was being fed, until you came along and ruined everything," Bowie muttered.

"Now, now," Montoya soothed him, his eyes gleaming at Gaby's delighted face. "Tía Elena has made liver and onions, just for you."

Bowie pursed his lips. "Well, in that case, maybe I can save Gaby for dessert," he compromised, with a soft smile for her.

Gaby slid her hand into his big one. "We're going to a lynching," she told Montoya.

"Yes, I know," the older man said quietly, with a level stare at Bowie. "The rifle is cleaned and loaded, if you want it, and your pistol and holster are in the top drawer of the tallboy in your room."

Bowie nodded, the humor gone from his hard face.

"You can't legally carry a pistol into a gathering of people, even with a permit," she reminded him, cold chills running up her spine at the thought that he might need that pistol.

"I know that. I'll leave it with Bill or Jim at the door."

He glanced at her curiously. "Did you know the police chief and his sergeant were going to be there?"

She smiled shyly. "I asked them to."

He just shook his head. They ate a quick supper, and after Bowie got the pistol, they headed out to the Scorpio. It was dusk, with shadows falling everywhere. A couple of the ranch hands were just pulling up in the ranch pickup, and Gaby turned to wave at them. Something suddenly whizzed past her head and slammed into the palo verde tree overhead. A loud crack sounded in the stillness, and she was suddenly caught and thrown down by Bowie's big body.

He said something unprintable and whipped his pistol out of the holster under his arm. He cocked it and rolled away from a shaking, white-faced Gaby to level it and fire twice after a white blur. Tires squealed on sand and a dust trail rose behind the vehicle as it weaved violently down the driveway.

"Get after him!" Bowie yelled at the cowboys in the pickup. "Shoot back if you have to!"

"You bet, boss!" One of them was already pulling the shotgun out of the rifle rack behind his head as the other man wheeled the pickup around and shot off in the direction the sniper had taken.

Gaby was remembering another shootout—one in which she'd been slightly wounded. It brought back some sickening memories, and she couldn't seem to stop shaking. She was aware of Bowie's hard arms around her, his lean hands faintly trembling as they went over her.

"My God, are you all right?" he demanded quickly, his eyes wild and fiercely concerned.

"Yes, I'm fine," she whispered, trying to smile. "I'm just a little shaky. How about you?" She touched him hesitantly, her eyes all over him, looking for marks. It was just dawning on her how very dangerous this situation was. He could have been killed. Because he had a firm opinion and had stuck to it, he'd actually been shot at. He could have died right here, over a few thousand acres of land! How did dust and water compare to a man's life?

He helped her to her feet and wrapped her up tightly in his arms, his blond head bent over her dark one, his big body trembling with belated terror as he realized how close the bullet had come to her pretty head. He couldn't bear the thought.

Montoya and Tía Elena came running from the house, so excited and frightened that they were incoherent in Spanish. Bowie answered them in that same tongue, his deep, measured tones contrasting with the fine tremor in the arms holding Gaby.

"¡*Dios mio*!" Montoya crossed himself. "Look where the bullet hit." He moved toward the green trunk of the palo verde tree, the bark visibly torn from the impact of the bullet.

Bowie drew Gaby along with him and looked at it. "Leave it there," he said. "I want the sheriff to see it. His boys can dig it out and do a ballistics test if my men can run down the yellow-bellied coward who fired it."

"The meeting," Gaby said huskily. She looked up at Bowie, her face still pinched and pale. "I have to go."

"Hell, yes, we do," he agreed, fear giving way to the same anger she was feeling. "Backing down now would be the biggest mistake I ever made."

"No!" she moaned. "Bowie, you can't! Don't you realize that he tried to kill you? It isn't worth it; it isn't worth this . . . !"

He shook her gently. "Stop that. I won't live in fear. Nobody is going to take away my right to decide what I do with my land—not with words, not with a bullet. And shame on you for asking me to back down. You're still shaking, but you're game, aren't you? You'll go to the meeting anyway, won't you?"

"Of course," she agreed unsteadily. "It's my job. But I want combat pay down at the office," she added with a ragged attempt at humor.

He searched her pale face. "Sure you're okay?"

She nodded.

"Then let's go. Maybe we can catch the pickup."

"Be careful!" Montoya called after them as he watched Bowie put Gaby in the car and then climb in beside her.

He threw up a hand and roared off down the long, dusty drive to the main road.

There was a dust cloud far in the distance. Gaby watched it with a sinking feeling of nausea. She didn't really want Bowie to catch up with his assailant—not if it meant he could be hurt. She hadn't realized how volatile the situation was becoming in Lassiter, and now it looked as though her determination to keep the story in the public eye might have led to what happened. Publicity and controversy always fanned hot tempers. If something happened to Bowie, she'd have to live with the knowledge that she could have been a party to it, however innocently. She looked across at him while he drove, his hands rocksteady on the wheel, his eyes intent on the road. Her world, she thought shakily, and she could lose him to a bullet. Her eyes closed on the sick thought. Now he was going with her to a meeting where he'd be the main dish on the menu. He was risking his life to protect her. If that wasn't love, she thought wonderingly, she didn't know what was. And she'd broken off the engagement over a comparatively little thing like physical reticence. She could have groaned. His feelings were only beginning to impact in her mind. He loved her. He was risking everything for her. Couldn't she find it in her own heart to take the same risk for him, in a different way? She had to get past the scars. She had to!

Bowie's booted foot pressed down on the accelerator, throwing up an even bigger dust cloud behind them on the wide, sandy road. Many back roads in this part of the state were unpaved, but the roads were well-kept and incredibly wide, making them easy to travel. They were almost to Lassiter when they caught up with the ranch pickup.

"We lost him, boss," the man in the passenger side said, "but we put a bullet in his spare tire. He was driving one of those four-by-fours—a white one. You tell the police chief we creamed the cover over his tire, too. He won't be hard to spot!"

"Sure thing. Thanks, boys. I'll see to it that your next check reflects my appreciation." Bowie grinned.

"Say, thanks!" they chorused.

He pulled out and drove on into Lassiter. The city hall was overflowing. The parking lot was already full, but there was no white four-by-four to be seen.

Bowie and Gaby went inside and found seats. Few people knew Bowie on sight, but he was getting a warm welcome from a few unattached females, and even from some attached ones. He sighed angrily at the unwanted attention, until Gaby slid her hand into his and calmed him down magically with a smile.

Only when Mayor White opened the meeting did the buzzing of voices stop. There were so many people in the big room that it was hotter than the devil. It wasn't the sweetest aroma in the world, either, because a lot of the people had just come from local ranches and jobs and they smelled like it.

Gaby got out her tape recorder and her pad and pen, and took a few quick shots with her .35 mm camera to show the size of the angry crowd. She hated this type of meeting, where emotions ran high and tempers flared.

Alvin Barry was on the front row—the real estate agent who was the front man for the agricultural syndicate. Sitting with him was Jess Logan, the acquisition man for Bio-Ag, and beside him was a man who looked oddly familiar. Gaby was sure she'd seen him somewhere before.

"The first order of business is an announcement about a new industry for Lassiter—or a proposed new business for Lassiter," Mayor White began, with a pointed glare at Bowie. "I'd like to introduce Mr. Alvin Barry, of Barry Land Company; Mr. Jess Logan, acquisition agent for the Bio-Ag Corporation; and Mr. Terrance Samuels, the vice-president of Bio-Ag, who's come all the way from Los Angeles to talk to us about his proposed enterprise here in the valley."

"Thank you," Samuels said with a big grin. He got up and went to the podium where the mayor was standing. "I've met a lot of you in recent weeks," he told the crowd, "and hope to meet a lot more. We have some big plans for Lassiter, and I'd like to share them with you. Our corporate engineer, Mr. Bill Frazier, was supposed to have come with us, but he had to deal with a problem that cropped up in our newest project in Texas. Mr. Logan and I have brought some charts and maps with us, and some projections. I'd like to give those to you now, if I may."

Mayor White nodded, smiling. Gaby knew at once that he'd probably been the major force behind Bio-Ag's desire to locate here. The mayor was known for his gung-ho efforts to recruit industry. Only two years before, he'd tried to locate a nuclear waste dump nearby, until the environmentalists had fought him to a standstill. He was much more concerned with raising the tax base than he was concerned for the environment. Not a conservationist himself, he couldn't understand anyone who preferred barren land to fat industry.

"I've heard of that man," Bowie said coldly.

Gaby's eyebrows arched. "Him, and not his company?"

He shook his head. "I don't remember. I just remember the name. There was an article about him in one of the cattlemen's bulletins I subscribe to. Not favorable, I think."

There was an interesting tidbit. Gaby made a quick note, which she didn't let Bowie see, and turned her attention back to what Mr. Logan was saying.

He had convincing statistics, but he said nothing about water, she noticed. Nothing about the ecology. Nothing about contaminants. Nothing about laser leveling. And most damning, nothing about the kind of crops he intended planting.

At the end of the presentation, Mr. Logan cautiously threw the floor open for questions, but nobody was asking any.

Bowie leaned back with deceptive laziness and lifted one big hand.

"Yes, sir?" Mr. Logan smiled, because he didn't know who Bowie was.

"What kind of crops do you plan to maintain here—assuming that you can get the land you want. I'm sure you know that water is becoming a dangerous issue here in the desert, and that we have some areas near Lassiter where you'd have to drill over five hundred feet to even hit the aquifer."

"Oh, the land we're looking at has water barely a hundred feet down," Mr. Logan assured him. "And we're positive that we can talk the landowner into selling to us. It's just a matter of persistence . . ."

"And a bullet?" Bowie stood up, and there were some quiet mutterings nearby. "Because the land you're discussing is my land. And not an hour ago, someone in a white four-by-four put a bullet two inches from Gaby Cane's head."

There were mingled gasps and frank outrage from some of the spectators. The mayor was stunned.

"That's not true," the mayor said. "Bowie, nobody here would shoot at Gaby..."

"He was shooting at me, but he damned near hit Gaby," Bowie returned, his black eyes level and cold. His cobra look, Gaby thought with faint amusement. The mayor shifted restlessly under it. "The bullet lodged in a palo verde tree just outside the house. One of the policemen has gone to dig it out and have a ballistic check run on it." Bowie smiled coldly. "I'll have something to say to the poor marksman who fired it, and so will my attorney, when we find him. The police, of course, have first claim on his time. Attempted murder is a crime, I'm told."

A white-faced man whom Gaby recognized as a local farmer out of work stood up. "Did you say a white four-by-four?" he asked huskily.

Bowie stared at him. "That's right, McHaney," he returned coldly. "Just like the one your oldest son drives. And if the police find a spare tire with a shotgun blast through it on that truck, your son is going to find himself in one hell of a mess."

"Riley wouldn't," he said heavily. "He just wouldn't!"

"Good for Riley!" one of the younger men piped up. "We need jobs here in Lassiter, not desert!"

"Do we need them badly enough to kill for them?" came a quiet, feminine voice from nearby. "Tell me that, Jake Marlowe," she added. "Well, do we?"

The man sat back down, glowering at her.

"Now, now," the mayor said. "This can't turn into a slinging match. We're here to discuss how the town can help."

"The town could help the most by not involving itself in a plot to force landowners to sell their land," Bowie told him coldly. "Now, let me ask you something. You're free and easy with the water on my land, but the aquifer here is dropping, and we're in trouble. You've already got a ban on outdoor watering. You tell me what you're going to do when you find that aquifer being pulled down even more by a huge conglomerate that depends on enormous stores of groundwater. What about herbicides and pesticides contaminating that fragile water store? What about the erosion that's going to result from wholesale tilling of dry soil when the topsoil starts blowing away? What about the damage to the ecology and the threat to ranchers and housing developments and tourist areas?"

"That's right!" Mrs. Lopez seconded, standing. "Let me show you these photographs." She held them up and explained them.

She was only the first; there were others. The ecology societies had representatives, who seconded Bowie's concerns, outnumbering the venomous people who wanted those jobs Bio-Ag would provide without counting the cost.

It very nearly became a riot, but the police calmed it down, and the mayor finally adjourned because not one item of regular business could be heard. He mumbled something about a meeting to discuss raised water rates and new contracts for police cars and grading, but he didn't make another sound in Bio-Ag's favor.

Mr. Logan came up to Bowie outside, after the meeting. "I just wanted to tell you that I'm genuinely sorry about the attempted shooting," he said, and meant it. "I wouldn't have bloodshed over this thing for the world. We really think we can help the local economy. I wish you'd talk to us, and give us a chance to explain our position. Miss Cane changed her mind when she heard me out."

Bowie glanced at Gaby and then back to Mr. Logan. "Gaby will have controlling interest in Casa Río in a few weeks," he said. "You can always try to coax her out of her part, but I'll warn you that the water is on my part," he added dryly, "and I won't sell. I've heard of your Mr. Samuels. I'm twice as determined now to hold on to my water rights. You can tell him I said so."

Mr. Logan frowned. "I don't understand."

"How long have you been with Bio-Ag?" he asked Logan levelly.

"Well, for about six months . . ."

"I suggest you find out a little something about your employer, Mr. Logan," Bowie said quietly. "You need to know exactly what you're fighting for. And now, you tell me what kind of crops you mean to plant, or I'll go to the media."

Mr. Logan swallowed. "I don't know," he confessed. "Mr. Samuels won't say. He keeps mentioning soil surveys and studies."

"I'll bet you ten to one he's planning to plant cotton on that land," Bowie said, surprising even Gaby. "Cotton is what it's best suited for. It takes more water than you'd believe to irrigate that crop, and it exhausts the soil and lowers the aquifer. If you don't believe that, you look at the soil studies back in the southeast, where cotton was grown until it wore out the ground it was planted in. It's a good cash crop for a quick profit, but it's devastating in the long run. It has to be extensively sprayed, and you won't need a handful of people to take care of it. You understand me? You're talking about one or two combines and few trucks—that's all. That will do the economy about as much good as opening a laundry here."

"I'm sure Mr. Samuels has good intentions. You might speak to him . . . oh, there he goes," he sighed, nodding toward the gray Mercedes that was just pulling out of the parking lot and speeding away.

"He won't speak to me," Bowie said. "He knows what I have to say. Good evening, Mr. Logan." He caught Gaby's arm and led her to the Scorpio.

"Do you mind?" she laughed breathlessly. "I wanted to talk to him."

"You can talk to him later, honey. I want to see about that bullet. By God, if it was McHaney's son, I'll beat the hell out of him! He could have hit you."

She was frightened and delighted at his reaction. "I'm okay. It was you I was worried about. Bowie, it's going to get worse. You won't even consider selling?"

"Not now," he replied as he cranked the car, his face set in determined lines. "I'll be damned if I'll be intimidated by bullets, or public opposition, or anything else."

She leaned her head back against the headrest and sighed.

The police found the man who took the shot—and it was McHaney's eldest son, Riley, a wild boy with a quick temper. Gaby felt rather sorry for the old man, because he was a hard worker. But the boy should have known better than to try such a stupid thing, and on Bowie, of all people.

She set up the story for the next week's edition, and then she began to make telephone calls. She'd been given blanket permission from Bob to do that while she checked out the Bio-Ag story. She played on every source she could think of, finally calling the *Phoenix Advertiser* and going directly to Johnny Blake.

She explained the problem and he promised to see what he could find out and get back to her.

She didn't even realize that she'd worked right through lunch. Bowie had gone back to Tucson late the night before, worried and scowling, his reluctance to leave obvious as he kissed Gaby good night and made her promise not to venture out after dark until he was back on the weekend. She knew that if he hadn't had an early morning meeting in Phoenix, he'd never have left her. Besides, they had a new closeness that alleviated all her fears. The only thing she was worried about now was Bio-Ag.

Three hours after lunch, she was poring over every bit of information she'd gleaned on Bio-Ag and waiting for phone calls to be returned. It was Friday, so she had to hurry before everything closed for the weekend. She had hardly missed lunch, so she was surprised to find Harvey, of all people, standing at her desk with half a ham sandwich in his pudgy hand.

"You haven't eaten," he said gruffly. He put the sandwich down and walked out, without a word.

She was touched beyond words. Amazing, when he was doing everything he could to make life hard for her, that he'd do such a thing. She frowned at the sandwich, wondering if maybe he'd put a poisonous mushroom in it, or sprinkled it with arsenic. But hunger got the best of her and she ate it, washing it down with lukewarm coffee.

She stopped by his office on the way out. "Thanks for the sandwich," she said hesitantly. "I know you don't want me here, and I'm sorry, but I wasn't really trying to foul up your job, you know." She shrugged helplessly. "I just wanted to be near Bowie, because we were engaged. I broke off the engagement, but Bowie's mother had already split the property between us. Now I'm staying to sort of look after my half. I've burnt my bridges in Phoenix. I don't have a place to go back to."

Harvey shifted uncomfortably. "It isn't that I mind your being here," he said after a minute, and a ruddy flush moved over his cheeks. "Bob made a big fuss over you, and I had visions of being tossed out on my ear," he confessed.

"How silly," she told him. "You're a marvelous reporter, even if you don't like controversy that much. You're great on politics and think pieces, and you get along well with local officeholders. They'll tell you things that they won't tell me."

He nodded. "Sometimes." He pursed his lips. "Has it occurred to you that Bowie may have a valid point about the agricultural project?"

"More and more," she agreed. "Especially after he got shot at. I'm digging as deeply as I can. I've got one contact in Colorado who thought he remembered a company with a similar name causing some trouble up there," she added. "And another contact is looking down in south Texas for me. But I don't have much time."

He frowned. "I've got some contacts of my own. Could I help?"

She grinned. "Would you? That would be super, Harvey."

"I'll do what I can," he promised. "Actually, I'm in agreement with your... with Bowie. I talked to a friend of mine at the U.S. Soil Conservation Service office across the mountain." He pulled his pad closer and began to decipher his notes for Gaby.

There was a big cotton growing operation in the area some years ago, he said, and water in the wells was falling five feet per year because of the increased usage. There was also a possibility that water pollution from fertilizers, pesticides, and herbicides could get into the San Pedro and into the shallow aquifer. There was, as he already knew, no reliable surface water for irrigation, so it would have to come from wells, and they required a permit.

"That could be a way out," Harvey told her. "If worst comes to worst, the opposition could protest the permit."

"There are plenty of wells on Casa Río property," she told him, "although Bowie uses them for his livestock. But they might require more than he's pumping if they had wholesale irrigation. Okay, what about efficiency if they don't use tail-water from a pit and reuse it for irrigation?"

He grimaced. "Fifty percent. In some instances, only twenty-five."

"Then, why do they want the land?" she persisted. "Just

for the water rights? Or could there be some more unsavory purpose?"

"There are outfits that buy up land as sites for dumping toxic wastes," he reminded her. "There are others that buy it as a front for some potential polluter. There are still others that purport to plant cotton and then go after government subsidies to keep from having to plant it."

She whistled. "I don't like this."

"Neither do I. What are we going to do about it?"

She grinned. "Get on the telephone," she said.

"You bet," he said, and grinned back.

She went back to her office and started phoning. It looked like she and Harvey just might make a team yet.

CHAPTER
Sixteen

By quitting time, Gaby was frustrated and gnawing her lips numb. She couldn't pin anyone down on anything. One of her contacts in Texas had suspicions, but it was going to require some deep checking into legal action, which meant spending the better part of a morning in the county courthouse poring over old newspaper stories in the bound editions of the county organ—the weekly newspaper there.

Her other contact in Colorado had drawn a temporary blank and had been sent out of town to cover a breaking story in California. She'd hoped to wrap it up over the weekend, and now she was back to first base. Harvey hadn't had any more luck than she had, unfortunately. If there was any free time this weekend, she had one more card to play. She'd managed to get the home telephone number of the prosecuting attorney in the small Texas town where Bio-Ag had last reported an operation. None of the new officials knew anything, but the then-district attorney might. She'd tried the number, only to be told that he was out of town until Sunday. Good enough. She'd try him then, and hope for the best.

Bowie came in very late Friday night. Gaby had been lying awake, worrying over Bio-Ag and the continuing controversy in town over the project. She worried about Bowie, even if he refused to worry about himself. Some of that concern was centered on Aggie, too. Aggie had looked bad when she had left, and Gaby still hadn't managed to track her down. She'd tried calling the people in Nassau with whom the older woman had been staying, but they hadn't heard from her, either.

It was one thing after another, Gaby thought miserably— broken engagements, her helpless fear of the past catching up with her, the unreasonable fear of intimacy that had cost her Bowie, the attempted shooting, the controversy over land use, Bowie's new tenderness with her that might only be pity, and Aggie's continuing absence. It was a good thing that she wasn't prone to ulcers, she told herself.

There was a faint tap at the door and Bowie came in, smiling at the picture she made sitting up in bed in her pale blue negligee, with her dark hair around her shoulders as she halfheartedly scanned the pages of a new novel.

He was wearing gray slacks, and his white shirt was open down the front, as if he'd just come in and was starting to get ready for bed.

"I thought I'd say good night," he mused. "Unless you'd rather I called it from the doorway?"

She smiled shyly. "Well, no, I wouldn't," she said.

He sat down beside her, casually eyeing the book before he tossed it aside on the coverlet. "Any trouble today?" he asked, his black eyes narrowed.

She shook her head. "Not really, except that old man McHaney's son was arrested and bail hasn't been set."

"I didn't want him arrested," he murmured. "I wanted ten minutes alone with him."

"He missed," she reminded him.

"By an inch." He sighed heavily. "Heard from Aggie?"

"No. Have you?"

He laughed gently. "Would she be likely to call me? The whole thing's my fault."

"Not really. They just disagreed." Her fingers touched his big hand where it rested on the bed. She loved its very bigness, its lean strength. "Sometimes people can't work things out, even when they love each other," she said wistfully.

"Like us?" He sighed, closing his fingers around hers. His dark eyes slid over her face like a caress, and he brought her hand gently to his mouth. "I wish I could go back in time," he mused softly. "And that it was my family your father had worked for. I wish I'd found you in the barn. I wouldn't have been drunk, and you'd have been secretly in love with me. Of course, you'd have had to be three or four years older than fifteen at the time." He brushed his lips over her palm, feeling her finger curl with pleasure. "I'd have taken you into one of the empty stalls—there would have been plenty of clean, fresh, unbriared hay, since we're imagining," he grinned. "And then I'd have undressed you, very, very slowly." The smile faded as his eyes cut into her fascinated ones. "I'd have shown you what physical pleasure was long before I took off my own clothes. And then," he breathed, bending toward her mouth, "I'd have eased you down into the hay and tasted you with my mouth until you began to moan, and then to twist under me, and then to cry out with the anguish for fulfillment." His lips touched her trembling ones, his voice deep and slow and soft in the stillness. "I'd have put my mouth against yours, just like this, Gaby," he breathed, fitting it to hers. "And then I'd have done this to you, with my body. . ."

His tongue went slowly, silkily into her mouth and she moaned. The words had been arousing, but the gentle, deep thrust of his tongue was so graphic that it was like possession. Her brows drew together and her body went rigid with unexpected desire as his hands slid under her shoulder straps. He half lifted her and slowly peeled the gown away. She felt his hands, gentle on her bare breasts. He was kindling a fever in her skin, in her mind.

Her fingers stroked his thick, cool hair and speared into its softness with helpless pleasure. She lifted up against his hands, savoring their expert tenderness on her body. She opened her mouth to admit an even deeper penetration from his tongue, and heard him groan softly.

She whispered his name, her old fears forgotten in her first flush of real desire. It was more than a spark this time. It was a fierce, urgent need that made her body move restlessly under the soft caress of his hands. She felt him sliding the gown around her hips and down her legs, but it was more a relief than a threat. It was sweet to feel the cool air on her heated flesh, to feel his hands smoothing over her soft skin.

"Sweet," he breathed against her swollen lips. "You're so sweet, Gaby."

She pulled his mouth down to hers again, hungry for its hard pressure. She hardly felt what he was doing until his fingers slid down her soft belly, and then it was suddenly too late to protest.

His mouth caught the first frightened cry and lazily stilled it, his touch sure and swift and determined. He felt her begin to move with him, and when he was certain of her response, he lifted his head to look at her face.

"Don't be afraid," he whispered, because there were remnants of fear in her eyes, despite her shivering helplessness and the rhythmic gasps that were pulsing out of her throat. "I want you to feel it," he breathed, bending again to her parted lips, feeling the excitement trembling in them as his own mouth lay gently against them. "I want you to feel it shuddering through your body like flame."

She felt her nails digging into his shoulders with a sense of shock, because there was a faint violence building in her, along with a tension that stretched her helpless body into unbearable torment. She couldn't breathe. He seemed to know that, because his mouth lifted and smoothed down over her taut breasts, stroking them as tenderly as his hand was working its magic.

When he felt her sudden rigidity and heard the shocked little cry that was torn from her throat, he smiled against her breast. He wanted to look, but that might have embarrassed her.

She clung to him, crying softly, tears softly tumbling down her cheeks. He lifted his head when he heard her. His mouth smoothed the tears away, tenderly caressing her flushed face and neck, comforting her.

"Oh, Bowie," she whispered tearfully. She couldn't meet his eyes. She buried her face in his warm throat and clung to him, feeling his big body stretch out beside her, his arms around her, holding her close.

"That's what you were afraid of," he said softly. "It isn't so very terrifying now, is it?"

"But it wasn't . . . all the way," she whispered.

"All the way is just like that, Gaby," he murmured against her throat, "except that I'll have to hurt you just a little, the first time. You're very much a virgin."

"I wouldn't have felt pain," she whispered, spellbound by what she'd experienced. "My goodness, I wouldn't have felt a bullet . . . !"

"I know." He rolled over onto his back with a heavy sigh, bringing her gently closer against his side. "I didn't want to shock you, but I thought it might help if you understood what lovemaking is like."

She was hardly breathing at all. "Would it feel like that?"

"Eventually. I won't lie to you. At first you're going to be uncomfortable, and there may not be a great deal of pleasure."

Her cheek moved onto his hair-roughened chest. "Show me," she whispered, surprised at her own forwardness.

He chuckled softly. "No. Not tonight. Petting is one thing, sex is something else."

She lifted her head and searched his face. "I don't understand."

"I don't have anything with me," he explained. "Sweetheart, I could make you pregnant."

Arrows of feeling penetrated her skin, sensation piling on sensation. She thought of a small boy with blond hair and black eyes, and his father laughing as he wrestled with him in front of the television. Her eyes grew soft with longing. She'd never had much of a childhood, and neither had Bowie, but their child would be wanted and loved.

"We could have a son," she said quietly. She smiled. "And maybe a daughter, too. We could give them the love we never really had from our parents."

That was a profound thought. He raised up and eased her onto her back to look down at her intently. "Do you want them enough to give yourself to me?"

"We won't know until we try," she whispered.

He was tempted. He wanted her beyond all reason. But despite what she'd felt with him, there was every chance that she would draw back at the last minute. It wouldn't be good for her when they began, and he could scar her even more if she tried to stop him and couldn't. He knew his own limitations. He was on fire for her now, but he didn't dare take the chance.

"Not tonight, honey," he said softly. "Let's go easy."

She didn't know if she was relieved or disappointed. She stared up at him with plain confusion until he smiled and kissed her gently, before getting to his feet.

He looked down at her with soft, loving eyes. She realized only then that she was completely bare and gasped, seizing her gown to hold it in front of her.

"So shy," he murmured softly. "And after what we did."

She colored. "Shame on you."

"You loved it," he said with pure male malice. He bent and kissed her roughly. "You're going to love what comes next, too, but I'm going to make you wait for that. We'll go sightseeing in the morning, so get to bed."

"Sightseeing?"

"Out to the old camp," he reminded her. "To see the ruins." His black eyes twinkled. "And make love on one of those big, smooth boulders . . . ?"

"Someone would see us," she murmured, blushing.

"Not there, they wouldn't," he chuckled. "It's as remote as the moon during the summer. And it's on our land, so tourists don't stray past the 'No Trespassing' signs."

She wasn't certain if he was serious or not, but she didn't press it. Her body still ached with what he'd done to it, and she tingled from head to toe with new knowledge of him and herself. She smiled at him as he went out the door, delighted to find that she hadn't thought about the past even once.

"Bowie?"

He paused with the doorknob in his hand. "What?"

"What about you?" she asked hesitantly, worried.

"I'm fine," he said firmly, and managed a smile. "Go to sleep."

She slid her gown back on when he was gone, and despite a faint niggling of shame at the freedom she'd given him with her body, she couldn't help but delight in the promise of womanhood. She'd never dreamed such sensations were possible, but what she'd felt with Bowie gave her hope. If that was what possession felt like, then it was nothing to be afraid of—except that she might become addicted to it.

The next morning, Montoya packed them a picnic lunch and they headed out toward the canyon.

"What about Aggie?" Gaby asked worriedly. She was

wearing jeans and a gray pullover knit top with her Western straw hat and boots.

Bowie glanced at her with a grin. He was wearing jeans and a cream-colored Western shirt with his own hat and boots, and he looked as Western as a rodeo. "Aggie will turn up. The private detective still hasn't come up with Courtland, but he's more hopeful about Aggie. The one piece of information he delved was that Courtland didn't register under that name on the cruise. The next step is to check out the passenger list. We know his age, so that eliminates a good many of them."

"I hope we can find Aggie," she replied. "Although it would be interesting to find out who Mr. Courtland really is."

"That it would." He turned on the radio, deep in thought, as they drove the miles to the box canyon.

There was something new—a chain across the small trail that led into the canyon. Bowie unlocked the gate, drove the truck through it, and locked it back again.

"I don't want anyone in here defacing the ruins," he explained. "Now this, little one, is what your friends at Bio-Ag want to level and plant."

He drove down a long, flat plain that led to the small mountain chain rising right off the desert floor. There was creosote and agave and ocotillo at first, and then mesquite, palo verde, cottonwood, and oak trees leading back to the increasingly dense vegetation of the mountains. He pulled off the road at a grouping of huge, smooth rocks.

"It reminds me of Texas Canyon," she remarked. "Although that's much farther away."

"It reminds me of Cochise Stronghold," he returned, helping her out of the truck, "which is much closer. I wouldn't be a bit surprised if Cochise and his band spent time here, too. Come on."

He took her by the hand and led her through the rocks to

the ruins of an ancient camp. "There isn't a lot left," he said, indicating adobe walls and scattered artifacts. "I've done some digging here, and I've let some archaeologists putter around, but I won't allow anything to be carried away. The Hohokam were here before any of us—even the Pima and Tohono O'odham. They were the ancients. They had the most sophisticated irrigation systems in existence in their time period, and elegant philosophies about life, and time, and the equality of the spirit."

She smiled, touching one of the walls. "I remember hearing you talk once about their priests—men who lived in places where the 'white winds' blew. They were very poetic, weren't they?"

"Yes. They had a simple philosophy—that you mustn't harm your brother in any way, for any reason, even an innocent one. Life was to be lived so that you didn't disturb the fabric of it, by anger or evil." He smiled. "They had a strong sense of democracy as well. Even the rich and powerful had houses only a little bigger than the others. They were special people. This is one of the last ruins left on private property. I'd hate like hell to see it go down for a cotton field."

"I can understand that," she said, forcing herself not to say one word about Bio-Ag.

He turned and looked down at her. "Gaby, do you know what used to sit in that grove of trees?"

She gazed toward where he was pointing. "No."

"A small house that once served as a wayside inn for the Overland Stage. I don't have to tell you about the people who passed through this area in the late 1800s. The owner kept a diary, and two pages of it told about a visit he had from the Earps and Doc Holliday soon after Virgil Earp was gunned down in Tombstone."

"I didn't remember that," she confessed.

"There are two big palo verde trees through here that were used by my great-great-grandfather to lynch rustlers in past times," he added. "And it was here that he made a peace treaty with the Apache when they joined forces to fight Mexican bandits who were raiding the area."

"I can see the historical aspects," she agreed. "But, Bowie, there's so little left . . ."

"Is there?" He turned her around and stood behind her, with his big hands on her waist. "Close your eyes and listen."

She humored him, but all she heard were natural sounds. "I hear the wind," she murmured. "And birds. Tree limbs brushing against each other. I think I heard a cactus wren . . ."

"That's what I mean. Civilization hasn't impacted here. This is natural, just the way it was a hundred years ago. It's untouched. The water from the spring that flows down the mountain is pure and clean and unpolluted. The groundwater below us is the same way." He turned her around to face him. "This is our children's heritage, Gaby. Do you want to see it leveled for a quick profit, and all this," he waved a long arm toward the unspoiled beauty, "destroyed forever?"

That was a hard question. She moved away from him, to sit on one of the big boulders. It was smooth and very comfortable, warm from the sun but not directly in it, because it was shaded by a big juniper tree.

"I like this rock," she hedged, because she didn't want to argue with him. She probably wouldn't be able to sell her land to Bio-Ag, because she was more distrustful of them by the day. But she didn't want to talk about Bio-Ag today— she just wanted to be with Bowie.

She closed her eyes and drank in the air, then opened them to savor the solitude. The path they'd driven down led into a box canyon, where trees grew thick beside a trickle of a stream, and huge, smooth boulders surrounded a small pool where water trickled down from the mountains.

"It's beautiful," Gaby enthused.

"It was a good place for the Apache to camp, too," he murmured, sliding onto the big flat rock beside her. "There was water for the horses and the people, a good level place to set up wickiups." He smiled at Gaby. "Do you see those depressions in the stones? They were used by the women to grind corn into meal."

"Fascinating." She leaned over to rub her hand over one and felt Bowie move suddenly, easing her onto her back on the sun-warmed stone. It wasn't terribly hard on her back, and it seemed to curve to her spine as she lay there, looking up at him, his head blocking out the sun as its rays turned his hair to spun gold.

"And very likely, when they weren't using them to pound corn, beat clothes, or dry rawhide and pemmican," he said softly, balancing his weight over her on his arms, "they made love here."

Her lips parted. "Here?"

He eased one powerful long leg in between both of hers so slowly and lazily that she was left without a protest, especially when his mouth moved down to whisper over hers and tease her lips apart.

The sun beat down on them, and the wind whispered around them. She lifted her arms to his neck and let his broad chest settle over her soft breasts, glad that she hadn't worn a bra so that she could feel the hard, warm muscles of his chest in almost direct contact with her skin. The two thin layers of fabric were hardly noticeable. He was careful with her, conscious of his size and her slenderness, keeping his body poised so that she didn't have to take the brunt of his weight.

His lean hands slid under her tank top and onto her rib cage. His head lifted, so that he could see her eyes. "We did more than this last night. I want to touch you that way again, very badly."

"Yes. I want it, too," she whispered huskily. And she did.

She'd dreamed of him, of what he'd done to her, all night. And all morning she'd ached with the need to feel those sweet, new sensations all over again. She was breathing unsteadily already, but she didn't want him to stop. Her eyes searched his black ones. "I dreamed of you," she breathed.

"Did you?" He smiled. "I dreamed of you, too."

His eyes held hers as one hand smoothly tugged up the tank top and peeled it away from her body. Even then, he didn't look. His hand slid to her waist and unfastened first her belt and then the snap and zipper of her jeans. He eased them away while she lay helplessly watching him, in thrall to a need so new and devastating that she could only give in to it.

His hand found her and she gasped and gave in all at once, so in thrall to him that she wasn't capable of even the slightest protest.

"It's all right," he said gently, and his dark eyes smiled at her. He touched her and watched her force her body to lie still, to permit the intimacy. "No one will see us."

"Oh, Bowie," she whispered, her face contorting as the pleasure came more swiftly this time because her body was familiar with it.

His fingers moved suddenly and his eyes were quiet with a new knowledge of her. "Yes. I know." He slid one arm under her head to pillow her neck while the other hand teased gently until she gasped. "Lie still," he whispered. His mouth brushed hers, tasting her tiny cries as he built the tension, second by exquisite second. When she was shuddering, her lifted his head to watch her expression. As it began to contort and her cries became frantic, he leaned over her and increased the pressure delicately. Her eyes widened, her face stilled, and she cried out piercingly in the stillness. Her body lifted and fell in the throes of her fulfillment.

He gathered her up against him and rocked her, smiling at the feel of her soft breasts against his chest through the fabric. But it wasn't enough. While she was trembling back to reality, he unfastened his shirt lazily and drew her inside it, loving the sensation her soft breasts sent through him as they crushed against his hard chest.

"Bowie?" she whispered, lifting her shocked, shy eyes to his.

"I want more," he whispered back, brushing his mouth against hers as he pressed her back against the rock again and slowly kissed his way down her body. All the while, he was removing fabric, baring her to his eyes and his lips and his seeking hands.

He pulled off his boots and his shirt and then, while she watched, astonished, his jeans and everything under them. He turned to let her look at him, enjoying the feel of her eyes on his body.

"You're beautiful," she whispered, lifting her rapt eyes from his body to his face. She was amazed that his arousal didn't frighten her.

"Not as beautiful as you are, Gaby," he said. He eased onto the rock beside her, drawing her body slowly to his in a sunburst of sensation that made her gasp as she felt all the differences between his flesh and hers in the intimacy of the embrace.

"Bowie!" she gasped, clinging. Her face nestled in the thick hair over his chest and she trembled with aching pleasure at the newness of touching without clothing.

She put her lips against his chest and felt him tremble, too. That made her a little afraid—the thought that he might lose control. She didn't know what she might do if she felt his weight over her . . .

While she was deliberating, he caught her hand and slid it down his body. When she protested, his mouth slid over hers with a tenderness she hadn't dreamed him capable of. And then it seemed so right to do what he wanted, to let him whisper, guiding her, until the silken concussion he'd kindled in her own body was threatening to erupt in him. He couldn't control it. With his last rational thought, he realized his mistake in coaxing her to touch him, but the need was too great, and abstinence far too long, Gaby's soft body far too accessible and beloved.

"Let me," he whispered huskily. His body moved over hers without warning, his hands guiding hers to his hips as he slid into a shocking new intimacy with her. His mouth ground into hers, and his breath came like a runner's, quick and shaking. "Oh, God . . . let me, baby . . . !"

She couldn't seem to move. She looked up at his hard face. His eyes were glazed, his jaw taut, his features already distorting.

He held her eyes. "I'm sorry," he bit off as his hands caught her hips. "My . . . God," he groaned. He drew in a harsh breath. "I love you . . . so. Forgive me . . . !"

She didn't understand until she felt the first hard thrust, like fire against her. She cried out, but he was beyond hearing. She felt her back being buffeted against the hard rock, the skin scraping faintly, as he drove violently for fulfillment, his big hands biting into her hips, his body overwhelming hers, possessing it.

He cried out hoarsely, stiffening, and then he began to shudder rhythmically while he moaned against her throat, his body racked with pleasure that he couldn't hide or control. It seemed to go on forever before he collapsed, shaking and damp with perspiration, on her cold body.

She felt his damp skin with fascination. So that was what it was like, she thought. The pleasure had only been an illusion, and this was the reality. It was just as he'd said it would be—she'd had no enjoyment from it. But even then, it came to her that she hadn't once thought of the past, of the terror. This was Bowie, and despite his loss of control, he loved her and she loved him. She touched his hair hesitantly and held his face against her body, overwhelmed with what had happened. He was her lover; they'd made love.

"Oh, my God," Bowie groaned. He rolled away from her, his face a study in agonized regret as he bent over to run his hands angrily through his damp hair. He couldn't bear to look at her, to see the revulsion and fear he knew were going to be on her white face. "My God, I'll never forgive myself for that," he said roughly. "Not the longest day I live."

Gaby studied him curiously. He looked as if he wanted to throw himself off a cliff. She couldn't have that . . .

"It's all right, Bowie," she whispered. She reached up and tried to touch his face, but he actually flinched away from her. "Bowie!"

He got back into his jeans and boots, his movements jerky and rough with subdued anger. He glanced at her and grimaced, as if the sight of her nude body was actually painful to him. "Get dressed, sweetheart," he said quietly.

At least his anger didn't seem to be directed at her. She sat up, touching her raw back, and gasped.

He turned, his eyes narrowing with pain as he saw her. If anything, his face grew harder. "There's a first aid kit in the truck," he said through his teeth. "Get your clothes on and I'll put something on that scratch."

She managed to get her clothes back on and sat docilely while he raised the back of her blouse and dabbed antiseptic on the short, wide scratch. It hurt, but she didn't flinch. She couldn't bear to make him feel worse than he already did.

"Will I get pregnant?" she asked under her breath, because that delightful possibility had just occurred to her. She felt dazed with wonder. She was a woman, and she hadn't fought or screamed. She'd actually given herself. That was the first step out of her nightmares and into the sunlight, but Bowie didn't seem to realize what a momentous experience it had been for her. He was blaming himself for losing control. She didn't. It was like getting over a hurdle.

His hands stilled and tautened on her back. "I don't know," he said. "I didn't hold anything back. It's possible that you might."

She smiled to herself. "Well, I . . . I wouldn't mind."

He seemed to have stopped breathing. "Gaby . . . this is why we broke off the engagement," he reminded her. "Because you hated the thought of intimacy with me."

"Not with you," she corrected. She glanced at him and then away. "With anyone. I . . . you were the only man I was ever able to . . . to want."

"You didn't want me just now," he said coldly. "I forced you . . ."

"No!" she whirled, her hand going to his lips, her eyes wide with regret. "No, no! I let you touch me and kiss me and . . . and . . . do that to me," she added, stammering and averting her eyes as she flushed with remembered pleasure. "I didn't fight you, you know. There was never any question of force between us. I'd give you anything I have, Bowie— anything I am. I belong to you now."

His arms contracted, and he grimaced when she cried out. "Your back," he sighed heavily. "I'll never get over this."

"It's all right," she repeated. "I understand."

"Do you?" His dark eyes searched hers. "Can you understand that I would have killed to have you? That my body was in such agony that I didn't even know what I was doing? Or can you imagine that kind of passion, little one?"

She couldn't. There was a reserve in her that wouldn't seem to let her feel violent emotion, even with Bowie. She knew pleasure now, but she didn't understand how to give it, or how to participate in it. Perhaps that was what he meant. She lowered her eyes to the shirt he was buttoning. "I knew you wanted me," she said.

"Well, now you know how much." He got up, running an angry hand through his hair. "The fat's in the fire now. Come on."

He took her hand and pulled her up, smoothing back her hair. "Do you own a white dress?"

She stared at him. "What?"

"Do you own a white dress?" he persisted, his eyes dark and stormy and irritated.

"Well, yes," she faltered. "Why do you want to know?"

CHAPTER

Seventeen

Several hours later, standing beside Bowie in front of a Mexican official, Gaby understood his question about the white dress. They were married almost before she realized what was going on. Bowie had bought her a bouquet of daisies from a Mexican vendor, and the ring he'd given her had been one he had taken from the safe. It had been his grandmother's—a delicate little band of rubies and diamonds that was supposed to have come with the Spanish land grant that started Casa Río.

"I can't believe this," Gaby faltered when he'd kissed her and signed the necessary documents and they were back in the car headed home.

"You'd better believe it," he murmured. "You certainly will when those photos hit the paper."

"Yes." She went quiet. There had been an American photographer in the small Mexican town, doing a photo layout on weddings. When he found out who Bowie and Gaby were, he insisted on making some shots of them for his article. Bowie seemed to enjoy it, but Gaby was all but frantic, trying not to let her face be photographed fully. Bowie was an important man, and naturally, their wedding would bring publicity. But she was afraid of wire services picking it up and splashing her picture in papers back east. She was, in fact, terrified of it.

She clutched her wilted bouquet of flowers. "Bowie, is this what you really wanted?"

"I made love to you," he said quietly. "Not that it was the kind of love I wanted to express. But I do love you with all my heart. And yes, this is what I want. I want you, for the rest of my life."

"I don't want you to feel forced . . ."

"You and I go to church together on Sundays, don't we?" he asked, glancing at her. "How would you like to go with me tomorrow if we hadn't married today?"

She colored and stared blindly out the window.

"We're both of us too old-fashioned and rigid in our beliefs to be intimate without a commitment. We were engaged. Now we're married, and we'll work things out, somehow." He sighed. "I'm only sorry your first time had to be so brutal—especially after what was done to you when you were in your teens."

The pain in his deep voice made her feel guilty. She turned in her seat to look at him. "It had to happen eventually," she replied. "I love you, too, Bowie," she added shyly, averting her eyes. "I couldn't have let anyone except you touch me, ever."

He glanced at her, a little less concerned when he saw the serenity of her face. But the guilt ate at him, all the same. He turned the radio on and sat back, smoking his cigarette, until they got home. They could talk then, he decided, and maybe iron out what was to become of them.

But when he pulled up in front of Casa Río, the front door opened before he could open Gaby's door for her, and Aggie came out into the courtyard to meet them.

Gaby's eyes lit up and she cried out with pure relief and joy as she ran to Aggie, laughing, arms wide.

"Oh, you scoundrel!" she accused, hugging the older woman with delight. "Where have you been? Why didn't you call or write, or something?!"

Aggie hugged her back, her eyes dull and accusing as they met Bowie's over her shoulder. "I've been busy," she said. "Hello, Bowie."

"Hello, yourself," he said. His black eyes searched hers. "You damned nuisance," he said with soft laughter, "we've been out of our minds."

Aggie felt exceptionally pleased by that remark. She'd convinced herself that her son really hated her, and that he was his father all over again, with the same mercenary attitudes. But that looked like real concern in his face, and he sounded as if he'd been worried.

"I'm sorry I didn't get in touch with you," she said. She let go of Gaby and allowed Bowie to hug her, too. "I didn't think you'd be worried."

"You're my mother," he said firmly. "I may disagree with you—I may even stick my nose in where it isn't wanted—but I love you. And when you vanish, I worry."

Aggie shifted restlessly. "I'm sorry. I've had some things to work through." She looked up hopefully. "You haven't heard from Ned?"

Bowie shook his head.

Aggie's face fell. "Oh. I had hoped..." She sighed. "Well, that's that, isn't it?" She fought back tears, and Gaby grimaced at her expression. "Montoya said you and Gaby went to Mexico and got married today," she said, as if she'd only just remembered it. Her gray slacks and red and gray top hung on her. She'd lost weight, although it only enhanced her very nice figure. "Did you just decide to annex her part of Casa Río anyway, or did you seduce her and feel guilty?" she asked levelly.

Bowie had to fight not to give the show away, schooling his features not to so much as blink. "I love Gaby," he said, and meant it. His eyes went past Aggie to Gaby's soft face and searched it hungrily. "I'd give up Casa Río in a minute before I'd give her up," he added, his voice husky with emotion.

Gaby blushed at the soft hunger, and smiled at him.

"Well, well," Aggie sighed. "So now you understand, do you?" she added, searching his face.

He looked at her. "Oh, yes. I understand better than you realize. I'm sorry I ran your Teton man off," he added with reluctant apology. "If he feels this way about you, I imagine he's loaded a gun and is thinking about blowing his head off by now. I'll have him on my conscience for a long time, along with you."

Aggie hugged him, her eyes flooding with tears. "I can't find him," she wailed. "I thought I could find his address on the passenger manifest, but they said there was no Ned Courtland on the cruise! And I've spent all this time down in Del Río, Texas, learning how to milk cows!" she sobbed.

Bowie stared at Gaby over the older woman's head, his shocked expression mirroring hers.

"Milking cows?" they burst out in unison.

Aggie pulled away. "Yes, milking!" she said irritably. "I was staying with Cousin Agnes—you do remember her, Bowie? She has a small farm. I've learned how to toss hay and weed a garden and do all sorts of unpleasant and some frankly disgusting things since I've been away. I can cope with a small ranch, and I don't even mind the work." Her lower lip trembled. "And now that I've put myself through the tortures of the damned to settle for what Ned can give me, I can't find him!"

"I've got a private detective working on it," Bowie said. "Any day, he'll come through. He's been looking for you, too," he added ruefully. "We were worried."

"I would have called, but I was just too tired," Aggie said with a sheepish grin. "I didn't know that hard work was so hard. But after your father died, I guess I just drifted into social get-togethers without realizing how empty my life had become. I'm on the right track now."

"Of course you are," Gaby murmured, hugging her warmly. "He'll turn up. We'll find him, honest we will."

Aggie studied the wan face. "You look terrible."

"I was kissing her, out at Cochise Stronghold, and she scratched her shoulder on the rocks," Bowie said with a regretful glance at Gaby, who'd gone scarlet.

"Shame on you," Aggie muttered. "Kissing people on rocks, for heaven's sake."

"Sofas are in short supply in the desert."

"That's no excuse. And you're married," she sighed, smiling warmly at Gaby. "What a delightful surprise. Are you going to have lots of children?"

"Oh, yes," Gaby said dreamily.

But Bowie turned away, still distressed by the way it had all come about. "I've got to make some phone calls," he said. "I'll check with the detective first."

"He's very solemn," Aggie remarked.

"He's never been married before," Gaby reminded her, trying not to notice the coldness in Bowie's face, the lack of affection. He probably hadn't wanted to get married just yet, but he'd felt obliged to. She hated that. She should never have let things go so far. But now that they had, she was less afraid of intimacy than she'd ever been before. In fact, just remembering the tenderness Bowie had shown her before he lost control made her go hot all over with pleasure. Could it be like that for her, she wondered? Perhaps it was his lack of women that had made him so hungry for her and so impatient. If she could satisfy him, then next time, things might be very different. She blushed just at the thought.

She and Aggie sat and talked for a long time and ate

supper together. Bowie didn't come out of the study. Finally, Aggie discreetly excused herself and left Gaby to go and find her new husband.

He was sitting in his swivel chair behind the big oak desk with his booted feet propped on it. His shirt was unbuttoned, and his blond hair, usually so immaculately combed, was disheveled and down in his eyes. He gave her a blank smile when she opened the door.

"Aren't you hungry?" she asked hesitantly.

He raised a whiskey glass. "I've had mine, thanks."

She didn't know what to say. Bowie hardly ever touched liquor. He might have a brandy from time to time, but whiskey and other hard forms of spirits were something he studiously avoided. And she didn't have to look very hard for the reason he was putting it away. She didn't have to look past that morning.

She closed the door and went to him, her face quiet and concerned. "How much have you had?" she asked gently.

He sighed. "Not enough."

She touched the lean hand that was holding the glass. "Why don't we go to bed?"

His jaw firmed and hardened. "That's just what you need now, isn't it?" he asked. "Another painful experience with a selfish man to scar your mind even more."

"You stop that," she said. She took the glass away from him. "I was a virgin. Of course you hurt me—it was unavoidable. Now come to bed, Bowie."

She tugged at his hand until he let himself be pulled to his feet, but he was staring at her as if she'd lost her mind.

"Aren't you afraid of me?" he asked softly.

"I'm afraid you may fall on me, yes," she muttered, getting under one big arm to help support him when he swayed slightly. "My gosh, how much do you weigh?"

"About two hundred and twenty-five pounds, I think," he said. "You aren't afraid of me—even after this morning?"

She was guiding him toward the door. "Maybe we have different memories of this morning," she said, flushing.

He stared down at her until her face lifted, and his black eyes slid over her features like searching hands. "I didn't want to hurt you, Gaby," he whispered.

"I knew that, even then," she said, smiling tenderly. "You aren't superhuman. You just keep expecting more of yourself than the rest of us do. I know it had been a long time. It wasn't that bad, either," she added shyly. "It wasn't horrible at all. Just . . . very intimate."

He framed her face in his big hands and bent to brush his whiskey-scented mouth over hers. "I wish I hadn't opened that bottle, you know. But I got to thinking about what I'd done to you, and I couldn't live with it."

"You're the only one heaping coals of fire on your head," she said, smiling. "I'm not. You've been terribly patient and gentle. One lapse isn't going to make me forget the pain I've caused you since the first time you kissed me."

"I didn't think you'd stay with me," he said, his voice only faintly slurred. "I thought you'd want to leave."

"Oh, no," she said gently. "I want you. Maybe not quite in the way you want me—not just yet—but I didn't fight you, and I didn't scream." She smiled lovingly. "Bowie, didn't you even notice that I wasn't afraid?"

"No," he murmured ruefully. "I was too far gone. Then, afterwards, I couldn't look at you for the shame of what I'd done."

She slid her arms around him and hugged him close. "You love me," she sighed, nestling her cheek on his hard, bare chest. "You said so, several times."

His hands touched her shoulders experimentally. "I don't remember that," he said.

"I do." She lifted her face. "First times are always uncomfortable, or so I've been told. The most important thing is that I've overcome the fear, and the memories of the past,

Bowie. I'm . . . still a little uncomfortable right now, but in a few days, we could . . ." she cleared her throat. "That is, if you want to . . . ?"

His lean hands closed around her waist and he lifted her up on a level with his eyes. "Are you offering me a second chance?"

"I'm offering you a beginning," she whispered. "I want to live with you, always, and have your babies and take care of you." She leaned forward and brushed her mouth gently over his eyes, closing them. "I love you so much, my darling—more than anything in the world."

He groaned, as if he were in pain, and gathered her close, his body shuddering as he held her, his face buried in her warm, softly scented neck. "You're my whole world," he breathed. "All I want—everything."

She held him fiercely, drowning in the shared need, in the pleasure of his firm hold and the knowledge that he was just as hopelessly in love as she was.

But he'd gone altogether too far into the whiskey bottle and he began to sway again.

"My God, I'm drunk," he murmured dazedly.

"I did notice that you were a bit tipsy. I really think we'd better get you upstairs," she remarked when he set her back on her feet.

"How had you planned to accomplish that?" he asked with a vague smile. "Throw me over your shoulder and carry me up?"

Her eyes measured all six foot three of him and she whistled through pursed lips. "I'd need a crane," she murmured.

"I can make it. Just guide me in the right direction."

"I remember a scene in a movie," she said. "A John Wayne movie. He was trying to help the housekeeper up the staircase, but they were both sauced, and they fell down it several times."

He chuckled. "I remember. Not to worry, little one, I won't fall."

He didn't, but by the skin of his teeth. Gaby managed to get him into his bedroom, and he sprawled on his back in the king-sized bed with a sigh of relief.

"Don't go to sleep," she said. "You have to help me get you out of these things."

One eye opened and he studied her amusedly. "No, I don't. Undress me, Gaby." His voice dropped an octave. "Come on, I dare you," he prodded, liking her red face and hunted expression.

"I can't undress you," she faltered.

"Why not? You're my wife."

She stared at him. Yes, she was. She lifted her hand and stared at the dainty ring on her wedding finger, then began to smile. "Well, yes, I am."

"I undressed you this morning," he murmured. "And last night." He frowned. "Didn't I undress you one other time?"

"No. Hold still."

She had the shirt off, and then she fumbled and fussed with his big boots until she got them off. But when it came to that big belt buckle and the snap and zipper of his pants, she stood looking down at him as if she were trying to undo a double combination lock.

"You've seen me," he reminded her. "All of me, without a stitch."

"Yes, but getting you that way is . . . unnerving," she murmured. "I can't!"

He laughed through his haze and sat up, pulling her across him to lie on her back beside him. "Coward," he teased. "What's so hard about pulling down a zipper?"

He guided her hands and made her do it, enjoying her shy reticence. "I'll teach you to do this a different way when I'm more sober and you're less uncomfortable," he said when his trousers were on the floor and he was stretched out in his dark briefs. "You'll lose that shyness one day. But not too soon, I hope—I enjoy it."

"So I see," she mumbled with a glare that quickly turned into a laugh at his expression.

"Go get your gown and come back." He grinned at her expression. "It's all right. We're married. You can sleep with me all night, and we don't have to worry about what the household will say about it."

She grinned back. "They didn't say anything the only time we did," she reminded him. "Okay. I'll get my gown."

He watched her go, amazed at the change in her—at the new tenderness, the acceptance, the lack of fear. He was sorry for the way he'd treated her, but he wasn't sorry that he'd let it go too far. She was his wife now. She loved him, and very soon he'd show her the ecstasy that she'd only sampled in his arms. He'd prove his love, in the best way of all.

She slept in his arms, drowsy with pleasure, stiffening when the telephone jangled very early and roused them. He lifted his aching head with a groan to answer it.

"Where's Montoya?" he muttered, glaring at the clock. But it was after nine already, and whoever was on the phone had him sitting straight up in bed. "Who?" he asked. "Where? Just a minute."

"Who is it?" Gaby murmured sleepily.

He got up, searching through his drawer for a pen and paper. He jerked up the receiver. "Give me that name and address again. Yes. Yes. No, never mind about Aggie, she came home all by herself. Send the bill to my home. Casa Río, that's right. And thanks!"

He hung up. He sat down heavily on the bed and stared at the paper with eyes that mirrored his shock and fascination.

"What is it?" Gaby demanded, punching his bare shoulder.

"Mr. Courtland," he replied absently. "Only he isn't Mr. Courtland. Do you know the name Ted Kingman?"

"My gosh, yes," she replied, a rodeo fan from way back. "He was world's champion calf roper, and world's champion saddle bronc rider a couple of years running, and best all around cowboy for another two years. He always took top money, but then, that was expected. The Kingman family is one of the oldest and most respected ranching families in Texas."

"That's right," Bowie agreed. "Guess who Ned Courtland is?"

Her eyebrows shot up. "But Ted Kingman gave up rodeo years ago. He made a killing on the rodeo circuit and invested that money in race horses. He gave that up some years back, after he'd made a million dollars at it, and went back to ranching, specializing in quarter horses. He almost wrote the book on training cutting horses...oh, my! No wonder he was so good with a rope, and knew so much about horses. Quick, we've got to tell Aggie!"

He caught her arm and held her back. "No."

"But she doesn't have to milk cows—he's a millionaire," she argued.

"The whole point of his coming here was to make sure she wasn't after his millions," he pointed out. "He wanted to see if Aggie McCayde of Casa Río could marry Ned Courtland who had no money and only a small ranch. Don't you see? He wasn't a gigolo. He was afraid she was a gold digger. It would almost be funny, if it hadn't become so damned tragic." He put his head in his hands. "I never should have interfered. I've put us all on the block because I was obsessed with keeping Casa Río intact."

"What are you going to do?"

"I'm going to Jackson, Wyoming, of course," he said. He looked up with a bloodshot grin. "And bring papa home where he belongs."

"But Aggie . . ."

"Honey, Aggie can't know. She mustn't know. He might think she's found out what he's worth and wants him for his money. No, she has to think he's still poor—just for the time being. And not a word to Montoya. He'd tell her." He got up, a little shaky. "Damn, my head hurts!"

She got up, too, and pressed against him. "Want an aspirin?"

"Make it two, and a cup of black coffee." He looked down at her in her pale blue gown and smiled a little. "That's sexy."

"I'm glad you like it. It's one of Aggie's that I borrowed. My gowns are kind of plain." She blushed. "I thought this one looked feminine."

"I'd like very much to show you how feminine it looks," he sighed. "But I don't have the time." He bent and brushed his mouth lazily over hers. "You even smell nice."

She drew his hands to her body and smiled against his shocked lips. "I like this," she whispered.

"So do I," he murmured, "but if you do much of that, I won't get to Wyoming. And you're not quite up to what I'll want, either."

She drew back. "Spoilsport," she sighed.

He ripped the shoulder straps away and jerked the gown down to her waist with a slow, predatory smile. "I like it this way best," he breathed, and bent to put his mouth hungrily against soft, warm flesh. She gasped, going under in a veil of pleasured memory, her hands holding his mouth against her. But before she could sink back on the bed, he'd picked her up and tossed her there, his black eyes slow and appreciative on the treasures he'd bared.

"That's sexy," he pointed out. "Damn the gown."

She sighed, and smiled up at him with pure delight. "I'll remember that you said that. How long will you be gone?"

He was still staring at her breasts. "God knows. Overnight, I suppose, if he doesn't hang me up in his barn and let his men shoot me. I probably deserve it, if he's in half the state Aggie is."

"He can't shoot you," she said firmly. "I haven't . . ." She cleared her throat. "He can't shoot you yet."

"I'll tell him you said so," he murmured sensuously. "Black coffee," he repeated, pulling her up with deft, cool hands. "Two aspirin. And have Montoya get me a ticket on the next plane to Jackson."

"All right," she sighed. "I guess I can live until you get back."

He laughed with exquisite delight. "My God. And just think how we started out."

"I'm much more interested in the way we'll wind up," she said, tongue in cheek, and smiled at him lovingly as she got into her robe and went downstairs.

The flight to Jackson gave Bowie time to collect his thoughts and decide what he was going to say to his prospective stepfather. An apology wasn't going to do it—not after the things he'd said and done. He cringed, remembering how he'd accused Edward Courtland Kingman of being a gigolo. That was damned funny, considering what the man was worth. Casa Río was big, but Kingman had holdings in two states, and probably overseas as well. He was a keen businessman, and not only in livestock. Bowie had never seen a photo of him, but he'd heard plenty about the man in cattlemen's circles.

He hired a taxi at the airport and gave the drive Ted Kingman's name, but before he could give the address, the driver said, "Yes, sir!" and pulled out of the airport parking lot.

"You know of Kingman, I gather?" Bowie probed delicately.

"Gosh, who doesn't?" he chuckled. "Mr. Kingman's a square shooter. Not everybody likes him—he can be a hardnosed so-and-so when he has to—but everybody respects him. He was champion calf roper two years running, and best all around twice. We're pretty proud that he chose Jackson to call home."

"I guess so." Bowie leaned back, wondering how he was going to approach Kingman. He still didn't have the slightest idea about what to say.

The driver pulled through a big wrought-iron gate with a scrolled "K" on both sides and up a long, paved driveway to a sprawling two-story gray stone house on a hill with its own spectacular view of the Tetons. Casa Río would have fit in one wing of it, with enough room left over to ride horses. Bowie laughed ruefully at his misconceptions about their mysterious guest.

Bowie paid the cab driver. "How about waiting for ten minutes or so, just in case?" he asked the man. "I may come through the door feet-first, and I'd hate like hell to have to walk back to Jackson."

"Sure thing." The cab driver cut off his engine and pulled his cap over his eyes, apparently content to sit and nap.

Bowie walked up the wide steps and rang the doorbell. It echoed in a cavernous hall and he heard footsteps.

The door opened. "Yes?" a middle-aged woman asked, and when she saw his face, her eyes widened and she stood just staring at him without another word.

She was at least fifty, Bowie imagined, thin, dark-haired and dark-eyed, and severe looking with her hair drawn back into a huge bun.

"Is Mr. Kingman at home?" Bowie asked hesitantly. The way she was staring at him made him uncomfortable. He shifted restlessly.

"What?" she asked. "Oh. I'm sorry," she said and smiled sheepishly. "Yes, Ted's home. I'm his younger sister, Ilene. Come in, won't you, Mr.—?"

He wondered if she'd recognize his name. "I'm Bowie McCayde," he said, watching her face closely.

The hard face grew briefly harder. Her eyes narrowed and she studied him with the same unnerving stare her brother had used once or twice. "You're Aggie's son," she said finally.

"I don't deserve to be," he murmured dryly. "And I hope your brother isn't in the same shape she is, or I may not get out of here in the same condition I came in."

The hardness fell away. "You know who he is now. Did that help?"

"Not much. But seeing Aggie look like death and worn to a nub learning how to milk cows did."

Ilene frowned. "I don't understand."

"She doesn't know who your brother is," he said patiently. "She thinks he's got a little farm up here in the Tetons and needs a full-time ranch wife to help him do chores. She didn't know how, so she went to Del Río to live with a cousin, who taught her. Now she's back home, bristling with success, and she can't find Ned Courtland to show him how capable she is."

Ilene's jaw fell. "Well!"

"So I came up here to see if your brother would like to come down to Casa Río and watch my mother milk a cow."

Ilene burst out laughing. She excused herself and ran to the doorway of another room, motioning frantically. She was joined by an older, slightly heavier version of herself who listened, gasped, and then burst out laughing.

"This is Joanne," she introduced the older woman. "Joanne, this is Aggie's son."

Joanne sighed and took the hand Bowie offered. "If Aggie looks like you, no wonder our poor Ted sits and broods all day."

Bowie moved restlessly. "Aggie's small and dark," he said. "I take after my father."

"We all look like our father," Ilene offered. "Our mother was small and blond. Dad adored her. She died when I was born, and we all paid for it in various ways. But that's another story. Do come and see Ted. Uh, your insurance is paid up . . . ?"

Bowie chuckled. "Yes. I told my wife he might hang me up and let his men use me for target practice, so I came prepared."

"You're married, Mr. McCayde?"

"Just recently. Oh, there's a cab outside. I asked him to stay until I scouted the area for mines and such."

"We'll take care of him. Here you go." Ilene knocked briefly on the study door and then opened it. "You have a visitor, Ted," she told the man behind the desk.

He looked up and saw Bowie, and his dark eyes flashed fire.

CHAPTER

Eighteen

"You look like hell," Bowie remarked conversationally. He stared at the older man reflectively, noting the new lines in that dark, hard face, the new gray hairs that had appeared among the black.

"Thanks to you, I guess I do," Ted Kingman said icily. He got up from the chair, elegant in slacks and a patterned green silk shirt. He looked the very picture of a successful businessman, and nothing like the poor cowboy who'd come with Aggie McCayde from Jamaica. "You've got one hell of a nerve coming here."

Bowie shrugged and bent his head to light a cigarette. "I've made so many mistakes in the past few weeks that I don't think I've got many nerves left." He blew out a cloud of smoke and stood his ground. "Go ahead. Throw a punch at me if it will help."

Kingman looked as if he just might. He came closer and his whole lean, fit body tensed. But after a minute, he sighed heavily and went to the liquor cabinet. "Do you want a drink?"

"No thanks," Bowie said with a grimace. "I tied one on last night."

"You don't get drunk," Kingman said, his narrow eyes piercing as he filled a snifter with brandy and went back to sit behind his desk. "Aggie said so."

"Aggie doesn't know what I did to Gaby before I married her, though," Bowie said. He dropped lazily into one of the big leather chairs facing the desk and crossed his long legs.

"You married Gaby? Quick work," the older man mused.

"So it was." He hitched up his pants leg and studied his highly polished tan boot. "Aggie just got home from Del Río."

Kingman's brows lifted. "Del Río, Texas?"

"She's got a cousin down there. She's been having farm lessons."

"I beg your pardon."

"Farm lessons," Bowie repeated. "She's learned how to pitch hay and milk cows and muck out barns." He smiled wickedly. "Then she came home to look for you, to show you how good she was at it. She couldn't find you, of course. She was looking for a man named Ned Courtland who had a few head of cattle in Wyoming."

"That reminds me. How did you track me down?" Kingman asked.

"I hired a private detective," Bowie replied. His eyes narrowed. "I think you knew I would."

"Well, it's what I would have done in your place," the older man replied. "I don't guess I blame you for being suspicious about me. You had every reason." Kingman leaned back with a hard sigh. "I've been chased for nine years," he remarked. "Ever since my wife died. I'm rich, you see." He glared at his brandy snifter. "I thought Aggie had guessed, even though I didn't dress like I had much money. But the real thing was to find out what kind of person she was, where she lived, what her lifestyle was like."

"So that you wouldn't wind up married to a gold digger," Bowie offered.

Kingman smiled wistfully. "Something like that. I had high hopes for Aggie and me, until she balked at the first test. I thought if I could get her to agree to marry Ned Courtland, who had nothing, it would surely mean that she loved me." He shrugged. "But it didn't work out that way."

"She's been used to wealth all her life," Bowie said. "She wasn't sure that she could be what you wanted. I guess she had other ideas, though, because she left a palatial estate in Nassau to muck out stables in Del Río."

The older man was still staring into his brandy. "I was too proud to try and get in touch with her," he said quietly. "I didn't know how she'd react to the truth, either." He looked up. "What did she say when you told her who I was?"

Bowie took a draw from the cigarette. "I didn't tell her."

"What?" Kingman sat up straight. "You haven't told her? She doesn't know you're here?"

"That's right," Bowie told him. "She's been mooning around Casa Río like a ghost, half listening to what's said and looking like death warmed over. Gaby and I agreed that it wouldn't help things to lay it on the line just yet."

"Well, I'll be damned." Kingman stared at him. "Then why did you come here?"

"I thought you might like to come down to Casa Río and watch mother milk a cow."

Kingman lit a cigarette of his own and took another sip of brandy. "What would be the use?" he asked. "She didn't want me the way I was."

"For God's sake," Bowie muttered. "You didn't give her a chance. All right, neither did I," he agreed when the older man opened his mouth to speak. "I stuck my nose in where it wasn't wanted or needed." He lowered his eyes to his cigarette. "My old man never gave a damn about me," he said stiffly. "I was his heir. Business was his whole life.

There never seemed to be much room in it for me, or even for Aggie. We had our uses, but we never came first. Then, when he died, Aggie had plenty of time for Gaby, but she figured I didn't need her anymore." He laughed bitterly. "I've never had much affection. I guess I was jealous of the attention Aggie paid Gaby. It was a lot worse when you came along out of nowhere, apparently dead busted, and set your sights on her."

Kingman finished his cigarette and put it out. He watched it smouldering in the ashtray for a long moment. "Business has been my solace for the past nine years," he said then. "Then Aggie came along, and I lost the taste for conferences and working weekends and spread sheets."

"Aggie seems to have lost hers for high living," Bowie volunteered. "The thing is, she's looking bad—really bad." He averted his eyes. "She's at the stage where she might do something desperate."

The older man was very still. "What do you mean?"

"Nothing. Just that she's a little disoriented, now that she can't find you. She even mentioned that life had lost its appeal." That wasn't quite the truth, but didn't they say everything was fair in love and war?

Kingman let out a long breath. "I didn't realize she cared that much," he said. "I thought she was rather relieved when she broke it off."

"She told me that love hurts like hell at our ages." Bowie's chest rose and fell. "She was right. If I lost Gaby now, I don't know what I'd do."

Kingman studied the younger man for a long minute. "I might fly back with you, just for the day," he said. "Just to see her. That's all."

"That might be just the thing," Bowie said, and grinned.

Kingman glared at him. "No matchmaking," he said. "It's just a quick visit."

"Sure."

Kingman jerked up the phone and dialed. "Frank? Get the Navajo checked out and gassed up. I'll be there in thirty minutes."

"Your own plane, too?" Bowie murmured. "We've got a corporate jet, but my pilot scares the hell out of me, so I fly commercial."

"I've got a Learjet," Kingman offered. "I fly it on long trips, but the Navajo is more my speed. Let me tell the girls where I'm going before we leave."

His sisters were smiling smugly when he and Bowie went out the front door and down the steps, to climb into a dark blue Mercedes for the trip to the airport. Bowie tried not to look too smug himself, but things might yet work out for Aggie.

Back at Casa Río, Gaby was still digging into Bio-Ag's past, trying to fight her way out of the delightful sensual web Bowie's ardor had slid around her. It was hard to work at all, but this was part of the job, and she had to do it. Bowie's life might depend on what she found.

She took long enough to go to church, her heart so full that she radiated happiness. Aggie had asked where Bowie was, but Gaby hadn't told her. She'd only smiled and taken Aggie to church to divert her from her dogged questioning.

Afterwards, she went into the study and phoned the district attorney in Callahan, Texas, and found him home.

After a brief explanation of who she was and why she was bothering him, Gaby got down to business.

"A company called Bio-Ag is trying to locate here," she explained. "We only know what they've given us in the press kits, but they're leaving a lot of holes in their explanations, and we can't seem to get at the truth. We thought you might remember something about them. I understand that they located in your community some two or three years ago."

There was a pause. "Bio-Ag?"

"Yes. It's short for Biological Agri-market, they say."

He made a soft sound. "I'm sorry, but that isn't a name I remember. I prosecuted an outfit that was involved in some cases of animal poisoning around here . . ."

"It wasn't Bio-Ag?" she interrupted. "You're sure?"

"Oh, I'm sure. I wouldn't forget a name like that."

She sighed. She'd been so certain. "Well, I appreciate your time anyway, Mr. James." She paused. "Just a minute. Do you remember the names of any of the officials of the company?" she added quickly. "A Mr. Samuels, perhaps? Or a Mr. Logan?"

"Samuels? Samuels . . ." There was another long pause, and Gaby held her breath. "Yes. That was the man's name. The company was called Cotton West. There was a class action lawsuit filed by several ranchers here who lost cattle because of pesticides leaching into the surface water table. I was the prosecutor in the case, and Cotton West was fined. But as I recall, they declared bankruptcy and the ranchers never recovered a dime. Yes, that's right."

"Mr. James, may I quote you?"

"Oh, I'll do better than that, young lady—I'll send you a transcript of the trial. Give me your address."

"The newspaper will gladly reimburse you if you can send it express, so that we have it early Tuesday morning," she said. "Better yet, one of our reporters can fly out there to get it tomorrow."

"Very well. If you'll have the reporter call me from the airport, I'll be glad to provide transportation for him," he added kindly. "I hate to see a polluter get away with anything, Miss Cane. You can count on my help. There's an environmentalist here who might like to say a few words, too."

Gaby could hardly believe her luck. Finally, something concrete! She almost danced around the telephone. She called Bob, and he said that he'd have Harvey fly out there this very afternoon and be waiting when the federal and state offices opened Monday morning. She hung up, very pleased with her efforts. This would delight Bowie, if only she had a chance to tell him. If he managed to bring Mr. Kingman back, she doubted that she'd have five minutes to tell him anything, in all the excitement. She only hoped that things worked out for Aggie and her beau. They had to. She wanted Aggie to be as happy as she was herself.

Bowie settled his big frame into the co-pilot's seat next to Ted Kingman and put on the headphones. He'd watched the older man go over the preflight checklist and he'd done his own walkaround, checking the fuel tanks and examining the hull.

Kingman had looked up from his clipboard, frowning. "What are you doing?"

"Double-checking," Bowie muttered. "Just to be safe."

"I've been flying since you were a kid," came the terse reply. "I'm instrument-rated."

Bowie had stared back at him. "So am I. I've got a license and I can fly, too."

Kingman's eyes widened. "And you fly commercially?"

"Well, I'm the pilot whose flying scares me," he'd confessed with a sheepish grin. "We've got another one who works for my board of directors and executives. I go up all right, and I fly all right. But I'm a holy terror on landings. Never could get the hang of crosswinds . . ."

Kingman chuckled softly. "I might be able to give you a hand there," he mused. "I had the same problem once."

"I might take you up on it," he replied.

They'd climbed into the cockpit at last and soon were in the air and on their way.

"I didn't notice a landing field at the ranch," Kingman remarked.

"There isn't one. I hate concrete on open land."

Kingman glanced at him. "How's the water battle going?"

Bowie filled him in, smoothing over the gunshots and the council meeting, but the older man was sharp. He didn't say a lot, but his expression spoke volumes.

"What will Gaby do about her share of the land?" he asked.

Bowie sighed. "Sell it, I imagine. I can't blame her. She feels as strongly about progress as I feel about the past."

"A few jobs won't replace the groundwater that's ruined," Kingman replied. "You're right—she isn't. I hope she finds out in time."

Bowie was oddly touched that the man sided with him. He hadn't really expected him to. "Why did you get out of rodeoing?" he asked suddenly.

Kingman's hands tightened on the joystick. "I caught my hand in a rope, bareback bronc riding. It tore it up pretty bad. They put me back together again, but I could never use that hand well enough again to come out on top." He shrugged. "Never could stand being second best at anything."

"Well, you're tops with quarter horses," Bowie murmured. "I should have realized who you were when you saved that Mexican boy from the bronc."

"I'm glad you didn't. It's important to me that Aggie takes me at face value."

"I think you'll find that Aggie would take you if you came covered in catsup and wearing a bun."

Kingman chuckled. "We'll see."

They flew to the Tucson airport and drove down to the ranch in Bowie's Scorpio. Kingman smoked more and talked less as they neared Casa Río, and by the time they pulled up in the driveway, the older man was rigid.

Bowie had to fight not to grin at the Kingman's discomfort. If that wasn't love, he didn't know what was.

He went into the house first, but there was no one in sight. He peeked into the dining room, where Montoya was setting the table.

"Where's Aggie?" Bowie whispered.

"In the living room. Gaby has gone upstairs for a minute."

Bowie motioned out the front door to Kingman and led the way to the living room.

Aggie was sitting on the sofa watching the news, her wan face barely interested in what was on the screen.

"Hello, Aggie," Bowie said.

She glanced at him. "Hello. Where have you been?"

"Just flying around. Look what I found."

He stood aside and let Ted Kingman walk into the living room.

Aggie didn't faint. She was good Arizona stock and not given to swoons, but she stood up with wobbly legs and a voice that sounded strained.

"Ned?" she croaked.

"Bowie says you've been getting your diploma in farm management," Kingman said easily. "He invited me down to watch you milk cows."

Aggie swallowed, her eyes soft and liquid with love as she studied his dark face hungrily. "I'd be delighted," she faltered. She tried to smile. "How have you been?"

"Miserable, thanks," Kingman replied. "How about you?"

"Just the same. And so alone." Her voice broke.

Kingman's face was a study in restraint gone to the wind. "My God, how do you think it's been for me?" he ground out. "Come here!"

He held out his arms and Aggie ran into them. He half lifted her, searching her eyes for the space of a heartbeat, and then he was kissing her. The fierce possession in the embrace would have been obvious to a blind man. Aggie moaned, and Kingman muttered something under his breath before he caught her closer and bent again.

Bowie discreetly closed the door behind him and turned, to see Gaby coming down the staircase.

"Mr. Courtland?" she asked, nodding toward the closed door.

He grinned. "Mr. Kingman," he corrected. He moved toward her.

"Miss me?"

"Terribly." She slid down the staircase into his arms and kissed him warmly. "He didn't shoot you."

"I thought he might, at first. Let's have coffee, and I'll tell you all about it." He glanced at the study door as they passed it and grinned at the faint sound coming out of it. "My, my, and here I thought she was over the hill."

Gaby blushed, still new to that kind of innuendo. She clung to his strong hand and followed him into the dining room.

"Tía Elena and I have prepared a late lunch," Montoya said when Bowie asked for coffee. "I will bring in the taco salads. What is happening?"

Bowie stared at him without answering.

"Tell me!" Montoya almost danced with impatience to know what was going on.

"Tell you what?" Bowie asked innocently.

"What are they doing?"

"Why not peek in the keyhole and find out?" Bowie grinned.

Montoya gave him a glare. "If you do not tell me, I will have Tía Elena starch your sheets."

"All right, Mr. Kingman is as miserable as Aggie is," the younger man said as he sat down beside Gaby. "He kissed her and she kissed him back, and I'll give you three guesses what they're doing right now."

Montoya grinned. "I will fetch the salad."

"Was it hard to convince him to come down here?" Gaby asked, her eyes soft on his face.

"It looked that way at first," he replied. "But he's crazy about her. I don't think he really needed much incentive, especially after I told him she was suicidal," he added, tongue-in-cheek.

"You didn't!" she gasped. "Aggie will shoot you herself!"

"Not right away," he murmured with a dry glance in the general direction of the living room. "Besides, he was getting stubborn. I had to make him see how desperate the situation was."

"And you were the one trying to run him off in the first place," she reminded him.

He took her soft hand and raised it to his lips. "I didn't understand what they felt, at the time." His black eyes began to glitter. "My God, I understand it now!" he said huskily.

Gaby's hand began to tremble where his held it. She was still getting used to having Bowie look at her like that, even if all the old fears were gone. There was only one last hurdle, and even that wasn't the terror it had been.

Before she could speak, there was the sound of a door opening, and two disheveled, breathless older people came into the dining room, hand in hand.

"We're starved," Aggie said with a shy glance at Ted Kingman. "What's for lunch?"

"What do you care?" Bowie grinned. "You'd more than likely eat cardboard and not notice right now."

"Stop that," Aggie muttered uncomfortably. She and Ted sat down next to each other, casting shy, curious glances at each other. Gaby and Bowie, watching, found the byplay amusing.

Montoya brought in a platter of taco salads and a huge bowl of chili, grinning from ear to ear. "Good to see you again, Señor Courtland," he greeted.

The older man shifted restlessly, his eyes going to Aggie. "Actually," he began, "Courtland is my middle name."

"Is it?" Aggie asked.

"My first name is Edward, but I usually go by Ted. And my parents are Kingmans from Texas."

Aggie didn't even blink, but her face went slowly red while she stared at him. "The Kingmans from near San Antonio?" she asked.

Kingman nodded. "The very same."

Aggie didn't move. She sat very still. "I've been mucking out stables," she began. "And pitching hay, and milking cows, and shoveling feed, and carrying water . . . you said I'd have to work on the ranch." Her black eyes began to burn. "You don't have a small ranch, you have a small empire!" she burst out, getting to her feet to glare down at him. "You thought I was after your money! You thought that I got lost deliberately . . . oh, my God!"

"Now, listen, Aggie," Kingman began. "You don't understand."

"Oh, yes, I do," she said, her voice shaking with rage. "You came down here to see where I lived and meet my kinfolk and decide whether or not I was good enough for you." Tears welled up in her eyes. "Well, thank you for coming back long enough to tell me the truth. And now you can go back to your quarter horses and your cattle and leave me alone! I don't want you!"

"That sure as hell wasn't the impression you gave me just now in the living room," Kingman returned, his own eyes glittering.

"That's true," Bowie told Gaby lazily. "I thought she was going to kiss him to death."

"Shut up!" Aggie wailed.

"And she's all but stopped eating, and all she's been doing is mooning around here," Bowie continued. "She sure doesn't act like a woman who doesn't want you," he added to Kingman.

"Whose side are you on?!" Aggie demanded of her son.

"His," Bowie nodded toward Kingman, whose eyebrows arched. "Well, Aggie, we men have to stick together."

"You can just put him right back where you found him," Aggie muttered, turning to leave the room. "A gold digger. He thought I was a gold digger!" she muttered on the way.

"Well, don't just sit there," Bowie glared at Kingman. "Go after her!"

"I won't," Kingman said shortly. "If that's the way she wants it, that's fine with me."

"You can't come all this way and give up so quickly."

"Sure I can," Kingman replied. He got up, his face stiff with anger and sadness. "You heard her. Put me back where you found me."

Bowie sighed angrily. "Some father you're turning out to be," he muttered as he got up from the table. "Leaving me here alone to cope with a rabid mother."

Kingman had to fight back a grin. "Never mind all that. I'm too old to be anybody's father."

"I'd let you take me to ball games," Bowie offered. "We could go to aerobatic shows, too." He frowned thoughtfully. "And I've always wanted to learn how to rope. I never could get the hang of it."

"For God's sake!" Kingman burst out.

Gaby had her face in her hands, trying not to giggle. Bowie just shrugged. "Okay. If that's the way you want it. Come on, I'll drive you to the airport."

"Goodbye, Gaby," Kingman said uncomfortably.

"Goodbye, Mr. Kingman," she said, stifling laughter. "I hope this won't be the last goodbye."

"This is how Aggie wants it," he returned coldly.

"Aggie wants you to follow her and kiss her half to death and tell her that you don't think she's a gold digger," Bowie told him. "But I guess that's a tall order for a man your age. I mean, Aggie's only fifty-six and she listens to Spanish music—very passionate Spanish music." He glanced at the rigid face of the man beside him as they walked toward the front door. "I guess she'd be more woman than you could handle."

"Damn it!" Kingman burst out. He whirled on his heel and went into the living room, where Aggie was sprawled, weeping, on the couch. "Now you listen to me, woman," he said furiously, and slammed the door behind him, hard.

There were muffled angry voices and the sound of something hitting the floor, followed by a different muffled sound, and then silence. Bowie grinned and went back into the dining room.

"You devil," Gaby accused, her olive eyes twinkling. "You did that deliberately."

"Well, he's the best father prospect I've had since my own died," he said reasonably. "Besides, he's on my side against the agricultural people." He glared at Gaby. "Something I can't even say for my own wife."

She touched his big hand. "Don't let's argue," she said softly. "I've got a lot to tell you about that later. Okay?"

He sighed heavily and sat down beside her. "Okay," he said with obvious reluctance. "Here, have some guacamole on that salad."

It was a long time before Aggie and Mr. Kingman came out of the living room, but there was no doubt in anyone's mind that they'd reached a truce. The engagement was back on again, and Aggie announced plans for a wedding the very next week. Bowie didn't bat an eyelash, although he did wink at Mr. Kingman.

Gaby had waited with bated breath in her own bedroom for Bowie to come to her. She'd been uncertain about going to his—being married was still new to her. She hadn't made him an invitation in so many words, but they'd been very comfortable with each other since the night before, when he'd had too much brandy. She'd rather expected that he might want to sleep with her again, even if she was still a little too uncomfortable for anything else.

But he didn't come. She lay awake with the lights on, hoping against hope that the cold wall between them had come down at last. Mr. Kingman had flown back to Wyoming to get a few things and to delegate some authority before he flew back to spend some time with a delighted Aggie before the wedding—which his sisters would attend as well. But after Bowie drove the older man to the airport, he didn't come straight home. Gaby and Aggie had been frantic, after the shot McHaney's son had taken at him already. They paced and mumbled until he finally showed up about nine o'clock in the evening.

He barely spoke to Gaby, directing his sparse conversation at Aggie instead. And when bedtime came, he excused himself and went into his study, where he closed the door firmly behind him.

Aggie had offered to talk, but Gaby was still shell-shocked by her sudden wedding and Bowie's odd behavior, so she had murmured something about being sleepy and escaped into her own bedroom.

Now she was hoping that Bowie would remember his married state and come to her, but it was midnight, and he didn't.

She heard footsteps finally and sat up in bed, arranging the covers just so, straightening the sheet, pushing her long hair back to make sure that every strand was in place. The gown was white—a very revealing one that she'd begged from Aggie while Bowie was gone. It was seductive and pretty, and it made her feel very feminine.

She held her breath as heavy footsteps came to her door and paused. But after a terse second, they continued lazily down the hall to Bowie's room. A door closed firmly.

Gaby could have screamed. For one minute, she thought about bursting into his room and demanding to know what he was up to, but her nerve failed her. She turned out her light and lay down. She couldn't think of anything she'd done—until she remembered the angry remark he'd made about her lack of loyalty in her dealings with Bio-Ag. He thought she was going to sell her share of Casa Río to them, and he was furious about it. She wasn't. She was on his side. But if he didn't trust her enough to know that she wouldn't ever sell him out without giving him a chance to protest, then he didn't know her at all.

She rolled over and pulled the covers up over her head. Men, she thought furiously, would just never understand the female mind. On the other hand, Bowie was a puzzle she didn't expect to fathom in the near future.

Down the hall, Bowie was lying awake himself, wondering why Gaby had gone to her own room. He'd been occupied all night trying to cool down his ardor. He loved Gaby and he wanted her, but she wasn't in any condition for what a few sweet kisses would inevitably lead to. He had to put her welfare first. So he'd stayed out late, removing himself from temptation, and then gone into his study for the same reason. He cared far too much for Gaby to put his pleasure before hers. And he guessed she'd realized that, since she'd gone to her own room. She probably knew he'd understand that she was asking him to wait. He smiled to himself. Sweet Gaby, so thoughtful. He closed his eyes with a contented sigh. It hadn't been a bad couple of days' work. He had a new daddy and a new wife, and now all he had to do was show Gaby how sweet lovemaking could be. He'd smoothed away her fears—God knew how, in his impatience—and she wasn't afraid of him anymore. Once she was better, he could show her how ungrounded those fears really were. He fell asleep on the thought.

CHAPTER

Nineteen

Harvey was already at his desk, spreading out information, and Bob Chalmers was bending over it looking at what Harvey had found.

"What have you got?" Gaby asked breathlessly as she joined them.

"Enough to cause a lot of trouble," Harvey said quietly. "Take a peek."

Gaby read over Bob's shoulder. The neatly typed notes documented Bio-Ag's two lawsuits—in Texas they accused Bio-Ag of causing groundwater contamination from careless use of dangerous pesticides resulting in dead cattle. Cotton West had also refused to spend the extra money for proper drains in the fields. Several landowners had sued because the eroded land had blown onto their fields and covered them in dust. There was another case pending in Texas, involving the deliberate laying by of fields to obtain government subsidies.

"Can you prove that?" Bob asked Harvey. "About the government subsidies?"

"You bet I can," Harvey replied. "The lawsuits are a matter of public record. Although," he added with a tiny grin, "they're public record in a town nobody ever heard of—"

"Your friend Johnny Blake called from Phoenix, too," Bob told her. "He said that the mysterious Mr. Samuels has something of a reputation for making money at the expense of the land. He gave me some numbers to call and asked if he could have access to your information. Considering that I stole you from him, I thought it was the least we could do—after we run the story first, of course." He chuckled wickedly.

Gaby sighed. Bowie had been right all along. His instincts had been good, and hers hadn't. Well, so much for her idealistic goals of providing new jobs for Lassiter's unemployed. This would take the small community out of the frying pan and into the fire.

"Shall I phone Mr. Barry, Mr. Logan, and Mr. Samuels, tell them our intentions, and offer them the chance to say something in their own behalf?"

"Sure." Bob grinned. "But do it quick. I want you and Harvey to get this thing together and in type before the end of the day. We're going to run a hell of a front page story Thursday." He smiled ruefully at Gaby. "And I'll go right to my terminal and write a nice editorial praising your stepbrother . . ."

"My husband." Gaby blushed as she extended her left hand, complete with wedding band. "We went down to Mexico Saturday."

"What a story! And you didn't call me to take pix?" Bob accused.

"There was a wire service photographer there," Gaby said, frowning a little. "He took plenty. I suppose they'll show up somewhere." The thought of them showing up back in Kentucky worried her, and it showed in her face.

Harvey took one look at it and got up abruptly. "Why don't we go phone those Bio-Ag people?" he suggested.

"Bob, I want to ask you about something. Oh—congratulations, Gaby," he added with a warm smile.

Gaby went on to her office, grateful for the momentary reprieve. Odd that Harvey should realize how upset she was and intervene. She wondered just how much he'd found out about her past, and then dismissed it. He hadn't had time, and if Bowie couldn't find anything, then surely Harvey couldn't. Or could he?

She sat down at her desk, still worried. She hadn't thought about the past in several days, but now it stared her right in the face. What was she going to do, now that she and Bowie were married? If she'd had time to think, she'd probably have found a way to get out of it, but things had gone too quickly. Her mind had shut down, and by the time it was working again, the ring was on her finger.

She loved Bowie—that was the one inescapable fact. But if her past ever caught up with her, what would she do? She couldn't even tell Bowie the whole truth—she couldn't confess what had really happened that night in Kentucky, because it would involve him. And if he ever let it slip, and anyone else found out, the ensuing scandal could ruin the McCaydes. Worse, it would even involve Mr. Kingman and Aggie now, because the Kingman fortune would ensure that Ted got his share of notoriety, too.

She felt the blood draining out of her face. What in the world was she going to do?

"Better get busy," Harvey murmured, peeking around the door. "We don't have a lot of time."

"Oh. Sure thing." She smiled at him. "Thanks."

He seemed to know without asking what she was thanking him for. He only smiled. "No sweat."

He left her to pick up the phone and start dialing.

Mr. Barry was shocked. Mr. Logan blustered and fumbled for words while Gaby read him part of what was going into print. But Mr. Samuels, when she reached him in Los Angeles, was supremely nonchalant.

"Well, you win a few, you lose a few," he replied carelessly. "We do make an impact on the local economy, you know, and there would have been a goodly number of jobs."

"There would have been a devastating amount of damage to the land," Gaby replied, "and the aquifer."

"Minor details," he replied, "and they don't really concern us. We use the land and then, when we make our money, we find more. That's big business, Miss Cane. We feel it's up to the local citizens to decide between progress and the ecology. We're in the business of making a profit."

"Yes, I can understand that," Gaby said quietly. "But don't you really care about the damage you do?"·

"Of course we care," he said. "But we can't afford to care too much—not in this day and time. Some of the things big corporations do to protect the land—installing expensive drains, laser leveling the land, adding chemicals to prevent salinization—take more money than we can afford to spend."

"Of course they're expensive," she returned, "but they guarantee that the land can be used over and over again. One of your major plantings is cotton, and nothing exhausts the land more quickly and more permanently."

"True," he agreed. "But it's a good cash crop, and it's more economical to grow than some others." He sighed. "You're good at your job, Miss Cane. Lassiter would have suited us very well. But, then, there are richer areas with better water, and we'll find them. Good day."

With those ominous words ringing in her ears, she put the receiver down belatedly.

"The thing is, he's right, in his way," she told Harvey later. "You can't afford too much sentiment in business. But Bowie's right, too—you can't replace history and the ecology once they're gone." She put her head in her hands. "Oh,

I hate being a reporter. Life was so much easier when I could only see one side of an issue."

"I know what you mean," Harvey said. "But at least we're objective. I know a lot of reporters who aren't. They deliberately slant news to suit their own viewpoints. Some papers do it, too—hatchet jobs, yellow journalism." He shook his head. "No wonder the media's been attacked so often in recent years. Honor used to be such an integral part of it. Now it's reporters after Pulitzers, and to hell with how they get them."

She was scrolling her copy as he talked. "I don't feel right about having my byline on this with you," she said. "You did all the work."

"I did not," he returned. "You came in with all the questions about effluent and drains and groundwater tables. I had to learn about those things before I could even ask the right questions." His broad face went a little red. "It embarrassed me that I didn't know already—that I took Bio-Ag's word as gospel. No good reporter takes anything at face value. You laid the groundwork for the story—I just helped follow it up."

She smiled at him. "Harvey, I didn't have the sources you have, and I lacked a lot of experience that you had. I think we're about even on embarrassment. But it's great to be working with you."

He cleared his throat. "I like working with you, too." He went redder. "By the way, I've given up trying to dig up your past. We all have skeletons. Yours are safe from me."

"Thanks, Harvey," she said huskily. He only nodded, and left. She wondered if he'd learned much. Hopefully he hadn't.

The day passed all too quickly, but Gaby and Harvey had finished their joint project by quitting time. They stayed late going over it for errors, so that it was almost dark by the time Gaby finally got to Casa Río.

Bowie was waiting on the front porch, pacing. Her heart lifted at his thunderous expression.

"Where the hell have you been?" he demanded, his black eyes flashing at her. "It's almost dark. I know you're Bio-Ag's biggest fan, but there are people around here who don't. I don't want anybody shooting at you."

She looked up at him. She almost told him what she and Harvey had done, but the mockery in his voice stung her pride. She pushed back her hair. "Nobody will," she assured him. "Is Mr. Kingman back?"

"Not until tomorrow," he said curtly. "Don't change the subject. You've got no business riding around in the desert at night."

"It isn't night, and I've been shot at before."

He ground his teeth together. "Don't remind me." He threw up his hands. "I thought if you worked on a small paper, you'd be out of danger."

Her eyebrows lifted. "I wasn't the one who stirred up this hornet's nest in the first place," she reminded him.

"No, you're all for progress, aren't you?" he asked with a steady glare. "To hell with the ecology and the land itself, let's have plenty of jobs!"

"Oh, yeah?" she shot back with her hands on her hips. "You're a builder! How many trees have you cut down? How many birds and squirrels are homeless because of you?!"

"You have to cut down an occasional tree . . . !"

"Could you two please keep your voices down?" Aggie grimaced, leaning out the front door. "Montoya and Tía Elena are threatening to go on strike."

"That'll be the day," Bowie muttered.

"There was a Buddy Holly song by that name," Gaby said brightly. "Supposedly taken from John Wayne's favorite expression in the movie, *The Searchers*."

Bowie glared at her. "I don't need any historical tidbits, thank you."

"Besides, darling, he doesn't remotely resemble John Wayne," Aggie returned. "I met him once, you know, when he was filming in Old Tucson. He was quite a gentleman, and a frequent visitor to Tucson."

"You never told me," Gaby beamed.

"I didn't think of it. Bowie, I never did get a chance to thank you for going after Ted," she added, smiling up at her tall, irritable son.

"It was that, or watch you moon around here until you faded away," he said lazily. "As it turned out, he was just as miserable as you were, but his pride was keeping him in Jackson."

Aggie stared at him. "Then, how did you get him here?"

"Oh, I told him I'd let him take me to ball games," he shrugged. "I think that was what did it."

Aggie laughed delightedly. "You didn't!"

"And I offered to let him teach me how to rope. You did know that he was world champion calf roper two years running?"

"No," Aggie returned, wide-eyed. "Was he, really? I don't keep up with the rodeo circuit, although most people know of the Kingmans."

"He was best all around two years running, too," Gaby offered.

"But I thought you disliked him," the older woman murmured, searching Bowie's hard face.

"I disliked the idea of him," he corrected gently. "Then it dawned on me from something he said that you aren't dead from the neck down just because you're past the hopscotch stage. I guess you can fall in love at any age."

Aggie smiled gently. "Yes, you can. I never expected to —Not like this." She sighed. "But he's all I want."

"That works both ways. His sisters said he was driving

them crazy. They were glad to see him leave, I think." He chuckled.

"What are they like?" Aggie asked hesitantly.

"Just like him, but they smile more," he replied. "You'll like them. I did."

Aggie relaxed visibly. "I was afraid of more infighting. Not that I'd have minded enough to give him up a second time. I'm just not that strong."

"When's the wedding?" he asked.

"Soon." She eyed Bowie and Gaby. "Why not make it a double ceremony? We're having it in the Baptist church, with Reverend Jackson doing the honors. I don't really like Mexican weddings."

"Neither do I," Bowie said, surprisingly. His black eyes went to Gaby. "I want something a lot more permanent."

She couldn't look away from that quiet, possessive gaze. It made her ripple with feeling. "Oh, so do I," she whispered.

"Then, we'll have the blood tests, and get another license, and do it properly," Bowie said, without removing his eyes from hers. "Okay?"

"Okay," she said huskily.

They went inside and had a companionable supper, but Bowie's black eyes were saying things that Gaby's body responded to in an alarming way. She had high hopes for the night ahead. But right after he finished eating, there was a phone call which required him to be locked up in the study for the rest of the night.

Gaby said a gentle good night to Aggie finally, after they'd spent the evening discussing clothes and future plans, and decided to have a relaxing shower.

She was enjoying the warm water on her tired shoulders when she heard a faint noise and then felt two big, warm hands on her waist, pulling her sharply back against a hard, bare, and definitely masculine body.

She gasped. "Bowie!"

"You know what a fanatic I am about water conservation, Gaby," he murmured at her ear with laughter in his deep voice. "How's this for saving water?"

She vibrated like a guitar string as his lean hands worked their way up her body. They were soapy, and the sensation of the silky substance on her bare skin was very arousing. She leaned back, letting him take her weight, while he rubbed soap gently over her taut breasts and down to her thighs, his hands magic, touching her in remembered ways, making her moan softly with the riotous sensations her body had enjoyed once before.

"I've missed you," he whispered, and pulled her around. The shower stall was enormous, with a huge tiled wall beside it. He eased her back against that, his feet firmly placed on the nonskid floor mat with hers, and his body levered down while his hard mouth found her soft lips and possessed them.

She felt the delicious abrasion of body hair rubbing against her breasts and flat belly and thighs, and her arms slid around him, holding him hungrily.

His mouth did the most intimate things to hers, teasing and lifting, probing softly, tasting, biting, and her body began to react in a new and helpless way. Her hips lifted and fell against his in an invitation she couldn't help.

"All right, honey," he whispered huskily, as if she'd spoken. His hips moved slightly, his knee edged between her legs, and he shifted.

Her tiny cry was buried in his warm mouth. She felt her body absorbing him, so easily, with none of the discomfort she'd felt before. This time, it was like slipping into velvet. The sensation was growing with each slow, gentle movement of his body. She was barely aware of the cool tile at her back, the sound of the shower running. She knew they should cut it off, but her mind was steadily becoming clouded by the pleasure he was giving her body.

Her fingers clung to his shoulders and then, impulsively, ran down his spine to his hips and she held him there, feeling the movements with something like awe. It hadn't been like this the first time—she hadn't really felt anything. But the sensations stabbing through her now took her breath, made her heart run wild, tensed her slender body until she thought she couldn't bear the muscular rigidity.

A sound broke from her—a hoarse cry that throbbed with sweet anguish as he shifted.

"There?" he whispered, and his voice sounded strained, too.

"Yes," she bit off.

His hands were flat against the wall beside her head. His mouth brushed against hers in slow, tender movements while the fever between them grew to flashpoint. Gaby's mouth slid to his hard chest and she bit him helplessly in her passion, her teeth tenderly nipping the hard muscle.

She heard him groan, and all at once she felt an urgency that she didn't even understand. She arched up at him, her voice breaking on his name, her hands clutching at his hips. She began to cry because the fury of what she was feeling had torn reason and sanity from her. She clung to him, begging him not to stop. The shower kept pouring beside them, the sound drowning her moans, and the frantic movement of their bodies.

She cried out and he lifted her, his hips pinning her to the wall. A kind of explosion of heat shot through her veins like pure fire, and she all but lost consciousness. She held on to Bowie as tightly as she could, barely aware of his own terrible stillness, his heavy shudder, the harsh groan that seemed endless. And then she felt his weight, all of it, crushing her, but even that was reverent, somehow.

She was trembling. She couldn't move, and she could

hardly breathe. She held him tight, shaking, feeling him shake, too. The water was cold now and uncomfortable, but her mind was only beginning to grasp that fact.

His lean arm reached out and turned it off. "Thank God we washed the soap off first." he whispered with a weary laugh. "I hate cold showers."

"Yes. So do I."

He moved away at last, and she averted her eyes quickly from his body and blushed.

He chuckled at her embarrassment. "We don't have any more secrets from each other," he mused. "That was the last one—the mystery of passion. And now you know how it feels, don't you?"

She lowered her eyes to his broad chest. "Oh, yes," she whispered, drowning in the memory of the pleasure she'd felt. "It was . . . unbelievable."

"Yes."

He dried her and then himself, chuckling at her fascinated gaze. "Why, Mrs. McCayde, you'll make me blush," he murmured.

She laughed delightedly. "Not a chance," she said. "Oh, Bowie, it was wonderful, and I wasn't afraid!"

"I did notice." He picked her up lazily and carried her into her bedroom, putting her gently on the sheets. The covers had been turned down before she went into the bathroom. "I don't like your bed. It's too short."

"Are you going away?" she asked sadly.

"Only if I take you with me," he murmured, smiling. "Want to sleep with me from now on?"

"Yes, please."

"Then, we'll have to find you a robe. You won't need a gown," he added with a wicked glance.

"What about you?"

"I'll borrow a towel. We can have Tía Elena move your things into my room tomorrow." He got a towel and wrapped it around his lean hips, then stuffed Gaby into a robe. He picked her up like a pirate, grinning from ear to ear, and carried her down the hall to his own room, pausing to lock the door behind them.

He laid her down on the bed and searched her eyes gently. She reached up to him. He unfastened the robe and whipped off his towel and followed her down.

She learned things then that she hadn't known before about him. Tenderness seemed as much a part of him as his black eyes, because he wooed her, slowly and with great patience. He made her wait for fulfillment until she was crying with her need, pleading with him for relief, and still he refused it. Not to salve his ego, he whispered, but to increase her own pleasure until the culmination was so violent that it all but left her unconscious. Afterwards, she lay in his hard arms and wept for several minutes, so overcome with the ferocity of pleasure that she could barely get her breath.

"Better now?" he whispered, drying her eyes.

"I'm sorry," she whispered back, reaching up to kiss his eyes closed. "It's just that it was so incredibly sweet . . . and violent . . . and devastating . . ."

"I can think of a few other adjectives," he whispered at her lips. "Reverent would be the first. You and I touch heaven when we do this."

"Yes." She nuzzled her face into his warm, damp throat. "I'm not taking anything."

"I'm not using anything." He brushed his mouth lazily over her forehead. "I love you. If a child comes of that love, it won't bother me in the least. How about you?"

She smiled. "I'm twenty-four. I've had my adventures, and a long taste of freedom. I wouldn't mind a baby—especially yours," she whispered huskily. "I love you, too."

He took a deep breath, swelling with pride and possession. "No more nightmares?"

"None."

"No more buried fears of intimacy?"

"Not anymore." She laughed mischievously.

His arms tightened around her and he tugged the sheet over them. "If you get pregnant, are you going to keep on working?"

"For a while," she said. "But reporting isn't really a fair profession for a mother. I might have to put it on hold until he's school age. I could do features, or in-depth pieces, of course, just to keep my hand in."

"He?" he probed, glancing down at her. "Until he's school age?"

She shifted. "I like little boys, don't you?"

"I like little girls just as much, you female chauvinist pig," he murmured dryly.

She laughed, hugging him close. "I'll do my best to have twins—one of each."

"Good girl. That's what I like—an equal opportunity mother. Come here."

He wrapped her up tight, kissed her gently, and turned off the light. She was asleep almost at once, so close to heaven that she could almost hear harps.

She hadn't told Bowie what was going on. She had meant to, but she'd been so lazy with pleasure that the unpleasantness was pushed to the back of her mind. She'd tried not to think about the past, and she'd shut out the story and its aftershocks. She didn't really want to tell him until the story was in print and she was sure that Bio-Ag wasn't going to try and slide out from under the charges.

As it turned out, she didn't have the chance to tell him. He was called out of town again on a construction job up in Scottsdale, which kept him tied up all day Tuesday. He stayed in Phoenix overnight and didn't get back until late Wednesday. By then, Gaby had an eyeful for him.

When she handed the paper to him, with its banner headline proclaiming the truth about Bio-Ag, he sat down heavily and let out an explosive breath. The look on his face was worth all the secrecy.

"You told me you were digging, honey, but you never mentioned this," he said accusingly.

"We were too involved Monday night for my mind to work properly," she said with a wicked grin. "And you were gone yesterday and most of today."

"Does Aggie know?"

She shook her head. "I'll tell her today. She's been mooning around, waiting for Mr. Kingman to come back. They keep the phone lines busy." She smiled. "They're very happy."

"So are we," he mused, smiling at her. "This is a hell of a story," he added, after he'd scanned it. "I knew you were good, cupcake, but this is exceptional. I don't think I'll let you give up that newspaper career, even if you insist. You're too good to keep in the kitchen."

"Montoya wouldn't like me in there, anyway," she assured him. She sat down in his lap with an easy affection that wouldn't have been possible for her even weeks ago. "I was so afraid somebody was going to put a bullet into you," she said seriously. "Thank God it's all worked out now."

"Amen. But you'll be sued to hell and gone, you know."

"I don't think so. Bob has good lawyers, and Mr. Samuels wasn't raving about being found out. He was very philosophical. He'll find another community," she added quietly. "He said there were other places."

"There are, and it will be up to the people who live in them to decide if they want progress at such a price." He searched her soft eyes. "I'd almost have done it for you," he said. "I'll try to come up with something to make it up to Lassiter. I've got contacts of my own. You can help."

She put her mouth lovingly to his. "I'd be delighted."

"Speaking of delight . . ."

She was being kissed breathless before Aggie came in and interrupted them, with Ted Kingman holding her hand.

"Don't mind us," Kingman mused, chuckling when Gaby extricated herself and stood up, flushed and laughing, while Bowie grinned at her.

"Don't worry, we won't." He handed the paper across the desk so that Aggie and her beau could get a good look at the headline. They read it, and Kingman laughed with pure delight.

"I told you he was right," he told Aggie.

Kingman stared at Bowie and then smiled. "That's great, both of you," he returned. He colored a little and turned to Aggie. "Suppose we go unload the car."

"You didn't bring the plane?" Bowie asked him.

"Well, it wouldn't fit in the trunk of my car," Kingman pointed out.

Bowie chuckled, taking Gaby's hand as they followed the older couple outside.

There were fireworks all over town when the paper hit the stands Thursday morning. The local radio stations aired the story, and the telephone rang off the hook at the newspaper office. The mayor was apologetic; the city councilmen were shell-shocked. Even old man McHaney called to apologize again for what had happened, and to tell Gaby how much he appreciated Bowie dropping the charges against his son. Gaby, who hadn't known, was delighted to see that her husband didn't hold grudges, even when he was justified.

CHAPTER

Twenty

Aggie and Ted announced that they were flying up to Jackson to spend a few days with his sisters. Ted drew Aggie close to his side with a warm, loving smile. "They'll like you," he told her. "You'll fit in very well at the ranch. Ilene's already said that she and Joanne plan to move into the big guest house after we marry. We'll see them, of course, but they want the main house to be strictly ours."

"They won't resent me, will they?" Aggie asked worriedly.

"No. They were convinced that I was going to live and die alone for the rest of my life. They're delighted about the wedding." He grinned at Bowie, who was talking to Montoya nearby. "Your son has them starstruck. They'd like to have him visit again."

Aggie laughed and so did Gaby. "I think he might be convinced to do that. You might have to take him to a ball game or something, though," Aggie said, tongue in cheek.

Kingman smiled. "I wouldn't mind that at all. I've enjoyed being around him. He's intelligent and honest. Those are good qualities."

"I think so, too," Gaby agreed, her heart in her eyes as she stared at her husband.

"Was he surprised when he read the paper yesterday?" Aggie asked.

"Shocked to the back teeth," the younger woman replied. "And very pleased, I think." She sighed. "I hope I don't get Bob Chalmers sued, but Harvey and I can verify everything we printed. It's so hard doing a story like this. I hate to see the jobs lost, but the ecology would have suffered terribly."

"There will be other enterprises," Kingman said. "I hope your politicians learned something from this. Industry is important, but the quality of industry is the prime criterion."

"I think they'll remember the lesson they've learned," Gaby said. "Most people are getting ecology-minded. None of us can afford to take the environment for granted anymore—the planet's getting too small. Still," she added wistfully, "it's hard to explain that to people with children they can't feed properly."

Bowie joined them in time to hear her last remark. "I agree wholeheartedly," he said, smiling down at her. "And I've got a couple of ideas about that. I'll tell you when I work them out."

"Are you going to get secretive now?" she teased.

"Stand back and watch me." He hugged her close, and she knew they'd never been quite as happy as they were now. She felt completely at peace with herself. If only the past wasn't still hanging over her like a sword.

She and Bowie spent the weekend exploring the area. They visited Tombstone and walked in the footsteps of the Clantons and Earps and Doc Holliday. They saw the huge rose tree and the old courthouse and the Bird Cage Saloon and the Crystal Palace. They drove down to Bisbee and looked into the awesome Lavender Pit, and had coffee in the Copper Queen Hotel, which had been a mecca of civilized comforts in the late 1800s. They paused to walk around the old country store at Pearce, look at the memorabilia, and talk to the proprietor, and then they struck out for Douglas and had lunch in the Gadsden Hotel. There were marvelous stained glass windows there, one done by Tiffany. Legend had it that Pancho Villa had ridden his horse up the marble staircase, and the chips in the clear surface attested to the rough treatment.

"There's a lot of history in Douglas," Bowie told her as they paused on the town square. Many of the stores were deserted now, and there were only a few pedestrians milling around. "Back during Villa's day, the townsfolk would rush up onto the rooftops to watch the fighting across the border in Agua Prieta. There's a rumor that they changed armbands when the politics changed over the border, so that they wouldn't be accosted for supporting the wrong side." He grinned. "There's another rumor that when Pancho Villa wanted to buy something, he put down a treasure chest and told the shopkeepers to take what they needed for their supplies. It's colorful, even if it isn't all true."

She clung to his hand. "Can we go over into Mexico?"

"Sure, if you want to."

They drove past the small border station and down into Agua Prieta where they bought colorful serapes and carved wooden candles and figurines. When they started back to the border, however, Gaby wanted to cry. Mexican children stood in a line almost all the way, offering for sale such items as homemade candies and food, proffering their services as car washers and window washers. Their huge black eyes pleaded with the well-dressed American tourists, and it was all she could do not to empty her purse out the window.

"The annual income down here is so low it would shock you," he told her as they stopped at the border station and then crossed back into Douglas. "Jobs are few and far between." He sighed. "Just like in Lassiter, only worse." He glanced at her. "I suppose you'll never forgive me for blowing up your idealistic hopes for the unemployed?"

"On the contrary," she said gently. "I think you were extraordinarily brave for sticking to your guns despite all the opposition—especially when Mr. McHaney started shooting. Why did you drop the charges?"

"McHaney's got a wife and two kids," he said simply. "I offered him a choice between staying in jail or giving me five minutes with him out behind his house." He smiled faintly. "I got even, believe me. He won't be shooting at me again."

She laughed. "You're a surprising man."

"I'm a happy man," he corrected, glancing her way. "And there will be some jobs for Lassiter. I'm working on that."

She gave up asking about his plans, because it was obvious that he wasn't going to tell her.

Every night she slept in his arms, and on Sunday, they went to church. It was sublimely sweet, sitting next to him in the pew and thinking about bringing their children here later on to Sunday school and church. Family life might be outdated in some places, but it was alive and well in Lassiter, and Gaby thanked God that she and Bowie had found each other. A career alone would never have suited her half as well as having Bowie's children and living at Casa Río, although reporting was still close to her heart, and she'd continue to do it.

Monday morning came all too soon. At work, things seemed a little tame after the big exposé. The morning went so smoothly that the last thing on her mind was complications. They came suddenly.

As Gaby returned to her office after lunch, she found a message on her desk, with a number for her to call. She wasn't sure where the call was from, so she looked up the area code in the telephone directory. It was Lexington, Kentucky.

Gaby sat down heavily, shaking all over. It couldn't be them—surely, it couldn't be—but who else in Kentucky would want to get in touch with her? It had to be about what had happened ten years ago. They wanted revenge, that was it. They'd finally tracked her down, very likely from the wedding picture of herself and Bowie, and now they were going to make trouble. But the trouble wouldn't be just hers —it would affect every single person she loved. It might even destroy them.

She could hardly bear the pain, but she knew what she was going to have to do. If they knew she was living at Casa Río, she had to leave—quickly. She had to do it without a trace, and let no one know where she was going—especially Bowie.

Her eyes closed and she began to cry—great heaving sobs of pure misery. There was a possibility that she was pregnant, and she and Bowie had shared a happiness that surely few couples truly knew. Now it was all over. The past had finally caught up with her, with a vengeance. There wasn't anyone she could turn to. She hadn't a friend in the world, except for Bowie himself, and he was the last person on earth she could tell.

Harvey was out covering a story, and Bob Chalmers didn't know anything about the telephone number when she asked. Judy did.

"It was a woman," she told Gaby, frowning. "She sounded elderly, and very gruff. She asked for you, and when I told her you weren't here—it was while you were out getting that ad from the drugstore—she left the number and asked to have you call her back."

"Was that all?" Gaby asked with false cheer.

"Yes. She wasn't very talkative. She didn't give her name, either."

"I'm not surprised," Gaby said, staring at the piece of paper in her hand.

"You look terrible," Judy said, concerned.

"It's just the heat," Gaby hedged. "I'll be fine. I'll, uh, return this call at home."

She got through the rest of the day, praying that the woman wouldn't call again. It must have been Mrs. Angus Bartholomew, the grand dame of the racing family, who'd hired Gaby's father. The old lady's son had been killed, and Mrs. Bartholomew wanted Gaby to pay for it. No doubt she'd been looking for her all these long years, and the hatred had grown until it had reached flashpoint. Gaby didn't know what she was going to do. If Mrs. Bartholomew was her old self, she'd probably think nothing of calling the media in and giving them the story.

Hiding her terror from Bowie was harder than she'd thought it would be. She put on her old mask and laughed at the supper table, telling him about the giant squash she'd photographed, listening to his woes about the snags the Canada project had run into, but her eyes were haunted, and he saw it.

"You're worried," he said unexpectedly, his black eyes probing, seeing deep, as usual. "You're trying to hide it, but you can't. I know you too well."

"It's the story we ran," she fabricated. "I'm still worried about a lawsuit."

He relaxed, smiling. "Well, don't worry. We can handle a lawsuit. I've got terrific lawyers. So has Chalmers. Eat your apple pie and ice cream and stop looking for trouble."

But I'm not, she wanted to say—it's looking for me. She smiled at him and dipped her fork into the deliciously flaky crust of Tía Elena's apple pie.

She didn't return Mrs. Bartholomew's call. In fact, she carefully put a match to the telephone number and asked Judy to tell the lady she wasn't there if any calls came again. She made up a story about an old enemy, and Judy was nice enough not to question what she was told. She liked Gaby, and agreed to do as she was asked.

Meanwhile, Gaby started getting her things together. It broke her heart to think about leaving her husband and Casa Río, Aggie and all her friends, but there wasn't any other choice. If she stayed, she could put them all at risk. It was far better to sacrifice her own happiness than to put them on the firing line with her.

She planned to leave on the following Saturday. Somehow, she got through until Friday night, but it was hard not to give the show away. Bowie was all too perceptive, and she disliked hiding anything from him.

Montoya and Tía Elena went into Tucson to visit relatives. Aggie was still in Jackson with Ted. Bowie went swimming in the pool house. It would have been a perfect time to slip away, but Gaby couldn't go—not just yet.

She stood at the edge of the pool, clad in her long blue silk robe, watching Bowie. He'd gotten into the habit of swimming nude just lately, and occasionally she joined him, but still in her bathing suit. Tonight was different. Tonight would be the last night. She was going to give him a memory that would last them both all the long years ahead when they wouldn't see each other.

He leaned his arms on the pool edge, smiling at her. "Well, come on in," he taunted. "You won't melt."

"Won't I?" She laughed softly, and all at once, she let the robe drop.

The smile faded. His face hardened with pure desire as his black eyes slid from her high, firm breasts down her soft body to her full hips and long, elegant legs.

"Have I ever told you how beautiful you are?" he asked softly.

"I could say the same thing about you, Bowie," she whispered, her voice carrying in the stillness. "And I'd mean inside as well as out. You're the most beautiful person I've ever known."

Her voice broke and he frowned. "What's wrong?"

"Nothing." She smiled and slid into the water with him, her arms curling around his neck. "No questions," she whispered as she eased her lips against his. "No more questions. I want you."

The shock of her uninhibited behavior made his mind fog. As soon as he felt her soft skin against his and returned her warm, hungry kisses, reason vanished.

"Gaby," he breathed. His hands slid to her hips and brought them in a slow, erotic motion to his.

"Yes, I like that," she murmured against his hardening mouth. Her nails scraped gently against his nape and then down his shoulders to his hips. She pressed herself against him, drowning in the sudden fury of his need and her exquisite certainty that she could satisfy it as never before.

"What are you doing?" he asked roughly when she moved back a little and her hands began to touch him in new, exciting ways.

"Learning things," she laughed tenderly. "Don't be afraid, honey," she whispered, nuzzling his nose with hers. "I'll be gentle."

He burst out laughing, and the laughter turned into a groan. His mouth found her neck and brushed there, his breathing rough and sharp, his hands clenching her hips.

She turned her mouth against his and kissed him with all her heart, levering her body so that she was even with his hips. "Help me," she whispered into his parted lips. "I . . . I'm not . . . yes! Oh, yes!"

His big, lean hands were under her spine, under her thighs, lifting, positioning. He pulled gently, lifting his head so that he could see her eyes as he probed, and then surged upward in one slow, tender movement of his powerful body.

"Not here," he whispered. "It's too deep."

He eased her into shallow water, backing her up against the side of the smooth pool, but so that they were standing waist-deep in the cool water.

"Take a long time," she whispered huskily. Her hands touched his hard face, tracing his eyebrows, his cheekbones, his mouth and nose, as he moved with exquisite slowness. "Take a long, long time." She gasped, and his mouth touched hers with easy affection.

"Marriage gets better every day," he breathed. He looked down and so did she, catching her breath at the contrast between his dark, hair-roughened body and her soft, pink one, at the intimacy of seeing where they touched, how they touched.

Her face turned red as he looked up. "Yes, it awes me, too," he whispered huskily. "And I've seen it before. But with you, it's a miracle of togetherness, a sharing of all we are. I love you very much, Mrs. McCayde."

"Oh, Bowie . . . I love you," she moaned. Tears filled her eyes, but she kissed him so that he wouldn't see them. Her arms lifted around him and she moved sensuously against him, which made him even hungrier, incited him to urgency.

"Don't let me hurt you," he breathed roughly.

"You couldn't," she whimpered. Her eyes closed. Her teeth ground together. "You couldn't, not . . . ever!"

The side of the pool was hard at her back, but his hands slid there, protecting her from the abrasion. He groaned into her open mouth as his hips began to echo the feverish urgency of his tongue penetrating her lips, probing the soft sweet darkness of her mouth, finding the emptiness there and making it throb with the need to be filled.

She felt her legs twining around his, holding him, as the rhythm grew shuddery and strong. She whispered something, and cried out. The heat was there again, like a brand, burning her, filling her with molten flame. She bit into his shoulder helplessly as the waves washed over her and lifted her, convulsively, into heaven.

She opened her eyes at that moment and saw his face— saw it corded and contorted with the anguish of fulfillment; even as the sound broke from his tight lips and his body arched into hers with the savage throb of ecstasy in his voice.

His eyes opened as his coiled muscles relaxed. He looked directly into Gaby's eyes. Incredibly, the sight of her watching him made his body begin to shudder all over again. He caught her hair and held her face while his mouth burned down into hers, and he waded into the shallows, with her body still part of his.

He lifted his head when they were knee-deep and his eyes were black as night. "Again," he breathed roughly. "I have to have it again."

She smiled faintly as she met his lips. He put her down to get out of the pool, a tremor in his arms as he helped her out and lifted her onto one of the loungers under the sun roof.

"Will it hold us?" she whispered as he came down over her.

"Who the hell cares," he ground out. "Gaby!"

His stamina overwhelmed her. He kissed her until she was dizzy, touched her in ways he never had, took her to the brink and pulled her back, over and over again, until she sobbed.

"I can't stand it!" she wailed.

"Yes, you can," he bit off against her mouth. His hands contracted hungrily on her hips. "Lift up. Hard. Hard!"

He controlled her movements, her mind, her heart. He rolled over and lifted her onto him and held her while she learned the rhythm and let him guide her. It was incredible the second time. She almost fell in her anguished release, his hands holding her thighs to keep her upright, his voice breaking with the sweet pain of fulfillment.

He pulled her down at last and his big hands soothed her while they both strained to breathe, their heartbeats shaking each other.

"I've never done it like that," he whispered finally, when she was still and faintly trembling against his broad, damp chest.

"Before," she whispered, smiling as she lifted up to put her mouth gently over his.

"Before," he agreed. His soft eyes searched hers. "I couldn't love you more if I worked at it all my life," he whispered. "You're my world, Gaby." His eyes darkened. "You're my very life. I know how Ted felt when his wife died and he ran the truck into the river. I'd just as soon be dead if I had to face a future without you in it."

"No," she whispered, her eyes tearing up again as she put her fingers to his hard mouth. "No, you're strong. You'd go on . . ."

"No, I damned well wouldn't," he said curtly, moving her hand to his chest. "I've never loved before. I never could again—not like this."

Terror shot through her. She bit her lower lip and tried to find the right words. How could she tell him that she was leaving him? How could she admit that she was going away?

"Stop looking so terrified," he murmured as he brought her back down against him and sighed. "You're not going anywhere, and neither am I—except to bed," he mused, chuckling, "before Montoya and Tía Elena get the shock of their married lives."

"They won't be back until ten," she murmured lazily.

"It's five after ten," he whispered.

She shot up, her wide eyes stunned. He lifted his waterproof watch and showed her the dial.

"Doesn't time fly when you're having fun?" he mused, his black eyes twinkling.

"They might come in here!"

"Yes, they might."

She jumped up, grabbing at her robe. She shouldered into it, still damp, and threw Bowie's towel to him. "Get up, do," she coaxed. "What will they think if they see us?!"

He chuckled as he got up, lazily, and wrapped the towel around his hips. "They'll think we've been swimming," he murmured, tongue in cheek. "Unless you blush like that in front of them."

"I can't help it," she said shyly.

"Amazing," he sighed. "Especially in view of the fact that you seduced me," he added wickedly. "I've never enjoyed anything as much in my whole life. You might keep that in mind."

"Oh, I will," she assured him. *I'll live on it all my life*, she added silently.

They came out of the pool area together just as Tía Elena and Montoya came in the door. Gaby greeted them, mumbled something about changing out of her wet bathing suit, smiled sheepishly, and shot up the staircase like a bullet.

Bowie was still laughing about it when he came to bed minutes later.

She got up before dawn, careful not to rouse Bowie, and dressed in a suit and high heels, barely pausing to put on makeup and brush her hair. Then she stood beside the bed and looked down at him, tears misting her vision as she let her eyes adore him one last time. It was for his own good. She had to remember that, and not weaken. If she stayed, she put him at risk—him, Aggie, Casa Río, and everything he held dear. She didn't dare think about what he'd said—about what he'd do if he lost her. She had to believe that he'd go on, because he was strong. He was very strong. He'd make it.

She wanted to kiss him, just once more, but she was afraid she might wake him. He was a light sleeper at best, despite the way she'd tired him out the night before. She still blushed, remembering how sweet it had been to make love with him. Amazing, she thought, that just when her old nightmares and fears were put to rest, the past should come back to threaten her again.

With a weary sigh, she forced her eyes away from him and turned. She opened the door silently and closed it. Then, with tears hot in her eyes, she crept down the staircase.

Montoya and Tía Elena would still be asleep. They arose just past dawn. She had less than ten minutes to get her suitcase and get out of the house before she was discovered. She didn't dare let anyone see her with her things in a bag, leaving Casa Río. She had to just disappear.

She reached into the hall closet where she'd hidden the suitcase, past the sports equipment, and gently pulled it out. She'd taken only what she had to have. She had her savings passbook in her purse, with enough money in her account to tide her over until she could get another job.

With a heart like lead in her chest, she gently closed the closet door and picked up the bag.

She turned to leave, and ran straight into Bowie, who'd been standing at the foot of the staircase, watching her.

CHAPTER

Twenty-one

Gaby couldn't even speak. She tried to get words out, but they wouldn't come. Bowie looked down at her without any particular surprise on his lean face. He was wearing jeans and nothing else, so obviously he'd dressed in a hurry. And he was smiling, tenderly, as his black eyes held hers.

"I can explain," she began finally, knowing she couldn't.

"I already know," he replied. "Everything."

"But you couldn't!" she burst out. "You said you'd tried already . . . !"

He took the bag from her and put it down. Then he picked her up gently and carried her into his study, kicking the door shut. "I did try, years ago," he agreed. He sat down in his big armchair with Gaby in his lap. "Mrs. Bartholomew isn't the kind of woman who gives up. She called me yesterday at my office."

Gaby burst into tears. She put her face in her hands and cried until her throat hurt.

Bowie held her close, rocking her. "Shhh," he whispered softly. "It's all right, baby. There's nothing in the world to be afraid of. It's all over. You're safe. You're with me, and you're safe."

"They'll hurt you." Her voice broke. She lifted eyes dark with terror. "My father killed Mrs. Bartholomew's son when he attacked me! We ran, oh, God, we ran, and I hoped . . . But she found me . . . and now she'll put it in all the papers. I can run away!" she whispered feverishly. "If they can't find me, they'll leave you alone!"

"Gaby." He put his fingers gently across her wild mouth. "Hush. I said it's all right. Mrs. Bartholomew doesn't want to hurt you, or me, or any of us."

She shuddered a little with reaction. "What?"

"It's a long story, but I can abbreviate it," he replied quietly. "Your father didn't kill her son."

"But he did, I saw . . . !"

"Your father hit him, and there was a lot of blood," he whispered. "There was even a preliminary and very premature story in one of the local papers to the effect that he had been murdered. But he didn't die that night, Gaby. He died in the hospital, two days later, of a heart attack. An autopsy was performed, at the request of the family. He died of valve disease—calcification of the heart valves. He must have known he had a heart problem for a long time, because the symptoms would have been obvious. But he drank heavily, and he wouldn't see a doctor. The blow concussed him. It didn't kill him."

Gaby buried her face in his chest and wept. She wept for her father, who'd died in a mental institution, overcome by the thought that he'd murdered another human being. She wept for herself, for all the long years that she'd been haunted by what had happened that night. She wept for the Bartholomews, who'd suffered so much because of their son.

Bowie smoothed her long hair. "Mrs. Bartholomew said they'd looked for you and your father for years. They finally traced him to the place he'd died. He was a minister at one time, wasn't he, Gaby, and that was why what happened was so horrible for him. Taking life was against everything he believed in."

"Yes," she whispered, wiping away the tears. "We were poor, but he was a good man, Bowie. He was never affectionate, but he was good to me, and he took care of me the best way he knew." She sniffed. "I've lived with it for so long," she whispered, shaking. "I've been so afraid that they'd find me one day."

"They did, from the wire service photo of our wedding," he continued. "They wanted you to know the truth. It was important to Mrs. Bartholomew that you weren't hiding or afraid that you might be prosecuted even today. There was no crime. There was no guilt—only theirs, that they hadn't known he was harassing you. She is delighted to know that you're married to a moderately successful man, and that you're happy. And you are, aren't you, honey?" he asked tenderly.

She clung to him hungrily and kissed him—tender little kisses, all over his face. "Oh, I'm happy," she whispered brokenly. "So happy! Bowie, I was going away..."

"Yes, I know." He kissed her back. "I wanted you to tell me. I was hoping, up until the last minute, that you'd trust me enough—especially after what happened in the pool last night. That was goodbye, wasn't it?" he asked gently.

She nodded, wiping away the tears. "I wanted to leave you a good memory."

"It was that. But losing you would have killed me." He searched her eyes, and he wasn't smiling. "I wasn't kidding. I meant every last word I said to you. You're my world—all of it."

The tears came back. She kissed him with her whole heart. "I couldn't bear to see you hurt because of me," she whispered. "It killed me to leave, but they could have ruined you."

He shrugged. "So I'd have gone back to construction work. But I'd much rather lose the business, and Casa Río, than lose you," he said simply. "A man can't live without his heart, little one."

She leaned her forehead against his with a soft sigh. "That's how I felt, because you're my heart, too." She closed her eyes. "I don't have to go? I can live with you forever?" she asked in a small, awed voice.

His big arms pulled her to him. "All my life, and all yours." His eyes closed on a hard sigh. "I hope I can live up to you," he added quietly. "You can't know how it touches me, that you'd have sacrificed your happiness for me."

She pulled back and looked into his haunted eyes. "Bowie . . . wouldn't you have done exactly the same thing for me?" she asked gently, smiling at him.

He took a slow breath and smiled back. "Yes."

"Now who's going to have to live up to whom?" she teased, and smiled against his warm, hard mouth.

"Just what is your real name?" he asked several heated minutes later.

"Gabrielle Cane," she replied.

He frowned. "But you said that was an assumed name."

She grinned. "Yes, I did. To throw you off the track, so you wouldn't try to find out anything."

"For God's sake," he said.

"Didn't it ever occur to you that I'd have had to falsify all my records—Social Security, learner's license, and so forth?" She gave him a demure glance through her lashes. "The authorities have unpleasant ways of dealing with people who do that sort of thing."

"No, it never occurred to me." He chuckled. He pulled her down again and wrapped her up with a heartfelt sigh. "It doesn't matter in the least, now. You're Mrs. McCayde—all mine."

"That works both ways. I never dreamed I'd be free of the past one day," she said, still stunned by the suddenness of it all. She stared across his bare chest to the window. "I've been haunted for so long, Bowie. I can't believe I'm actually free."

"Yes, you can. I'll make you believe it." He kissed her forehead with breathless gentleness. "We start here, Gaby. Together."

She smiled and looked up at him with her heart in her eyes. "Yes. No more nightmares. No more lies. No more secrets. And I guess that means I can unpack, doesn't it?"

"Later," he said when she tried to get up. His mouth found hers, and she melted into him, wrapped up like his greatest treasure in his big, loving arms.

Once the past was put into proper perspective—it took a few days for Gaby to resolve it all—life seemed to move at a slower, less taxing pace. Work went on as usual, and there were no lawsuits.

The one sour note in her life was that she wasn't pregnant. She hadn't told Bowie what she suspected until she'd gone to the doctor, but what she thought was pregnancy was only a missed period. There was still hope, of course, and Bowie's ardor didn't cool a bit as time went by. She knew that one day her fondest hope would be realized, so she was content to take it one day, one lovely day, at a time.

Gaby had found the prospect of a double wedding with Aggie and Mr. Kingman delightful, and it was. She and Aggie chose matching street-length dresses in an antique white color, styled like wispy feminine dresses from the 1920s, with matching veils. Aggie blushed like a girl as she spoke her vows. Bowie and Gaby took their own vows a second time, and with even more reverence, because the love they shared was deeper now, and stronger than ever.

It seemed as if half of Arizona came to Casa Río for the reception. Gaby's friends from the Phoenix and Lassiter newspapers were in attendance, along with Bowie's construction gang chiefs and board of directors. Mr. Kingman had plenty of family attending besides his two sisters, and with them came his foreman, and a number of familiar faces from the rodeo circuit.

Gaby was staring adoringly at her husband when Harvey paused beside her with a second glass of champagne, which he put into her empty hand.

"Congratulations, again," he said.

She grinned at him. "I think we both deserve some. We're the toast of two newspapers, lest you forget, and if we threatened to resign, I really think Bob might offer us a partnership."

He laughed himself. "Imagine, and we didn't even get sued."

She shrugged. "Mr. Samuels is apparently used to being sued. He does make money, and I can understand that some communities would be desperate enough to let him in." She glanced at Harvey somberly. "The worst of it was that I felt like I was coming out against agriculture, and that isn't so. Nobody is more on the side of farmers and ranchers than I am."

"This was a different situation," he reminded her. "We did what we had to, to protect the ecology. We can't resent that."

"I suppose not. But it worries me that we've cost Lassiter a lot of jobs."

"We'll find a way to get more—without having to sacrifice the quality of life for it."

"Will we?" She smiled sadly. "I hope so."

"Stop glowering." Bowie grinned as he joined them. "We're supposed to be celebrating."

"We already are," Harvey assured him. He lifted his glass. "Congratulations."

"On my wife or my stepfather?" Bowie asked with a wry glance at a beaming Mr. Kingman. "I'm quite happy with both, thanks."

"It shows," Gaby told him, leaning against his side with a warm, happy sigh. "I'm pretty happy myself."

"That shows, too," Harvey said, smiling. "I'd better go and rescue Bob from the competition. See you."

Gaby nodded, watching him go. "He's not a bad man at all, you know," she mused. "He's a good reporter, too."

"I know another good one." His arm brought her close. "Have I ever told you how proud I am of you?" he asked sincerely. "You did a hell of a job on that story."

"I did my best," she corrected. "I hope it was good enough. But I still worry about having done what was best for the community," she confessed. "Bowie, all those jobs . . ."

He bent and kissed her gently. "Don't carry the weight of the world on your shoulders—especially not today. Come on. I want you to meet my new in-laws."

She was delighted with Mr. Kingman's sisters and family, and so was Aggie. As the reception wound down, she wondered at the ease with which the two families seemed to fit together. Staring up at her handsome husband, she sighed with pure pleasure at the way things had happened in her life—at the random factors that had led her to Arizona, and to Bowie. It was enough to convince her that there was no such thing as coincidence. She slid her arm around his hard waist and smiled up at him, her eyes soft with love. It couldn't get better than this, she thought. Nothing could be as wonderful as standing in the arms of the man she loved, with a whole lifetime ahead of them to discover everything there was to know about each other.

But, Bowie was still keeping one secret from Gaby. For the next few weeks he worked unusually long hours and attended meetings with city council members that he kept from her newsy nose. Until one Monday afternoon, when he put her in the ranch pickup and drove her out to the site where he'd made love to her for the first time. There he showed her the blueprints and pending council approval for his development project.

She sat down heavily on the running board of the truck with the plans in her hands.

"Bowie, this is incredibly big," she burst out. "What is it?"

"A retirement complex," he said. "It will cater to elderly people—an age group that can't do much damage to the surroundings. There'll be a shopping mall, complete with grocery store and pharmacy, and a resident doctor and clinic —even a vet." He grinned. "And over here," he pointed to another square on the blueprint, "is a small museum and library which will house all the artifacts and history of this area. The entire complex won't use a fraction of the water an agricultural outfit would, and we've designed it with water conservation in mind, right down to the plant material in the landscaping. The whole thing will cost $3.5 million. We can get some federal funding, and the city council is kicking in a bit. There are grants we can apply for from private industry, and I'm furnishing the construction labor. You wanted jobs for Lassiter, honey. Here they are."

She couldn't even think. She jumped up and threw her arms around him, laughing as she hugged him. "I think you're terrific," she murmured happily.

"I'm glad you appreciate me," he returned, grinning. "It's nice to know that I have my uses."

She grinned back. "I can think of a couple . . ."

"Can you?" He bent and kissed her lazily. "The first time was here," he said, the smile fading. "I hurt you."

She put her hand over his mouth. "I loved you," she replied. "And I left the past behind here. There aren't any scars on me from what happened—not even one."

He let out a heavy breath. "Thank God for that. It haunted me for a long time."

"You more than made up for it," she mused. She hugged him hard. "When do you get council approval on this project?"

"At the next meeting, unless there's a lot of public opposition. And I don't see how there can be," he added with a chuckle, "because I own the land."

"How long will it take to build?"

"A couple of years, I imagine," he replied. "These things take time. But it will give people something to hope for, something to look forward to."

"Indeed it does. Can I break the story?" she probed.

"Along with the rest of the media," he replied. "I don't play favorites, even when they're married to me," he added, tapping her on the nose with his forefinger.

"Oh, well," she sighed. "I guess I'll just melt into the crowd with the rest of the unappreciated press."

"You'll never be that." He kissed her gently. "Aggie and Ted are coming down for the weekend."

"I know. Aggie said that Ted had tickets for the rodeo in Phoenix. He thought you might like to go with him."

He chuckled. "Yes, I would. You and Aggie can go shopping."

"Are you kidding?" she burst out. "Go shopping, when there's a rodeo to watch?!"

He looked down at her. "Fanatic."

"So is Aggie; it runs in the family. Besides, one of Ted's

cousins from Texas is competing in the calf roping. We have to go and support him."

"If you say so," he said. He put an arm around her and leaned back against the truck to watch the sun going slowly down behind the Dragoon Mountains. They were turning dark burgundy, their jagged peaks outlined against the orange and yellow and red of the sunset. "This is one hell of a beautiful country, Gaby," he said.

"It certainly is." She leaned her head against his shoulder. "Bowie, you don't really mind sharing the past with the future, do you? I mean, the compromise isn't going to keep you awake nights or anything?"

He pulled her closer. "I had to make a decision. It wasn't an easy one, at first. But you're right about people being important. The thing is to find ways to help the economy without sacrificing too much of the ecology. I think it can be done. I'm going to do my part."

"I'm glad."

"So am I." He sighed pleasantly, smiling to himself at the way it had worked out for him and Gaby. He looked down at her, loving every line of her face, every facet of her personality. "I know we said no more secrets. Can you forgive me for keeping this last one?"

"Of course. In fact, I've been keeping one of my own."

"Have you? What?" he asked with lazy affection.

She took his free hand and pulled it to her flat stomach. Then she looked up at him, the light from the setting sun reflected in her eyes.

The action was enough, without the words. He knew he couldn't get words out. It was a miracle that he had Gaby, that she loved him, but this made the miracle complete. This would complete the circle of their love.

He bent and kissed her mouth with soft tenderness. She smiled, thinking that his lips felt like a firebrand in the late afternoon, touching her with the heat of desire, the flame of possession, the mark of love in the shadow of the past. She closed her eyes, and felt the sun warming her eyelids. Love, she thought, endured as surely as Bowie's precious ruins, as strongly as the land itself.

Far away, there was a sound. Wind through the trees or ancient chants in the fiery sunset, voices whispering of sacred places, of white winds and soft wonder. Gaby heard them. Their children would hear them, too, now.

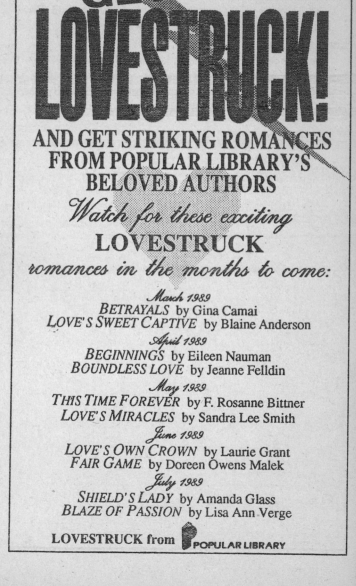